THE JEFFERSON LIBRARY

Once Upon A
CRIME II

Once Upon A
CRIME II

STORIES FROM
Ellery Queen's Mystery Magazine

edited by Janet Hutchings

ST. MARTIN'S PRESS ❦ NEW YORK

Library of Congress Cataloging-in-Publication Data

Once upon a crime II: historical mysteries from Ellery Queen's mystery magazine / edited by Janet Hutchings. —1st ed.
    p.   cm.
  ISBN 0–312–14386–9
    1. Detective and mystery stories, American. 2. Detective and mystery stories, English. 3. Historical fiction, American. 4. Historical fiction, English. I. Ellery Queen's mystery magazine.
PS648.D4O52 1996
813'.087208—dc20   96–1204

First edition: July 1996

10 9 8 7 6 5 4 3 2 1

CONTENTS

ACKNOWLEDGMENTS

Thanks to Steve Stilwell of Minneapolis, Minnesota, for letting us borrow the name of his bookstore, Once Upon A Crime, for this series of historical mystery anthologies. Thanks are also due to editor Keith Kahla of St. Martin's Press for his intelligent suggestions and dedicated support of this project, as well as to Dorothy Cummings of *Ellery Queen's Mystery Magazine* for help in preparing the manuscript.

INTRODUCTION

B ooks, are each a world," Wordsworth wrote, ". . . a substantial world. . . . Round these, with tendrils strong as flesh and blood, / Our pastime and our happiness will grow."* As every reader and writer knows, the creation of a book's world is a process in which the active imaginations of both reader and writer play a part, though not in equal or consistent measures. The author who wishes to create a fictional world from times long past must usually supply more elements of the creation than a counterpart who works with contemporary themes, for readers will fill in for themselves a myriad of details in a contemporary story, where actions have meanings recognizable from their own experience. The historical writer, who works without this shared bond of time and place, has the daunting job of building, brick by brick and stone by stone, the world which readers are to see.

This second volume of *Once Upon A Crime* contains a panorama of fictionally reconstructed worlds: ancient Greece, Cicero's Rome, medieval and Renaissance Europe, Victorian England, early twentieth-century America. Its architects are scholars and humorists, crime writers and journalists, and, interestingly, several authors who also specialize in science fiction and fantasy. Perhaps the jump from science fiction or fantasy to historical fiction is natural, for all three types of story demand large-scale world creation (whether in time, another galaxy, or pure imagination) and the capacity for big—one could even say "galactic"— leaps of the imagination. Yet the historical writer must bring to the word processor something that does not encumber the fantasy writer, and that is a regard for facts. Facts about historical events; facts about

---

*Personal Talk. Sonnet I

historical personages; and, if the story is a mystery, also facts about the state of criminology in a given era.

Ellery Queen thought the historical the hardest type of mystery to write, especially when centered around real historical figures. "It is really a monumental task," he said, "—so herculean a labor that your editors have never had the temerity to attempt it." And it isn't only the need for factual accuracy that makes the task herculean. "The historical figure has to be convincing as well as authentic," he went on to say, "and the scene, time, speech, and manners have to be projected with equal authenticity." The character that emerges must, in other words, be congruent with the picture an historian would paint of him and at the same time possess traits that make him believable as an investigator.

In drawing together this collection, we discovered a number of talented authors who had the temerity to cast great men and women of history in their mysteries. Some of the historical luminaries were clearly chosen for qualities of mind: Who better than Socrates, the ultimate seeker of truth through logic, to solve a mystery?—unless it be Galileo, champion of unbiased observation and experimentation. Or Jane Austen, a master at dissecting human motivation.

Historical detectives may also be chosen because of the authority they wielded in life, for in most societies prior to our own, there were no organized police forces from which a writer might resurrect a great detective. London's Scotland Yard, for instance, only assumed the crime-solving responsibilities with which the name resonates in 1829, and in the United States no metropolitan police force existed at all until 1844, when the New York City force was incorporated. A writer in search of a figure with the power to enact justice might therefore look instead to a head of state—a king or queen, or a conqueror like Alexander the Great.

The place occupied in modern societies by police forces was, of course, filled in different ways in the various cultures which were without them. The variety of means of maintaining justice from culture to culture provides an opportunity for a writer who chooses his period carefully to create a detective unique in the genre. One of the most interesting sleuths to come on the scene in recent years is Peter Tremayne's Sister Fidelma, a medieval Irish *religieuse*, whose training in law gives her the kind of clout even contemporary women might envy. Also sounding a curiously contemporary note is Steven Saylor's

Gordianus the Finder, by any other name a private eye. Private investigators were common in the Rome of which Steven Saylor writes, where there were no police to investigate even crimes of a serious nature. Gordianus's trade is mostly with the highborn and wealthy, but our collection does not neglect the common man. The fabled outlaw Robin Hood, benefactor of the poor, plies new skills as a detective in an adventure by Clayton Emery, and Edward D. Hoch portrays that peculiarly Wild Western entity, the vigilance committee, in a case in which early labor unions clash violently with management.

The sixteen stories that make up this book do not all treat of real historical persons, though this second volume contains more of that monumentally difficult type of detective story than the first. They do, however, all take pains to flesh the bare bones of fact that readers who are not historians will bring to each period. "Background, language, thought, and tone" must all be given, Ellery Queen said, in order for the historical writer's canvas to be complete. When, with the last stroke of the brush the light of murder has been added to the eye, the writer has a story, and the anthologist a book, round which the tendrils of a crime reader's imagination may grow.

Janet Hutchings

SOCRATES SOLVES A MURDER

Brèni James

Our collection begins with a literary "first." Brèni James's "Socrates Solves a Murder" is one of thirteen first stories that won special awards in Ellery Queen's Mystery Magazine's *Ninth Annual Worldwide Short Story Contest. The year was 1953. Forty-two years later, her story still stands as one of best EQMM debuts. The durability of the story derives from the perfect marriage of theme to character. Anyone who has read the dialogues of Plato must remember the relentlessness of Socrates' questioning of his interlocutors. The great philosopher's style is no different when the subject is murder.*

Aristodemus was awakened towards daybreak by a crowing of cocks, and when he awoke, the others were either asleep, or had gone away; there remained only Socrates, Aristophanes, and Agathon . . . And first of all Aristophanes dropped off, then, when the day was already dawning, Agathon. Socrates, having laid them to sleep, rose to depart; Aristodemus, as his manner was, following him . . . to the Lyceum.

—PLATO: SYMPOSIUM *(JOWETT TRANS.)*

S ocrates strolled along barefoot, having left his sandals behind at Agathon's. Aristodemus, barefoot as always, ran on short legs to catch up with his friend.

Aristodemus: Here, Socrates; you left your sandals.

Socrates: You seem to be more interested in what I have forgotten, Aristodemus, than in what you ought to have learned.

Aristodemus: Well, it is true my attention wandered a bit, and I missed some of your discourse, but I agreed with your conclusions.

Socrates: My dear friend, your confidence is like that of a man who drinks from a goblet of vinegar because his host has recited a paean in praise of wine.

The philosopher, after this nettling remark, obliged his companion by stopping to put on the sandals; and they resumed their walk through the town, passing out of the two eastern gates. The sun was rising above Mount Pentelicus, and Hymettus glowed before them in shadows as purple as the thyme which bloomed on its slopes.

They were soon climbing the gentle rise which led them to the shrine of Apollo Lyceus. It was a small, graceful temple whose columns and caryatids had been hewn from sugar-bright marble.

At the hilltop shrine they saw the fading wisps of smoke rising from its eastern altar. The priestess, her sacrifices completed, was mounting the stairs to enter the golden doors of her sanctuary. She was clothed in the flowing white robes of her office; her hair fell in a tumble of shimmering black coils about her shoulders; and a garland of laurel leaves dipped on her forehead. Her gray eyes were serene, and on her lips played a smile that was not gentle.

Socrates: What omens, Alecto?

Alecto: For some, good. For some, evil. The smoke drifted first to the west; but now, as you see, it hastens to the god.

Indeed, as she spoke, a gentle gust of wind rose from the slope before them and sent the smoke into the shrine.

Alecto withdrew, and the two men proceeded down the short path which led to the Lyceum itself and to their destination, the swimming pool.

It appeared at first that their only companion this morning would be the statue which stood beside the pool, a beautiful Eros that stood on tiptoe as if it were about to ascend on quivering wings over the water that shivered beneath it.

The statue was not large—scarcely five feet high even on its pedestal; but the delicacy of its limbs and the airy seeming-softness of its wings gave an illusion of soaring height. The right arm of the god was extended; in the waxing light it appeared to be traced with fine blue veins. The hand was palm upward; and the face, touched with a smile that was at once roguish and innocent, was also turned to the heavens.

When Socrates and Aristodemus came closer to the edge of the pool, they perceived for the first time a young man, kneeling before the statue in prayer. They could not distinguish his words, but he was apparently supplicating the god of love with urgency.

No sooner had they taken note of this unexpected presence than a concussion of strident voices exploded from the palaestra adjoining the pool, and a party of perhaps a dozen young men bounded into view. All laughing, they raced to the water's edge and leaped in one after another, with much splashing and gurgling.

Socrates led his companion to a marble bench a few yards from the pool, and bade him sit down.

"But," frowned Aristodemus, "I thought we came to swim. Surely you have not become afraid of cold water and morning air?"

"No," replied his friend, tugging at his paunch with laced fingers, "but I consider it prudent to discourse in a crowd, and swim in solitude."

Socrates turned from Aristodemus to watch the sleek young men at their play in the pool, and he listened with an indulgent smile on his satyr's face to their noisy banter.

Suddenly a piercing *Eee-Eee, Eee-EEE* screeched at the south end of the pool, where stood Eros and knelt the pious youth.

"A hawk!" Socrates pointed to a shadow that sat on the fragile hand of Eros. The bird, not a large one, seemed a giant thing on so delicate a mount.

Its screams had not attracted the young men in the water. Their laughter was incongruous and horrible as the marble Eros swayed on its pedestal and then crashed to the ground at the pool's edge, sending the evil bird crying into the sun.

The two friends rushed to the assistance of the youth who, with only a glance at the bird, had remained at his prayers. The body of Eros was rubble; but its wings—which had seemed so tremulous, so poised for flight—had swept down like cleavers. One wing had cleanly severed the youth's head.

Socrates knelt beside the broken bodies, marble and flesh, the one glistening in crystalline fragments, the other twitching with the false life of the newly dead. He gently tossed a dark curl from the boy's pale forehead, and he looked into the vacant blue eyes for a long time before he drew down the lids.

Aristodemus, fairly dancing with excitement and fright, shouted, "Socrates, you know him? It is Tydeus, the Pythagorean. What a fool he was to try to bargain with Eros! The god has paid him justly!"

The philosopher rose slowly, murmuring, "Eros dispenses love, not justice." His eyes strayed over the rubble, now becoming tinted with the red of sunlight and the deeper red. A white cluster of fat clung to the shattered marble fingers of the god.

"The sacrifice," said Aristodemus, following his glance. "Tydeus was going to sacrifice that piece of lamb."

By this time the crowd of swimmers, glistening and shivering, had run to see what had happened. They chattered like birds, their voices pitched high by death.

"Someone must run to tell his friend Euchecrates," cried Aristodemus.

At this, the group fell silent. Socrates looked intently on each of the young men. "You are unwilling," he said mildly, "to tell a man of his friend's death?"

At last a youth spoke up: "We were all at dinner together last night, Tydeus and Euchecrates among us. Our symposiarch suggested that we discourse on the theme of Fidelity, for we all knew that Tydeus found it difficult to remain loyal to his friend Euchecrates. The symposiarch thought to twit him about it."

"But," broke in one of the others, "Tydeus immediately took up the topic and spoke as though he, not Euchecrates, were the victim of faithlessness!"

The first boy nodded. "It became a personal argument between them, then, instead of a discussion among friends. They began to rail at each other about gifts of money and gamecocks and I know not what. All manner of fine things, from what Tydeus said."

Socrates: Then these gifts were from our dead friend Tydeus to Euchecrates?

Youth: Yes, Socrates; and Tydeus was angry because Euchecrates had given them all away to someone else.

Socrates: To whom did Euchecrates give the gifts of Tydeus?

Once again silence fell, and the young men exchanged puzzled looks. But a bronzed athlete who had been standing outside the circle blurted out: "Even Tydeus didn't know who it was!"

Socrates: Why do you say that?

Athlete: I came here to the palaestra before any of the others, just at daybreak, and I met Tydeus on his way to the god. I recall that I asked him if he were going to swim, and he said, no, he was about to offer a prayer to Eros for a misdeed. Then I teased him about losing his gifts . . .

Socrates: And asked him who Euchecrates's admirer was?

Athlete: Yes, but Tydeus flew into a rage and began to say things in a distracted fashion about "that person," as he put it, "whoever it may be." I wanted to speculate with him on the identity, but Tydeus said he must hurry to Eros, for he wished to complete his prayer before the sun rose above the horizon.

Socrates: And he said nothing further? Well, then, will you now please go to Euchecrates's house and tell him what has befallen his friend Tydeus, and ask him to meet Socrates at the Shrine of Apollo Lyceus?

The bronzed youth agreed to do so, and Socrates took his companion Aristodemus by the arm, leading him back up the path to the shrine. "I shall return with water," he said, passing through the crowd, "that you who have touched the body may purify yourselves."

When they were out of the hearing of the young men, Aristodemus said in a low voice, "I know, Socrates, that you seek answers by the most devious questions; but I cannot discover what it is you attempt to glean from all that you have asked of those boys."

Socrates: I believe you said that the piece of fat which we saw in the rubble was sacrificial lamb?

Aristodemus: I would say so. And we saw Tydeus sacrificing, did we not?

Socrates: We saw him praying. Do you recall that the bronzed fellow told us that when first he saw Tydeus, he asked Tydeus if he were going to swim?

Aristodemus: Yes, I remember.

Socrates: And would it not be an exceedingly odd question to ask of a man who was carrying a sacrifice?

Aristodemus: That is true, Socrates; but what does it mean?

Socrates: You recall, too, that you spoke of Tydeus as a Pythagorean?

Aristodemus: Yes, I know that he was.

Socrates: Then perhaps you will also remember that, among Pythagoreans, it is a custom never to offer living sacrifice, or to kill any animal that does not harm man?

Aristodemus: I had forgotten, Socrates. And I see now that it could not have been possible that Tydeus intended to sacrifice.

Socrates: Yet we saw a piece of lamb, did we not? How else could we account for it, if it were not brought to be sacrificed?

Aristodemus: It seems unaccountable.

Socrates: Do you remember where you saw it?

Aristodemus: It was on the hand of Eros.

Socrates: And so, also, was the hawk. Does that not suggest another reason for the fat?

Aristodemus: Why, yes! It must have been placed on the hand as bait for the bird!

Socrates: Clearly, that is what was intended. And I think it must have been fastened there in some manner, for the hawk did not pick it up and fly off, but rather balanced himself on the fingertips and pulled at it until the statue was overbalanced.

The two had walked, in their preoccupation, to the very steps of the altar before the Shrine of Apollo Lyceus. The eastern doors of the marble sanctuary were still open, and they could see the god within, gold and ivory, gleaming softly now in the full morning light.

But at that moment they heard shouts from a footpath on their right, and they saw the bronzed athlete running toward them. He pulled up abruptly and panted heavily.

"He's dead, Socrates! Euchecrates is dead! I found him at Tydeus's house, in the doorway. He'd hanged himself from a porch beam!"

Socrates: Are you certain Euchecrates took his own life?

Athlete: Quite certain, Socrates. For he had scrawled a message on the wall, and I recognized his writing.

Socrates: What was his message?

Athlete: "Hide me in a secret place." Does not that mean he was ashamed?

Socrates: That is so.

"Who wishes to be hidden?" asked a woman's voice, and the three men turned to see Alecto, the priestess of the shrine, slowly and gracefully descending the marble steps.

Socrates: Euchecrates, who has killed himself, Alecto.

Alecto: It is indeed a dreadful thing to hear, Socrates.

Aristodemus: Oh, there is more! See where the statue has fallen? Tydeus lies dead beneath it.

Alecto: He must have displeased Eros mightily to have been felled by the god's own image!

Aristodemus: No, I think it fell because Euchecrates contrived that it should.

Alecto: How could it have been contrived, Aristodemus?

Socrates: Alecto, we came to ask you for some water which we will take to the Lyceum, for there are those of us who have not yet purified ourselves.

The priestess nodded and left. She returned in a few moments with a vessel of water.

Socrates: I should have asked also on behalf of this young man, so that he may take some to the place where he found Euchecrates.

Athlete: No, there is not need of that, for there was water there.

Socrates: Indeed? Then, Alecto, who preceded us with such a request?

Alecto: For water? Why, no one.

Socrates: Can purificatory water be simply drawn out of a well, or a pool, or any other ordinary source?

Alecto: No, of course it must be obtained from a priest or a priestess.

Socrates: And there is no other priest or priestess so close to the house of Tydeus, where Euchecrates lies?

Alecto: No, I am the closest.

Socrates: Then can we not assume the water was obtained here? Do you not recall such a request?

Alecto: Only that of Tydeus, several hours ago. I didn't know why he asked for water, but it would now seem to be for that reason.

Socrates: And we know also from this, do we not, Aristodemus, that Euchecrates was already dead when Tydeus went to pray to Eros? Tell me, Alecto, when Tydeus came for water, do you recall that he asked for anything else?

Alecto: I recall nothing else.

Socrates: Tydeus had told this young man that he could not stand and talk with him, since he wished to complete his prayers before the sun's rise. Does that not indicate that Tydeus knew beforehand that his prayers would be of some length?

Alecto: Yes, surely it does.

Socrates: And since he stayed to complete them even though the sun had already risen, and was not even distracted from his intentions by the presence and noise of the bird, what is the likely conclusion?

Aristodemus: I would say that he had a particular prayer to complete.

Socrates: Excellent. That would be my conclusion. Now, Alecto, do you think it likely that a young man still angry from a quarrel—indeed distraught—would sit down and compose a lengthy prayer?

Alecto: He would be more likely to pray spontaneously.

Socrates: But these things seem not to agree. The prayer, we may suppose, was planned beforehand; yet the young man was not prepared to plan the prayer. What may we surmise, then?

Alecto: That someone else composed the prayer for him?

Socrates: I believe so. And who would be likely to have done that?

Alecto: It would be someone expert in such matters, no doubt.

Socrates: Such as a priest or priestess?

Alecto: Yes, it must be so.

Socrates: And since Tydeus called, as you have said, upon yourself, Alecto, does it not seem inevitable that he asked you to compose his prayer?

Alecto: I am compelled to admit he did just that, Socrates.

Socrates: And one last matter: You were sacrificing lamb here at dawn?

Alecto: Yes, lamb and honey.

Socrates: And where is the fat of the lamb which you sacrificed this morning, Alecto? While Tydeus was within memorizing his prayer, did you not go down to the statue of Eros and affix some of the fat to that extended hand?

Alecto: You have a daemon advising you, Socrates!

Aristodemus: Oh, no, Alecto. It is as Cebes has said: Socrates can put a question to a person in such a way that only the true answer comes out! But, Alecto, how did Tydeus dare come to you?

Alecto: He did not know that it was to me his friend Euchecrates had given his gifts. But when Tydeus confessed to me that he had caused my lover's suicide, I could not but avenge the death!

The priestess turned her cold eyes proudly on Socrates. "I was named Alecto for good reason," she said with fierce triumph; "for like that divine Alecto, the Well-Wisher, I too found myself singled out by the gods to wreak vengeance!"

"But remember," cautioned Socrates quietly, "we call the divine Alecto the 'well-wisher' only to placate her. She is still one of the Furies. She still pursues the blood-guilty to death or madness. And think, Alecto: You are only mortal, and you have done murder."

Alecto's eyes widened with the sudden, horrible knowledge of her own fate.

The priestess wept then, and drew the heavy black coils of hair about her face like a shroud.

ALEXANDER THE GREAT, DETECTIVE

Theodore Mathieson

Six decades after the death of Socrates, Alexander the Great was laying claim to the Hellenic world. No man of might is without enemies, and Alexander's were born of several conquered peoples. Theodore Mathieson brought to life more than a dozen of history's giants in the pages of EQMM from 1956 to 1973. The following mystery is one of Mathieson's most poignant, for in it Alexander the Great confronts a crime that concerns him in the most intimate way possible.

I, Jolas of Philippi, returned to Babylon on the first day of the month of Hecatombaeon bearing a heavy heart and fearing lest the word I carried from our homeland, Macedonia—whereunto I had gone at the express wish of my dearest friend Alexander—should make my king turn against me. I left the caravan, with which I had travelled so many weary stadia through the steppes of Asia, in the western part of the city, and crossing the Euphrates by means of the ferry, went at once to my house by the edge of the palace gardens.

From my servant Bessus, who was exceedingly glad to see me, I learned that the city had the previous day held a great festival to celebrate Alexander's planned campaign against the coasts of Arabia. He was to leave Babylon in five days with the fleet under the command of Nearchus, and I knew I had come barely in time to tell the king my news.

With many sighs for what lay before me, I bathed briefly and put on clean garments and sandals, for the opportunities for bathing upon my journey had been few, and I knew that no matter how glad Alexander would be to see me again, except when he was upon the battlefield, he was most fastidious about the cleanliness of those about him.

I went then to the palace, passing the guards at Ishtar Gate who gave me familiar greeting, and ascended the steep stairway to the great terrace. There I learned the king was preparing for his bath, so upon the decision to surprise him I went at once to the lavacre, which was as yet deserted, although the warm water in the deep pool steamed invitingly in the evening air.

Sitting upon a bench beside the bath, surrounded by the paraphernalia for vigorous exercise, I played musingly with a ball until I heard footsteps, and then considering my activity unseemly in view of the portentous news I had to impart, I threw the ball aside.

Shortly thereafter Alexander himself entered with his attendants, and when he saw me, his joy was great.

"My thoughts have been with thee constantly, Jolas," said he, embracing me. "Since dear Hephaestion died, I have been quite lonely, and I waited eagerly for thy return."

Indeed, although Alexander was a big man, compared with myself who am slight but agile in the games, he was so well proportioned and carried himself with such grace that one felt not overwhelmed by his proximity. His features were strong and proud, with a fresh pink color to his skin that Apelles, who painted Alexander holding lightning in his hand, did not accurately reproduce, making him somewhat black and swarter than his face indeed was.

Alexander disrobed and descended the tile steps into the pool, where he swam as we talked casually and I told him of the rigors of the journey and its adventures, but did not touch upon the burden of my intelligence, which he seemed unwilling to hear knowledge of. Whenever our talk verged upon the serious he would start cavorting like an aquatic mammal, disappearing beneath the surface, and rising again to cough with the access of water into his mouth.

When he had done this thrice, I rose concerned and said, "Wilt thou hear now what news I bear, Alexander?"

He looked reproachfully at me, but left the pool and, motioning away the attendants who came to anoint him with oil, put on his gown. Then he signalled me to follow him and we went to his chambers. There he dismissed his servants and stood looking at me with a frown.

"Thou hast ill news for me about Antipater?" he asked at last, with a flicker of suspicion in his eye. I knew Alexander feared the growing power of his regent in Macedonia; that is why he had sent me to discover how affairs went in the home country.

"Not about Antipater," said I, "but from him. Antipater is loyal to thee, Alexander, and governs as thou wouldst. But he sends this news: Leanarchus, governor of Phrygia, has engaged mercenaries and is occupied in plundering Thrace, and boasts of descending upon Macedonia itself!"

"Cannot Antipater deal with this traitor as he deserves?" Alexander demanded.

"He has already put soldiers into the field against Leanarchus, and no doubt will be successful. But that is not the worst. Leanarchus, as thou knowest, is uncle of Medius, thy captain of the Macedonian forces here in Babylon. It is upon Medius's strategic skill thou wilt depend for conquest of Arabia. And yet, Antipater wishes to inform thee that Leanarchus has spoken of his nephew's desire to rule all Asia in thy place. Leanarchus has hinted that Medius heads a plot to assassinate thee. I prayed I would return in time to bear thee this news."

Alexander's face and chest grew red, as they always do when he falls into a rage, and he turned upon me as if I were his adversary.

"By the divine fury of Bacchus! I do not believe Antipater. *I trust Medius!* Together we have fought five years, from the Hindu Kush to the Great Ocean. 'Twas he who saved me from death at the siege of Multan when I received this!" Alexander touched the scar upon his breast. "With the help of Medius's ingenuity we have rebuilt the phalanx, which we shall use with crushing effect against the Arabians. We have planned our victory side by side—he is like a very brother to me. I love him not less than I have loved thee, Jolas—until thou came to me with such impossible news!"

It was as I had feared. Alexander, my dearest friend, had turned against me at my words. I shrugged and made obeisance and turned to leave the chamber, but Alexander stopped me by smiting his hand into his palm.

"Stay, Jolas," he said, less wildly. "Thou must give me time to think." But even as I turned there came a knock upon the door and Medius himself entered. He is a heavy-set, plethoric man, with a weighty chin and a forehead that bulges aggressively over deep and canny eyes. Because Alexander favors me, Medius also shows a liking which I am sure he does not feel.

"Welcome back to Babylon, Jolas," said he, touching me. "I come to fetch Alexander to a private drinking bout, but if he is willing, thou must join us as well."

"Yes, dear Jolas," Alexander said with his customary affection. "Do join us. We drink again to the health of the Gods but talk of the exaltation of mortals through the conquest of Arabia!"

"Thank thee, Alexander," I said, "but I am weary with many days of travel. With thy permission I shall return home."

"Of course, thou must be tired," Alexander said. "Come tomorrow at noonday, and we shall talk further of—Antipater."

I bowed and left the chamber, and at my last look at Alexander he was frowning at Medius.

But Alexander did not wait until midday for my visit. Next morning, as I stood upon my balcony watching the shadows vanish upon the terra cotta bosom of the Euphrates, a messenger brought me a letter from him, telling me to put all business asunder and hasten to his side at once, as he had urgent need of me.

I returned to the palace, and within the vast reception chamber—from whose windows one can see past the fertile greenery that lines the Euphrates into the blank desert beyond—I found Alexander lying upon a couch.

At once he arose and spake to his attendants, telling them to leave him, and when we were alone he sat upright upon the couch and with a sigh covered his face with his hands. When he drew them away I was shocked to see how ravaged was his visage, and wondered at his great will power that hid what must be intense suffering from the eyes of his court.

Then he stepped down from the dais and clapped his hands upon my shoulder.

"Oh, thou bosom friend of Hephaestion, who once quarrelled with him how much thou loved me more than he, I need now thy help in my extreme moment!"

His hand upon my shoulder burned with fever, and his words came in unsteady gusts, as if he drew breath with painful difficulty. I could see the gleam of fever behind the swart steadiness of his eye, and smell the good savor of his body which always clung like incense about him.

"I am ever thy faithful servant, dear Alexander," I said.

"Yes, I trust thee. And therefore thou must know, and no one else— *that I have been poisoned, and am dying.*"

The fervent words that sprang to my lips he stemmed by upraised hand, while with the other he withdrew his ring with which he sealed his letters, and pressed it firmly against my lips.

"Thus thou must swear to keep silent," he said.

"I swear," I said, when Alexander removed the seal.

"Listen then, Jolas," spake my king, sinking in sudden lassitude upon the couch. "Last night, as thou knowest, Medius came to carry me off to a drinking bout in Nearchus's chambers in the palace. There were only four of us—Medius, Nearchus, Susa the Persian treasurer, and myself. The chamber was guarded without, and no one entered nor left the whole time; we poured wine for one another as we listeth, and we quaffed greatly, for the wine was sweet. If I had not dulled my palate I would have complained sooner of the sudden bitter cup that was poured me, but it was near daybreak and my senses were lulled; as it was, I drained it all but a third, and then remembering with a sudden stab what thou had said, I demanded to know why I was served bitter vintage, and cried treason in my cup. Nearchus said he had served me, and that I did but taste the dregs of the flagon. Medius, whom I accused, picked up the very cup and himself drained the remainder. That calmed me, and I forgot my accusations until this morning. But while I knelt at the sacrifice within the temple, I felt a flush come over me, and later when I tried to write in my journal, I felt weak and faint. I knew then that I had been poisoned."

"Perhaps it is some passing ague that thou feelest," I said, but Alexander shook his head.

"Nay, Jolas, because I know this poison well. When Calisthenes languished in his prison at my command, I had him given it myself and watched the progress thereof. It waits from six to eight hours to make itself felt, and then one is taken with fever, which grows day by day for six days, until the life has been burned away. See, it is a poison I myself carry ever with me should I be taken captive!"

He seized his sword and pressed a spot upon the silver hilt close to the haft, and I beheld a lid suddenly spring open, revealing tiny white crystals within.

"It is gathered as liquid, and is formed into crystals which are cold to the touch.* Knowest thou of this poison, Jolas?"

"Nay, Alexander," said I.

"It is that which was put into my cup last night," said he. "And if

---

*Plutarch, Alexander's biographer, tells that this poison falls as liquid from a rock in the territory of the city of Nonacris, where it is gathered as they would gather dew, into the horn of the foot of an ass, for there is no other kind of thing (except silver) that will keep it.

Medius had not drained the remainder I would have had him quartered at the first flush in my cheek!"

"But perhaps you drank with him earlier in the day, Alexander," I said. "It would not be unusual."

"True. But for two days I have fasted to the Gods for a successful expedition to Arabia. *Neither food nor drink has passed my lips in all that time until I went to drink with Medius last night.* Nay, Jolas, as certain am I of the time of my poisoning as that I am Alexander."

He closed the little receptacle, and held his sword over his knee, his hand gripping the hilt. Then with an access of violent energy he rose and swept down from his dais, swinging his sword as if at an imaginary enemy, and I withdrew for safety to an alcove while he raved.

"Would that I could kill them, all three!" he shouted. "Then I would be sure of punishing my assassin! There was a time I would have done it! But not now. I must at the last use stealth, and pusillanimous *investigation* to discover the culprit, for the power of Macedonia must not be weakened, and each one of those men is part of the keystone in the arch of that power!"

"But Medius," I insisted, "has he shown signs of poisoning also?"

Alexander straightened and breathed deeply, and when he spake his voice was calm, and I knew his mind had gained control. "He was here just now. I had a servant feel of his forehead and his body. He has no fever. The poison has not touched him."

He turned to me and smiled, and the sight of its implacability chilled me.

"That is my problem, you see. The poison was in that cup. Until I find how I could be poisoned and Medius not, I cannot act. For not only had Medius reason to kill me, if thy report from Antipater be accurate, but Nearchus, the admiral of my fleet also, as thou shalt see. And 'twas Nearchus, remember, who admittedly poured my drink."

"And Susa the Persian?"

"He too, and for the best reason of all: that I have conquered his homeland."

Somewhere a gong sounded. Alexander pulled a cord, and presently the doors to the reception chamber opened. Two Persian slaves entered and prostrated themselves upon their knees, and a Macedonian servant in exquisite tunic bowed low and announced Nearchus and Susa the Persian.

The admiral of the fleet entered with regal stride and stood at attention before the dais as Alexander returned to his couch. The Persian stood behind Nearchus and a little to his right.

"We have come, Susa and I, at thy command," said Nearchus, his face showing the strain of the occasion; at the same time he gave me a sidelong glance that told me he cared not much for my presence. He was a stern-faced man with hollow cheeks and the pale blue eyes of an anchorite, and was perhaps the most powerful man among the Macedonians, for Alexander trusted and honored him highly.

"Yes, Nearchus, be seated," Alexander said, and Nearchus sat upon a stool below the king and watched with wary eyes as Alexander, showing now no signs of his illness, picked up several scrolls from a cushion beside him.

"These have been found among thy possessions, Nearchus," said Alexander. "Letters from my step-brother Arideus in Lydia, arguing the futility of further conquest in Arabia. He urges thee to return to Macedonia, where Olympias, my mother, will heap honors undreamed of upon thee."

"I have told Alexander of these letters," Nearchus said quietly.

"Yes, but thou didst not tell me thy decision. Should thou have decided to go, I would first have to be dead. Because alive I would not permit it!"

"Have our plans for the Arabian campaign ever suffered the slightest reservation of my enthusiasm, or diminution of my efforts on their behalf?"

Alexander's eyes fell before the cool inquiry of the other, and he shook his head. Then Nearchus turned to me and pointed an unwavering finger.

"There stands one whom thou should suspect, Alexander. Jolas is the troublemaker, the one who pours false asssertions into thine ear."

"I think Alexander dost not doubt my love for him," said I.

"Nor do I," said Alexander. "My welfare has ever been uppermost in Jolas's mind."

"Unless Antipater has corrupted him," said Nearchus.

"Is it likely," I said, "when my life has been spent at Alexander's side, and I was in the company of Antipater only a few days?"

"Antipater is subtle at corrupting," Nearchus persisted. "Perhaps thou wouldst not know it."

"I would know it," said I.

"Enough!" Alexander cried, dismissing Nearchus, and the latter went out stiffly. The king then pointed his finger at Susa the Persian, who approached with a low obeisance.

"Last night Susa, thou toldest of great treasure buried beneath the ground by thy emperor Darius at Opia, a day's journey to the north. Thou sayest that thy love for me bade you tell me of it, so our campaign to Arabia might prosper with such wealth to sustain it."

"It is true, O King," the Persian said. He was an elderly man, clad in the garishly dyed Persian garments, wearing a high headgear which rose as far above his face as his white beard fell below it.

"Now thou wilt have a chance to prove thy fealty. Thou wilt assemble porters and carriages and soldiers, and go to Opia to fetch the treasure here to me. At once. I will give thee three days—one to go, one to load the treasure, and one to return. If thou art not here three days hence, I shall send swift messengers to kill thee. When I see the treasure, my doubt concerning thee shall be cleared."

"I understand, O King," said Susa, bowing low.

"And thou, Jolas, wilt accompany him to see that all goes well."

I stood stiffly with surprise at the sudden appointment, and Alexander smiled gently.

"Thou hast often complained of the boredom of litigating among the Macedonians, dear Jolas," he said. "Now I give thee opportunity for treasure hunting and adventure."

With a wave of his hand he dismissed the Persian, who backed out of the chamber, and then Alexander descended from the dais and took my hand.

"I am relying upon thee, Jolas, to get the treasure safely to Babylon. Whilst thou art gone I shall continue probing the matter here. And take no longer than three days, dear friend, *for I shall be dead in six!"*

Of the outward journey to Opia I shall not dwell, except to mention that we left Babylon with fifty foot soldiers and ten carts, and twenty mounted horsemen, including Susa and myself, and all went well. Since Opia lies like most other Persian towns along the river, we did not digress into the desert, and never lost sight of trees and greenery.

There was the matter of digging for the treasure, which lay in a cemetery to the east of Opia; and among the bones of departed natives, Susa indeed did reveal great wealth, and thus establish his fealty to Alexander—amphorae of gold, masks of silver, heavy bronze chests filled with darics—gold coins with the figure of an archer impressed upon one side—as well as urns filled with tiny golden siglos, and much other wealth besides.

By sunset of the second day, the whole of the treasure, well worth an emperor's ransom, lay battened down securely within the carts, and I had to promulgate the warning that any soldier found with treasure upon his person would instantly be put to death.

Planning to return to Babylon early the following morning, we retired early—I to my tent, Susa to his. But in the middle of the night I was awakened by a sound outside, and rose to investigate. I had but stepped out into the moonlight when an arrow whirred by my cheek, penetrating the fabric of my tent, and turning, I saw the archer behind a tall dark cypress and set out after him. He fled at once among the graves and I followed as best I could; but so busy was I watching lest I tumble into the great holes we had dug and thus keep their ancient occupants company, I soon lost sight of him and stopped and stood in the quiet moonlight, smelling the odor of decay and trembling in the cool breeze that blew from the river.

On sudden thought I returned at once to the camp and looked in upon Susa in his tent, and found the Persian sleeping soundly there.

But that proved nothing. Susa could have hired an assassin to kill me. As well as could Nearchus—or Medius.

I returned thoughtfully to my tent, but did not sleep the remainder of the night.

On our return to Babylon I found that Alexander had quit the palace for a garden villa across the river, and thence Susa and I repaired upon the ferry.

While crossing, Susa praised Alexander exceedingly for his policy of integrating the conquered peoples of Asia into the governmental fabric of the new empire, which stretched from the Aegean to the borders of India, and said how fortunate a man was he, Susa, a Persian, to have Alexander's trust in being appointed treasurer to the royal coffers. I replied that Susa's predecessor, Harpalus, a Macedonian, had proved himself faithless by stealing from the treasury, and Alexander had thought it fair and wise to entrust it thereafter to a native.

"But there are many, especially in Macedonia," I added, "who do not favor Alexander's policy of racial equality, and should like to reverse it."

Whereupon Susa fingered his beard and fell silent.

At the villa, which lay in lush gardens close to the edge of the river where it was cooler, we were shown into Alexander's presence by an elderly doctor, who when I questioned him as to our king's condition murmured, "It is truly a strange disease which works in him. I cannot mark the end of it."

And when I saw Alexander I knew why the doctor shook his head so doubtfully. The king sat upon his bed in a terrace overlooking the river, playing at dice with Medius, and his face looked white and strained, like a mask stretched into place by the fingers of Death himself. My heart smote me with pity as I knelt by Alexander and told him of the treasure we had brought from Opia.

"Good, Jolas," he said, laying aside the dice and smiling upon Susa. "Thou hast proved my trust, Susa. Nevertheless, thou wilt lodge here in this villa with me, as do Medius and Nearchus."

Thereupon Alexander dismissed the Persian and turned to Medius who sat opposite him and who was flushing redly and scowling at me the while.

"Why glowerest thou at Jolas, Medius?" Alexander asked. And when Medius did not answer, I spake up thus, "Perhaps Medius is surprised that I am here, dear Alexander. My life was set upon while at Opia, and if the archer had not aimed poorly, perhaps Medius would be smiling now."

With an oath Medius leaped to his feet, his hand upon his sword.

"Go, Medius!" Alexander cried, rising, and with an obeisance and a final black look at me, Medius left the terrace. Alexander sighed and walked unsteadily to the balcony, saying, "A furnace rages within me, Jolas, and consumes me steadily. In three days hence I will be dead."

"No, dear Alexander," said I, stung with anguish. "The Gods will not permit thy passing."

Alexander stooped to the edge of a small fish pond set into the floor of the terrace and picked up a cup of greenish glaze and held it before my eyes.

"This cup poisoned me," said he, "and will help me to discover who my murderer is. I have not been idle these three days. Come, I will show thee what I have done."

In one room of the villa the king pointed out several near-naked men lying chained upon the floor. Two looked at us with fever-clouded eyes, and one was unconscious with great beads of sweat standing upon his forehead.

"I had several condemned criminals brought to me and gave them a choice: They could drink the poison I gave them, and let me watch the results, or be put at once to the sword, which was their just punishment. On the other hand, if they recovered from the poison, they would be free. Several volunteered gladly. Unfortunately, two have already died from the heavy dosage I gave them."

"But what dost thou seek to determine?" I asked as we returned to the terrace.

"How little of the poison is required in a third of a cup before it brings no fever. I think I quaffed the major lethal portion from the top, for the crystals are instantly soluble. Doubtless there was *some* mingling below, and if I can find a minimum dose that will leave the drinker unaffected . . ."

"Then it would explain how Medius could drink without being poisoned?"

"Yes," said Alexander, his lips turning cruel.

"But, dear Alexander, has not another thought occurred to thee? A man bitten by an asp, who lives, may be bitten again with less effect, and yet again. Could not Medius have accustomed himself to small doses of the poison by taking first a grain and then a larger quantity?"

Alexander breathed heavily in sudden anger, and for the first time spake sharply to me.

"Of course I did think of it," he said. "But I do not have time to determine whether this could be done!"

He rang a bell and when the attendants arrived he ordered that Nearchus should bring him the final prisoner.

"Thou shalt watch the end of my experiment, Jolas," said he, equable once again. "This poison is most powerful. Five crystals are lethal—but so are four; three bring fever and so do two, and both are probably lethal in the long run. Now if a *single* crystal brings fever by tomorrow, I shall know at least that Medius is in all probability innocent, for it means one is not immune from the smallest possible dosage."

Thereupon Alexander filled the green-glaze cup a third full of wine, and from the receptacle in his sword picked out a single crystal of the poison with a fine tweezers, his hand shaking in sudden weakness, and dropped the crystal into the liquid.

By then Nearchus had entered with a bearded, half-naked prisoner of tremendous proportions and the yellowish skin of a Paphlagonian. The man had a truculent expression and Nearchus watched him carefully as Alexander stepped forward, holding the cup out to him.

"Drink," he commanded. "I think perhaps freedom lies ahead for you, who are the last."

The dull eyes of the Paphlagonian looked first at Alexander and next at the cup. Then I beheld a spark rise in his orbs, and the following moment he raised his hand and dashed the cup out of the king's hand so that it crashed against the edge of the fish pond, the contents spilling into the water.

Almost at the sound of the shattering of the cup, Nearchus stepped forward, swung his sword aloft, and swept it down with tremendous force at the point where the prisoner's neck met his shoulder. The Paphlagonian fell with his head half severed and lay athwart the coping of the fish pool, covering the shards of the poison cup, while his heart, still beating, pumped blood into the clear water.

Meanwhile I saw Alexander back unsteadily towards his couch, his face flushing scarlet, beads of sweat forming upon his upper lip.

"I am aflame," he murmured, and I took him by the arm and helped him to his couch.

"Thou must cover thy feet for they are cold," I said as the sight of my weakened king made my own heart bleed, "and support thy back for the sharp pain that is in it." And I put a cushion gently behind him.

By the time Alexander lay resting easily, with his eyes closed, Nearchus had ordered the body of the Paphlagonian removed and I stood alone with the admiral in an antechamber.

"Thou art a troublemaker," Nearchus said, looking at me with loathing. "With thy talk of conspiracy, thou hast caused many deaths, and will bring ruin upon us all! Could it not be that Alexander has caught a mere disease and will recover? Must thou call us all assassins?"

"It is no disease," I said simply.

"Thou art a liar!" Nearchus cried, and left the chamber.

I returned at once to the terrace.

"Wilt thou have me at thy side?" I asked softly. But Alexander watched me not, so absorbed was he gazing upon the shards of the green glaze and the blood mingled with the wine that still spread, staining the limpid waters of the pool, and now making invisible the fish within it.

For the remainder of the day, every time I sought admittance to Alexander's chambers, the doctor turned me away, saying the king was too ill to grant an audience. At the evening meal Alexander was absent, and

Susa and Nearchus and Medius and I sat together without a word, and I could feel the united force of their dislike directed against me. I could not finish my supper, and rose to walk along the river bank until sundown, returning to my quarters at the villa and retiring early, for I was greatly fatigued.

I was awakened in the middle of the night by the doctor, who told me to come at once, that Alexander had expressed a wish to see me.

At the sight of him I knew death was not far away. He put out a dry hand as I sat beside him, and I felt the heat of it burn my wrist.

"Dear Jolas," he said weakly. "Again I have cut the Gordian Knot. I know now who has poisoned me, and thou must help me to see justice done. Call Nearchus and Susa and Medius here at once. We shall make the final judgment!"

I went at once and awakened the others, and when they all stood before the king he spake again.

"Nearchus—Medius—thou hast known me long, hast stood beside me in battle, hast abided by my decisions and rarely found me wanting in wisdom. Susa, thou knowest me for a fair sovereign, and one who governs wisely. I tell thee now. *Thou must trust me.* I have discovered my assassin, but I wish to reveal my knowledge in my own way. Jolas—" he extended a hand in my direction. "Upon the table is a tray with three cups, filled with wine. Give one to each of them."

I handed a glazed cup, much like the one the Paphlagonian had recently shattered, to the two Macedonians and the Persian.

"Now believe me when I say this: *that the ones who are innocent of poisoning me need fear nothing.* But the one who is my murderer will himself be poisoned tonight! Now then, I command thee to drink, Susa!"

Susa blinked at Alexander and I thought his lip trembled, but he seized the cup with both hands and drank the contents in three great draughts. Then he put down the cup, rubbing his beard with the back of his hand.

"Drink thou, Nearchus," said Alexander.

Nearchus did not hesitate, but drained the cup as quickly as Susa had done.

"And now thou, Medius," said Alexander.

Medius raised the cup to his lips and then lowered it.

"But suppose thou art wrong, Alexander?" he asked quietly.

"I asked thee to trust me. I am not wrong."

Thereupon Medius raised the cup and drank, having trouble halfway through, as if his throat had closed against the liquid; but finally he managed to drain the cup and looked at Alexander defiantly.

Nearchus spake up then. "We have all three drunk, trusting thee, Alexander, but thou has raised Jolas of Philippi above us, as if he alone were free of thy suspicion. Why not have him drink as well?"

"But I have not forgotten him," Alexander said. "Jolas, there stands a cup of water upon the table for thee to drink. If thou, too, participate in this test, perhaps the anger of the others against thee will be diminished. I say unto thee as I said to the others; if you are innocent, thou hast nothing to fear. Drink the water."

I raised the glass to my lips and as I did Alexander spoke again.

"It is as pure as the water of my bath, Jolas."

At that I hesitated and looked at Alexander with staring eyes and beating heart—and put the cup down upon the table.

"Thou art my murderer, Jolas," said Alexander, his eyes burning. "Thou wert sitting beside the pool when I arrived there four nights ago. How didst thou poison it?"

"With some of the poison, which I tossed into it," said I, almost crying now that my perfidy was so inevitably disclosed. "But I did not mean to kill thee, Alexander," I pleaded. "Antipater assured me that he had tested the poison upon others, and that taken through the pores the poison merely induces a fever that will pass away. But I saw thee *swallow* some of the water!"

"Antipater knew thee for a fool! He meant Alexander should die!" Nearchus cried, stepping towards me, but he stopped as Alexander raised his hand.

"And what reason did Antipater give thee?" he asked.

"He wished Medius dead and disgraced, so members of Medius's family in Macedonia, who have been troublesome to Antipater, could be removed from authority. He knew Medius was thy great drinking companion. I was to poison thee harmlessly, plant the knowledge of Medius's desire to assassinate thee, then when the effects of the poison became manifest, to indicate their origin, and accuse Medius of administering it in thy drink."

Alexander nodded with satisfaction.

"And what was to be thy reward, Jolas?"

"Antipater would beg thee to release me from duty here in Babylonia, and once in Macedonia he would give me the governorship of Sestos, a position thou, Alexander, wouldst never give me, since thou wouldst have me litigate in Babylonia until the end of my days."

"Not now, Jolas, not now!" Alexander said. Then, rising unsteadily, he pointed at Medius.

"Thou wert to be the victim, Medius," he said. *"Make Jolas drink the water!"*

With Medius's all-too-ready sword at my throat, I had no alternative and I drained the water to the last drop.

In the silence that followed I asked, "How didst thou know that it was I, Alexander?"

"The other day I asked thee if thou knewest this poison, and thou denied any knowledge of it. Yet when the Paphlagonian was killed I was stricken with a sudden seizure and thou helped me to my couch. 'Warmth for thy feet,' thou said, 'and a pillow for the great pain in thy back!' *But how couldst thou know my back hurt, feeling as if someone thrust a sword between my shoulder blades, if thou didst not already know the effects of the poison?* I had not told it to anyone. That began a train of thought, and when I saw the poisoned wine spreading within the pool and wondered how soon the fishes would die, I remembered the bathing water, and realized why Medius had not been poisoned by the third of the bitter cup, and why all my investigation had been fruitless. *There was no poison in the cup!* I had been poisoned *before* the drinking bout, not during it! . . ."

Alexander was too weak to go on, so Nearchus had me sent under guard to my house at the edge of the palace gardens and confined there. Medius wished to kill me at once, which was but natural, since it was he who had sent the archer after me, but Alexander and Nearchus were against it. It would be better for the ruling officers if it were thought Alexander died of disease, and so it will be told that I, too, died of the same, from my contact in the service of the king.

It is two days now since the great Alexander died. There is the sound of weeping and mourning in the streets of Babylon, and a hush in the palace gardens. The fever that burns me makes my pen cold to the touch, but I must finish this so the world will know that I did not mean that my dearest friend Alexander should die.

I have no use for men who would kill merely to satisfy their ambition.

KING BEE AND HONEY

Steven Saylor

The period between the Roman civil wars (79 B.C.–72 B.C.) was characterized by excess and insecurity. Yet it is not hard to believe that there were bucolic interludes, a striving after harmony and balance, in the history of even the most debauched of Romans. It is such a chapter in the lives of those of the patrician class that we come upon in "King Bee and Honey." "All the bee lore is authentically Roman," the author tells us, and so is the role a "finder" such as Gordianus would play. Like a modern private investigator, Gordianus is susceptible to the lure of money, but he's on holiday in this adventure, and his services are strictly gratis.

Gordianus! And Eco! How was your journey?"

"I'll tell you as soon as I get off this horse and discover whether I still have two legs."

My friend Lucius Claudius let out a good-natured laugh. "Why, the ride from Rome is only a few hours! And a fine, paved road all the way. And glorious weather!"

That was true enough. It was a day in late Aprilis, one of those golden spring days that one might wish could last forever. Sol himself seemed to think so; the sun stood still in the sky, as if enraptured by the beauty of the earth below and unwilling to move on.

And the earth was indeed beautiful, especially this little corner of it, tucked amid the rolling Etruscan countryside north of Rome. The hills were studded with oaks and spangled with yellow and purple flowers. Here in the valley, groves of olive trees shimmered silver and green in the faint breeze. The orchards of fig trees and lime trees were in full leaf. Bees hummed and flitted among the long rows of grape leaves. There was bird song on the air, mingled with a tune being sung by a group of

slaves striding through a nearby field and swinging their scythes in unison. I breathed deeply the sweet odor of tall grass drying in the sun. Even
my good friend Lucius looked unusually robust, like a plump-cheeked
Silenus with frazzled red hair; all he needed to complete the image was
a pitcher of wine and a few attendant wood nymphs.

I slipped off my horse and discovered I still had legs after all. Eco
sprang from his mount and leaped into the air. Oh, to be a fourteen-
year-old boy, and to never know a stiff muscle! A slave led our horses
toward the stable.

Lucius gave me a hearty slap across the shoulders and walked me
toward the villa. Eco ran in circles around us, like an excited pup. It was
a charming house, low and rambling with many windows, their shutters all thrown open to let in the sunlight and fresh air. I thought of
houses in the city, all narrow and crammed together and windowless
for fear of robbers climbing in from the street. Here, even the house
seemed to have sighed with relief and allowed itself to relax.

"You see, I told you," said Lucius. "It's a beautiful place, isn't it? And
look at you, Gordianus. That smile on your face! The last time I saw you
in the city, you looked like a man wearing shoes too small for his feet. I
knew this was what you needed—an escape to the countryside for a few
days. It always works for me. When all the politicking and litigation in
the Forum becomes too much, I flee to my farm. You'll see. A few days
and you'll be a reborn man. And Eco will have a splendid time, climbing
the hills, swimming in the stream. But you didn't bring Bethesda?"

"No. She—" I began to say *she refused to come,* which was the exact
truth, but I feared that my highborn friend would smirk at the idea of
a slave refusing to accompany her master on a trip. "Bethesda is a creature of the city, you know. Hardly suited for the countryside. She'd
have been useless to me here."

"Oh, I see." Lucius nodded. "She refused to come?"

"Well . . ." I began to shake my head, then gave it up and laughed out
loud. Of what use were citified pretensions here, where Sol stood still
and cast his golden light over a perfect world? Lucius was right. Best to
leave such nonsense back in Rome. On an impulse I reached for Eco, and
when he made a game of slipping from my grasp I gave chase. The two
of us ran in circles around Lucius, who threw back his head and laughed.

That night we dined on asparagus and goose liver, followed by mush-
rooms sautéed in goose fat and a guinea hen in a honey-vinegar sauce

sprinkled with pine nuts. The fare was simply but superbly prepared. I praised the meal so profusely that Lucius called in the cook to take a bow.

I was surprised to see that the cook was a woman, and still in her twenties. Her dark hair was pulled back in a tight bun, no doubt to keep it out of her way in the kitchen. Her plump cheeks were all the plumper for the beaming smile on her face; she appreciated praise. Her face was pleasant, if not beautiful, and her figure, even in her loose clothing, appeared to be quite voluptuous.

"Davia started as an assistant to my head cook at my house in Rome," Lucius explained. "She helped him shop, measured out ingredients, that sort of thing. But when he fell ill last winter and she had to take his place, she showed such a knack that I decided to give her the run of the kitchen here at the farm. So you approve, Gordianus?"

"Indeed. Everything was splendid, Davia."

Eco added his praise but his applause was interrupted by a profound yawn. Too much good food and fresh air, he explained, gesturing to the table and to the breath before his lips. Eco's tongue was useless, due to a fever that had nearly claimed his life, but he was a skillful mime. He excused himself and went straight to bed.

Lucius and I took chairs down to the stream and sipped his finest vintage while we listened to the gurgling of the water and the chirring of the crickets and watched thin clouds pass like shredded veils across the face of the moon.

"Ten days of this, and I think I might forget the way back to Rome."

"Ah, but not the way back to Bethesda, I'll wager. I was hoping to see her. She's a city flower, yes, but put her in the country and she might put out some fresh blossoms that would surprise you. Ah well, it shall be just us three fellows, then."

"No other guests?"

"No, no, no! I specifically waited until I had no pending social obligations, so that we should have the place all to ourselves." He smiled at me under the moonlight, then turned down his lips in a mock-frown. "It's *not* what you're thinking, Gordianus."

"And what am I thinking?"

"That for all his homely virtues, your friend Lucius Claudius is still a patrician and subject to the snobbery of his class; that I chose a time to invite you here when there'd be no one else around so as to avoid having you seen by my more elevated friends. But that's not the point at all. I wanted you to have the place to yourself so that *you* wouldn't have to put up with *them!* Oh, if you only knew the sort of people I'm talking about."

I smiled at his discomfort. "My work does occasionally bring me into contact with the highborn and wealthy, you know."

"Ah, but it's a different matter, socializing with them. I won't even mention my own family, though they're the worst. Oh, there are the fortune hunters, the ones on the fringes of society who think they can scrape and claw their way to respectability like a ferret. And the grandpas, the boring, self-important old farts who never let anyone forget that some ancestor of theirs served two terms as consul or sacked a Greek temple or slaughtered a shipload of Carthaginians back in the golden age. And the crackpots who claim they're descended from Hercules or Venus—more likely Medusa, judging from their table manners. And the too-rich, spoiled young men who can't think of anything but gambling and horse racing, and the too-pretty girls who can't think of anything, but new gowns and jewels, and the parents who can't think of anything but matching up the boys and girls so that they can breed more of the same.

"You see, Gordianus, you meet these people at their worst, when there's been a dreadful murder or some other crime, and they're all anxious and confused and need your help, but I see them at their best, when they're preening themselves like African birds and oozing charm all over each other like honey, and believe me, at their best they're a thousand times worse! Oh, you can't imagine some of the dreadful gatherings I've had to put up with here at the villa. No, no, nothing like that for the next ten days. This shall be a respite for you and me alike—for you from the city, and for me from my so-called circle of friends."

But it was not to be.

The next three days were like a foretaste of Elysium. Eco explored every corner of the farm, as fascinated by butterflies and ant beds as he was by the arcane mechanics of the olive-oil press and the wine press. He had always been a city boy—he was an abandoned child of the streets when I adopted him—but it was clear he could develop a taste for the country.

As for me, I treated myself to Davia's cooking at least three times a day, toured the farm with Lucius and his foreman, and spent restful hours lying in the shade of the willows along the stream, scrolling through trashy Greek novels from Lucius's small library. The plots all seemed to be the same—humble boy meets noble girl, girl is abducted by pirates/giants/soldiers, boy rescues girl and turns out to be of noble birth himself—but such nonsense seemed to fit my mood perfectly. I allowed myself to become pampered and relaxed and thoroughly lazy in body, mind, and spirit, and I enjoyed every moment.

Then came the fourth day, and the visitors.

They arrived just as the light was beginning to fail, in an open traveling coach drawn by four white horses and followed by a small retinue of slaves. She was dressed in green and wore her auburn curls pinned in the peculiar upright fan-shape that happened to be stylish in the city that spring; it made a suitable frame for the striking beauty of her face. He wore a dark blue tunic that was sleeveless and cut above the knees to show off his athletic arms and legs, and an oddly trimmed little beard that seemed designed to flout convention. They looked to be about my age, midway between thirty and forty.

I happened to be walking back to the villa from the stream. Lucius stepped out of the house to greet me, looked past me, and saw the new arrivals.

"Numa's balls!" he exclaimed under his breath, borrowing my own favorite epithet.

"Friends of yours?" I said.

"Yes!" He could not have sounded more dismayed if he was being paid a visit by Hannibal's ghost riding a ghostly elephant.

He, it turned out, was a fellow named Titus Didius. She was Antonia, his second wife. (They had both divorced their first spouses in order to marry each other, generating enormous scandal and no small amount of envy among their unhappily married peers.) According to Lucius, who took me aside while the couple settled into the room next to mine, they drank like fishes, fought like jackals, and stole like magpies. (I noticed that the slaves discreetly put away the costliest wines, the best silver, and the most fragile Arretine vases shortly after they arrived.)

"It seems they were planning to spend a few days up at my cousin Manius's place, but when they arrived, no one was there. Well, I know what happened—Manius went down to Rome just to avoid them. I wonder that they didn't pass him on the way!"

"Surely not."

"Surely yes. So now they've come here, asking to stay awhile. 'Just a day or two, before we head back to the city. We were so looking forward to some time in the country. You will be a dear, won't you, Lucius, and let us stay, just for a bit?' More likely ten days than two!"

I shrugged. "They don't look so awful to me."

"Oh, wait. Just wait."

"Well, if they're really as terrible as that, why don't you let them stay the night and then turn them away?"

"Turn them away?" He repeated the phrase as if I'd stopped speaking Latin. "Turn them *away?* You mean, send away Titus Didius, old Marcus Didius's boy? Refuse my hospitality to *Antonia?* But Gordianus, I've known these people since I was a child. I mean, to avoid them, like cousin Manius has done, well, that's one thing. But to say to them, to their faces—"

"Never mind. I understand," I said, though I didn't, really.

Whatever their faults, the couple had one overriding virtue: They were charming. So charming, indeed, that on that first night, dining in their company, I began to think that Lucius was wildly exaggerating. Certainly they showed none of the characteristic snobbishness of their class toward Eco and me. Titus wanted to hear all about my travels and my work for advocates like Marcus Cicero. ("Is it true," he asked, leaning toward me earnestly, "that he's a eunuch?") Eco was obviously fascinated by Antonia, who was even more remarkably beautiful by lamplight. She made a game of flirting with him, but she did so with a natural grace that was neither condescending nor mean. They were both witty, vibrant, and urbane, and their sense of humor was only slightly, charmingly, vulgar.

They also appreciated good cooking. Just as I had done after my first meal here, they insisted on complimenting the cook. When Davia appeared, Titus's face lit up with surprise, and not just at the fact that the cook was a young woman. When Lucius opened his mouth to introduce her, Titus snatched the name from his lips. "Davia!" he said. The word left a smile on his face.

A look of displeasure flashed in Antonia's eyes.

Lucius looked back and forth between Davia and Titus, speechless for a moment. "Then you . . . already know Davia?"

"Why, of course. We met once before, at your house in the city. Davia wasn't the cook, though. Only a helper in the kitchen."

"When was this?" asked Antonia, smiling sweetly.

Titus shrugged. "Last year? The year before? At one of Lucius's dinner parties, I suppose. An odd thing—you weren't there, as I recall. Something kept you home that night, my dear. A headache, perhaps . . ." He gave his wife a commiserating smile and then looked back at Davia with another kind of smile.

"And how is it that you happened to meet the cook's helper?" Antonia's voice took on a slight edge.

"Oh, I think I must have gone into the kitchen to ask a favor of the cook, or something like that. And then I . . . well, I met Davia. Didn't I, Davia?"

"Yes." Davia looked at the floor. Though it was hard to tell by the lamplight, it seemed to me that she was blushing.

"Well," said Titus, clapping his hands together, "you have become a splendid cook, Davia! Entirely worthy of your master's famously high standards. About that we're all agreed, yes? Gordianus, Eco, Lucius . . . Antonia?"

Everyone nodded in unison, some more enthusiastically than others. Davia muttered her thanks and disappeared back into the kitchen.

Lucius's new guests were tired from traveling. Eco and I had enjoyed a long, full day. Everyone turned in early.

The night was warm. Windows and doors were left open to take advantage of the slight breeze. There was a great stillness on the earth, of a sort that one never experiences in the city. As I began to drift into the arms of Morpheus, in the utter quiet I thought I could hear the distant, dreamy rustling of the sheep in their pen, the hushed sighing of the high grass far away by the road, and even a hint of the stream's gentle gurgling. Eco, with whom I shared the room, began to snore very gently.

Then the fighting began.

At first I could hear only voices from the next room, not words. But after a while they started shouting. Her voice was higher and carried better than his.

"You filthy adulterer! Bad enough that you take advantage of the girls in our own household, but picking off another man's slaves—"

Titus shouted something, presumably in his defense.

She was not impressed. "Oh, you filthy liar! You can't fool me. I saw the way you looked at her tonight. And how dare you try to bring up that business about me and the pearl diver at Andros? That was all in your own drunken imagination!"

Titus shouted again. Antonia shouted. This went on for quite some time. There was a sound of breaking pottery. Silence for a while, and then the shouting resumed.

I groaned and pulled the coverlet over my head. After a while I realized that the shouting had stopped. I rolled onto my side, thinking I might finally be able to sleep, and noticed that Eco was standing on his knees on his sleeping couch, his ear pressed against the wall that ran between our room and theirs.

"Eco, what in Hades are you doing?"

He kept his ear to the wall and waved at me to be quiet.

"They're not fighting again, are they?"

He turned and shook his head.

"What is it, then?"

The moonlight showed a crooked smile on his face. He pumped his eyebrows up and down like a leering street mime, made a circle with the fingers of one hand and a pointer with the opposite forefinger, and performed a gesture all the street mimes knew.

"Oh! I see. Well, stop listening like that. It's rude." I rolled to my other side and pulled the coverlet over my head.

I must have slept for quite some time, for it was the moonlight, traveling from Eco's side of the room to mine, that struck my face and woke me. I sighed and rearranged the coverlet and saw that Eco was still up on his knees, his ear pressed fervently against the wall.

They must have been at it all night long.

For the next two days Lucius Claudius repeatedly drew me aside to fret over the intrusion on my holiday, but Eco went about his simple pleasures, I still found time to read alone down by the stream, and to the extent that Titus and Antonia intruded on us, they were in equal measure irritating and amusing. No one could be more delightful than Titus at dinner, at least until the cup of wine that was one cup too many, after which his jokes all became a little too vulgar and his jabs a little too sharp. And no one could be more sweetly alluring over a table of roasted pig than Antonia, until something happened to rub her the wrong way. She had a look which could send a hot spike through a man as surely as the beast on the table had been spitted and put on to roast.

I had never met a couple quite like them. I began to see how none of their friends could refuse them anything. I also began to see how they drove those same friends to distraction with their sudden fits of temper and their all-consuming passion for each other, which ran hot and cold, and could scald or chill any outsider who happened to come too close.

On the third day of their visit, Lucius announced that he had come up with something special that we could all do together.

"Have you ever seen honey collected from a hive, Eco? No, I thought not. And you, Gordianus? No? What about you two?"

"Why, no, actually," said Antonia. She and her husband had slept until noon and were just joining the rest of us down by the stream for our midday meal.

"Does that water have to gurgle so loud?" Titus rubbed his temples. "Did you say something about bees, Lucius? I seem to have a swarm of them buzzing in my head this morning."

"It is no longer morning, Titus, and the bees are not in your head but in a glen downstream a bit," said Lucius in a chiding tone.

Antonia wrinkled her brow. "How *does* one collect the honey? I suppose I've never given it much thought—I just enjoy eating it!"

"Oh, it's quite a science," said Lucius. "I have a slave named Ursus whom I bought specifically for his knowledge of beekeeping. He builds the hives out of hollowed strips of bark tied up with vines and covered with mud and leaves. He keeps away pests, makes sure the meadow has the right kind of flowers, and collects the honey twice a year. Now that the Pleiades have risen in the night sky, he says it's time for the spring harvest."

"Where does honey come from? I mean, where do the bees get it?" said Antonia. Puzzlement gave her face a deceptively vulnerable charm.

"Who cares?" said Titus, taking her hand and kissing her palm. "You are my honey!"

"Oh, and you are my king bee!" They kissed. Eco made a show of wrinkling his nose and shuddering. Faced with actual kissing, his adolescent prurience turned to squeamishness.

"Where *does* honey come from?" I said. "And do bees really have kings?"

"Well, I shall tell you," said Lucius. "Honey falls from the sky, of course, like dew. So Ursus says, and he should know. The bees gather it up and concentrate it until it becomes all gooey and thick. To have a place to put it, they gather tree sap and the wax from certain plants to build their combs inside the hive. And do they have kings? Oh yes! They will gladly give their lives to protect him. Sometimes two different swarms go to war. The kings hang back, plotting the strategy, and the clash can be terrific—acts of heroism and sacrifice to rival the *Iliad!*"

"And when they're not at war?" said Antonia.

"A hive is like a bustling city. Some go out to work in the fields, collecting the honey-dew, some work indoors, constructing and maintaining the combs, and the kings lay down laws for the common good. They say Jupiter granted the bees the wisdom to govern themselves as repayment for the favor they did him in his infancy. When Jupiter was hidden in a cave to save him from his father Saturn, the bees sustained him with honey."

"You make them sound almost superior to humans," said Titus, laughing and tracing kisses on Antonia's wrist.

"Oh, hardly. They're still ruled by kings, after all, and haven't yet advanced to having a republic, like ourselves," explained Lucius earnestly, not realizing that he was being teased. "So, who wants to go and see the honey collected?"

"I shouldn't want to get stung," said Antonia cautiously.

"Oh, there's little danger of that. Ursus sedates the bees with smoke. It makes them dull and drowsy. And we'll stand well out of the way."

Eco nodded enthusiastically.

"I suppose it would be interesting . . ." said Antonia.

"Not for me," said Titus, lying back on the grassy bank and rubbing his temples.

"Oh, Titus, don't be a dull, drowsy king bee," said Antonia, poking at him and pouting. "Come along."

"No."

"Titus . . ." There was a hint of menace in Antonia's voice.

Lucius flinched in anticipation of a row. He cleared his throat. "Yes, Titus, come along. The walk will do you good. Get your blood pumping."

"No. My mind's made up."

Antonia flashed a brittle smile. "Very well, then have it your way. You shall miss the fun, and so much the worse for you. Shall we get started, Lucius?"

"The natural enemies of the bee are the lizard, the woodpecker, the spider, and the moth," droned the slave Ursus, walking beside Eco at the head of our little procession. "These creatures are all jealous of the honey, you see, and will do great damage to the hives to get at it." Ursus was a big, stout man of middle years and lumbering gait, hairy all over, to judge from the thatches that showed at the openings of his long-sleeved tunic. Several other slaves followed behind us on the path that ran along the stream, carrying the embers and hay-torches that would be used to make the smoke.

"There are plants which are enemies of the bees as well," Ursus went on. "The yew tree, for example. You never put a hive close to a yew tree, because the bees will sicken and the honey will turn bitter and runny. But they thrive close to olive trees and willows. For gathering their honey-dew they like red and purple flowers; blood-red hyacinth is their favorite. If there's thyme close by, they'll use it to give the honey a delicate flavor. They prefer to live close to a stream with shaded, mossy pools where they can drink and wash themselves. And they like calm and quiet. As you will see, Eco, the secluded place where we keep the hives has all these qualities, being close by the stream, surrounded by olives and willows, and planted with all the flowers that most delight the bees."

I heard the bees before I saw them. Their humming joined the gurgling of the stream and grew louder as we passed through a hedge of cassia shrubs and entered a sun-dappled, flower-spangled little glen that was just as Ursus had described. There was magic to the place. Satyrs and nymphs seemed to frolic in the shadows, just out of sight. One could almost imagine the infant Jupiter lying in the soft grass, living off the honey of the bees.

The hives, ten in all, stood in a row on waist-high wooden platforms in the center of the clearing. They were shaped like tall domes, and with their coverings of dried mud and leaves looked as if they had been put there by nature; Ursus was a master of craft as well as lore. Each hive had only a tiny break in the bark for an entrance, and through these openings the bees were busily coming and going.

A figure beneath a nearby willow caught my eyes, and for a startled instant I thought a satyr had stepped into the clearing to join us. Antonia saw it at the same instant. She let out a little gasp of surprise, then clapped her hands in delight.

"And what is this fellow doing here?" She laughed and stepped closer for a better look.

"He watches over the glen," said Ursus. "The traditional guardian of the hives. Scares away honey-thieves and birds."

It was a bronze statue of the god Priapus, grinning lustfully, with one hand on his hip and a sickle held upright in the other. He was naked and eminently, rampantly priapic. Antonia, fascinated, gave him a good looking-over and touched him for luck.

My attention at that moment was drawn to Eco, who had wandered off to the other side of the glen and was stooping amid some purple flowers that grew low to the ground. I hurried to join him.

"Be careful of those, Eco. Don't pick any more. Go wash your hands in the stream."

"What's the matter?" said Ursus.

"This is Etruscan star-tongue, isn't it?" I said.

"Yes."

"If you're as careful about what grows here as you say, I'm surprised to see it. The plant is poisonous, isn't it?"

"To people, perhaps," said Ursus dismissively. "But not to bees. Sometimes when a hive takes sick it's the only thing to cure them. You take the roots of the star-tongue, boil them with wine, let the tonic cool, and set it out for the bees to drink. It gives them new life."

"But it might do the opposite for a man."

"Yes, but everyone on the farm knows to stay away from the stuff, and the animals are too smart to eat it. I doubt that the flowers are poisonous; it's the roots that hold the bee tonic."

"Well, even so, go wash your hands in the stream," I said to Eco, who had followed this exchange and was looking at me expectantly. The beekeeper shrugged and went about the business of the honey harvest.

As Lucius had promised, it was fascinating to watch. While the other slaves alternately kindled and smothered the torches, producing clouds of smoke, Ursus strode fearlessly into the thick of the sedated bees. His cheeks bulged with water, which he occasionally sprayed from his lips in a fine mist if the bees began to rouse themselves. One by one he lifted up the hives and used a long knife to scoop out a portion of the honeycomb. The wafting clouds of smoke, Ursus's slow, deliberate progress from hive to hive, the secluded magic of the place, and, not least, the smiling presence of the watchful god, gave the harvest the aura of a rustic religious procession. So men have collected the sweet labor of the bees since the beginning of time.

Only one thing occurred to jar the spell. As Ursus was lifting the very last of the hives, a flood of ghostly white moths poured out from underneath. They flitted through the smoky reek and dispersed amid the shimmering olive leaves above. From this hive Ursus would take no honey, saying that the presence of the bandit moths was an ill omen.

The party departed from the glen in a festive mood. Ursus cut pieces of honeycomb and handed them out. Everyone's fingers and lips were soon sticky with honey. Even Antonia made a mess of herself.

When we reached the villa she ran ahead. "King bee," she cried, "I have a sweet kiss for you! And a sweet reason for you to kiss my fingertips! Your honey is covered with honey!"

What did she see when she ran into the foyer of the house? Surely it was no more than the rest of us saw, who entered only a few heartbeats after her. Titus was fully dressed, and so was Davia. Perhaps there was a fleeting look on their faces which the rest of us missed, or perhaps Antonia sensed rather than saw the thing that set off her fury.

Whatever it was, the row began then and there. Antonia stalked out of the foyer, toward her room. Titus quickly followed. Davia, blushing, hurried off toward the kitchen.

Lucius looked at me and rolled his eyes. "What now?" A strand of honey, thin as spider's silk, dangled from his plump chin.

The row showed no signs of abating at dinner. While Lucius and I made conversation about the honey harvest and Eco joined in with eloquent flourishes of his hands (his evocation of the flight of the moths was particularly vivid), Antonia and Titus ate in stony silence. They retired to their bedchamber early. That night there were no sounds of reconciliation. Titus growled and whined like a dog. Antonia shrieked and wept.

Eco slept despite the noise, but I tossed and turned until at last I decided to take a walk. The moon lit my way as I stepped out of the villa, made a circuit of the stable, and strolled by the slaves' quarters. Coming around a corner, I saw two figures seated close together on a bench beside the portico that led to the kitchen. Though her hair was not in a bun but let down for the night, the moon lit up her face well enough for me to recognize Davia. By his bearish shape I knew the man who sat with one arm around her, stroking her face: Ursus. They were so intent on each other that they did not notice me. I turned and went back the way I had come, reflecting that the hand of Venus reaches everywhere, and wondering if Lucius was aware that his cook and his beekeeper were lovers.

What a contrast their silent devotions made to the couple in the room next to me. When I returned to bed, I had to cover my head with a pillow to muffle the sounds of them still arguing.

But the morning seemed to bring a new day. While Lucius, Eco, and I ate a breakfast of bread and honey in the little garden outside Lucius's study, Antonia came walking up from the direction of the stream, bearing a basket of flowers.

"Antonia!" said Lucius. "I should have thought you were still abed."

"Not at all," she said, beaming. "I was up before dawn, and on a whim I went down to the stream to pick some flowers. Aren't they lovely? I shall have one of my girls weave them into a garland for me to wear at dinner tonight."

"Your beauty needs no ornament," said Lucius. Indeed, Antonia looked especially radiant that morning. "And where is—mmm, dare I call him your king bee?"

Antonia laughed. "Still abed, I imagine. But I shall go and rouse him at once. This day is too beautiful to be missed! I was thinking that Titus and I might take along a basket of food and some wine and spend most of the day down by the stream. Just the *two* of us . . ."

She raised her eyebrows. Lucius understood. "Ah yes, well, Gordianus and I have plenty to occupy us here at the villa. And Eco—I believe you were planning to do some exploring up on the hill today, weren't you?"

Eco, not quite understanding, nodded nonetheless.

"Well then, it looks as though you and the king bee will have the stream all to yourselves," said Lucius.

Antonia beamed. "Lucius, you are so very sweet." She paused to kiss his blushing pate.

A little later, as we were finishing our leisurely breakfast, we saw the couple walking down toward the stream without even a slave to bear their baskets and blanket. They held hands and laughed and doted on each other so lavishly that Eco became positively queasy watching them.

By some acoustical curiosity, a sharp noise from the stream could sometimes carry all the way up to the house. So it was, some time later, standing by Lucius in front of the villa while he discussed the day's work with his foreman, that I thought I heard a cry and a hollow crack from that direction. Lucius and the foreman, one talking while the other listened, seemed not to notice, but Eco, poking about an old wine press nearby, pricked up his ears. Eco may be mute, but his hearing is sharp. We had both heard Titus's raised voice too often over the last few days not to recognize it.

The spouses had not made up, after all, I thought. The two of them were at it again. . . .

Then, a little later, Antonia screamed. We all heard it. It was not her familiar shriek of rage. It was a scream of pure panic.

She screamed again.

We ran all the way, Eco in the lead, Lucius huffing and puffing in the rear. "By Hercules," he shouted, "he must be killing her!"

But Antonia wasn't dying. Titus was.

He was flat on his back on the blanket, his short tunic twisted all askew and hitched up about his hips. He stared at the leafy canopy above, his pupils hugely dilated. "Dizzy . . . spinning . . ." he gasped. He coughed and wheezed and grabbed his throat, then bent forward. His hands went to his belly, clutching at cramps. His face was a deathly shade of blue.

"What in Hades!" exclaimed Lucius. "What happened to him, Antonia? Gordianus, what can we do?"

"Can't breathe!" Titus said, mouthing words with no air behind them. "The end . . . the end of me . . . oh, it hurts!" He grabbed at his loincloth. "Damn the gods!"

He pulled at his tunic, as if it constricted his chest. The foreman gave me his knife. I cut the tunic open and tore it off, leaving him naked except for the loose loincloth about his hips; it did no good, except to show us that his whole body was turning blue. I turned him on his side and reached into his mouth, thinking he might be choking, but that did no good either.

He kept struggling until the end, fighting to breathe. It was a horrible death to watch. At last the wheezing and clenching stopped. His limbs unfurled. The life went out of his staring eyes.

Antonia stood by, stunned and silent, her face like a petrified tragedy mask. "Oh no!" she whispered, dropping to her knees and embracing the body. She began to scream again and to sob wildly. Her agony was almost as hard to watch as Titus's death throes, and there seemed as little to be done about it.

"But how in Hades did this happen?" said Lucius. "What caused it?"

Eco and the foreman and I looked at each other dumbly.

"Her fault!" wailed Antonia.

"What?" said Lucius.

"Your cook! That horrible woman! It's her fault!"

Lucius looked around at the scattered remains of food. Crusts of bread, a little jar of honey, black olives, a wineskin, a broken clay bottle—that had been the hollow crack I had heard. "What do you mean? Are you saying she poisoned him?"

Antonia's sobs caught in her throat. "Yes, that's it. Yes! It was one of my own slaves who put the food in the basket, but she's the one who prepared the food. Davia! The witch poisoned him. She poisoned everything!"

"Oh, dear, but that means—" Lucius knelt. He gripped Antonia's arms and looked into her eyes. "You might be poisoned as well! Antonia, do you feel any pain? Gordianus, what should we do for her?"

I looked at him blankly. I had no idea.

Antonia showed no symptoms. She was not poisoned, after all. But something had killed her husband, and in a most sudden and terrible fashion.

Her slaves soon came running. We left her grieving over the body and went back to the villa to confront Davia. Lucius led the way into the kitchen.

"Davia! Do you know what's happened?"

She looked at the floor and swallowed hard. "They say . . . that one of your guests has died, master."

"Yes. What do you know about it?"

She looked shocked. "I? Nothing, master."

"Nothing? They were eating food prepared by you when Titus took ill. Do you still say you know nothing about it?"

"Master, I don't know what you mean. . . ."

"Davia," I said, "you must tell us what was going on between you and Titus Didius."

She stammered and looked away.

"Davia! A man is dead. His wife accuses you. You're in great danger. If you're innocent, the truth could save you. Be brave! Now tell us what passed between you and Titus Didius."

"Nothing! I swear it, by my mother's shade. Not that he didn't try, and keep trying. He approached me at the master's house in the city that night he first saw me. He tried to get me to go into an empty room with him. I wouldn't do it. He kept trying the same thing here. Following me, trapping me. Touching me. I never encouraged him! Yesterday, while you were all down at the hives, he came after me, pulling at my clothes, kissing me. I just kept moving away. He seemed to like that, chasing me. When everyone finally came back, I almost wept with relief."

"He harassed you, then," said Lucius sadly. "My fault, I suppose; I should have warned him to keep his hands off my property. But was it really so terrible that you had to poison him?"

"No! I never—"

"You'll have to torture her if you want the truth!" Antonia stood in the doorway. Her fists were clenched, her hair disheveled. She looked utterly distraught, like a vengeful harpy. "Torture her, Lucius! That's what they do when a slave testifies in a court. It's your right—you're her master. It's your duty—you were Titus's host. I demand that you torture her until she confesses, and then put her to death!"

Davia turned as white as the moths that had flown from the hive. She fainted to the floor.

Antonia, mad with grief, retired to her room. Davia regained consciousness, but seemed to be in the grip of some brain fever; she trembled wildly and would not speak.

"Gordianus, what am I to do?" Lucius paced back and forth in the foyer. "I suppose I'll have to torture the girl if she won't confess. But I don't even know how to go about such a thing! None of my slaves would make a suitable torturer. I suppose I could consult one of my neighbors—"

"Talk of torture is premature," I said, wondering if Lucius could actually go through with such a thing. He was a gentle man in a cruel world; sometimes the world's expectations won out over his basic nature. He might surprise me. I didn't want to find out. "I think we should have another look at the body, now that we've calmed down a bit."

We returned to the stream. Titus lay as we had left him, except that someone had closed his eyes and pulled down his tunic.

"You know a lot about poisons, Gordianus," said Lucius. "What do you think?"

"There are many poisons and many reactions. I can't begin to guess what killed Titus. If we should find some store of poison in the kitchen, or if one of the other slaves observed Davia doing something to the food . . ."

Eco gestured to the scattered food, mimed the act of feeding a farm animal, and vividly performed the animal's death—a hard thing to watch, having just witnessed an actual death.

"Yes, we could verify the presence of poison in the food that way, at the waste of some poor beast. But if it was in the food we see here, why wasn't Antonia poisoned as well? Eco, bring me those pieces of the clay bottle. Do you remember hearing the sound of something breaking at about the time we heard Titus cry out?"

Eco nodded and handed me the pieces of fired clay.

"What do you suppose was in this?" I said.

"Wine, I imagine. Or water," said Lucius.

"But there's a wineskin over there. And the inside of this bottle appears to be as dry as the outside. I have a hunch, Lucius. Would you summon Ursus?"

"Ursus? But why?"

"I have a question for him."

The beekeeper soon came lumbering down the hill. For such a big, bearish fellow, he was very squeamish in the presence of death. He stayed well away from the body and made a face every time he looked at it.

"I'm a city dweller, Ursus. I don't know very much about bees. I've never been stung by one. But I've heard that a bee sting can kill a man. Is that true, Ursus?"

He looked embarrassed at the idea that his beloved bees could do such a thing. "Well, yes, it can happen. But it's rare. Most people get stung and it just goes away. But some people . . ."

"Have you ever seen anyone die of a bee sting, Ursus?"

"No."

"But with all your lore, you must know something about it. How does it happen? How do they die?"

"It's their lungs that give out. They strangle to death. Can't breathe, turn blue . . ."

Lucius looked aghast. "Do you think that's it, Gordianus? That he was stung by one of my bees?"

"Let's have a look. The sting would leave a mark, wouldn't it, Ursus?"

"Oh yes, a red swelling. And more than that, you'd find the poisoned barb itself. It stays behind in the flesh when the bee flies off. Just a tiny thing, but it would be there."

We pulled off Titus's tunic, examining his chest and limbs, rolled him over, and examined his back. We combed through his hair and looked at his scalp.

"Nothing," said Lucius.

"Nothing," I admitted.

"What are the chances, anyway, that a bee happened to fly by—"

"The bottle, Eco. When did we hear it break? Before Titus cried out, or after?"

After, gestured Eco, rolling his fingers forward. He clapped. *Immediately* after.

"Yes, that's how I remember it, too. A bee, a cry, a broken bottle . . ." I pictured Antonia and Titus as I had last seen them together, hand in hand, doting on one another as they headed for the stream. "Two people in love, alone on a grassy bank—what might they reasonably be expected to get up to?"

"What do you mean, Gordianus?"

"I think we shall have to examine Titus more intimately."

"What do you mean?"

"I think we shall have to take off his loincloth. It's already loosened, you see. Probably by Antonia."

As I thought we might, we found the red, swollen bee sting in the most intimate of places.

"Of course, to be absolutely certain, we should find the stinger and remove it. I'll leave that task to you, Lucius. He was your friend, after all, not mine."

Lucius located and dutifully extracted the tiny barb. "Funny," he said. "I thought it would be bigger."

"What, the stinger?"

"No, his . . . well, the way he always bragged, I thought it must be . . . oh, never mind."

Confronted with the truth, Antonia confessed. She had never meant to kill Titus, only to punish him for his pursuit of Davia.

Her early morning trip to the stream had actually been an expedition to capture a bee. The stoppered clay bottle containing her prize had been hidden under the flowers in her basket. Later, Titus himself unwittingly carried the bee in the bottle down to the stream in the basket of food.

It was the Priapus in the glen that had given her the inspiration.

"I've always thought the god looks so . . . *vulnerable* . . . like that," she told us. If she could inflict a wound on Titus in that most vulnerable of places, the punishment would be not only painful and humiliating but strikingly appropriate.

As they lazed on their blanket beside the stream, cuddling with their clothing on, Titus became aroused, just as she planned. Antonia reached for the bottle and unstoppered it. Titus was lying back with his eyes closed and a dreamy smile on his lips. The wound was inflicted before he realized what was happening. He cried out and knocked the bottle from her hand. It broke against the trunk of a willow tree.

She was ready to flee, knowing he might explode with anger. But the catastrophe that followed took her completely by surprise. Her shock and grief at Titus's death were entirely genuine.

Antonia could hardly admit what she had done. Impulsively, she chose Davia as a scapegoat. She partly blamed Davia anyway, for tempting her husband.

It was agreed that Lucius would not spread the whole truth of what had happened. Their circle of friends would be told that Titus had died of a bee sting, but not of Antonia's part. His death had been unintentional, after all, not deliberate murder. Antonia's grief was perhaps punishment enough. But her scapegoating of Davia was unforgivable. Would she have seen the lie through all the way to Davia's torture and death? Lucius thought so. He allowed her to stay the night, then sent her packing back to Rome, along with her husband's body, and told her never to visit or speak to him again.

Ironically, Titus might have been saved had he been a little more forthcoming or a little less amorous. Lucius later learned, in all the talk that followed on Titus's death, that Titus had once been stung by a bee as a boy and had fallen very ill. He had never talked of this to any of his friends, or even to his wife; only his old nurse and his closest relatives knew about it. When he hung back from seeing the honey harvest, I think he did so partly because he wanted time alone to pursue Davia, but I suspect he was also quite reasonably afraid to approach the hives, and unwilling to admit his fear. If he had told us then of his susceptibility to bee stings, I am certain that Antonia would never have attempted her vengeful scheme.

Eco and I saw out the rest of our visit, but the days that followed Antonia's departure were melancholy. Lucius was moody. The slaves, always superstitious about any death, were restless. Davia was still shaken, and her cooking suffered. The sun was as bright as when we arrived, the flowers as fragrant, the stream as sparkling, but the tragedy cast a pall over everything. When the day came for our departure, I was ready for the forgetful hustle and bustle of the city. And what a story I would have to tell Bethesda!

Before we left, I paid a visit to Ursus and took a last look at the hives down in the glen.

"Have you ever been stung by a bee yourself, Ursus?"

"Oh yes, many times."

"It must hurt."

"It smarts."

"But not too terribly, I suppose. Otherwise you'd stop being a bee-keeper."

Ursus grinned. "Yes, bees can sting. But so can love. I always say that beekeeping is like loving a woman. You get stung every so often, but you keep coming back for more, because the honey is always worth it."

"Oh, not always, Ursus," I sighed. "Not always."

THE HICCUP FLASK

James Powell

The secular and religious head of a traditional Muslim state—the caliph—is often depicted in story as a man both clever and wise. To be most effective, such stories must create the mood of fable, their natural beginning being "Once upon a time." The caliph in James Powell's fanciful story has the wisdom to employ a thief. We must leave it up to the reader to decide whether the explanation underlying the thief's solution to the caliph's problem involves magic or plain human nature.

Know, my masters, that there once lived in Bagdad a Caliph named Amalik the Proper. His grandfather, a famous wager of wars, had filled the country's cemeteries to bursting and then left a son behind him who emptied the treasury to support the extravagances of his court. When at last the key of the Great Door of Bagdad passed to Amalik, a ruined and exhausted land was his inheritance.

Now though the new Caliph was a shy, unexceptional man with a stiff carriage and a cool manner, he loved his people well. And in his heart he believed destiny had chosen him as the proper one to lead the Caliphate away from war's crimson trumpets and the spendthrift lutes of pleasure back to the humbler songs of plow, forge, and marketplace.

According to custom, the Caliph discoursed publicly on the sacred writings in the palace courtyard at sunset on the last Friday of every month. Though no scholar, Amalik discharged this obligation faithfully, speaking from a canopied dais while beneath him the worthies of Bagdad nodded and blinked away the tears of suppressed yawns. Halfway through one of these addresses it happened that the Caliph was seized by an attack of hiccups so violent he was obliged to rush back into the palace, red-faced with embarrassment.

The Caliph's doctors hurried to attend him. But though they worked long into the night, their master's hiccups grew until each rang like a hammer on an anvil, rattling his bones from toes to teeth. Finally, Amalik dismissed them and ordered drummers to be sent throughout the city offering a reward of a thousand gold dinars to whoever cured him of his affliction. Then, exhausted from his ordeal and ashamed to appear in his condition among his wives, the Caliph had a bed made up deep in the cellars of the palace, where he spent a dreadful night with the stone walls echoing each hiccup and (or so it seemed to him) broadcasting it across the Bagdad rooftops.

Early the next morning, a crowd gathered outside the palace, each man eager to share some ancient hiccup nostrum. Over the next several days Amalik submitted to wearing dried toads around his neck, being tickled with peacock feathers, and having his ears and nostrils closed up with wool and beeswax. In addition, he consumed every vile concoction and vaunted tisane presented to him, sat for hours in the smoke of burning rhinoceros horn, and recited a thousand incantations, standing first on one leg, then on the other. Finally, he allowed himself to be ambushed by the three Abdullah brothers wearing garish masks and armed with bells and gongs.

When his heart had returned to his body, the haggard-eyed, hiccuping Caliph sent the drummers out into the streets again, ordering them to announce the reward had been raised to two thousand dinars—with the warning that whoever tried and failed to rid the Caliph of his affliction would receive two hundred lashes from the public executioner. Abruptly, the cures stopped coming.

For the next several days, Amalik, made snappish and short-tempered by his misfortune, paced the palace gardens. Now the servants jumped when he spoke and the vizier advised without condescension and even the Caliph's youngest ceased to pull his beard when they sat in his lap. Amalik resolved that even when he was cured he would maintain this stern manner and use it to drive his city along the road to prosperity. Perhaps one day the historians of his reign would speak of "the hiccups that saved the Caliphate."

And if he was never cured? Then by my beard, thought Amalik, I will ride forth at the head of my Army hiccuping like thunder, and, hearing my approach, my enemies shall flee before me! So swore the Caliph to himself. But in the next moment he had fallen to his knees, touched his forehead to the path, and prayed that his affliction be taken from him.

That very day, the public executioner ushered an old man dressed in mantle and turban of the deepest blue-blackness into the throne room. This gaunt-faced newcomer's deep-set eyes burned with a wild fire. He bowed before the Caliph.

Amalik hiccuped and fixed him with as stern a gaze as the situation would allow. "Can you rid me of this?" he demanded.

"I have had some success in such things, Your Honor," said the old man with a thin-lipped smile. "A hiccup, Lord, is a sigh which has been turned malignant by some passing Jinn of the Evil tribe. It breaks forth on the outward breath and returns on the inward, bent on destroying whomever it afflicts as slowly and surely as a water drop will eventually split the purest adamant."

Here the Caliph hiccuped mightily. The old man's flashing fingers seemed to pluck something out of the air under Amalik's nose. From inside his mantle, he pulled a flask of green glass with a band of silver beneath the lip and made motions as if pushing something into the bottle with his fingertips. With his palm over the mouth, he rummaged in a pocket until he found the stopper. When the flask was sealed, the old man held it up to the light for the Caliph to see.

Amalik looked and saw nothing. He cocked an unhappy eyebrow. He had listened to the man's story of wicked Jinns and watched his pitiful dumb show. Now he was tired and wanted to be left alone. He was about to give the signal to have the old man taken out and flogged when he realized his hiccups had left him. He laid his hand on his breast, which was still at last. When he looked at the flask again it now seemed to him that something fluttered there. The joyful Caliph embraced the old man gratefully and pressed the purse of gold dinars on him. Then he swept from the room to inform his wives of the miraculous cure.

The old man slipped the flask inside his garment and the purse after it. Pausing only to blink with wonder at the splendor of the throne room, he followed the public executioner out of the palace.

Amalik spent the next month like one resurrected from the dead. Every day was a bright gift and each small pleasure came clad in fresh garments. So when he rose again to address Bagdad on the sacred writings he spoke with an enthusiasm his listeners had not come to expect.

But midway into his exhortation, the Caliph suddenly observed the old man in the mantle of deepest blue-blackness listening on the edge of the crowd. Seeing he had the Caliph's eye, the curer of hiccups raised the flask of green glass and smiled. Amalik understood. He knew that if the old man removed the stopper, his affliction would wing its way back to him like a dove to its cote. Pretending to refresh his throat with a sip of fruit juice, Amalik whispered an urgent command to his vizier. Then he returned to his speech and soon had the satisfaction of seeing guards seize the flask from the old man and lead him off.

His discourse behind him, Amalik hurried to the throne room, where the guards and their prisoner waited.

"So," declared the Caliph, "you dared to come here to extort money from me. But you see how things stand now. I have the flask and I have you."

"My Lord baffles me," insisted the old man. "I came only to be edified by Your Honor's words. That empty flask was in case the evil Jinn passed by again as you spoke."

And indeed the flask the Caliph held had no stopper. Ashamed at having so misjudged the man, Amalik began to pull a massive ring from his finger as recompense. But then the old man said, "And yet I am happy to have this word with Your Honor. With the hiccups of ordinary men, I merely buried them deep and had done with it. But in your case I have felt obliged to guard the flask in my humble residence to keep it safe from breakage, brigands, and pretenders to Your Honor's station who might use it against you. The burden of this responsibility has distracted me from profitable studies."

"Then return the flask," said the Caliph in a smooth voice. "I will place it in my treasure house for safekeeping."

The old man bowed low. "Sire, I am not able to obey your command. For curiosity bedevils caliphs as much as lesser men. One day it would force you to unstop the flask to see if your affliction really dwells within. And, alas, incompetent fool that I am, I am seldom successful in recapturing a hiccup grown wary by imprisonment."

The Caliph's brow grew dark. "What is it you wish?"

"A hundred gold dinars for my trouble," said the old man. "Call it a monthly rental on the flask."

Amalik was quick to realize that for the moment at least he had no choice but to pay the few gold pieces demanded. As they waited for the money to be brought, the old man wet his lips and with a canny look said, "A while back, Sire, I thought Your Honor was about to make me a gift. Indeed it is a mighty ring." Without a word, the Caliph slipped the ring off his finger and handed it over.

But he had the old man followed when he left the palace.

The extortionist rode his donkey to a wine house near the alchemists' bazaar. There he joined a table of shabby old men of the learned sort. The table talked long and heatedly on subtle subjects and drank wine, napkins in fists like gentlemen. A waiter informed the Caliph's man that the one he followed was an alchemist who searched for the Philosopher's Stone which could transmute base metals into gold, another at the table sought the Elixir of Life, a third pursued the system of Perpetual Motion, and a fourth contemplated the Universal Dissolvent.

When at last the old man took his leave, he rode for two hours and reached the ragged foothills of the ancient mountains where a high tower stood atop a crag. The alchemist knocked thrice and loudly at the base of the tower. When a servant opened the stout broad door, he rode inside. A few minutes later, a light appeared in the single window high in the tower. When the light blinked out again, the Caliph's man returned to his master.

Amalik did not like what he learned. It would be impossible to take the old man and his servant by surprise. And any thought of moving against the tower by force brought visions of the flask being thrown from the high window to the rocks below. So for the next few months he continued to pay the alchemist's modest extortions and resigned himself to the gifts which the old man invariably extracted at each visit—this month a silver cup, the next a valuable prayer rug, and so on.

Then one last Friday of the month, while the old man stood in the throne room examining a vase of rare cobalt-blue glaze with that appreciative eye the Caliph had come to dread, Amalik's favorite daughter, a smiling girl of a marriageable sixteen summers, rushed in to present her doting father with the first apricot from the tree in the family garden. She came and went like a breeze from the incense forests of Hadramaut. But the Caliph's smile died when he saw the look in the old man's eyes as he watched her go. A chill found Amalik's marrow, for then and there he knew what the impudent old man would demand on his next visit.

The moment the alchemist left the palace with the cobalt-blue vase under his arm, the Caliph hurried across the courtyard to the royal prison. He mounted to the roof, where a soldier stood guard over a man-sized steel cage hanging from a tripod. Each bar of the cage was graven with verses from the sacred writings so powerful that none would dare cut them. Inside, his legs dangling through the bottom bars, sat the famous Thief of Bagdad, a weathered, quick-eyed man with the look of a desert bird of prey.

"Hail, Thief," said the Caliph.

"Hail, Caliph," answered the Thief. "What would you have me steal?"

"May the Most High give you patience, Thief," prayed the Caliph, making a sign for coffee to be brought. For a good part of an hour they drank from wafer-thin porcelain and watched the sun set behind the city walls. Then the Caliph dismissed the sentry, and as the darkness took on weight he explained his dilemma in the fullest detail.

"If I am to steal this flask, then first you must give me my freedom," said the Thief at last.

Amalik looked sad as caliphs always do when they are helpless. "No power on earth can release you from the cage where my father placed you."

"Oh, I know this cage is my fate," said the Thief quickly. "Still you could let me return to the bosom of my family, cage and all. My eldest boy has been apprenticed to a burglar. I would like to take his education in hand myself and direct it along a loftier road."

The Caliph pulled his lower lip thoughtfully. Another Thief of Bagdad? Well, he seemed to have no choice. "Let it be so," he declared.

In the next morning's dim, a boy led a camel out through the Great Gate of Bagdad, a litter covered with a purple cloth bobbing like a cork on the sea-swell of the animal's back. Boy and camel did not stop until they reached the mountain foothills not far from where the alchemist's tower stood. Here the camel knelt and, throwing back the purple cloth, the son helped his caged father clamber to the ground. Then the Thief gathered up the cage in either hand as a man might carry two satchels and walked along inside it until the road passed an olive grove whose shade made an attractive headquarters. Ordering his son to reconnoiter the tower on foot, the Thief tethered the camel and settled down to wait. Then, as the sun dropped behind the line of mountains, he hitched up the cage again and waddled about, starting a fire and getting dinner ready.

The lad returned, and as they ate he told his father what he'd learned. It was their misfortune that the skill of the masons had left no toeholds between the building stones of the tower's exterior face. But while the lad was hanging about, the alchemist's servant, a simple country soul, had come out to put the donkey to pasture and gather firewood in a stand of trees off from the tower. The Thief's son had offered to help him collect faggots. Later they'd sat on a hillock together and shared some sweetmeats the lad had brought with him in a kerchief. ("I told him I was a sweetmeat peddler's son," said the boy, displaying a knife with a curiously wrought brass handle and giving his father a sly wink. "In return for his knife I promised to come back with a supply to satisfy any sweet tooth. And he believed me." "My son," said the father sternly, "you are a thief, not a swindler."

The lad then reported that the alchemist went into town each Friday to shop and socialize with his learned friends. The servant had strict orders to unlock the doors to no one during his absence. This injunction the servant obeyed most scrupulously. The poor soul believed the alchemist had stolen his wits one day, luring them out of his head with a saucer of milk and then snatching them up and imprisoning them in a small ebony box inlaid with ivory which he kept in his pocket. By obeying the alchemist in all things, the poor soul hoped one day to earn them back.

"Taking your servant's wits is like pulling your watchdog's teeth," observed the Thief. Then he fell into a deep revery. Finally he said, "When next the alchemist goes to the city, the sweetmeat peddler's son will visit the tower."

When Friday arrived, the Thief moved his headquarters deeper into the olive grove and watched the alchemist ride out of sight on his donkey. Then he and his son approached the tower. A knock brought the servant's inquiring voice. The lad identified himself and said he'd brought the promised sweetmeats. The servant could be heard smacking his lips through the oak door. "But I can't let you in, you know," said the poor soul in a fearful voice. "I dursn't open the door the smallest crack. I'd lose my wits forever if I durst."

"Then lower a rope from the window and I'll send up your sweet-meats in a kerchief," urged the boy. "But hurry! My father saw me at his saddlebag. He follows short behind me with his stick. Ah, I see him coming now. Quick, I must hide! Tie the rope to the bar in the win-dow—I'll attach the kerchief when the coast is clear. Hurry!"

They could hear the servant's quick step on the stairs inside. A minute later the Thief's son peered around the tower and announced that the rope was hanging within reach. Then the Thief struck the door three times, as was the alchemist's custom. Down from the top of the tower came the sound of alarmed footsteps, followed by a tumbling crash as though the hurrying servant had tripped over his own feet and arrived at the bottom of the flight of stairs headfirst. "Is that you, mas-ter?" he asked in a voice wracked with pain. "I'd never, never open the door if it wasn't."

"I am known as Mansur the Delectable," announced the Thief, "pur-veyor of gustatory sweetnesses and delights to the Caliph himself."

"Your son isn't here! Oh, no, indeed!" blurted the servant. "I've never, never set eyes on him! Oh, I shall lose my wits for good for sure!"

When father and son met again in the olive grove the Thief asked, "And can you get past the window bar, my eldest?"

The lad nodded. "Where the shoulders can go, the rest of the body may surely follow." Then he added in a puzzled voice, "But, Father, there are flasks of green glass everywhere in the room at the top of the tower. On the floor, on the books, on the workbench, and on shelves along one wall."

The Thief brightened. "Things might be worse."

"But, Father," added the lad slyly, "I know the stall in the bazaar where such flasks can be had two for a penny."

"What are you saying, my son?"

"Father, we could buy a flask. 'Here, Caliph, is your affliction,' we could say. 'Guard it well.' "

"My son, that would be dishonest. In our business above all others, we must give full measure. Besides, what you suggest would be futile, as I will explain. Nevertheless, these flasks do answer one important question. The alchemist is no fraud. He does really believe he can cap-ture hiccups. Were it otherwise, we would be helpless. For even if we were able to steal the flask, he would appear with another and claim it was the one he used. And I don't doubt whom the Caliph would believe. Yes, for a fraud any flask would do. But our alchemist has chosen to hide one flask among many others. Therefore, it alone is important to him."

As they spoke, they saw the alchemist return on his donkey in the moonlight, cursing and muttering to himself, for wine does not make all people sing. The name of a man called Abul-Abbas sat bitter on his lips.

The lad showed the brass-handled knife. "Father, I could strike him down here and now. And who would come before the Caliph to discredit whichever flask we brought him?"

"My son," said the Thief in a tone of self-reproach, "you have been out of my care too long. Understand that we do not murder. We steal."

"How can we steal when we cannot tell the right flask among so many?"

"He will have to show us," said the Thief.

Now when the Thief's son had scampered up the tower on the servant's rope to peer in the window, he had trailed a clew of silk thread after him, which he passed behind the bar and let drop to the ground. This thread enabled him to pull a stout cord up and around behind the bar and back down to him whenever he wished. In this way he could climb up and observe the alchemist tinkering amid his alembics and aludels, or writing in his great clasp-bound book, or poring through his ancient library, or muttering at his cat—one of Prince Attab's breed, who watched from workbench, hearth, or lap.

The lad also observed that some flasks were stacked so that a careless touch might send them crashing down. (These, his father later informed him, and those on the floor as well, were clearly noisy obstacles for intruders. Somewhere among the others must be the one they sought.) And some nights—always, it seemed, when the moon was dimmest and the shadows thickest beyond the fireplace glow— the old man would step into the darkness and reemerge with a flask in hand. And he would sit for the longest time holding the glass up to the firelight, staring inside, and chuckling with black satisfaction.

And so the weeks became a month. At last it was Friday eve. As the Thief's son watched, the alchemist unlocked a humpbacked chest in a corner and drew out a scarlet vest worked with gold and matching turban cloth and slippers. Then he took out another outfit of horizon-blue. He pursed his lips and compared both suits of clothes thoughtfully by candlelight. He scratched at a gravy stain on the scarlet vest with his fingernail for a minute and then chose the horizon-blue.

When the lad had returned to the campfire and told the Thief what he had seen, he added sharply, "The old man has chosen his betrothal outfit, Father. But we still don't know which flask is which."

"Tomorrow before the sun has risen, you will go into the city and return with a fleet horse," said the Thief. "Leave the rest to me."

The Thief's son had gone and returned long before the alchemist appeared on his donkey bound for Bagdad, the very picture of a man on his way to present himself to the father of his beloved. To the horizon-blue vest and turban had been added a snow-white tunic and a mantle which he gathered up under one arm to show off his slippers. But when the old man came upon the Thief sitting cross-legged in his cage by the side of the road, he reined in the donkey and looked him over. The alchemist's curiosity quickly got the better of him. "Peace, stranger," he said. "Who brought you to this sorry state?"

"My son, who has been hired as a shepherd in the vicinity," said the Thief.

"I meant how do you come to be in a cage," said the alchemist briskly, for he did not tolerate fools well.

"I am the Thief of Bagdad."

The old man's eyes narrowed. But the sight of what was graven on the steel reassured him. He threw a leg over the donkey and dismounted. "Ah, yes, I recall you were caught in the amber merchant's strongroom with the pride of his jewel casket in your hand."

"A pearl as black as a moonless night sky reflected in a summer pool. Its beauty stopped my ears to the watchman's step."

"And our fool, the Caliph, set you free on some amnesty or other, no doubt. If you can be called free." The alchemist swaggered back and forth in front of the cage, displaying at once his freedom and his finery. "And how does it feel, you who were master of the night, to be caged like a parrot? Speak."

"At least it's silenced the constant slandering of my good name," said the Thief. "Time was when the disappearance of every third-rate diamond or flawed ruby was laid at my door. Actually, I never took anything."

"At last I've found an honest man—and he's in a cage," laughed the alchemist sarcastically.

"The most I ever did was share things that weren't mine," said the Thief. The alchemist's incredulous snort prompted him to continue. "When I was old enough, my father taught me our family's secret art: the power to send one's spirit out of one's body and across great distances in a twinkling. Like him and his father before him, I can be in two places at once. That is why this cage is no prison for me. Whenever I wish, my spirit can leave this cage like the smoke from a wood fire. Each noon I pray in Mecca. If I wish, I can travel back to Bagdad in the instant and enter into any lattice window or under any strongroom door and there become as solid again as the wood from which the smoke sprang. This power makes every man's house, harem, garden, larder, and wine cellar mine. And his black pearls as well. Of course, I can carry nothing away when I go. But why should I? Why steal what is there for me to admire whenever I wish? Certainly not for money. I sleep sounder in another man's bed than he does when business and ambition let him sleep at home. This art my father taught me I am now teaching my son. Unfortunately, we must always interrupt his education for him to earn his livelihood."

The alchemist was smiling into the distance and stroking his beard. "What a power that would be," he mused aloud. "No secret could be hidden from you." The old man thought for a moment. Then in a confidential tone he said, "There is one named Abul-Abbas whom I fear. We both seek the method of turning base metals into noble, I by the power of projection, he by philosophical elixirs." The alchemist belittled these obscure liquids with a contemptuous fluttering of his fingers. "Had you the power you claim, you could visit his workroom this very afternoon while he and I drink with others in a wine house. A great book sits on his workbench. Its last two pages committed to memory would be worth a hundred gold dinars to me."

"I told you I have no need of money."

"Yet your son must spend his days watching over other men's sheep to earn his bread when he could be sitting at your feet learning this great art which would make him happy for the rest of his life."

"True," admitted the Thief. "For his sake, I might perhaps take on your commission. But the money would have to be paid in advance."

The alchemist gave a tired laugh. " 'How the Famous Thief of Bagdad, Though Confined to a Cage, Swindled a Fool of His Gold'? No, I don't wish to go down to posterity that way. After all, what proof have I you possess this power you claim?"

"Put me to the test, then," said the Thief. "Send me somewhere and have me describe it."

The alchemist had never traveled far and knew few places in Bagdad that the ubiquitous Thief might not know as well. But all of a sudden, the old man caught sight of the tower standing on the crag. Laughing, he bent over the cage. "See that window high in that tower? Go in there and describe the room to me."

"I hear and obey," said the Thief, grabbing his elbows in his palms, jutting his jaw, and squinting shut his eyes. In the next instant he announced, "I have arrived. I am standing beside a table cluttered with scientific paraphernalia."

"Of course you would describe an alchemist's room. But tell me what you see against the north wall."

Without moving a muscle, the Thief said, "A fireplace, a bellows, a small crucible for heating metals. And the remains of a bowl of gruel on the hob."

This staggered the alchemist. "And in the corner?"

"A small humpbacked trunk."

"Unlock it," said the old man.

"There are flasks in the way," said the Thief.

"They are nothing but my collection of gases," said the alchemist. "Tell me what's inside the trunk."

"Let's see, now," said the Thief. "One scarlet vest sewn with gold, one turban cloth ditto, and one, two scarlet slippers. A gravy stain on the vest."

The alchemist's jaw went slack. "Even my servant didn't know that," he acknowledged. "The last time I wore that I was a young man searching for the elusive polypharmack, the cure for all diseases. But my betrothed died before I could find it." He averted his eyes. "All right, close up the trunk and return here."

"Son of a donkey!" exclaimed the Thief. "Son of two donkeys!"

"What is it?" demanded the alchemist.

"Surely you heard the racket? I closed the blasted trunk on the tabby cat's tail. It leaped to the topmost shelf of flasks. The shelf collapsed onto the shelf below, sending flasks crashing to the floor."

"Were any on the third shelf broken?" demanded the alarmed alchemist.

"Startled, I stepped backward, lost my balance on an overturned flask, and reached out for that very shelf to steady myself."

"The second bottle from the wall!" screamed the old man. "The one with the bubble in the glass just below the silver band! Tell me, did that break?"

"Let me take a look," said the Thief. In a moment he reported, "No, it is safe and sound."

"The Most High be praised," said the alchemist, adding, "That of all my gases was rare. Come back, then. Come back at once."

"I hear and obey," said the Thief. He relaxed and turned toward the old man.

"You've proven your powers well, if clumsily," said the alchemist. "When I return, I will pay you the gold and direct you to where this Abul-Abbas lives."

And so the old man set off for the city, confident that by nightfall he would possess both the hand of the Caliph's daughter and his rival's secrets. He did not concern himself with the fast horse which overtook and passed him before he was halfway to Bagdad or what the young rider carried in his saddlebag. When he swaggered into Amalik's presence, he was astonished to find his precious flask in the Caliph's hand.

Before delivering over the alchemist to his dungeon master, the Caliph fulfilled the Thief of Bagdad's request that a certain black box inlaid with ivory in the man's possession be opened. Some say at that very same moment it occurred to the alchemist's servant to better himself by leaving a cruel and niggardly master for more congenial service. And so he left the tower, never to return.

For his part, the Caliph had the mouth of the flask dipped in molten lead and impressed with the ancient signet of Solomon the Great to ward off tamperers. Then he entrusted it to the best horseman in the Caliphate. Nor did he feel safe from a growing curiosity until the rider had vanished over the horizon. The man rode and rode until he came to the blue ocean sea. There, as the Caliph had commanded, he cast the flask from a high promontory into the waves.

Here, my masters, I should recommend my bowl to those of you who prefer endings to be happy and bid you good day until you honor me with your ears again. But for the rest of you who enjoy the fruit when it is sour as well as sweet I will add that Amalik spent many a sleepless night over the matter of the Thief of Bagdad's pardon. For he knew that weak rulers serve a people ill. And subjects always see an act of mercy as one of weakness. So for the general good, the Caliph broke faith with the Thief. He pardoned him but ordered him banished from the city.

Things did not go well for the Thief in exile. Damascus, where he finally settled, was uncongenial. And it is hard to discipline a headstrong son from a cage. The Thief of Bagdad lived to see that son join a low band of robbers and die by the knife in a dispute over the division of paltry spoils. And he lived to see his grandson apprenticed to a common cutpurse. The Thief died of a broken heart and was buried, cage and all, in the very same month when the Caliph Amalik was fatally injured by a falling roof tile. The Caliph's death was lingering, and in his final delirium he spoke the Thief of Bagdad's name, for it came to him that the tile would have done him no harm had he, too, been wearing a steel cage. At last life fled his body, which was buried in the family's secret mountain tomb.

Years became generations. Then one day the blue ocean cast up a flask of green glass at the feet of a faraway beachcomber. The seal and something aflutter inside made him think he had a Jinn in his grasp, one obliged to grant his liberator three wishes. Hurrying homeward, the beachcomber saw himself husband of his heart's desire, master of a gold palace, beloved ruler of a prosperous people. And he imagined himself and his beautiful wife stepping out onto a balcony to greet the acclaiming population with a loving gesture, arms outspread. Here the flask slipped from his fingers and smashed on the shingle.

At precisely that moment two seas away, the moon was rising over a line of barren mountains. Below the crags, deep in the darkest gully, four men huddled about a meager fire and cursed the moonlight. No ghouls coveted the darkness more than these, the very outcasts of the underworld. The largest of the men squatted a bit apart with his elbows on his knees, face pitted and pocked, hard eyes staring defiantly into the flames. A wolfish skull among the others spat and said hoarsely, "Gold? There's no gold. No jewels." And another face, with a scar where one eye should be, asked, "How long will we let him lead us about by the nose?" The fourth, with lips like a camel's, jeered in someone else's high-pitched voice, "But his father's father's father was the Thief of Bagdad." Wordlessly, the big brooding man swung a heavy fist and knocked this last speaker over backward into the darkness. "Shut your mouths, too, the rest of you. A man can hardly hear himself think."

In the quick silence, he rose and moved away from the fire. Then he stopped and cocked his head as though he heard a noise in the darkness. He moved deeper into the gully shadows and stopped again. Then he scratched his head in amazement. A spectral sound like echoing hiccups was issuing from a crack in the rock at his feet.

"Here!" he shouted. "Here!" Obediently, the men jumped up from the fire and hurried over with shovel, mattock, and crowbar.

And that, my masters, is how it came to pass that the grave robbers discovered the lost tomb of the Caliph Amalik.

A CANTICLE FOR WULFSTAN

Peter Tremayne

Peter Tremayne is a pseudonym for the respected Celtic scholar Peter Beresford Ellis. He is also a former journalist and the author of two dozen fantasy novels. One might almost have expected a feminist writer to beat Peter Tremayne to his subject, for the Ireland of which he writes, circa A.D. 650, is one in which women held positions of power and respect that would not be equaled in the rest of Europe for many centuries to come. Medieval Ireland was also ahead of its neighbors in accepting Christianity and general learning—a fact that occasions bitterness in the visiting Saxons in the following story.

Abbot Laisran smiled broadly. He was a short, rotund, red-faced man. His face proclaimed a permanent state of jollity, for he had been born with that rare gift of humour and a sense that the world was there to provide enjoyment to those who inhabited it. When he smiled, it was no fainthearted parting of the lips but an expression that welled from the depths of his being, bright and all-encompassing. And when he laughed it was as though the whole earth trembled in accompaniment.

"It is so good to see you again, Sister Fidelma," Laisran boomed, and his voice implied it was no mere formula but a genuine expression of his joy in the meeting.

Sister Fidelma answered his smile with an almost urchin grin, quite at odds with her habit and calling. Indeed, those who examined the young woman closely, observing the rebellious strands of red hair thrusting from beneath her headdress, seeing the bubbling laughter in her green eyes, and the natural expression of merriment on her fresh, attractive face, would wonder why such an alluring young woman had taken up the life of a *religieuse*. Her tall, yet well-proportioned figure seemed to express a desire for a more active and joyous role in life than that in the cloistered confines of a religious community.

"And it is good to see you again, Laisran. It is always a pleasure to come to Durrow."

Abbot Laisran reached out both his hands to take Fidelma's extended one, for they were old friends. Laisran had known Fidelma since she had reached "the age of choice," and he, it was, who had persuaded her to take up the study of law under the Brehon Morann of Tara. Further, he had persuaded her to continue her studies until she had reached the qualification of *Anruth,* one degree below that of *Ollamh,* the highest rank of learning. It had been Laisran who had advised her to join the community of Brigid at Kildare when she had become accepted as a *dálaigh,* an advocate of the Brehon Court. In the old days, before the Light of Christ reached the shores of Éireann, all those who held professional office were of the caste of Druids. When the Druids gave up their power to the priests and communities of Christ, the professional classes, in turn, enlisted in the new holy orders as they had done in the old.

"Shall you be long among us?" inquired Laisran.

Fidelma shook her head.

"I am on a journey to the shrine of the Blessed Patrick at Ard Macha."

"Well, you must stay and dine with us this night. It is a long time since I have had a stimulating talk."

Fidelma grimaced with humour.

"You are abbot of one of the great teaching monasteries of Ireland. Professors of all manner of subjects reside here with students from the four corners of Ireland. How can you be lacking stimulating discourse?"

Laisran chuckled.

"These professors tend to lecture, there is little dialogue. How boring monologues can be. Sometimes I find more intelligence among our students."

The great monastery on the plain of the oaks, which gave it the name Durrow, was scarcely a century old but already its fame as a university had spread to many peoples of Europe. Students flocked to the scholastic island, in the middle of the bog of Aillín, from numerous lands. The Blessed Colmcille had founded the community at Durrow before he had been exiled by the High King and left the shores of Éireann to form his more famous community on Iona in the land of the Dàl Riada.

Sister Fidelma fell in step beside the abbot as he led the way along the great vaulted corridors of the monastery towards his chamber. Brothers and laymen scurried quietly hither and thither through the corridors, heads bowed, intent on their respective classes or devotions. There were four faculties of learning at Durrow: theology, medicine, law, and the liberal arts.

It was midmorning, halfway between the first Angelus bell and the summons of the noonday Angelus. Fidelma had been up before dawn and had travelled fifteen miles to reach Durrow on horseback, the ownership of a horse being a privilege accorded only to her rank as a representative of the Brehon Court.

A solemn-faced monk strode across their path, hesitated, and inclined his head. He was a thin, dark-eyed man of swarthy skin who wore a scowl with the same ease that Abbot Laisran wore a smile. Laisran made a curious gesture of acknowledgement with his hand, more as one of dismissal than recognition, and the man moved off into a side room.

"Brother Finan, our professor of law," explained Laisran, almost apologetically. "A good man, but with no sense of humour at all. I often think he missed his vocation and that he was designed in life to be a professional mourner."

He cast a mischievous grin at her.

"Finan of Durrow is well respected among the Brehons," replied Fidelma, trying to keep her face solemn. It was hard to keep a straight face in the company of Laisran.

"Ah," sighed Laisran, "it would lighten our world if you came to teach here, Fidelma. Finan teaches the letter of the law, whereas you would explain to our pupils that often the law can be for the guidance of the wise and the obedience of fools, that justice can sometimes transcend law."

Sister Fidelma bit her lip.

"There is sometimes a moral question which has to be resolved above the law," she agreed. "Indeed, I have had to face decisions between law and justice."

"Exactly so. Finan's students leave here with a good knowledge of the law but often little knowledge of justice. Perhaps you will think on this?"

Sister Fidelma hesitated.

"Perhaps," she said guardedly.

Laisran smiled and nodded.

"Look around you, Fidelma. Our fame as a centre of learning is even known in Rome. Do you know, no fewer than eighteen languages are spoken among our students? We resort to Latin and sometimes Greek as our lingua franca. Among the students that we have here are not just the children of the Gael. We have a young Frankish prince, Dagobert, and his entourage. There are Saxon princes, Wulfstan, Eadred, and Raedwald. Indeed, we have a score of Saxons. There is Talorgen, a prince of Rheged in the land of Britain. . . ."

"I hear that the Saxons are making war on Rheged and attempting to destroy it so they can expand their borders," observed Fidelma. "That cannot make for easy relationships among the students."

"Ah, that is so. Our Irish monks in Northumbria attempt to teach these Saxons the ways of Christ, and of learning and piety, but they remain a fierce warrior race intent on conquest, plunder, and land. Rheged may well fall like the other kingdoms of the Britons before them. Elmet fell when I was a child. Where the Britons of Elmet once dwelt, now there are Saxon farmers and Saxon thanes."

They halted before Laisran's chamber door. The bishop opened it to usher Fidelma inside.

Fidelma frowned. "There has been perpetual warfare between the Britons and the Saxons for the last two and a half centuries. Surely it is hard to contain both Briton and Saxon within the same hall of learning?"

They moved into Laisran's official chamber, which he used for administering the affairs of the great monastery. He motioned Fidelma to be seated before a smouldering turf fire and went to pour wine from an earthenware jug on the table, handing a goblet to her and raising the other in salute.

"*Agimus tibi gratias, Omnipotens Deus,*" he intoned solemnly but with a sparkle of humour in his eyes.

"Amen," echoed Sister Fidelma, raising the goblet to her lips and tasting the rich red wine of Gaul.

Abbot Laisran settled himself in a chair and stretched out his feet towards the fire.

"Difficult to contain Briton and Saxon?" he mused, after a while. In fact, Sister Fidelma had almost forgotten that she had asked the question. "Yes. We have had several fights among the Britons and the Saxons here. Only the prohibition of weapons on our sacred ground has so far prevented injury."

"Why don't you send one group or the other to another centre of learning?"

Laisran sniffed.

"That has already been suggested by Finan, no less. A neat, practical, and logical suggestion. The question is . . . which group? Both Britons and Saxons refuse to go, each group demanding that if anyone leave Durrow then it should be the other."

"Then you have difficulties," observed Fidelma.

"Yes. Each is quick to anger and slow to forget an insult, real or imaginary. One Saxon princeling, Wulfstan, is very arrogant. He has ten in his retinue. He comes from the land of the South Saxons, one of the smaller Saxon kingdoms, but to hear him speak you would think that his kingdom encompassed the world. The sin of pride greatly afflicts him. After his first clash with the Britons he demanded that he be given a chamber whose window was barred from ingress and whose door could be bolted from the inside."

"A curious request in a house of God," agreed Sister Fidelma.

"That is what I told him. But he told me that he feared for his life. In fact, so apprehensive was his manner, so genuine did his fear appear, that I decided to appease his anxiety and provide him with such a chamber. I gave him a room with a barred window in which we used to keep transgressors but had our carpenter fix the lock so that the door could be barred from the inside. Wulfstan is a strange young man. He never moves without a guard of five of his retinue. And after Vespers he retires to his room but has his retinue search it before he enters and only then will he enter alone and bar the door. There he remains until the morning Angelus."

Sister Fidelma pursed her lips and shook her head in wonder.

"Truly one would think him greatly oppressed and frightened. Have you spoken to the Britons?"

"I have, indeed. Talorgen, for example, openly admits that all Saxons are enemies of his blood but that he would not deign to spill Saxon blood in a house of God. In fact, the young Briton rebuked me, saying that his people had been Christian for centuries and had made no war on sacred ground, unlike the Saxons. He reminded me that within the memory of living man, scarcely half a century ago, the Saxon warriors of Aethelfrith of Northumbria had defeated Selyf map Cynan of Powys in battle at a place called Caer Legion, but then profaned their victory by slaughtering a thousand British monks from Bangor-is-Coed. He averred that the Saxons were scarcely Christian in thought and barely so in word and deed."

"In other words . . . ¿" prompted Fidelma when Laisran paused to sip his wine.

"In other words, Talorgen would not harm a Saxon protected by the sacred soil of a Christian house, but he left no doubt that he would not hesitate to slay Wulfstan outside these walls."

"So much for Christian charity, love, and forgiveness," sighed Fidelma.

Laisran grimaced. "One must remember that the Britons have suffered greatly at the hands of the Saxons during these last centuries. After all, the Saxons have invaded and conquered much of their land. Ireland has received great communities of refugees fleeing from the Saxon conquests in Britain."

Fidelma smiled whimsically. "Do I detect that you approve of Talorgen's attitude¿"

Laisran grinned.

"If you ask me as a Christian, no; no, of course not. If you ask me as a member of a race who once shared a common origin, belief, and law with our cousins, the Britons, then I must say to you that I have a sneaking sympathy for Talorgen's anger."

There came a sudden banging at the door of the chamber, so loud and abrupt that both Laisran and Fidelma started in surprise. Before the abbot had time to call out, the door burst open and a middle-aged monk, his face red, his clothes awry from running, burst breathlessly into the room.

He halted a few paces inside the door, his shoulders heaving, his breath panting from exertion.

Laisran rose, his brows drawing together in an unnatural expression of annoyance.

"What does this mean, Brother Ultan¿ Have you lost your senses¿"

The man shook his head, eyes wide. He gulped air, trying to recover his breath.

"God between us and all evil," he got out at last. "There has been a murder committed."

Laisran's composure was severely shaken.

"Murder, you say¿"

"Wulfstan, the Saxon, Your Grace! He has been stabbed to death in his chamber."

The blood drained from Laisran's face and he cast a startled glance towards Sister Fidelma. Then he turned back to Brother Ultan, his face now set in stern lines.

"Compose yourself, Brother," he said kindly, "and tell me slowly and carefully. What has occurred?"

Brother Ultan swallowed nervously and sought to collect his thoughts.

"Eadred, the companion of Wulfstan, came to me during the mid-morning hour. He was troubled. Wulfstan had not attended the morning prayers nor had he been at his classes. No one has seen him since he retired into his chamber following Vespers last night. Eadred had gone to his chamber and found the door closed. There was no response to his summons at the door. So, as I am master of the household, he came to see me. I accompanied him to Wulfstan's chamber. Sure enough, the door was closed and clearly barred on the inside."

He paused a moment and then continued.

"Having knocked awhile, I then, with Eadred's help, forced the door. It took awhile to do, and I had to summon the aid of two other Brothers to eventually smash the wooden bars that secured it. Inside the chamber . . ." He bit his lip, his face white with the memory.

"Go on," ordered Laisran.

"Inside the chamber was the body of Wulfstan. He lay back on the bed. He was in his night attire, which was stained red with congealed blood. There were many wounds in his chest and stomach. He had been stabbed several times. It was clear that he had been slain."

"What then?"

Brother Ultan was now more firmly in control. He contrived to shrug at Laisran's question.

"I left the two Brothers to guard the chamber. I told Eadred to return to his room and not to tell anyone until I sent for him. Then I came immediately to inform you, Your Grace."

"Wulfstan killed?" Laisran whispered as he considered the implications. "Then God protect us, indeed. The land of the South Saxons may be a small kingdom, but these Saxons band together against all foreigners. This could lead to some incident between the Saxons and the land of Éireann."

Sister Fidelma came forward from her seat, frowning at the master of the household.

"Let me get this clear, Brother Ultan, did you say that the chamber door was locked from the inside?"

Brother Ultan examined her with a frown of annoyance, turning back to Abbot Laisran as though to ignore her.

"Sister Fidelma is a *dálaigh* of the Brehon Court, Brother," Laisran rebuked softly.

The Brother's eyes widened and he turned hurriedly back to Sister Fidelma with a look of respect.

"Yes, the door of Wulfstan's chamber was barred from the inside."

"And the window was barred?"

A look of understanding crossed Ultan's face.

"No one could have entered or left the chamber through the window, Sister," he said slowly, swallowing hard, as the thought crystallised in his mind.

"And yet no one could have left by the door?" pressed Sister Fidelma remorselessly.

Ultan shook his head.

"Are you sure that the wounds of Wulfstan were not self-inflicted?"

"No!" whispered Ultan, swiftly genuflecting.

"Then how could someone have entered his chamber, slaughtered him, and left it, ensuring that the door was bolted from the inside?"

"God help us, Sister!" cried Ultan. "Whoever did this deed was a sorcerer! An evil demon able to move through walls of stone!"

Abbot Laisran halted uneasily at the end of the corridor in which two of his brethren stood to bar the way against any inquisitive members of the brethren or students. Already, in spite of Brother Ultan's attempt to stop the spread of the news, word of Wulfstan's death was being whispered among the cloisters. Laisran turned to Sister Fidelma, who had followed at his heels, calm and composed, her hands now folded demurely in the folds of her gown.

"Are you sure that you wish to undertake this task, Sister?"

Sister Fidelma wrinkled her nose.

"Am I not an advocate of the Brehon Court? Who else should conduct this investigation if not I, Laisran?"

"But the manner of his death . . ."

She grimaced and cut him short.

"I have seen many bodies and only few have died peacefully. This is the task that I was trained for."

Laisran sighed and motioned the two brothers to stand aside.

"This is Sister Fidelma, a *dálaigh* of the Brehon Court who is investigating the death of Wulfstan on my behalf. Make sure that she has every assistance."

Laisran hesitated, raised his shoulder almost in a gesture of bewilderment, then turned and left.

The two Brothers stood aside respectfully as Sister Fidelma hesitated at the door.

The chamber of Wulfstan was one which led off a corridor of dark granite stone on the ground floor of the monastery. The door, which now hung splintered on its hinges, was thick—perhaps about two inches thick—and had been attached to the door frame with heavy iron hinges. Unlike most doors she was accustomed to, there was no iron handle on the outside. She paused awhile, her keen green eyes searching the timber of the door, which showed the scuffing of Ultan's attempts to force it.

Then she took a step forward but stayed at the threshold, letting her keen eyes travel over the room beyond.

Beyond was a bed, a body laid sprawled on its back, arms flung out, head with wild staring eyes directed towards the ceiling in a last painful gape preceding death. The body was clad in a white shirt which was splattered with blood. The wounds were certainly not self-inflicted.

From her position, she saw a small wooden chair, on which was flung a pile of clothes. There was also a small table with an oil lamp and some writing materials on it. There was little else in the room.

The light entered the gloomy chamber from a small window which stood at a height of eight feet from the floor and was crisscrossed with iron bars through which one might thrust an arm to shoulder length, but certainly no more than that could pass beyond. All four walls of the chamber were of stone blocks, while the floor as well was flagged in great granite slabs. The ceiling of the room was of dark oak beams. There was little light to observe detail in the chamber, even though it was approaching the noonday. The only light that entered was from the tiny, barred window.

"Bring me a strong lamp, Brothers," Fidelma called to the two monks in the corridor.

"There is a lamp already in the room, Sister," replied one of them.

Sister Fidelma hid her annoyance.

"I want nothing in this room touched until I have examined it carefully. Now fetch me the lamp."

She waited, without moving, until one of the Brothers hurried away and returned with an oil lamp.

"Light it," instructed Fidelma.

The monk did so.

Fidelma took it from his hand with a nod of thanks.

"Wait outside and let no one into the room until I say so."

Holding the lamp, she stepped forward into the curious chamber of death.

Wulfstan's throat had been slashed with a knife or sword and there were several great stab wounds in his chest around the heart. His night attire was torn by the weapon and bloodied, as were the sheets around him.

On the floor beside the bed was a piece of fine cloth which was bloodstained. The blood had dried. She picked it up and examined it. It was an elegantly woven piece of linen which was embroidered. It carried a Latin motto. She examined the bloodstains on it. It appeared as if whoever had killed Wulfstan had taken the kerchief from his pocket and wiped his weapon clean, letting the kerchief drop to the floor beside the body in a fit of absent-mindedness. Sister Fidelma placed the kerchief in the pocket within the folds of her robe.

She examined the window next. Although it was too high to reach up to it, the bars seemed secure enough. Then she gazed up at the heavy wooden planking and beams which formed the ceiling. It was a high chamber, some eleven feet from floor to ceiling. The floor, too, seemed solid enough.

Near the bed she suddenly noticed a pile of ashes. She dropped to one knee beside the ashes and examined them, trying not to disperse them with her breath, for they appeared to be the remnants of some piece of paper, or vellum, perhaps. Not a very big piece either, but it was burnt beyond recognition.

She rose and examined the door next.

There were two wooden bars which had secured it. Each bar, when in place, slotted into iron rests. The first was at a height of three feet from the bottom of the door while the second was five feet from the bottom. She saw that one of the iron rests had been splintered from the wooden doorjamb, obviously when Ultan had broken in. The pressure against the bar had wrenched the rest from its fastenings. But the bottom set of rests was in place and there was no sign of damage to the second bar, which was lying just behind the door. Both bars were solid enough. The ends were wrapped with twine, she presumed to stop the wood wearing against the iron rests in which they lodged. On one of the bars the pieces of twine had become unwound, blackened, and frayed at the end.

Sister Fidelma gave a deep sigh.

Here, indeed, was a problem to be solved, unless the owner of the kerchief could supply an answer.

She moved to the door and suddenly found herself slipping. She reached out a hand to steady herself. There was a small pool of blackened grease just inside the door. Her sharp eyes caught sight of a similar pool on the other side of the door. Bending to examine them, she frowned as she noticed two nails attached on the door frame, either side of the door. A short length of twine, blackened and frayed at the end, was attached to each nail.

Sister Fidelma compressed her lips thoughtfully and stood staring at the door for a long while before turning to leave the death chamber.

In Abbot Laisran's chamber, Sister Fidelma seated herself at the long table. She had arranged with the abbot to interview any she felt able to help her in arriving at a solution to the problem. Laisran himself offered to sit in on her encounters but she had felt it unnecessary. Laisran had taken himself to a side room, having presented her with a bell to summon him if she needed any help.

Brother Ultan was recruited to fetch those whom she wanted to see and was straightaway dispatched to bring Wulfstan's fellow Saxon prince, Eadred, who had helped Ultan discover the body, as well as his cousin Raedwald.

Eadred was a haughty youth with flaxen hair and cold blue eyes that seemed to have little expression. His features seemed fixed with a mixture of disdain and boredom. He entered the chamber, eyes narrowing as he beheld Sister Fidelma. A tall, muscular young man in his late twenties accompanied Eadred. Although he carried no arms, he acted as if he were the prince's bodyguard.

"Are you Eadred?" Fidelma asked the youth.

The young man scowled.

"I do not answer questions from a woman." His voice was harsh, and that combined with his guttural accent made his stilted Irish sound raucous.

Sister Fidelma sighed. She had heard that Saxons could be arrogant and that they treated their womenfolk more as chattels than as human beings.

"I am investigating the death of your countryman, Wulfstan. I need my questions to be answered," she replied firmly.

Eadred merely ignored her.

"Lady." It was the tall muscular Saxon who spoke, and his knowledge of Irish was better than that of his prince. "I am Raedwald, thane of Staeningum, cousin to the thane of Andredswald. It is not the custom of princes of our race to discourse with women if they be not of equal royal rank."

"Then I am obliged for your courtesy in explaining your customs, Raedwald. Eadred, your cousin, seems to lack a knowledge of the law and customs of the country in which he is now a guest."

Ignoring the angry frown on Eadred's features, she reached forward and rang the silver bell on the table before her. The Abbot Laisran entered from a side room.

"As you warned me, Your Grace, the Saxons seem to think that they are above the law of this land. Perhaps they will accept the explanation from your lips."

Laisran nodded and turned to the young men. He bluntly told them of Fidelma's rank and position in law, that even the High King had to take note of her wisdom and learning. Eadred continued to scowl but he inclined his head stiffly when Laisran told him that he was under legal obligation to answer Fidelma's questions. Raedwald seemed to accept the explanation as a matter of course.

"As your countryman considers you of royal rank, I will deign to answer your questions," Eadred said, moving forward and seating himself without waiting for Fidelma's permission. Raedwald continued to stand.

Fidelma exchanged a glance with Laisran, who shrugged.

"The customs of the Saxons are not our customs, Sister Fidelma," Laisran said apologetically. "You will ignore their tendency to boorish behaviour."

Eadred flushed angrily.

"I am a prince of the blood royal of the South Saxons, descended through the blood of Aelle from the great god Woden!"

Raedwald, who stood silently with arms folded behind him, looking unhappy, opened his mouth and then closed it firmly.

Abbot Laisran genuflected. Sister Fidelma merely stared at the young man in amusement.

"So you are not yet truly Christian, believing only in the One True God?"

Eadred bit his lip.

"All Saxon royal houses trace their bloodline to Woden, whether god, man, or hero," he responded, with a slightly defensive tone.

"Tell me something of yourself then. I understand that you were cousin to Wulfstan? If you find speaking in our language difficult, you may speak in Latin or Greek. I am fluent in their usage."

"I am not," rasped Eadred. "I speak your language from my study here but I speak no other tongue fluently, though I have some knowledge of Latin."

Sister Fidelma hid her surprise and gestured for him to continue. Most Irish princes and chieftains she knew spoke several languages fluently besides their own, especially Latin and some Greek.

"Very well. Wulfstan was your cousin, wasn't he?"

"Wulfstan's father Cissa, king of the South Saxons, was brother to my father, Cymen. I am thane of Andredswald, as my father was before me."

"Tell me how Wulfstan and yourself came to be here, in Durrow."

Eadred sniffed.

"Some years ago, one of your race, a man called Diciul, arrived in our country and began to preach of his god, a god with no name who had a son named Christ. Cissa, the king, was converted to this new god and turned away from Woden. The man of Éireann was allowed to form a community, a monastery, at Bosa's Ham, in our land, and many went to hear him teach. Cissa decided that Wulfstan, who was heir apparent to the kingship, should come to the land of Éireann for education."

Sister Fidelma nodded, wondering whether it was the young man's poor usage of Irish that made him seem so disapproving of Cissa's conversion to Christ.

"Then Wulfstan is the tanist in your land?"

Abbot Laisran intervened with a smile.

"The Saxons have a different system of law from us, Sister Fidelma," he interrupted. "They hold that the eldest son inherits all. There is no election by the *derbhfine* such as we have."

"I see," nodded Fidelma. "Go on, Eadred. Cissa decided to send Wulfstan here."

The young man grimaced sourly.

"I was ordered to accompany him and learn with him. We came together with our cousin Raedwald, thane of Staeningum, and ten churls and five slaves to attend our needs, and here we have been now for six moons."

"And not the best of our students," muttered Laisran.

"That's as may be," snapped Eadred. "We did not ask to come, but were ordered by Cissa. I shall be pleased to depart now and take the body of my kinsman back to my country."

"Does the Latin inscription *cave quid dicis* mean anything to you?"

Eadred sniffed.

"It is the motto of the young Frankish prince, Dagobert."

Sister Fidelma gazed thoughtfully at the young man before turning to Raedwald. The muscular young man's face was flushed and confused.

"And you, Raedwald? Does it mean anything to you?"

"Alas, I have no Latin, lady," he mumbled.

"So? And when did you last see Wulfstan?"

"Just after Vespers."

"What happened exactly?"

"As usual, Wulfstan was accompanied by myself and Eadred, with two of our churls and two slaves, to his chamber for the night. We searched the chamber as usual and then Wulfstan entered and dismissed us."

Eadred nodded in agreement.

"I talked awhile with Raedwald in the corridor. We both heard Wulfstan secure the wooden bars. Then I went off to my chamber."

Sister Fidelma glanced again towards Raedwald.

"And you can confirm this, Raedwald?"

Eadred flushed.

"You doubt my word?" His voice was brittle.

"This investigation will be conducted under our law, Eadred," retorted Fidelma in annoyance.

Raedwald looked awkward.

"I can confirm what Eadred says, lady," he replied. "The thane of Andredswald speaks the truth. As soon as we heard the bars slide shut we both knew that the prince, Wulfstan, had secured himself in for the night and so we both departed for our sleeping chambers."

Sister Fidelma nodded thoughtfully.

"You can also confirm, Eadred, that Wulfstan was afraid of being attacked? Why was that?"

Eadred sniffed.

"There are too many mad *welisc* in this place and one in particular had made several threats against him . . . that barbarian Talorgen!"

"*Welisc*? Who are they?" frowned Fidelma, puzzled.

Laisran gave a tired smile.

"The Saxons call all Britons *welisc*. It is a name which signifies that they are foreigners."

"I see. So you left Wulfstan safely secured in his room? You did not seem to be as afraid of the Britons as your cousin. Why was that?"

Eadred laughed bitterly.

"I would not be thane of Andredswald if I could not defend myself against a pack of *welisc* cowards. No, I fear no barbarian's whelp nor his sire, either."

"And the rest of your Saxon entourage? Did they fear the Britons?"

"Whether they feared or not, it is of no significance. I command them and they will do as I tell them."

Sister Fidelma exhaled in exasperation. It would be difficult to live in a Saxon country if one was not a king or a thane, she thought.

"When did you realise that Wulfstan was missing?" she prompted.

"At prayers following the first bell . . ."

"He means the Angelus," explained Laisran.

"He did not come to prayers and, thinking he had slept late, I went to classes."

"What classes were these?"

"That weasel-faced Finan's class on the conduct of law between kingdoms."

"Go on."

"During the midmorning break, having realised that Wulfstan was missing, I went to his room. The door was shut, signifying he was still inside. I banged upon the door. There was no response. I then went to look for Brother Ultan, the house churl. . . ."

"The steward of our community," corrected Laisran softly.

"We went to Wulfstan's chamber and Ultan had to call upon two

other Brothers to help us break in the door. Wulfstan had been felo-
niously slain. One doesn't have to search far for the culprit."

"And who might that be⸮" invited Sister Fidelma.

"Why, it is obvious. The *welisc*-man, Talorgen, who calls himself a
prince of Rheged. He had threatened Wulfstan's life. And it is well
known the *welisc* practise sorcery. . . ."

"What do you mean⸮" Fidelma asked sharply.

"Why, the fact that Wulfstan had been slaughtered in his bedchamber while the window was barred and the door shut and secured from
the inside. Who else but a *welisc* would be able to shape-change and
perpetrate such a monstrous deed⸮"

Sister Fidelma hid her cynical smile.

"Eadred, I think you have much to learn, for you seem to be wal-
lowing in the superstition of your old religion."

Eadred sprang up, his hand going to his belt where a knife might be
worn.

"I am thane of Andredswald! I consented to be questioned by a
mere woman because it is the custom of this land. However, I will not
be insulted by one."

"I am sorry that you think that I insult you," Sister Fidelma replied,
with a dangerous glint in her eyes. "You may go."

Eadred's face was working in a rage but Laisran moved forward and
opened the door.

The young Saxon prince turned and stormed out. Raedwald hesitated a moment, made a gesture almost of apology, and then followed
the prince out of the room.

"Did I not tell you that these Saxons are strange, haughty people, Fid-
elma⸮" smiled Laisran almost sadly.

Sister Fidelma shook her head.

"They probably have their good and bad like all peoples. Raedwald
seems filled more with the courtesy of princes than his cousin Eadred."

"Well, if Eadred and his followers are to be judged, then we have had
their bad. As for Raedwald, although a thane and older than either
Wulfstan or Eadred, he seems quiet and was dominated by them both.
He is more of a servant than a master. I gather this is because his
cousins both stand in closer relationship to their king than he does."
Laisran paused and cast her a curious glance. "Why did you ask them
about the Latin motto—*cave quid dicis⸮*"

"It was a motto found on a piece of linen which wiped the weapon that killed Wulfstan. It could have been dropped by the killer or it could have been Wulfstan's."

Laisran shook his head.

"No. Eadred was right. That belligerent motto, Fidelma, 'Beware what you say,' is the motto of the Frankish prince—Dagobert. I have recently remarked on its pugnacity to the young man."

Sister Fidelma stretched reflectively. "It seems things do not look good for Dagobert of the Franks. He now stands as the most likely suspect."

"Not necessarily. Anyone could have taken and dropped the cloth, and there are many here who have come to hate the arrogance of the Saxons. Why, I have even heard the dour Finan declare that he would like to drown the lot of them!"

Fidelma raised her eyebrows.

"Are you telling me that we must suspect Finan, the professor of your law faculty?"

Abbot Laisran suddenly laughed.

"Oh, the idea of Finan being able to shape-change to enter a locked room, commit murder, and sneak out without disturbing the locks is an idea I find amusing but hardly worthy of consideration."

Sister Fidelma gazed thoughtfully at Laisran.

"Do you believe that this murder could only be carried out by sorcery, then?"

Laisran's rotund face clouded and he genuflected quickly.

"God between me and all evil, Fidelma, but is there any other explanation? We come from a culture which accepted shape-changing as a normal occurrence. Move among our people and they will tell you that Druids still exist and have such capabilities. Wasn't Diarmuid's foster brother changed into a boar, and wasn't Caer, the beloved of Aengus Og, condemned to change her form every alternate year?"

"These are ancient legends, Laisran," admonished Sister Fidelma. "We live in reality, in the here and now. And it is among the people of this community that we will find the person who slew Wulfstan. Before I question Dagobert, however, I would like to see Wulfstan's chamber once more."

Abbot Laisran pulled at his lower lip. His usually jovial face was creased in a frown of perplexity.

"I do not understand, Sister Fidelma. Everyone in our community here, at Durrow, had cause to kill Wulfstan and everyone is suspect. Is that what you are saying? At the same time that everyone is suspect, no one could have done the deed, for its implementation was beyond the hand of any human agency."

"Now that I did not say," Sister Fidelma admonished the abbot firmly, as she led the way along the corridor to halt at the open door of what had been Wulfstan's chamber.

The body of Wulfstan had been removed to the chapel of St. Benignus, where preparations were being made to transport its sarcophagus to the coast, from where Eadred and his entourage would accompany it, by sea, to the land of the South Saxons, which lay on the southern shore of Britain.

Sister Fidelma stared once again at the grey stone-flagged floor. She walked over the slabs, pressing each with her foot. Then she stared upwards towards the ceiling, which rose about eleven feet above the chamber floor. Her eyes eventually turned back to the bars on the window.

"Give me a hand," she suddenly demanded.

Abbot Laisran stared at her in surprise as she began pushing the wooden table towards the window.

Hastily, he joined her in the effort, grinning sheepishly.

"If the young novitiates of my order could see their abbot heaving furniture about . . ." he began.

"They would realise that their abbot was merely human," replied Fidelma, smiling.

They pushed the table under the barred window and, to Abbot Laisran's astonishment, Sister Fidelma suddenly scrambled on top of the table. It rose three feet above the ground and by standing on it, Sister Fidelma, being tall, could reach easily to the bars of the solitary window, whose bottom level was eight feet above the floor. She reached up with both her hands and tested each inch-thick iron bar carefully.

The lowering of her shoulders showed her disappointment.

Slowly she clambered down, helped by the arm of Laisran.

Her lips were compressed. "I thought the bars might have been loose."

"It was a good idea," smiled Laisran, encouragingly.

"Come, show me the floor above this," Sister Fidelma said abruptly.

With a sigh, Laisran hastened after her as she strode swiftly away.

The floor above turned out to be equally disappointing. Over Wulf-

stan's chamber stretched a long wooden floor which was the floor of
one of the long dormitories for the novitiates of the community. There
were over a dozen beds in the dormitory. Even had she not examined
the boards of the floor carefully, to see whether any had been prised
up in order that a person could be lowered into the chamber below,
and realised that none of the floorboards had been moved in many
years, Sister Fidelma would still have recognised the fact that such an
exercise would have necessitated the participation of everyone in the
dormitory.

She turned away with disappointment on her features.

"Tell me, Laisran, what lies below Wulfstan's chamber?"

Laisran shook his head.

"I have had that thought also, Fidelma," he confided. "Nothing but
solid earth lies below. There is no cellar, nor tunnel. The stone flags are
laid on solid ground, so no person could enter the chamber by removing one of the floor stones. Besides," he smiled wryly, "what would
Wulfstan have been doing during the commotion required to enter his
chamber by the removing of the ceiling planks or floor slabs, or the re-
moval of the bars of the window?"

Sister Fidelma smiled.

"The pursuit of truth is paved by the consideration and rejection of
all the alternatives, no matter how unlikely they may be, Laisran."

"The truth," replied the abbot, looking troubled, "is that it was impossible for the hand of man to strike down Wulfstan while he was
locked alone in his chamber."

"Now that I *can* agree with."

Abbot Laisran looked puzzled.

"I thought you said that no sorcery was employed. Do you mean
that he was not killed by the hand of a man?"

"No," grinned Sister Fidelma. "I mean that he was not alone in his
chamber. It is a syllogism. Wulfstan was stabbed to death. Wulfstan was
in his bedchamber. Therefore he was not alone in his bedchamber
when he was killed."

"But . . ."

"We have ruled out the argument that our murderer could have
come through the window. Do you agree?"

Laisran frowned, trying hard to follow the logic.

"We have ruled out the possibility that our murderer could have entered the chamber through the roof."

"Agreed."

"We have concluded that it would be impossible for the murderer to enter via the stone-flagged floor."

Abbot Laisran nodded emphatically.

"Then that leaves one obvious method of entry and exit."

Now Laisran was truly bewildered.

"I do not see . . ." he began.

"The chamber door. That is how our murderer gained entry and how he left."

"Impossible!" Laisran shook his head. "The door was secured from the inside."

"Nevertheless, that was how it was done. And whoever did it hoped that we would be so bemused by this curiosity that we would not inquire too deeply of the motive, for he hoped the motive was one that was obvious to all: the hatred of Wulfstan and the Saxons. Ideas of sorcery, of evil spirits, of Wulfstan being slain by no human hand, might cloud our judgement, or so our killer desired it to do."

"Then you know who the killer is?"

Fidelma shook her head.

"I have not questioned all the suspects. I think it is now time that we spoke with the Frankish prince, Dagobert."

Dagobert was a young man who had been brought from the land of the Franks when he was a child. It was claimed that he was heir to the Frankish empire, but his father had been deposed and the young prince had been taken into exile in Ireland until the time came when he could return. He was tall, dark, rather attractive, and spoke Irish almost as fluently as a native prince. Laisran had warned Sister Fidelma that the young man was well connected and betrothed to a princess of the kings of Cashel. There would be repercussions if Dagobert was not accorded the full letter of the Brehon Law.

"You know why you are here?" began Sister Fidelma.

"That I do," the young man smiled. "The Saxon pig, Wulfstan, has been slain. Outside the band of Saxons who followed the young whelp, there is a smile on the face of every student in Durrow. Does that surprise you, Sister Fidelma?"

"Perhaps not. I am told that you were known to have had an argument with him?"

Dagobert nodded.

"What about?"

"He was an arrogant pig. He insulted my ancestry and so I punched him on the nose."

"Wasn't that difficult to do, with his bodyguard? I am also told that Raedwald was never far away and he is a muscular young man."

Dagobert chuckled.

"Raedwald knew when to defend his prince and when not. He diplomatically left the room when the argument started. A man with a sense of honour is Raedwald of the South Saxons. Wulfstan treated him like dirt beneath his feet even though he was a thane and blood cousin."

Sister Fidelma reached into her robes and drew out the bloodstained embroidered linen kerchief and laid it on the table.

"Do you recognise this?"

Dagobert frowned and picked it up, turning it over in his hands with a puzzled expression.

"It is certainly mine. There is my motto. But the bloodstains . . . ?"

"It was found by the side of Wulfstan's body. I found it. It was obviously used to wipe the blood off the weapon that killed him."

Dagobert's face whitened.

"I did not kill Wulfstan. He was a pig but he simply needed a sound thrashing to teach him manners."

"Then how came this kerchief to be by his side in his chamber?"

"I . . . I loaned it to someone."

"Who?"

Dagobert bit his lip, shrugging.

"Unless you wish to be blamed for this crime, Dagobert, you must tell me," insisted Fidelma.

"Two days ago I loaned the kerchief to Talorgen, the prince of Rheged."

Finan inclined his head to Sister Fidelma.

"Your reputation as an advocate of the Brehon Court precedes you, Sister," the dark, lean man greeted her. "Already it is whispered from Tara how you solved a plot to overthrow the High King."

Fidelma gestured Finan to be seated.

"People sometimes exaggerate another's prowess, for they love to create heroes and heroines to worship. You are professor of law here?"

"That is so. I am qualified to the level of *Sai,* being a professor of law only."

The *Sai* was a qualification of six years of study and the degree below that of *Anruth* held by Fidelma.

"And you taught Wulfstan?"

"Each of us has a cross to bear, as did Christ. Mine was the teaching of the Saxon thanes."

"Not all the Saxons?"

Finan shook his head.

"No. Only the three thanes, as they refused to sit at lessons with churls, and only the express order of the Abbot Laisran made them attend class with the other students. They were not humble before the altar of Christ. In fact, I formed the opinion that they secretly mocked Christ and clung to the worship of their outlandish god Woden."

"You disliked the Saxons?"

"I hated them!"

The vehemence in the man's voice made Sister Fidelma raise her eyebrows.

"Isn't hate an emotion unknown to a Brother of the order, especially one qualified as a *Sai?*"

"My sister and brother took up the robes of the religious and decided to accept a mission to preach the word of Christ in the lands of the East Saxons. A few years ago I encountered one of the missionaries who had gone in that band. They had arrived in the land of the East Saxons and sought to preach the word of Christ. The heathen Saxons stoned them to death, only two of the band escaping. Among those who met a martyr's fate were my own sister and brother. I have hated all Saxons ever since."

Sister Fidelma gazed into the dark eyes of Finan.

"Did you kill Wulfstan?"

Finan returned her scrutiny squarely.

"I could have done so at another time, in another place, I have the hatred in me. But no, Sister Fidelma, I did not kill him. Neither do I have the means to enter a barred room and leave it as though no one had entered."

Fidelma nodded slowly.

"You may go, Finan."

The professor of law rose reluctantly. He paused and said reflectively, "Wulfstan and Eadred were not liked by any in this monastery. Many young men with hot tempers have challenged them in combat since they have been here. Dagobert the Frank, for one. Only the fact that such challenges are forbidden on sacred soil has prevented blood-shed thus far."

Fidelma nodded absently.

"Is it true that the Saxons are leaving tomorrow?" Finan demanded.

She raised her head to look at him.

"They are returning with the body of Wulfstan to their own land," she affirmed.

A contented smile crossed Finan's face.

"I cannot pretend that I regret that, even if it has cost one of their lives to prompt the move. I had hoped that they would have left Durrow yesterday."

She glanced up at the law professor, interested.

"Why would they leave?"

"Some Saxon messenger arrived at the monastery yesterday afternoon seeking Wulfstan and Eadred. I half hoped that it was a summons to return to their country. However, praise be that they are departing now."

Fidelma frowned in annoyance.

"Let me remind you, Finan, that unless we find the culprit, not only this centre of learning, but all the five kingdoms of Éireann will be at risk, for the Saxons will surely want to take compensation for the death of their prince."

Talorgen of Rheged was a youth of average stature, fresh-faced and sandy of hair. He already wore a wispy moustache, but his cheeks and chin were clean shaven.

"Yes. It is no secret that I challenged Wulfstan and Eadred to combat."

His Irish, though accented, was fluent and he seemed at ease as he sat in the chair Sister Fidelma had indicated.

"Why?"

Talorgen grinned impishly.

"I hear that you have questioned Eadred. From his manner you may judge Wulfstan's arrogance. It is not hard to be provoked by them, even if they were not Saxons."

"You do not like Saxons?"

"They are not likable."

"But you are a prince of Rheged, and it is reported that the Saxons are attacking your land."

Talorgen nodded, his mouth pinched. "Oswy calls himself Christian king of Northumbria, but he still sends his barbaric hordes against the kingdoms of the Britons. For generations now the people of my land have fought to hold back the Saxons, for their thirst for land and power is great. Owain, my father, sent me here, but I would, by the living Christ, rather be at his side, wielding my sword against the Saxon foemen. My blade should drink the blood of the enemies of my blood."

Sister Fidelma regarded the flushed-faced young man with curiosity.

"Has your blade already drunk of the blood of your people's enemies?"

Talorgen frowned abruptly, hesitating, and then his face relaxed. He chuckled.

"You mean, did I kill Wulfstan? That I did not. I swear by the living God! But hear me, Sister Fidelma, it is not that I did not want to. Truly, sometimes the faith of Christ is a hard taskmaster. Wulfstan and his cousin Eadred were so dislikable that I scarcely believe there is anyone in this community who regrets the death of Wulfstan."

She took out the bloodstained kerchief and laid it on the table.

"This was found by the body of Wulfstan. It was used to wipe the blood from the weapon that killed him. It belongs to Dagobert."

"You mean Dagobert . . . ?" The prince of Rheged's eyes opened wide as he stared from the kerchief to Sister Fidelma.

"Dagobert tells me that he gave you this kerchief in loan two days ago."

Talorgen examined the kerchief carefully and then slowly nodded.

"He is right. It is the same one, I can tell from the embroidery."

"How then did it get into Wulfstan's chamber?"

Talorgen shrugged.

"That I do not know. I remember having it in my chamber yesterday morning. I saw it was gone and thought Dagobert had collected it."

Sister Fidelma regarded Talorgen steadily for a moment or two.

"I swear, Sister," said the prince of Rheged earnestly, "I would not have hesitated to kill Wulfstan outside these walls, but I did not kill him within them."

"You are forthright, Talorgen."

The young man shrugged.

"I am sprung of the house of Urien of Rheged, whose praise was sung by our great bard Taliesin. Urien was the Golden King of the North, slain in stealth by a traitor. Our house is even-handed, just, and forthright. We believe in honesty. We meet our enemies in daylight on the plain of battle, not at night in the darkened recesses of some bedchamber."

"You say that there are many others in this community who held enmity against Wulfstan? Was there anyone in particular that you had in mind?"

Talorgen pursed his lips.

"Our teacher Finan often told us that he hated the Saxons."

Sister Fidelma nodded.

"I have spoken with Finan."

"As you already know, Dagobert quarrelled with Wulfstan in the refectory and bloodied his mouth two nights ago. Then there was Riderch of Dumnonia, Fergna of Midhe, and . . ."

Sister Fidelma held up her hand.

"I think that you have made your point, Talorgen. Everyone in Durrow is a suspect."

Sister Fidelma found Raedwald in the stables making preparations for the journey back to the land of the South Saxons.

"There is a question I would ask you on your own, Raedwald. Need I remind you of my authority?"

The Saxon warrior shook his head.

"I have learnt much of your law and customs since I have been in your country, Sister. I am not as Eadred."

"And you have learnt some fluency in our tongue," observed Fidelma. "More fluency and understanding than your cousin."

"It is not my place to criticise the heir apparent to the kingship of the South Saxons."

"But I think that you did not like your cousin Wulfstan?"

Raedwald blinked in surprise at her directness and then he shrugged.

"I am merely a thane in the house of Cissa. I cannot like or dislike my appointed king."

"Why were you not on guard outside the chamber of Wulfstan last night?"

"It was not the custom. Once Wulfstan had secured himself inside, he was well guarded. You have seen the chamber he asked Abbot Laisran to devise for him. Once he was locked inside, there was, apparently, no danger to him. I slept in the next chamber and at his call should he need help."

"But he did not call?"

"His killer slashed his throat with his first blow. That much was obvious from his body."

"It becomes obvious that he willingly let the killer into his chamber. Therefore, he knew the killer and trusted him."

Raedwald's eyes narrowed.

Fidelma continued.

"Tell me, the messenger who arrived from your country yesterday, what message did he bring Wulfstan?"

Raedwald shook his head.

"That message was for Wulfstan only."

"Is the messenger still here?"

"Yes."

"Then I would question him."

"You may question but he will not answer you." Raedwald smiled grimly.

Sister Fidelma compressed her lips in annoyance.

"Another Saxon custom? Not even your messengers will speak with women?"

"Another Saxon custom, yes. But this is a custom of kings. The royal messenger has his tongue cut out so that he can never verbally betray the message that he carries from kings and princes to those who might be their enemies."

Abbot Laisran gestured to those he had summoned to his study chamber, at Sister Fidelma's request, to be seated. They had entered the room with expressions either of curiosity or defiance, according to their different personalities, as they saw Sister Fidelma standing before the high-manteled hearth. She seemed absorbed in her own thoughts as she stood, hands folded demurely before her, not apparently noticing them as they seated themselves around. Brother Ultan, as steward of the community, took his stand before the door with hands folded into his habit.

Abbot Laisran gave Fidelma an anxious glance and then he, too, took his seat.

"Why are we here?" demanded Talorgen abruptly.

Fidelma raised her head to return his gaze.

"You are here to learn how Wulfstan died and by whose hand," she replied sharply.

There was a brief pause before Eadred turned to her with a sneer.

"We already know how my kinsman Wulfstan died, woman. He died by the sorcery of a barbarian. Who that barbarian is, it is not hard to deduce. It was one of the *welisc* savages, Talorgen."

Talorgen was on his feet, fists clenched.

"Repeat your charges outside the walls of this abbey and I will meet your steel with mine, Saxon cur!"

Dagobert came to his feet to intervene as Eadred launched forward from his chair towards Talorgen.

"Stop this!" The usually genial features of Laisran were dark with anger. His voice cut the air like a lash.

The students of the ecclesiastical school of Durrow seemed to freeze at the sound. Then Eadred relaxed and dropped back in his seat with a smile that was more a sneer than amusement. Dagobert tugged at Talorgen's arm and the prince of Rheged sighed and reseated himself, as did the Frankish prince.

Abbot Laisran growled like an angry bear.

"Sister Fidelma is an official of the Brehon Court of Éireann. Whatever the customs in your own lands, in this land she has supreme authority in conducting this investigation and the full backing of the law of this kingdom. Do I make myself clear?"

There was a silence.

"I shall continue," said Fidelma quietly. "Yet what Eadred says is partially true."

Eadred stared at her with bewilderment clouding his eyes.

"Oh yes," smiled Fidelma. *"One* of you at least knows how Wulfstan died and who is responsible."

She paused to let her words sink in.

"Let me first tell you how he died."

"He was stabbed to death in his bed," Finan, the dark-faced professor of law, pointed out.

"That is true," agreed Sister Fidelma, "but without the aid of sorcery."

"How else did the assassin enter a locked room and leave it, still locked from the inside?" demanded Eadred. "How else but sorcery?"

"The killer wanted us to think that it was sorcery. Indeed, the killer prepared an elaborate plan to confuse us and lay the blame away from him. In fact, so elaborate was the plan that it had several layers. One layer was merely to confuse and frighten us by causing us to think the murder was done by a supernatural agency; another was to indicate an obvious suspect, while a third object was to implicate another person."

"Well," Laisran sighed, "at the moment I have yet to see through the first layer."

Sister Fidelma smiled briefly at the rotund abbot.

"I will leave that to later. Let us firstly consider the method of the killing."

She had their complete attention now.

"The assassin entered the room by the door. In fact, Wulfstan let his assassin into the bedchamber himself."

There was an intake of breath from the usually taciturn Raedwald. Unperturbed, she continued.

"Wulfstan knew his killer. Indeed, he had no suspicions, no fear of this man."

Abbot Laisran regarded her with open-mouthed astonishment.

"Wulfstan let the killer in," she continued. "The assassin struck. He killed Wulfstan and left his body on the bed. It was an act of swiftness. To spread suspicion, the killer wiped his knife on a linen kerchief which he mistakenly thought belonged to Talorgen, prince of Rheged. As I said, if we managed to see beyond the charade of sorcery, then the assassin sought to put the blame for the murder on Talorgen. He failed to realise that the kerchief was borrowed two days ago from Dagobert. He did not realise that the kerchief prominently carried Dagobert's motto on it. It was a Latin motto which exhorts 'Beware what you say!' "

She paused to let them digest this information.

"How then did the killer now leave the bedchamber and manage to bar the door from the inside?" asked Dagobert.

"The bedchamber door was barred with two wooden bars. They were usually placed on iron rests which are attached to the frame of the door. When I examined the first wooden bar I observed that at either end there were two pieces of twine wrapped around it as if to protect the wood when it is placed in the iron rests. Yet on the second wooden bar, the curiosity was that the twine had two lengths of four feet still loose. Each end of the twine had been frayed and charred."

She grimaced and repeated herself.

"A curiosity. Then I noticed that there was a rail at the top of the door on which a heavy woollen curtain could be drawn across the door when closed in order to prevent a draught. It was, of course, impossible to see whether the curtain had been drawn or not once the room was broken into, for the inward movement of the door would have swept the curtain aside on its rail."

Eadred made a gesture of impatience.

"Where is this explanation leading?"

"Patience, and I will tell you. I spotted two small spots of grease on the ground on either side of the door. As I bent to examine these spots of grease I saw two nails fixed into the wood about three inches from the ground. There were two short pieces of twine still tied on these nails and the ends were frayed and blackened. It was then I realised just how the assassin had left the room and left one of the bars in place."

"One?" demanded Abbot Laisran, leaning forward on his seat, his face eager.

Fidelma nodded.

"Only one was really needed to secure the door from the inside. The first bar, that at three feet from the bottom of the door, had not been set in place. There were no marks on the bar and its twine protection was intact, nor had the iron rests been wrenched away from the doorjamb when Ultan forced the door. Therefore, the conclusion was that this bar was not in place. Only the second bar, that which rested across the top of the door, about two feet from the top, had been in place."

"Go on," instructed Laisran when she paused again.

"Having killed Wulfstan, the assassin was already prepared. He undid the twine on both ends of the wooden bar and threaded it around the wooden curtain rail across the top of the door. He set in place, or had already placed them during the day, when the chamber was open, two nails. Then he raised the wooden bar to the level of the curtain rail. He secured it there by tying the ends of the twine to the nails at ground level. This construction allowed him to leave the room."

Laisran gestured with impatience.

"Yes, but how could he have manipulated the twine to lower the bar in place?"

"Simply. He took two reed candles and as he went to leave, he placed a candle under either piece of the string near the ground. He took a piece of paper and lit it from his tinder box—I found the ashes of the paper on the floor of the chamber, where he had to drop it. He lit the two reed candles, on either side of the door under the twine. Then he left quickly. The twine eventually burned through, releasing the bar, which dropped neatly into place in the iron rests. It had, remember, only two feet to drop. The candles continued to burn until they became mere spots of grease, almost unnoticeable, except I slipped on one. But the result was that we were left with a mystery. A room locked on the inside with a corpse. Sorcery? No. Planning by a devious mind."

"So what happened then?" Talorgen encouraged, breaking the spellbound silence.

"The assassin left the room, as I have described. He wanted to create this illusion of mystery because the person he wished to implicate was one he felt his countrymen would believe to be a barbaric sorcerer. As I indicated, he wished to place suspicion on you, Talorgen. He left the room and talked to someone outside Wulfstan's bedchamber for a while. Then they heard the bar drop into place and that was the assassin's alibi, because it was clear that they had heard Wulfstan, still alive, slide the bar to lock his chamber door."

Raedwald was frowning as it seemed he struggled to follow her reasoning.

"You have given an excellent reconstruction," he said slowly. "But it is only a hypothesis. It remains only a hypothesis unless you name the assassin and his motive."

Sister Fidelma smiled softly.

"Very well. I was, of course, coming to that."

She turned and let her gaze pass over their upraised faces as they watched her. Then she let her gaze rest on the haughty features of the thane of Andredswald.

Eadred interpreted her gaze as accusation and was on his feet before she had said a word, his face scowling in anger.

Ultan, the steward, moved swiftly across the room to stand before Sister Fidelma, in anticipation lest Eadred let his emotions, which were clearly visible on his angry features, overcome him.

"You haven't told us the motive," Dagobert the Frank said softly. "Why would the thane of Andredswald murder his own cousin and prince?"

Sister Fidelma continued to stare at the arrogant Saxon.

"I have not yet said that the thane of Andredswald is the assassin," she said softly. "But as for motive, the motive is the very laws of the Saxon society, which, thanks be to God, are not our laws."

Abbot Laisran was frowning.

"Explain, Fidelma. I do not understand."

"A Saxon prince succeeds to the kingship by primogeniture. The eldest son inherits."

Dagobert nodded impatiently.

"That is also so with our Frankish succession. But how does this provide the motive for Wulfstan's murder?"

"Two days ago a messenger from the kingdom of the South Saxons arrived here. His message was for Wulfstan. I discovered what his message was."

"How?" demanded Raedwald. "Royal messengers have their tongues cut out to prevent them revealing such secrets."

Fidelma grinned.

"So you told me. Fortunately this poor man was taught to write by Diciul, the missionary of Éireann who brought Christianity and learning to your country of the South Saxons."

"What was the message?" asked Laisran.

"Wulfstan's father had died, another victim of the yellow plague. Wulfstan was now king of the South Saxons and urged to return home at once."

She glanced at Raedwald.

The big Saxon nodded silently in agreement.

"You admitted that much to me when I questioned you, Raedwald," went on Fidelma. "When I asked you if you liked Wulfstan you answered that it was not up to you to like or dislike your appointed king. A slip of the tongue, but it alerted me to the possible motive."

Raedwald said nothing.

"In such a barbaric system of succession, where the order of birth is the only criterion for claiming an inheritance or kingdom, there are no safeguards. In Éireann, as among our cousins in Britain, a chieftain or king not only has to be of a bloodline but has to be elected by the *derbhfine* of his family. Without such a safeguard it becomes obvious to me that only the death of a predecessor removes the obstacles of the aspirant to the throne."

Raedwald pursed his lips and said softly: "This is so."

"And, with Wulfstan's death, Eadred will now succeed to the kingship?"

"Yes."

Eadred's face was livid with anger.

"I did not kill Wulfstan!"

Sister Fidelma turned and stared deeply into his eyes.

"I believe you, for Raedwald is the assassin," she said calmly.

Finan made a grab at Raedwald as the muscular Saxon thane sought desperately to escape from the room. Dagobert leapt forward together with Ultan, the steward, to help restrain the struggling man. When the thane of Staeningum had been overpowered, Sister Fidelma turned to the others.

"I said that the assassin had a devious mind. Yet in the attempt to lead false trails, Raedwald over-excelled himself and brought suspicion down on him. In trying to implicate Talorgen, Raedwald made a mistake and caused confusion by thinking the kerchief to be Talorgen's. It bore Dagobert's motto in Latin. Raedwald has no Latin and so did not spot his mistake. This also ruled out Eadred from suspicion, as Eadred knew Latin to the degree that he could recognise Dagobert's motto."

She settled her gaze on Eadred.

"If you had also been slain, then Raedwald was next in line to the kingship, was he not?"

Eadred made an affirmative gesture.

"But . . ."

"Raedwald was going to implicate you as the assassin and then show how you tried to put the blame on Talorgen. He would have either had you tried for murder under our law or, if all else failed . . . I doubt whether you would have returned safely to the land of the South Saxons. Perhaps you might have fallen overboard on the sea voyage. Whichever way, both Wulfstan and you would have been removed from the succession, leaving it clear for Raedwald to claim the throne."

Eadred shook his head wonderingly. His voice was tinged with reluctant admiration.

"Never would I have suspected that a woman possessed such a meticulous mind to unravel the deviousness of this treachery in the way that you have done. I shall look upon your office with a new perspective."

Eadred turned abruptly to the Abbot Laisran.

"I and my men will depart now, for we must return to my country. With your permission, Abbot, I shall take Raedwald with me as my prisoner. He will stand trial according to our laws and his punishment will be prescribed by them."

Abbot Laisran inclined his head in agreement.

Eadred moved to the door, and as he did so, his eyes caught sight of Talorgen of Rheged.

"Well, *welisc*. It seems I owe you an apology for wrongly accusing you of the murder of Wulfstan. I so apologise."

Talorgen slowly stood up, his face trying to control his surprise.

"Your apology is accepted, Saxon."

Eadred paused and then he frowned.

"The apology notwithstanding, there can never be peace between us, *welisc!*"

Talorgen sniffed.

"The day such a peace will come is when you and your Saxon hordes will depart from the shores of Britain and return to the land whence you came."

Eadred stiffened, his hand going to his waist, then he paused and relaxed and almost smiled.

"Well said, *welisc*. It will never be peace!"

He strode from the room with Ultan and Dagobert leading Raedwald after him.

Talorgen turned and smiled briefly towards Sister Fidelma.

"Truly, there are wise judges among the Brehons of Ireland."

Then he, too, was gone. Finan, the professor of law, hesitated a moment.

"Truly, now I know why your reputation is great, Fidelma of Kildare."

Sister Fidelma gave a small sigh as he left.

"Well, Fidelma," Abbot Laisran smiled in satisfaction, reaching for a jug of wine, "it seems that I have provided you with some diversion on your pilgrimage to the shrine of the Blessed Patrick at Ard Macha."

Sister Fidelma responded to the rotund abbot's wry expression.

"A diversion, yes. Though I would have preferred something of a more pleasant nature to have occupied my time."

A LOAF OF QUICKSILVER

Clayton Emery

With a reputation based more in legend than reality, the twelfth-century out-law Robin Hood is readily adapted to an author's ends. Rather than being shown in the fabled redistribution of worldly goods that history usually attributes to him, Sherwood Forest's most famous denizen is often engaged in holiday making and rambling in the adventures designed by Clayton Emery. The author has cre-ated for his subjects Robin and Maid Marian a new role as itinerant detectives, and the husband-and-wife team fit the job to a tee.

Rouse, rouse!" Pounding at the door shook the cottage. Moaning on the sea wind came the doleful cry. "A boat's come back empty! Rouse!"

Robin and Marian were off their pallets instantly—sleepy outlaws didn't live long—with bows in hand. Their host, the fisherman Peter, unbarred the door. Sea wind, cold and salty, swirled in their faces and made the fire in the hearth gutter.

"What's happening?" asked Sidony. A barrel-shaped woman with a face like a dried apple, she was bundled in wool with a scarf over her head. Five sleepy-eyed children clustered around. "Whose boat?"

"Gunther's! Both him and Yorg are missing!"

"Oh my!" The fishwife put a gnarled hand to her mouth. "And Lucy and Zerlina so young to be widows!"

Robin Hood shrugged on his quiver, an instinct when trouble por-tended. He and Marian were dressed alike, in tattered wool of Lincoln green, laced deerhide jerkins, and soft hats sporting spring feathers. The outlaw chieftain and his wife stepped outside the tiny cottage.

With food lean in the Greenwood and a long winter over, they'd taken a holiday of sorts, walked from Sherwood east and then north, followed a Roman road through Lincoln, across the Humber, to the high cliffs at Scarborough, which Marian had never seen. They'd dawdled on the way back, followed the coast dotted with black wrecks, out to buy dried herring for Lent and "to smell the salt air."

They had salt air aplenty, for the wind never quit. It pulsed and blustered and boomed and tickled, never still. Sea and wind and clouds were half the world for tiny Wigby, sixteen cottages almost overwhelmed by wide Humber Bay, roiling with waves driven from the turbulent North Sea, called the German Sea hereabouts. Behind the village lay sandy dunes with grass atop, and a forest, The Wolds, like a fog bank in the distance. A long way to haul firewood, the outlaw thought.

Against a cloudy red-streaked sunrise, villagers clustered at the high-tide mark, an undulating wave of seaweed. Men and women were almost identical in salt- and scale-streaked smocks, shabby wool hose, and pitchy half-boots. Hats were tied under chins to confound the wind. Amidst the fisherfolk slumped two new widows, teary but resigned, as if they'd expected this day. Children clung to their skirts and stared at an empty dory.

As the fishing family and their guests straggled down the shingle, Sidony muttered, "It's their own fault. 'If two relatives go out in a boat, one will drown.' And sneaking out in the middle of the night."

"Sneaking out?" Marian listened close, for the local accent was guttural and garbled. The last phrase resembled "sneegin' gout."

"Aye. Gettin' a jump on the herrin'. You're not supposed to go ahead of the rest, t'ain't fair. You wait, pass your boat through the rope circle, get the blessing of the deacon. It's custom goes back forever. And they sailed under a full moon, too!"

The party squeezed in to examine the dory, floated in on the tide and hauled up from the surf, but there was little to see. The boat was a dozen feet long with a tombstone stern and flat bottom, broad-beamed and high-walled to ride blue water. Around the mast was a lateen sail of coarse yellowed linen. Nets were folded in heaps across the waist. A large rock in the bow served as anchor. The oars were missing while a worn boot had been left behind. Many villagers echoed Sidony's admonitions about tempting fate and taking advantage.

Robin Hood's keen eyes were busy. Peering, he handed Marian his bow and clambered over the gunwale, careful to tread on ribs and not the bottom planks. Still someone warned, "Not supposed to step in a boat ashore. S'bad luck." Robin rubbed his hand along the ribs, swirled his hand in the bilge slopping in the bottom. It might have been tinged red, but his callused hand came away clean.

A toothless elder sighed and let go of the gunwale, then so did the others, as if letting go of the lost fishermen. "Enough grievin'. Tide's makin'. Time to get the fish in." Instinctively people scanned the wind and waves and sky, then turned to breakfast and ready their own boats lined along the strand.

Robin and Marian lingered, as did their hosts. The outlaw scanned the dory from stem to stern as if he'd buy it. He used his Irish knife to poke the outer hull, felt the sea moss and barnacles. Then he stood back stroking his beard. Marian knew that sign: His curiosity was piqued.

They walked with Peter's family back to the cottage for chowder and ale. Sidony muttered, "Knew it would happen some day. I'm just surprised it took this long."

"What?" asked Robin and Marian together.

The fisherfolk looked at them, still unsure of their status. These were the famous outlaws of Sherwood Forest, they knew, and supposedly lords. They'd descended on Wigby unexpectedly, seeking lodging and paying in silver. Their hosts were unsure how to address them, but fishermen were a hard-headed lot who feared only God and storms. Husband and wife let the silence drag to underline their independence. Robin added, "Please. We're strangers hereabouts. Why are you not surprised?"

Peter remained silent, let his wife talk for both. "Well . . . The good Lord knows we lose enough men to plain accidents. There's more ways to die on the swan's road. Strike a rock, or a whale, a rogue wave, a sea serpent. But if anyone went hunting grief it was Gunther and Yorg. They were brothers and forever fighting. They even fought over who owned that boat when both helped build it. So squabbling's been the death of them, I'd say."

The outlaw nodded absently. " 'Most of our troubles we bring on ourselves.' "

The family stamped up the shingle. Marian lagged behind. "You're pensive, Rob. What's your guess?"

Robin turned and scanned the sea. "I'm a simple man given to simple explanations. There's no sign the boat struck anything: no planks stove in, no barnacles scraped off, the moss intact all over. The boat might've pitched them overboard, but the nets are still folded neat. And there's that boot."

"Yes . . . ¿"

"I don't know. . . . It's rare that ghosts or selkies or serpents pluck a man into the sea. Men bear enough evil we needn't blame the fays for murder."

"And . . . ¿"

"Perhaps nothing." Robin shrugged. "I don't wish to speak ill of the dead, especially newly dead. I don't need ghosts wafting over the waves for me."

Marian stared at the gray roiling sea. The breeze blew dark hair around her face and she combed it back. "Yes, let's curb our tongues."

After a subdued Mass and blessing of the fleet, and passing each boat through a rope circle, Wigby went fishing. And Robin Hood went with them.

He worked with Peter, who'd lost his eldest son in a storm the year before. Next eldest, too young to be married, was a squint-eyed, serious-faced girl of fourteen named Madge.

Robin rowed, for he liked the feel of the waves under the wooden blades, while Peter manned the tiller and sheets for the triangular sail. Madge watched from the bow. Other boats from Wigby had put out, a dozen of them, and farther off bobbed boats from other villages and towns: Aldbrough, Patrington, Hedon, Grimsby. Peter occasionally sheared by another boat, yelled a welcome or a friendly insult, asked for news, passed on gossip. Yet no one from Wigby mentioned that two brothers were drowned and missing, that two families had been wiped out.

After a time, Madge reported this spot might do. Robin glanced over the side and gasped.

The boat floated on a sea of silver backs.

Herring jammed the water nose to tail, tight-packed as if already in the barrel. Alike as leaves on a tree, all were a foot long, mouths open and eyes like jet targets.

With no sign of elation, Peter donned an oilskin apron and unfolded the nets with an easy grace. Robin helped, so clumsy he almost pitched overboard. Madge took the tiller and steered a lazy circle. In minutes Robin felt the boat slow as the nets dragged. Peter grunted to Madge, snapped at Robin, then tilted inwards a tiny corner of a net.

A silvery cascade washed the bottom of the boat. Fish boiled and roiled and flopped and flapped, some so hard they flipped over the gunwale back to their haven. In two hours of backbreaking, fingernail-ripping, clothes-soaking labor, the tiny crew made four more passes, hauling in nets until the gunwales were awash and Robin Hood was knee-deep in fish.

"S'enough," said Peter. He and Robin sat near the bow to keep the nose down and prevent the stern from foundering, while Madge turned her cheek to the wind and aimed for home.

Yet the fisherman took no ease, but honed a knife on a sea stone, handed it to Robin with a few terse instructions. Robin Hood knew better how to dress deer than clean fish, but managed to behead and gut, yet keep the fillet intact along the spine for hanging, all without losing fingers.

Always curious, Robin looked to expand his knowledge. "How many trips will you make today, Peter?"

Hands busy, the fisherman glanced instinctively at the sky. Gulls followed them, soaring and banking, crashing into the water after fish offal. "As many as God gives us. While the herring are here, we work, for they'll be gone soon enough."

"Oh? Why so?"

But the fisherman just shrugged and wouldn't answer.

Robin sought another topic. Examining the fish he cut, he found them not all the same. "Why are they different?" He tried to hide the chattering of his teeth. Though both were just as wet, the fisherman and his daughter gave no sign of being chilled. They ate slices of raw fish to keep their body heat up.

The man flipped a butterfly fillet into a wicker basket. "They ain't. They're all herrin'." At the stern, Madge laughed quietly.

Robin held up a fish in either hand, solid writhing muscles coated with scales and slime. Both were the same length, but one was slim as a snake while the other was fat and humpbacked. "But they ain't the same. These are—"

Clearly galled by his free help, the fisherman stopped cleaning to point with his knife. "The skinny one's a pilchard. The fat one is a gizzard shad; he's got a fat gizzard, see? That'n's 'n alewife, blessed by Saint Peter. See his fingerprints down his ribs? And here." He pinched a fish by its dorsal fin. "If 't hangs straight, it's a herrin'. If 't hangs tail down, it's a pilchard. Nose down is a sprat—little and spratty, see? But hell, man, if they come to shore in herrin' season, they're herrin'. Like women—they all taste the same in the dark."

Robin chuckled at his ignorance and flayed with slimy hands, one fish to every five of Peter's. He kept the man talking. "Why did you say the fish would be gone soon? I thought herring season lasted a full moon."

"Not now it won't. 'Herrin' dislike a quarrel,' they say. Now that blood's been spilt, they'll vanish." He nodded grimly over the side where the wind ripped whitecaps and sent spume flying. "This be all we'll see this year. It's a hungry winter we'll 've."

Robin didn't disagree, but the gray waves shone with fish deep as he could see. He failed to understand how they could disappear overnight. Shaking his head, he grabbed another fish. It squirted through numb hands and kissed him on the mouth.

While her husband toiled at sea, Marian helped on the strand. Women and girls rolled out barrels of salt dried in salt pans during the winter, broached them, and crushed the white clumps with wooden mallets. Girls returned from the woods with brush hooks and saplings to repair the yards-long drying racks. Then the first boats arrived, and women toted the fillets and fish in wicker baskets and set to with sharp knives at long plank tables.

They worked and sang and joked and gossiped of wedding plans. It was common for betrothed to marry after the herring season, when hands were idle and dirty weather kept folk home. "Weddings bring stormy weather," Marian was told a dozen times. Brides chattered about plans for improving homes and husbands while the matrons shook their heads. Marian noted some needed little advice, for their bellies were swollen from wintertime assignations.

Unmarried girls took time to dig fat from under the backbone of a proper herring, a glob of gooey silver, and hurl it against a hut wall. If it stuck upright, they were teased, their husband would be upright and true, but if the fat clung crooked, so would their husbands prove false.

The only ones quiet were Lucy and Zerlina, the new widows. They grieved but worked, for no one stood idle while the herring ran.

Yet one did. As Marian returned from the privy, she noted a dark figure silhouetted against the gray sky. The woman walked the bushy cliffs and lumpy headlands north of the village, where the tide smashed to spray on rocks.

Marian stood by Sidony, grabbed a fish and a knife, set to slicing. She nodded south. "Who's that? Why doesn't she help?"

Sidony answered without looking. "That'd be Mornat. She don't associate."

"Mornat?" said Marian. "What a queer name. What does it mean?"

" 'S'a queer woman. The priest named her after cutting her from her dead mother. It means 'living from the dead' or somewhat. A posthumous child. So she has the second sight, and can heal with her touch."

Marian touched up a blade, sliced off the hundredth staring head of the day. Her callused hands were pruney and blue. "Why doesn't she associate?"

"She's queer, is all. We go to her when we need potions and such. The rest of the time she's off wandering the cliffs and sea caves, or walking to Hull for her nostrums. We don't keep track of her comings and goings. She doesn't like us. She's touched. And today she'll be worse than ever."

Marian made silence her question.

"Mornat set her cap for"—she wouldn't say the name, so Marian knew it must be one of the drowned brothers—"one who's left us for a better place. When she turned thirteen, she washed her shift in south-running water, turned it wrong-side out, and hung it before the fire, as girls will, you know. They say the likeness of—him who's not with us—came into her hut and turned the shift right-side out. Mornat followed him everywhere then, and let him take liberties up on the cliffs in the grass, and told everyone they were to marry in spring. But it didn't happen, for he married Lucy over there and never spoke to Mornat again."

So, thought Marian, it was the elder brother, Gunther, that Mornat had fancied. "The poor thing. It must have torn her heart from her bosom."

"If she has a heart," Sidony sniped. "Them touched with the sight don't live entirely in this world. And good enough, I say."

More boats plowed the surf and disgorged heaping baskets of fish. Men and boys took warmed watered cider and bread and chowder, then returned to the waves. Robin, his beard flecked with scales, gave Marian a quick kiss before driving his oars through the surf once more.

All day they worked. Drying racks were hung with fillets that danced and dripped in the sea wind. More were packed in salt. When the group flagged, one woman began a song so old it was in another tongue and no one knew the words, yet every woman sang along, timing the beat to the rhythm of her hands. As the sun set, old men built driftwood fires. Girls threaded fillets onto whittled sticks and propped the dripping bundles on the drying racks higher than a dog could jump. Boys lugged baskets of guts to wash out on the evening tide as gulls squawked at their feet.

When it was too dark to fish even by torchlight, the men beached the boats and helped clean and thread before snatching a few hours' sleep and setting out at dawn to fetch more fish.

Robin and Marian worked together, cutting themselves often now, salt stinging the gashes. At one point in the long night, Marian asked her husband, "Well, Rob? Are you ready to eschew outlawry and take up fishing instead?"

Robin sliced, cursed as he shaved fine bones. "Nay, never. Not in this life or any other. You'd have to be daft to go fishing, cracked as a coal miner. It's safer riding into battle against Saracens than going head-to-head with the North Sea in a cockleshell. It's no wonder these lot are so superstitious, putting their lives in the hands of God with every scull."

Marian agreed. "I never saw such a lot for queer beliefs."

"I thought we were bad in Sherwood, what with crossing streams with the right foot foremost and never venturing into caves without making the sign of the cross and making sure the light of a full moon never falls on your face: sensible things. But these fisherfolk! Not once today did anyone mention two brothers had drowned for fear of provoking their ghosts. And I was told more how not to fish than to fish. Never point at a boat with your finger, use your whole hand. Never call the salmon by its name, call it the 'red fish' instead. Never mention rats or mice while baiting hooks or laying the nets. By Saint Dunstan, what's rats and mice got to do with baiting?"

Marian only shook her head. Oddly, her thoughts flickered to the ostracized Mornat, alone and wind-blown as she walked the cliffs, like some widow who had never known a husband.

As the eternal night dragged and breath frosted, both outlaws grew sick of the bloody-salty-seaweedy smell of flayed fish. The villagers were exhausted yet worked with a will, glad the time of plenty had finally arrived after the long dark winter.

Three days they toiled thus, a blur of dying fish and chilled blood and raw, chapped, bleeding hands, snatching sleep and food. By late in the third day, no one sang or laughed. Work was a soul-numbing chore, and only future survival kept everyone hauling in nets and flaying fish.

As the sun peeked over the horizon on the fourth day, the women braced at their plank tables, knives sharp and ready, not talking. Only the sough of the constant wind and crackle of fires was heard.

It got quieter when the boats did not return for hour after hour. Women left tables to warm at the fires, or found other chores neglected over the past frenzied days.

Finally three boats came in, riding high, the fishermen's faces long, and the women guessed. The men splashed over the sides and beached the boats. They lifted out two or three baskets of odd fish and a few herring.

An old man ran his tongue over toothless gums, husked, "They're gone, ain't they? It's happened. The curse. Blood's been spilt and the herrin've vanished."

More boats beached. With empty hearts and idle hands, villagers stumbled to their cottages to sleep. There was no more work, no more herring to flay and dry, nothing extra to trade.

Come the depths of winter, they'd go hungry.

"It's the witch's done it. Witches are the bane of us. Do more harm than good."

Next morning, Peter's family sat around a guttering fire in the tiny cottage. They ate meager portions of chowder, already rationing, and stared at the driftwood fire, winking blue and green from burning salt.

"Look out on Lewis there," said Sidony. "One time, starvin' times, a woman was 'bout to hurl herself into the sea. But a magic cow appeared, white she was, a beauty. Told her to fetch her milking pail. Everyone in Callinish could milk her every night long's they took but one pail. Then an old witch tried to milk her into a sieve. She roared once like a lion and disappeared. No more milk after that. And they say she become the Dun Cow of Dunchurch, tearing up the countryside until Guy of Warwick killed 'er. And you know 'hat's true, because one of her ribs is in a chapel dedicated to Guy in Warwickshire.

"Nothing's good for a witch but to hang her familiar, then cut crosses in her body to let the bad blood out. There was one village—I ain't saying which one, but it's near here—had its crops blighted. A witch bred big toads and hitched 'em to little plows, sent 'em across the fields and poisoned the soil. They had to move away and never came back.

" 'Twas probably Mornat done in—them that's missin'."

Marian disliked arguing with a host, but could not let this last comment pass. "How could one small woman harm two brawny seamen? I've seen the muscles on your menfolk. Any one of them could wrestle Little John, Cumberland-style, and take one bout out of three. And how could she get into their boat? You'll blame the poor woman for shooting stars next."

Sidony only looked at the fire. "There's ways o' working evil. There's ways."

Robin Hood rubbed his brow with a hunk of lard where the wind had streaked it with salt. "Is there some way to lift the blood curse? That would bring the herring back?"

Sidony and Marian both frowned in thought. Finally the fishwife said, "Might be possible. I've heard tell if you could raise the bodies and give 'em a Christian burial, lay their—" she skipped the word "ghosts"—"the herring *might* come back. But it's been three days now and they haven't come ashore."

Everyone knew what she meant. Lungs full of water, a drowned body sank at first. But after three days, gases from corruption bloated the body and raised it. Yet neither brother had floated ashore, though the wind stayed in the northeast.

Marian pondered. "Perhaps we could float a loaf. But would anyone have quicksilver?"

The fishwife stared at the fire. "Aye, we might. 'T would comfort the widows, too. . . . Mornat would have quicksilver. She uses it in potions."

Without further ado, Sidony left the cottage, Marian following. They stopped at a house where Sidony borrowed a fresh loaf of dark rye bread. The goodwife guessed its intention, but said nothing. So little needed be said in this village, Marian noted, as if everyone's mind lay open.

Sidony plodded towards the farthest cottage, removed from the rest, and Marian nodded again. A wise woman, a witch, was shunned but tolerated because she was needed.

The young woman who answered the knock seemed in need of healing herself. Thin as the railbirds that piped along the shore, Mornat was tall with skin boiled red—far more red than chapped cheeks. Her mouth pouted, lips puffed out, and her breath stank like a cesspit. Taciturn and curt, Mornat declined to look in Marian's eyes. "Yes? What is it?" Her voice quavered, and she wiped away drool with a shaky hand. She salivated like a hungry dog, and Marian wondered why.

"Good Maid Mornat," Marian suppressed distaste at the sinister name, "we wondered if you might spare some quicksilver. I can pay in true silver."

Mornat's answer was a short nod to enter. She walked, Marian noted, gracelessly, straight up and down like a man.

The windowless cottage was tiny and, lacking a man's hand, drafty. The fire guttered and backblew, a sign the chimney was stacked wrong or clogged with soot. There was a table and single stool, a messy bed, jars and crocks for nostrums, and little else. Fresh seaweed lay on the hearth, a charm against house fires.

Mornat also did not question their begging quicksilver. She reached under the table and drew out a hollowed stump packed with chunky white clay. Calomel, Marian knew, fetched from Hamburg. She recalled Mornat often walked to Kingston Upon Hull down the coast. There'd be ships from the Continent there.

Mornat broke the white clay into an iron spider with a spoon and propped it in the fire to roast it. As she waited for the quicksilver to ooze from the clay, Mornat wafted her hand through the sweetish fumes and inhaled deeply. To Marian's curious glance, she supplied, "The breath of quicksilver is good for the lungs." Yet she coughed.

Marian nodded, but other thoughts flickered through her head. One Merry Man, Gilbert of the White Hand, had been a prisoner in the Holy Land and learned medicine from the Saracens. Greeks and Persians believed quicksilver touched by the god Mercury: An alchemist fathoming its secret might gain immortality. Yet Marian had doubts, for Mornat looked sick, for all she was strong and intelligent and composed. Pity welled in her breast, but she suspected any kindness would only be rebuffed.

Eventually, the witch lifted the pan away. Amidst the burned clay skittered globs of quicksilver. This fractious metal, Marian knew, over time hardened into true silver, also found in Germany.

With her Irish knife, Marian slit the top of the bread. Tipping the pan, Mornat dribbled in the quicksilver. Marian mashed the crust to seal in the metal.

Giving Mornat silver pennies, Marian said, "Our thanks. If this aids in locating the missing men—"

" 'Twill mean naught to me," Mornat interrupted. She stared from deep-sunk pouchy blue eyes. "Good day."

Peter and Robin dragged the dory to the surf as a crowd watched. A stout man named Vamond brought a proper anchor, the only one in the village, a four-pronged iron hook. Marian handed her husband the metal-laden loaf.

"Where shall we float it?" he asked.

Peter said, "I know."

Men helped launch the boat. Robin rowed, Vamond steered, and Peter in the bow shielded the precious loaf from spray.

Peter directed them north by east, marking a low-breasted hill. A quarter-mile from the rocky shore, where the boom of surf was loud, he called, "Gunther and Yorg often fished off Turk's Head here. Thought it was lucky."

So saying, he leaned over the bow and laid the loaf on the waves. Robin shipped his oars, and all three men stood, sway-hipped, to see what the bread would do.

At first it only bobbed up and down. Peter ordered Robin to back water to reduce drag. Again they watched.

Vamond gasped. Robin felt hairs prickle along his arms.

As if towed by an underwater string, the bread moved towards shore. It bobbed up one side of a wave, crested, slid down, clearly moving towards land.

Not daring to speak, Peter signaled. Blades feathering the water, Robin rowed after the bread.

Row, pause, row, pause, row. They followed the waterlogged loaf for a furlong, close enough to shore to feel the boat tremble as green-gray waves exploded against seaweedy rocks. Robin noted dimples and cracks in the cliffs, the waves tortured them so. From the heights, gulls launched themselves at the boat, anticipating trash. Spooked already, Robin shuddered. The birds' cries were so mournful, like lost souls; the voices of the drowned, seafarers claimed . . .

"It's sinking!" Vamond yelped.

"It's sunk!" bawled Peter over the boom of surf. "Row up to it! Get the grapnel!"

Robin fought to keep the dory on the invisible sunken mark as the fishermen tangled rope and anchor in their excitement. Staring holes in the water, Peter finally lowered the grapnel straight down, Vamond feeding out. When the line bobbed slack, he'd hit bottom. Carefully, Peter swirled the rope, snapped it to make the anchor hop. Muttering, he told of thumping rocks, empty shells, a sand bar, more rocks. Still dredging, he ordered Robin to scull closer to shore.

Finally the anchor snagged and both fishermen groaned, for the drag on the rope told what it was. Robin steadied the oars and his stomach.

The men had no need to pull hard, for corruption had done its work. With a bubble and hiss and belch, a missing fisherman bobbed to the surface for the last time.

It took all three to haul the cold, clammy corpse aboard. Each man prayed aloud.

"Saint Peter protect us," breathed Peter. "It's Yorg. He had blond hair. Gunther was dark."

The hair was handy, for there was little else to identify the man. The body was naked, rough seas having stripped its clothes, and bloated twice normal size. Fish and crabs had chewed round its features.

Still, Robin Hood forced himself to squat and look. He'd seen worse, he affirmed, though not while pitching in a boat that reeked of dead fish and dead men. Grimly, he examined the remains as the fishermen set sail to veer from shore.

"You shouldn't defile the body," warned Peter.

"God values probity above propriety," Robin answered vaguely. Rolling Yorg over, he found the scalp cut cleanly, a flap of skin eaten away. The skull underneath was dented. The outlaw grunted. He'd seen enough open wounds to know living bone scratched easily.

"I don't understand," Vamond muttered. "How does the bread *know* where a body's sunk?"

"The quicksilver steers to the blood," Peter offered, "like an iron needle floated on water points north."

"More likely," suggested Robin as he poked, "the loaf is small enough to follow the strongest current. Weighted down, it floats like a body and stops in slack water, then just sinks on its own. . . . Unless I'm daft, this man was struck from behind. . . . But with what? . . ."

Immediately he knew, for the answer dug into his back: the shipped oars. He recalled both oars missing from Gunther's dory. And the bilge had been tinged red.

Peter shook his head as he took the tiller. "No surprise. They fought their lives long as only brothers can. And Gunther had a temper. So for him to cosh Yorg with an oar in a blind rage . . ."

Robin Hood cast about the gray roiling waves. "Where's Gunther then?"

"Where indeed?" asked Marian.

Robin shrugged. He walked the strand with Marian, glad to be off the water now he'd seen what it could do. Far behind, the village held a Mass for Yorg. The outlaws left them to it: Rather than weep and pray, they wanted to talk and think.

"Perhaps," mused Robin, "Gunther did fly into a rage, killed his brother, then threw himself after? Men with tempers are often mad turn and turn about."

Marian touched her little finger to her mouth. "Could someone *else* have killed *both?*"

"Who?" asked Robin. "*I* couldn't kill two fishermen with a sword, they're so tough and strong. . . ."

"He was struck from behind. A child could do that."

". . . Yorg was ready to come up: One tug freed him. Gunther should have washed up by now."

"Unless he went out to sea."

"Not with this wind. It'd peel the bark off a tree." Robin had tied his hat cord under his chin. "Wait. . . . What if Gunther's not a body?"

"Eh?"

Robin froze in his tracks. "If we don't have his body, when by all rights we should, maybe he's not—Jesus, Mary, and Joseph! The gulls!"

Marian glanced overhead, saw only tiny black-tipped terns. "What gulls?"

"Come on!" Robin snatched her hand and dragged her stumbling down the strand.

"Are you sure you're not just showing off?" Marian asked.

Robin took Peter's dory without asking permission. He and Marian manhandled it to the surf, then Robin grabbed his wife by the waist and heaved her aboard, pushed off, hopped belly-down over the gunwale. Rowing would take too long, he claimed, so he raised the sail and set the sheets as best he could. The sail luffed, flapping, but they steered in the right direction, the sharp prow slicing the waves, the bluff beam riding comfortably up and down.

"Will you *please* tell me what we're hunting?"

Robin told her. Afterwards, she was silent, straining to hear over the wind.

Off Turk's Head, the boat pitched as waves steepened near the rocks. Robin dumped the sail in a heap and grabbed the oars. He rowed closer to shore than last time. Marian watched waves boom and spume explode. "Rob, are you sure—"

"Hush and listen!" He ceased the creaking of oars. They bobbed, the rocks coming closer, the booming louder, listening until their ears rang.

Impatient, Robin shipped oars, braced his back against the mast, cupped his hands, and bellowed, "Hellooooooo!"

Listening. Slap of water under the prow. A warbling keen of disturbed gulls. The smash of surf.

Then, very faint, "Helllllll . . ."

"An echo!" bleated Marian.

"No! Hush! Helloooooooooooo!"

Fainter. "Helllllllpppp!"

Robin scanned the cliffside, head wagging. "Whence came it, Marian?"

The Vixen of Sherwood marked the rocks. A shoulder of cliff jutted like an upright axe blade. "I think there!"

"Methinks also! Hang on!"

"Rob!" Marian scrooched her bottom in the tiny seat at the prow, clung to the gunwales with white knuckles. "What are you *doing?*"

"*Hang on!*" he roared. Craning his head around, hauling with mighty sinews, Robin rowed for a gap in the rocks no wider than the dory's ribs.

"*Robbbbbb-iiiiinnnnn!*"

A steepening wave curled around their stern like a giant hand and hurled them towards shore. Kept arrow-straight by the outlaw's rowing, the dory lifted high, hung just under the breaking crest of the huge wave, and—

Marian screamed and covered her eyes.

—*crashed* down into the gap and stuck fast.

Waves clawed and sucked at the boat's strakes, but couldn't dislodge it, so gushed over the gunwales instead. Marian yelped, but her husband hoicked her from her perch, hugged her around the waist, and jumped.

They plunged breast-high. The swirling salty chill made them gasp.

Robin Hood fought for footing on shifting pebbles and slime. Straining against the undertow, he broke clear, trotted onto the narrow shingle, plunked his wife down with a grin.

Wet to her bosom, Marian could only gasp and nod at his brilliance. Robin jerked a shaking thumb towards the craggy cliff. "Wh-wh-wh-which?"

Marian couldn't talk, couldn't even point, so she led the way. The bright spring wind cut like the whips of Satan's imps.

Shuffling across rocks polished smooth by the pounding tide, they clung to the cliffside and crept towards the promontory, which rose before them like an upthrust knife blade. At half-tide, the surf swirled around their knees, sucked at their feet, tried to trip them again and again. Timing slack water, Marian, then Robin, zipped around the corner.

There, washed by waves, was a cave mouth not waist high. Marian, in front, saw daylight wink on swirling water inside. Watching the waves, with Robin bracing her waist, Marian scrooched inside the cave. After the next wave burst around his legs, Robin slid after her.

Inside was a chamber big as a cottage. Daylight spilled through a grass-edged hole at the top of the cave. A dirt slide angled down to a natural rock ledge just above their heads.

On the ledge lay a fisherman.

His face was pinched with hunger and cold, his clothes sopping. A huge scab marked the back of his head, and his right leg jutted at an odd angle.

But he was alive, staring with haunted eyes.

"Gunther," said Robin, "we've come to take you home."

The fisherman began to cry.

Robin offered Marian ten fingers up to the ledge. "You know more of healing than I. Tend him. I'll see if the boat's lifted loose on the tide. We'll need it to get him home, otherwise I'll have to carry him the long way 'round."

Marian took the boot-up, knelt beside Gunther. The fisherman had expended the last of his strength shouting for help. As he swooned, Marian checked for damage, tried to figure how to splint his leg for transporting.

Robin Hood crouched at the cave mouth, timed the incoming waves—higher now—crabbed through the hole, quickly grabbed the cliff, and inched back. He found the boat stuck fast, half-swamped. Foam churned along the port strakes: He'd stove them beaching. He wasn't sure he could have rowed the dory out against the tide anyway. Better he walked the bluffs with the wounded man on his back while Marian ran ahead for help.

Rising tide crashed about him. Fighting for footing, Robin would have been sucked away by the undertow if not for steely fingers on the cliff face. The cave mouth was almost drowned, and he had to hold his breath and half submerge to claw inside. Icy water almost stopped his heart.

Inside, gasping, blinded by seawater, he looked up at his wife and the fisherman. Gunther had blacked out, and Marian tussled to bind his legs together with rags.

Above them stood a third figure.

Dark-clad, wind-whipped, the woman loomed over the unsuspecting Marian, a knife held high.

"Marian!"

The Vixen of Sherwood looked down, saw her husband's expression, glanced behind—

—and jerked aside as the knife slashed down at her back.

Marian shrieked as Mornat's cold blade sheared her deerhide jerkin and wool skirt and kissed her ribs. The madwoman hurled the knife high again.

Robin had no bow to shoot, no rock to pitch, so he threw his big Irish knife. His famous aim held true. The weapon cartwheeled, spanked flat against Mornat's breast, hard enough to rock her.

Marian reared half-erect on the narrow ledge. Unable to turn, she slammed her elbow into the woman's brisket.

Arms flailing, the murderess toppled from the ledge backwards.

Marian and Mornat screamed together, until the madwoman's head struck the rock wall.

"She slid down that chimney hole, got behind me. I didn't hear her for surf noise," Marian hissed as Robin wrapped a crude bandage around her naked ribs.

"She must have seen us from shore. She was always walking the bluffs."

"Aye, alone," said Marian. "Gunther told me a little. Mornat was always pestering him. That night, while the men were readying their boat for the herring, she startled them in the dark. Furious, they told her to bugger off. She struck both from behind with an oar. She killed Yorg and stunned Gunther, beat him and broke his leg, then tumbled them in the boat and pushed out. Yorg she tipped overboard. Gunther she hid in this sea cave. She fed him potions to make him love her."

"The strength of the mad," Robin muttered.

It took awhile, but Robin eventually boosted Marian through the chimney hole, then Gunther. Marian helped hoist, gasping with pain from her burning ribs.

Dead Mornat they left to the sea for now.

Grunting, Robin shifted the fisherman across his brawny shoulders. From the top of Turk's Head they saw distant Wigby like a colony of hermit crabs. They started walking through the bent yellow grass.

" 'Twas some poison she mucked with, is my guess. It drove her mad," Robin huffed. When his wife didn't answer, he glanced over. "Marian, you're crying!"

"Yes, I'm crying!" Marian snapped. "You men! Quick to blame the moon and stars for your own faults! It wasn't quicksilver killed that poor woman! She was cursed before she was born! Cut from her dead mother, christened with that horrid name—'The living from the dead'!—so she's reminded of it every time someone speaks to her! And none would, for she was ostracized like a leper! Begged to heal all and sundry, then shunned for fear of ghosts or contamination or plain spite. Growing up without a mother, never learning a girl's graces and arts. Never to marry, never to know love! Suffering in silence while the girls chatter of wedding plans, knowing she'd never be a bride! It wasn't anything earthly killed that girl, it was lack of love!"

She sobbed now, chilled and wounded. Robin shifted his burden to catch her hand. "Don't cry, Marian. I hate to see you cry."

"Don't touch me! I need to cry! No one ever cried for that poor, lonely, love-starved creature, so it's time someone did, if only a stranger!"

Robin clucked his tongue, saved his breath for walking. Together they trudged along the bluff.

The sea wind pushed them along.

THE JESTER AND THE SAINT

Alan Gordon

A jester, like all those whose occupations allow them to masquerade as what they are not, is in a prime position to solve a crime. To him will be revealed things that to another would not be spoken; without the paraphernalia of his trade, he will scarcely be recognized by those he knows. Add to this that a jester in Renaissance Italy would have access to the highest circles as an entertainer and a wit, and you have the makings of a great detective. Author Alan Gordon came to write of a jester in Saint Francis's Assisi after penning award-winning stories in the field of science fiction.

I t is folly, perhaps, writing a history of a society that would prefer to remain unknown. Yet who better than a fool to take on such a task, to throw a pebble into the Adriatic hoping it might cause a wave to wash upon Egyptian shores. And our little troupe must keep its history if it wishes to continue to be effectual. So, to those of you who may read this, I salute you all, jesters and jongleurs, troubadours, trobairitzes and trouvères, minstrels, mimes and minnesingers, players of the Great Farce, my brothers and sisters of the Fools' Guild.

And if ultimately we are defeated, or *(mirabile visu!)* achieve our goal and happily disband, then this may be read in wonderment or scepticism by anyone who chances upon it, that he may learn of us, of the parts we have played, the history behind the history, and know that we strove without thanks, without expectation of success in this world or reward in the next, meeting our ends without dignity, shivering in a rain-filled ditch or succumbing to the assassin's dagger. And pray, my unknown reader. Pray for the souls who made others laugh and, more importantly, sought a world where others could laugh. For underneath the motley, the makeup, and the masks hid the most dedicated band of Christian soldiers that ever walked the face of this world. We did not crusade for Rome, nor did we take up pig bladders on staves for Byzantium. We regarded both with disdain, for they had lost their way. We looked instead to the First Fool, our Savior. We were fools for Christ's sake, as St. Paul had said, and the philosophical debate that began at the Council of Nicaea, whether God was three entities or one, did not interest us.

You might think that our goals and those of the Franciscans would coincide, then. Well, it's a long way from Francis to the Franciscans, even so short a time after his death. Already Rome is converting him into legend, the better to tame him. For they couldn't do it while he was alive. I hear Celano is already revising the *Vita,* removing all traces of humanity and ransacking Irish and Coptic folklore for inspiration. Pity. I always thought you could win more converts by showing how an ordinary man became good, rather than by making him a saint from birth. It's hard to be a saint all the time. But not according to the official historians of the Church, those noted sticklers for accuracy.

Giving credit where it is due, he did better than most. But I knew him before he was a saint, as the old troubadour joke goes. Oh, he wanted so much to be one of us, not knowing our true purpose. He fancied himself a singer, aspired to motley. Even after his great revelation, he kept it up. God's Fool, God's Troubadour, as if calling him one made it so.

I met him in 1198. He would have been fifteen or sixteen. I was passing through Umbria on my way back to the guildhall, having successfully completed my last assignment on two levels. Overtly, I entertained for several months at a great palace in Apulia, pleasing the lord there so much that he rewarded me with a weighty purse. Covertly, I caused two warring factions in the town to see the lunacy of their quarrel, while encouraging a marriage between members of each who, quite frankly, needed little encouragement. And so a peace was created where none had been before, and maybe it will last a few years. And I didn't have to kill anybody. This time.

Not wishing to empty my purse too quickly, I had spent a pleasant summer night on a bed of pine needles in a forest. I was hoping to make Arezzo in two days and inveigle my way onto a boat or barge as far as Firenze. I woke up to hear birds singing and, to my bewilderment, someone lustily bellowing a Provençal drinking song. Before the fog cleared from my brain, he stomped into the clearing in which I reposed, stopping in midstride and midlyric as he saw me.

He was a well-favored youth, black-haired and black-eyed. His clothes suggested some prosperity, as the cloak was new and unpatched, while the boots were sturdy and well made.

"Good morning, young sir," I greeted him both in langue d'oc and in the Tuscan dialect. "Are you of these parts? And if so, which parts are these? I had thought myself in Umbria, but think now to be in Provence. If the latter, I am come by miracle, for I was in Umbria when I went to sleep."

"And still are," he replied, laughing. "I apologize for disturbing your rest. I thought myself to be the only human for miles." I stood, removed my own cloak, folded it carefully, and placed it in my pack. "A troubadour!" he exclaimed with delight upon seeing my costume. "No, a jester," he decided after glancing at my face, which still bore traces of my makeup.

"Correct. And well met, good sir. May I have the honor of learning your name?"

"I was christened Giovanni de Bernardone, son of Pietro de Bernardone, a cloth merchant of this area. But my father calls me Francesco, for I have a French mother and, he says, a French disposition."

"And a fine French voice, Monsieur Francesco. I have sung that song with entire rooms of troubadours, and you sing it as well as any of them."

"I thank you, Master Fool. And I call you that only because you have yet to return the honor of the knowledge of your identity. What name do you go by?"

"I go by all of them until I stop at one that suits me. Pray, monsieur, what is the nearest town?"

"Assisi."

I thought for a moment. I liked to associate my *nom de bouffon* with the town I was in at any given time. "Then call me Balaam. That is as good a name for a fool as any. Now, tell me, monsieur, why are you singing in the forest at a time when farmers are at field and nuns at prayer?"

He began walking towards the roads, and I fell into step beside him. "Tell me, do you think that every creature and plant now in the world was present in the Garden of Eden?"

Casual answers to even more casual questions have led many a man to a heretic's stake.

"If they were all present, then it must have been a wondrous large garden," I answered. "But His powers are infinite, so it must have been so."

"I sometimes think that Our Lord continues to create them anew," he says. "For I keep finding even in our own forests such creatures that were never mentioned in the telling, creatures that could not have been named by Adam, yet who miraculously appear just the same. So, I often come here at sunrise, to listen to the birds greet the morning and to commune with the works of our Creator, for I believe that He is with us here in everything we see."

A nature mystic, I thought. Unusually young to be one, but a harmless enough vocation. He stopped abruptly, leaned against a beech trunk, and vomited.

"And," he continued, resuming his pace, "it helps clear my head after a night such as last."

"Communing with the grape, were you?" I said sympathetically. "Blessed is the fruit of the vine, as the Jewish prayer goes."

"We blessed it many times, and crossed that blessing with a few more. So, good Balaam, tell me a merry tale."

"Give me some cloth for free," I replied. He looked puzzled. "A fool lives by his wits, young master. Were I to tell my tales freely, they would travel faster than I can, pausing only to be mangled in the retelling. I need to be paid for my art. I will sing for my supper, dance for my dinner, tumble for lunch, and cut a caper for a capon, roasted slowly with herbs over a lemonwood fire. But I will not perform gratis for a hungover youth in the forest."

"Alas, I have no funds after last night." His face brightened. "Barter, perhaps? I will trade you a song for a song."

"I doubt that you know any songs that I do not."

"This one I wrote myself."

"A bad trade. You ask me to take a pig in a poke. Your voice I can vouch for, but your compositional skills are unknown."

He thought for a while as we reached the road. "I will sing you the song, and you tell me what you think. And if you like it, you may sing me one. That will pass the time until we reach the gate, and I'll ask my father if you could entertain us tonight in exchange for food, lodging, and whatever silver he wishes to bless you with."

It was a fair offer, and as I was in no hurry to reach the guildhall, I accepted. He sang an earnest if maudlin paean to Nature and her constituents. He was not without talent, but it needed work. I suggested a few improvements, which he took with grace and good humor, then

I unslung my lute, tuned it, and sang a chanson that lasted until we reached the walls of the town. The guard waved us through, staring curiously at my motley, as people do, and we soon arrived at the villa of the de Bernardones. He brought me to the stables. "You may leave your belongings here, if it suits you. The hayloft is quite comfortable, as many of the local lads will assure you."

After a night in the forest, a hayloft seemed a palace, and I told him so, but he wasn't listening, his eye having chanced upon a feather lying on the floor.

"Look at this!" he exclaimed. "I've never seen anything like it." It was a huge feather, nearly the length of my arm, colored black, gray, and white.

"Not a local bird?" I asked.

He shook his head decisively. "I know every bird that makes its nest in or passes through Umbria. None could produce a feather like that."

I climbed the ladder to the hayloft and paused when I reached the top. "Here's something else unusual, monsieur," I said. Something in the tone of my voice brought him immediately up the ladder, where he looked and then froze in horror.

She was perhaps fifteen, and what was left of her clothing suggested a housemaid. She appeared to have been stabbed several times. The blood had soaked the surrounding hay, and what still clung to her body was thick and pasty to the touch. Her expression was one of unspeakable terror.

"Do you know her?" I asked softly. He gulped and gave a short nod.

"She's a servant in my household," he whispered. I scanned his garments and saw no sign of blood. His shock at seeing her seemed genuine, and he seemed upon short acquaintance too guileless to be dissembling.

"Alert your father and summon the guards," I advised. "And a priest." He nodded and nearly fell back down the ladder. I followed him.

"Aren't you going to stay with her?" he asked.

"Can't help her, and I'd rather not be found with a body and no explanation. You'll vouch for me, I hope."

"Of course. Come with me."

He ran outside and collared a stableboy, ordering him to fetch his master. A gardener was dispatched to the guards. The two between them must have told a dozen others, for a crowd gathered within minutes.

Pietro de Bernardone arrived still tucking his tunic into his breeches. Merchants can afford to sleep late. He entered the stables accompanied by his son and the captain of the guard. I took advantage of the crowd's attention to duck behind a tree and reapply my makeup. They emerged moments later, the elder de Bernardone coughing into a handkerchief. By this time a man I figured by his administrative robe to be the podesta had arrived, trying to look officially concerned rather than rapaciously curious like the rest of the crowd. He, the two de Bernardones, and the captain conferred briefly. The captain looked around, saw me, and beckoned me forward.

"Your name, stranger?"

"I am Balaam the Jester, your worship," I replied, bowing low and jingling the bells on my cap for effect.

"What were you doing in there?"

"Young Master de Bernardone was kind enough to offer shelter in exchange for an evening's entertainment. We came in and found the unfortunate young woman."

The elder de Bernardone scowled at his son. "Another stray, Francesco?"

"Please, Father. He has a ready wit and a deft hand on the lute."

The captain continued to regard me with animosity.

"This was most likely done by a stranger," he said. "And you're the only stranger in town."

"Captain, if I had done this, I would scarcely make my way here. I would make myself scarce, wouldn't I?"

"Well spoken, Fool," applauded the podesta. "But a man of your wit may stay on after the crime just to throw us off the scent."

"Are you armed?" continued the captain.

"Only by my wits," I replied, giving the standard answer. "Oh, and a knife for eating." I pulled it out of my bag and handed it to him. He held it up to the sun and examined it closely.

"No blood," he pronounced finally, and gave it back to me.

"Good, good," said the podesta. "Well, Pietro, you must have us over for the entertainment tonight."

De Bernardone scowled even more, but found himself inviting several no doubt influential locals to dinner.

"And you, Fool, must stay in town until we've gotten to the bottom of this horrible matter," added the podesta. "We would find any sudden departure on your part to be most incriminating." I bowed low. A priest came running up and entered the stable, followed by most of the principal players. Francesco came over to me.

"I'll find you somewhere else to stay," he whispered. "Perhaps in the servants' quarters. Terrible, isn't it?"

"It is. And I thank you for vouching for me. You do well under pressure, young master. I've seen many a battle-hardened Crusader turn ill at a sight so grisly."

"I had the good fortune to throw up earlier," he reminded me. "I suppose I should be thankful." He led me to the servants' quarters where one of the men showed me a bench where I could sleep. I thanked him, and they left me alone to think.

I didn't like the position in which I found myself. A stranger arrives in town to discover a murder, and has only a callow youth who'd been walking off a night of carousing as his vouchsafe—surely I would be the chief suspect, regardless. In any case, an easy scapegoat for the murderer to blame. I usually don't like to meddle in affairs that are neither my nor the Guild's concern, but this one seemed to be pulling me under in spite of myself.

An investigation seemed to be in order, but I faced another problem. I was a stranger, which would not only hamper my ability to nose out any information, but would prevent me from denouncing any local villains with any credibility. I decided to cross that bridge when I came to it, and to burn it quickly behind me.

I was not expected to perform until dinner, which left me several hours to fend for myself. I divested myself of my heavier gear, slung my working bag and lute over my shoulders, and walked to the piazza. I found at that time of my life that juggling was an effective way of concentrating my mind as well as drawing a crowd, so I pulled three clubs out of my bag and kept them aloft as I strolled about. A group of children gathered almost immediately, followed by servants and signóras who were roaming the stalls at the market. I continued walking and juggling as if oblivious, then let one of the clubs fly too far to catch easily. A woman screamed as I snatched it from over her head, but by this time a second was heading the other way. I mimed increasing frenzy as I ran around in a circle, turning near-misses into miraculous recoveries while the children shrieked with laughter. Finally, I allowed one of the clubs to conk me directly in the forehead. I toppled onto the ground, and the other two landed simultaneously in my outstretched hands. The crowd applauded, and I stood and bowed.

"Good day, fair citizens of Assisi," I said. "I am Balaam the Fool."

"If you're Balaam, where's your ass?" shouted a young man who smacked of privilege by his fine clothes and the fact that he had nothing better to do than heckle me. I turned away from him, bent over, and wiggled my bottom in reply. No one ever said we had to be sophisticated all of the time, and you take your straight lines as you find them. The crowd laughed, including the youth.

"Indeed, though I share the name with the Balaam of legend, I am not quite such a fool as he," I continued. "For he would have passed by an angel without noticing, but I see an angel now." The crowd looked about curiously. "You do not see her?" I said with amazement. "Then I shall show you." I walked up to a beautiful little girl who was staring up at me from the front of the group of children, bowed low, and kissed her hand. She giggled with delight, and I had them eating out of my hand for the rest of the performance.

It was a mildly profitable morning, and I gathered enough coin to buy a decent lunch. I did not want to delve into my Apulian treasure. A jester is expected to earn his way as he goes, so I lived up to that.

I entered a tavern off the piazza, procured a dish of stewed chicken, some bread that wasn't too stale, and some cheese that was, and sat among a group of men who were taking a break from repairing the cathedral. Needless to say, I was an object of curiosity to them, but it wasn't for the usual reason.

"They say you found the body of that poor Sofia," one of them said.

"Yes," I answered shortly, and gave them enough gory details to satisfy their curiosity. "A terrible sight. Did you know her?"

"She came here a few years ago with her father," said another. "Just a little girl at the time. He died, and Bernardone took her into service. He was very fond of her."

"Too fond," muttered a third, but the others shushed him.

"A good girl," continued the second man. "We would see her helping the cook do her shopping most days."

"And she went to church on Sundays," added the first. "Never missed it. She was a good girl, Sofia was."

"Then she's in heaven, gentlemen," I said, and we all crossed ourselves piously. "God grant that her murderer be as quickly dispatched."

"Not likely," said one of them bitterly. "She's not the first to die like that. Three girls in the past year. And no one's been caught for it. The captain's been doubling the guard at night, searching all the town, but nothing's turned up."

"Are there no suspicions as to who it is?" I asked.

They all looked around fearfully. "When the Devil walks, he leaves no footprints, or so they say," said one, and they all crossed themselves again. We finished our meal and went our various ways. The man who had been silenced by the others lagged behind and beckoned to me.

"Many think that a man of wealth and power committed these horrors," he whispered. "That the captain is afraid to catch him."

"The podesta? De Bernardone?" I asked.

"Them, maybe one of the landholders outside the town. The podesta has the captain in his back pocket; he could stall the investigation if it was leading to him or one of his allies." He seemed willing to say more, but we came in sight of a guard. He put his finger to his lips briefly and walked away.

As I passed by the cathedral, a man called, "You, jester." I turned to see the priest who was at the stables earlier striding angrily towards me. I bowed low, and he caught me off guard with a backhanded blow that sent me tumbling in ways I do not normally tumble.

"I can tell you're a man of Christ," I said as I wiped the blood from my lip.

"How dare you!" he thundered. "A girl is murdered, and not an hour later you tell jokes in the piazza. Impious ruffian!"

"Yes, good Father, a girl lies dead, and the farmers keep on plowing. A girl lies dead, and the weavers keep weaving. The apothecary grinds his drugs, the baker bakes, the ropemaker braids his hemp, and the cooper rolls out another barrel to sell, all while a girl lies dead. Why should a jester be the only one not to practice his profession when there's a murder?"

He was livid. "Sacrilege! That you should care so little for one of God's perfect creatures. I am here to tell you, Fool, that the man who killed her is damned, and if my prayers have any power, he shall burn while he's still alive."

He looked straight at me when he said this. I knew better than to bait him, but I did it anyway.

"Such passion for a man of the cloth," I said idly. "What did she confess to you that has so stirred your blood?" I was reintroduced to the paving stones, though I was ready for it this time and broke the fall without much damage. I got up to see him running away, sobbing. His name was Father Arnolfo, I learned from an old woman selling beads from a stall, and he had been known to yearn for Sofia before his family forced him, as the youngest son, into the priesthood. To have so much passion bound up in cloth was a terrible thing, she said. I bought some beads and moved on.

Very possible, I thought. Celibacy does strange things to passionate men, and there were many accounts in Guild records of priests gone mad. All hushed up, of course. And black cowls make effective cover at night.

The market provided me with gossip but no useful information. Sofia was suspected of having lovers; she was a virgin who would become a nun soon; she was an orphan with no family; she was the secret daughter of the elder de Bernardone.

I gave up and went back to the villa. I came upon a manservant who was changing into fresh clothes for the evening's festivities and waylaid him.

"Tell me, friend, what manner of people will be here tonight? I need to know what kind of performance they will demand."

"There's the master," he said. "And the young master. The podesta, Signórs di Cambio and Grande, they've both got estates outside of town. And their wives, of course. And the captain's coming. And the bishop, maybe one or two of his people. That's it."

"And are they a sophisticated group? Have they traveled, and would they appreciate some big-city humor?"

"Ah, now that's a hard one. The master goes back and forth to Provence, of course, and the young master sometimes goes with him, learning the trade and all. The bishop goes down to Rome every now and then. The podesta's traveled. He went on the last Crusade, fought Saladin himself to hear him tell it, which he does over and over. The captain was in on that one, too."

"He fought with the podesta?"

"No, he wasn't here then. The captain's from Venice. He was a mercenary, before that a merchant, used to trade all over the Mediterranean. Went broke, became a mercenary, went on a ship with Philip Augustus's lot, met the podesta. Saved his life, they say, so the podesta brought him back here and made him captain. And that's all I know about that."

"It is a considerable amount, good friend, and I am grateful. I shall

be sophisticated enough to flatter the ladies into thinking they're sophisticated, and simple enough for everyone to understand me. And
then I'll come back here and tell you fine fellows all the dirty stories."

He brightened. "As to that, sir, we know a few ourselves. I'm fancied quite a jokester myself back here."

"Then we shall have a duel of wits, my friend, and he who is still
standing at the end of it didn't drink enough."

He guffawed, clapped me on the back, and went about his chores.

I was settling down for a short nap when Francesco poked his head
into the room. "May we speak?" he whispered. I beckoned him in. He
sat on the end of my cot. "I can't stop thinking of her," he said, looking down. "She was such a pretty, lively maid. She used to tease me
endlessly when we were younger. I can't believe that anyone would
want to kill her."

"What about the other girls who were killed?" I asked. "Why would
anyone want to kill them?"

"No one knows," he said. "One was a farmer's daughter, one was
traveling with a merchant from Pisa. I cannot believe that such sinful-
ness exists in the world."

"It does, unfortunately."

"I suppose she presented too great a temptation for the man."

"Nonsense," I said sharply. "Whoever it was, he's a monster with no
need for inspiration. He carries his evil with him."

"I stand rebuked," he said. "You're right, of course. It's just that I have
never encountered anything like this. Sometimes I think I'm better off
with animals than with people. They only kill for food."

"Maybe, young master. Anyway, there's the dinner bell. Go join
your guests. I'll be along shortly."

I had half a notion to recruit him for the Guild, but thought him still
a bit young. A decision I have regretted since, but not chief among my
regrets. That was still to come.

It's one thing to perform before anonymous crowds when a girl's
been murdered, but quite another to perform before the master of the
household where she had lived. A jester depends on his timing and
knowing his audience. I chose to become a troubadour for the evening,
singing heroic and mournful ballads, none too close to the unspoken
theme of the day, none in opposition to it. I threw in a few songs of
courtly love for the ladies, and retired to genuine applause. I learned
nothing at the dinner to help me.

But I had a theory now, one that needed evidence. So, after I bested the braggart manservant in ribald rivalry, I waited for them to fall asleep and pulled out my traveling bag. How does a jester disguise himself, fellow fools? By taking off his makeup and motley, of course. Without them, I am a nondescript fellow. On with some dark clothing, and I was ready to lurk among the shadows of the town.

And shadows there were. The captain had doubled the guards on the walls and gates, which meant that patrols in the town itself were sparse. That suited my purpose neatly. I passed through a series of alleyways until I located the house of my quarry, listened at a window, and confirmed that no one was there. I slipped inside, searched it thoroughly, and found what I was looking for. I rearranged things as they had been, slipped back out, and made my way back to the servants' quarters.

Well, a problem solved, and another awaiting. I had verified to my own satisfaction the identity of the murderer, but as a transient alien was in no position to convince the town. I was up all night thinking about it.

And then, in the morning, a miracle occurred.

I was sitting on a low wall in front of the villa when Francesco came by, stumbling as if in a trance.

"Young master?" I called to him. He started and stared at me, momentarily unable to remember who I was.

"Oh, Fool," he whispered. "It's unbelievable."

"What is?"

He shook his head suddenly and started running towards the center of the town. "I must tell them!" he shouted.

I followed him, concerned for his safety. He staggered through the streets to the piazza, then dashed across it, scattering children and pigeons in his wake, seized a rope that dangled in front of the cathedral, and started ringing a bell suspended above the entrance. "People of Assisi, hear me!" he shouted over and over. Not surprisingly, people did, leaving the market, the taverns, the cathedral itself, laughing and pointing at the noble youth apparently gone mad. He stopped his bell ringing and addressed them in awed tones.

"A vision . . . No!" he corrected himself. "A miracle! It was . . ." He stopped, seemingly unable to find the words. Come on, boy, I urged him silently. Get it out.

"I was in the woods south of the town," it started pouring out of him.

"I went to listen to the birds, to pray and think about the evil that dwells within us." You'll lose your crowd with that patter, I thought, but they hung in there and listened to him. "And then . . . it was a miracle! A robin spoke to me! Not like a bird, but in the voice of a man. No, not a man, an angel. A saint!"

Cries of wonder from the crowd. The hook was set. "He said, 'In the name of Saint John the Evangelist I am come to warn you. Listen to the birds, they shall lead you. One who has slaughtered such birds for their plumage wears it now to slaughter your maids. Seek the owner of the feather.' " The crowd looked puzzled. He reached into his doublet and produced the long feather he had found in the stable. "This was worn by Sofia's murderer," he explained. "I found it near where we found her body. Whosoever has feathers to match this killed her."

"The captain!" someone shouted.

"Where?" asked Francesco.

"No, no, he's the one." A burly man strode to the front. "When he came here, I helped carry his trunks to his quarters. I saw him remove a tunic covered with these feathers. I'd never seen their like, but he quickly hid it in his closet, and I never thought about it until now. It's the captain."

"The captain!" screamed others, and several ran in the direction of his quarters, returning with the garish garment with feathers clearly the match of the one in Francesco's hand. Dried blood splattered some of them.

The rest was simple and brutal. He was taken, tortured, and forced to confess. The details of his perversions and his frenzies I leave to your imaginations. Suffice it to say, he was sentenced quickly to depart this earth, and splattered it with blood one last time.

I did not stay for that. My job was done, and I preferred not to arouse anyone's curiosity. Francesco walked me to the north gate.

"I confess, good Fool, that I heard of such wonders, but never thought to see them for myself," he commented.

"The Lord works in mysterious ways, young master. Perhaps He will speak to you again. Perhaps not. You were His chosen vessel for ending a great evil, and maybe now that it's over, you will not be called upon again."

He looked disappointed, and I clapped him on the back. "Cheer up, monsieur. You have much in life to look forward to. The world awaits you. And I hope to meet you again someday."

He brightened. "I would like that. I would like to learn more of what it is to be a fool."

"Maybe we'll teach you. Until then, be merry, Francesco. Despite recent events, I truly believe the world is deserving of laughter and song. Your voice is a gift to be shared. Be generous with it."

We shook hands, and I left Assisi. We did cross paths a few times thereafter, but you know the way he took. Taken ill during the Papal Wars, a fever induced a revelation, or so the stories go. His first vision, they say. Perhaps. I've spent many a fevered night hearing all manner of angels and demons, but in the morning I was sober again. I say his first miracle was when a robin in the forest spoke with a saint's voice, and thanks to that we now have legions of fat gray friars arguing over who has betrayed his principles more. Oh, there's some that do some good, and God knows they're not as bad as the Dominicans (and the stories I can tell you about them, fellow fools!), but they've become just another branch of Rome now.

And it's all my fault. For I recognized the feather. It belonged to the ostrich, a fantastical creature that gallops across the African plains. And the only person in town who could possibly have traveled there was the captain, the one-time Venetian merchant. He also would have the greatest ease in avoiding the guards, for it was he who determined their patrols. It was his quarters that I targeted that night.

And then it was a simple thing to follow a simple boy into the woods. The bird spoke with my tongue, of course, for any fool who can't throw his voice was never meant for motley in the first place. And so, with the best intentions in the world, I created a saint.

The memory haunts me. I hear him singing in that boyish voice that song which would be transformed into the "Hymn of the Sun." I was secretly pleased when I heard it in its final form that he adopted some of my suggestions, but that doesn't compensate for all the efforts the Guild has been forced to make to counter these holy simpletons. I wish we had recruited him first, but who knew?

Brothers and sisters, I salute you across the years and pages, and bid that you remember a jester with no particular name, and pray for him. And if we meet in the hereafter, greet me with our ancient password and motto: Stultorum numerus infinitus est—the number of fools is infinite!

GALILEO, DETECTIVE

Theodore Mathieson

Only rarely does an anthologist include more than one story by a single author. We make this departure from convention in Once Upon A Crime II *in order to make more complete our pantheon of historical persons. And who could be more representative of the age of intellectual achievement and enthusiasm than the philosopher, mathematician, astronomer, and physicist Galileo? In his fictive re-creation of events in sixteenth-century Pisa, Theodore Mathieson has given Galileo Galilei one of the few roles history does not attribute to him in life, the part of the great sleuth. As always, the author bases his mystery on a real concern of his protagonist, Galileo's desire to contradict Aristotle on the laws of falling bodies.*

O n an evening in the spring of 1590, the young professor Galileo Galilei hurried along the Via S. Maria towards the river Arno, now and then glancing back at the empty moonlit streets. He paused for breath in the center of the Ponte di Mezzo and listened to the water swirling in full flood beneath the bridge.

The city of Pisa lay peacefully quiet around him, her skyline of belfries, cupolas, and thrust-up loggias black against the luminous night sky. Now the bells of the Duomo began to ring with reassuring sweetness through the still, warm air.

When he had rested a few minutes, Galileo continued across the bridge and into the southern section of the town, turning presently into a side street, where the way, although narrow, was lined with substantial homes. He stopped before a square, brown house, faced with white stone—the home of Jofre Tarrega, professor of philosophy at the university.

Galileo's knock brought to the door a buxom housekeeper who greeted him pleasantly in a broad Calabrian accent, and then showed him into the living room.

"The signorina is not at home, maestro," she said smiling. "She is visiting her aunt in Lucca, but we expect her to return tomorrow."

"I know, Guilia," Galileo said. "I came to see Signor Tarrega this time."

"I will tell him."

Jofre Tarrega appeared almost at once, clad in his riding clothes. He took off his leather gloves and threw them upon a table.

"Ah, Leo," he said opening his arms in greeting to the stocky red-haired young man. "I've just had a fine moonlight ride on the Cascina road. Guilia sounded concerned about you, and indeed, you do not look happy. Is there something I can do for you?"

Galileo looked soberly at the proud, thin-lipped man, who had the lean but powerful body of an expert swordsman.

"I need your counsel, Signor Tarrega," Galileo said. "As my colleague at the university, and the only one who has opened his home to me, perhaps you could tell me what I should do about this."

From his pocket Galileo drew a folded note and handed it to Tarrega. The latter stooped before a lamp and read the message slowly aloud.

" 'Your denunciation of the truths established by Aristotle is prompted by the Devil. Beware! He soon will come to claim his own.' Well, now, Leo, where did you get this?"

"I found it upon the lectern after my class left the hall this afternoon."

"And upon what have you lectured of late?"

"I have been investigating Aristotle's statement that bodies of different weights move in one and the same medium with different speeds. Today, for example, I demonstrated how wooden balls of unequal weight, when rolled down an incline, reach the bottom at the same time."

"Then you have successfully refuted Aristotle!" Tarrega exclaimed.

"Of course. I can prove it to anyone who will take the trouble to look."

Tarrega clicked his tongue. "You know, of course, that the faculty stands united against these demonstrations of yours. Isn't it likely this was written by one of them?"

"Yes. I am the youngest professor, and they resent my questioning their sacred Aristotle. But I suspect an outsider."

"Who, then?"

"Giovanni de Medici."

"Giovanni, the grand duke's brother?"

Tarrega appeared startled. A widower of Spanish origin from Catalonia, the professor was distantly related, through marriage, to the Medici family, and although Tarrega's fortunes had not waxed greatly through that connection, he was nonetheless passionately proud of the distinction.

"You see," Galileo continued, "shortly after I came to Pisa, Giovanni de Medici asked me if I would examine a model of a dredging machine which he had designed. I did, and told him it would never work."

"Tact is a quality you should cultivate, Leo."

"Perhaps. But it was the truth. Anyway, Giovanni was so stubborn he had a big dredger built and tried to dig out the harbor at Leghorn. All the machine did was sink so far into the mud that they couldn't get it out. Since then, when Giovanni passes me by, he makes a sign against the Devil."

"You apparently have a way of making dangerous enemies, Leo," Tarrega said. "And I cannot see how I can advise you."

"But what would you do? Confront Giovanni with the note and demand an explanation?"

"Look here, Leo, you must learn to control your impulse to fling down challenges—that is the reason you have more than one enemy on the faculty. My advice to you is to restrain yourself. Especially do not challenge Giovanni de Medici, or you will find yourself in serious trouble with the rector of the university."

Galileo shrugged uneasily. "I know, Signor Tarrega. You're right. I have a hot temper. I only hope that you are not now so angry with me that I cannot come to visit your daughter."

Jofre Tarrega smiled unexpectedly, and then placed his hands gently on Galileo's shoulders.

"You are always welcome in my house, Leo."

Soon after, as Galileo took his leave from Tarrega's house, he became aware that he was being followed. Twice he heard footsteps on the paving stones behind him—footsteps which stopped whenever he did. He quickened his steps, determined that he would lead his follower an exhausting chase. He kept to the broad avenues in a northeasterly direction, and passing the university came at last to a broad piazza where three lofty buildings, built of fair marble, rose like giant ghosts in the moonlight—the Duomo, the Baptistry, and the Leaning Tower.

Galileo, satisfied that his follower was still behind him, crossed a grassy corner of the piazza, passed the Leaning Tower, and entered the Campo Santo, the cemetery adjacent. Once in the concealing darkness he pressed himself against a wall and waited. Footsteps sounded, and as a man passed by him, Galileo spoke up sharply.

"Why are you following me?"

The man spun around, whipped out a dagger from his belt, and pressed the point against the young professor's chest.

"Diavolo!" the man whispered. "I should kill you now, Galileo Galilei. But take heed of my words, or I shall do it later, I swear!"

"What have I done?" Galileo demanded. "Why do you threaten me?"

He could see now in the moonlight that the man was young, tall, and strong, and that he wore a mask over the upper part of a gaunt face. Then, when his attacker whispered again, Galileo thought the voice sounded familiar.

"You will not visit the house of Livia Tarrega again!" the masked man cried.

"Why not? I respect and admire the signorina."

"Do you? That is why, I suppose, you visit her secretly at night, creeping along the back street, and atop the wall to her window."

"But I have not—ever!" Galileo protested. "I visit the signorina with her father's full permission, and always in the presence of her duenna."

"You lie! My friend has seen you at her window."

"Then your friend it is who lies. He wishes you to make a scandal, perhaps kill me—for something I have not done, nor, I vow, has anyone. The signorina would not permit anyone to visit her thus. Surely you could not love her and think that she would do such a thing!"

The sincerity of Galileo's speech had an effect upon the young man. The pressure of his dagger point upon Galileo's breast lightened, and he spoke only once more.

"Perhaps you are telling the truth. I hope so. *But keep away from Livia Tarrega!*"

And he was gone.

Quite unexpectedly, Galileo recognized his attacker the following day as he stood upon the banks of the Arno amid cheering crowds, watching the Giuoco del Ponte, or the Fight for the Bridge.

Once each year Mezzogiorno (that is, Pisa south of the Arno) challenged Tramontana (Pisa to the north) to fight upon the Ponte di Mezzo, the object being for the "fighters" of each side to penetrate to the opposition's half of the bridge.

Now as Galileo watched, each of the battalions assembled on its side of the river, and at the sound of a horn from the marshal, they rushed forward to meet in combat upon the bridge, armed, and in helmet and breastplate. One young fighter on the Tramontana side caught Galileo's eye at once. In his helmet, which descended low like a mask, he was instantly recognizable as Galileo's pursuer of the night before.

Galileo kept his eye upon him all through the fight, and when the marshal blew the horn which terminated the struggle, he saw him break away from the cheering crowds and set off by himself down the narrow lane of La Cervia. Galileo followed at once, and catching up with him, tapped him upon the shoulder.

"Oh, it is you," the young man said, removing his helmet and turning a sullen face towards the professor.

Galileo blinked with surprise. It was Paolo Salviati, who attended Galileo's course in mathematics—an outstanding student of law who was in his final year at the university.

"I never met you visiting at Signorina Tarrega's," Galileo said at last.

The other shrugged, as if scorning a denial.

"And now that you know who I am," he said, "what will you do?"

Galileo sat down upon the edge of a small marble fountain and folded his arms.

"I shall say nothing to anyone about the incident—provided you tell me who it was that told you the lie about me, that I visited the signorina secretly."

"I cannot do that."

"Then I shall report the matter to the rector."

"No, no! If it is known I assaulted a professor of the university, I shall be turned out, and all my work shall be for nothing!"

"Then tell me."

The young man clenched his fists and looked for a moment as if he might attack Galileo again. But finally he said, "It was one of the other professors. But do not ask me his name—"

"A colleague! Will one descend that low to stem the flow of truth from my rostrum? You must tell me his name, Salviati!"

But shaking his head, the law student hurried off down the lane.

Two nights later, as Galileo lay sleeping in his small house close by the university, he was awakened by a thump on the wall. He lay listening, but all the sounds he could hear were the distant clop-clop of a mule's hooves on the paving stones and, from the inn next door, the Padrona talking out loud in her sleep again. But the memory of the thump disturbed him, so presently he rose, lit a candle, and opened the street door.

He saw at once it was empty, and smelled the odor of fresh fish that always blew from the river at this hour. Then, as he turned to close his door, he espied the note upon the sill.

You are warned again—do not break idols in the marketplace!

Galileo crumpled the note in his hand. He looked again up the street as he heard the sound of singing which grew louder and louder until he recognized the voices.

"Vincenzio—Pettirosso," Galileo cried. "What are you doing here so late?"

Two of his most trusted and promising students appeared out of the shadows and smiled affectionately at him. One of them carried a jug of wine.

"You look troubled today, maestro, and we thought you might need cheering up," said the smaller student, who was called Pettirosso because he was preternaturally fragile-boned and light, like a bird.

"Well, perhaps you are right," Galileo said. "Come in."

And while his visitors sat down at the table, the young professor fetched three pottery cups and poured wine freely all around.

"This was just left at my door," Galileo said at last, throwing the note upon the table. "Did you see anyone upon the street?"

"Not a soul, maestro," Pettirosso said, reading the note and passing it to Vincenzio. "Who do you think wrote it?"

"At first I thought it was an outsider, but now I think it was a member of the faculty."

"And why should anyone write thus?"

"The faculty resents the fact that my statements do not accord with their venerable Aristotle's." Galileo smiled suddenly. "Tell me, Vincenzio, what do you think I should do? You're the bold one!"

Vincenzio Barbierini rubbed his hands and scowled. He was a broad fellow, handsome, with long blond hair that curled over his collar. Although he was often vain and given to preening himself over his accomplishments with the *meretrices,* or loose women of the city, to Galileo he showed only respect and devotion. Indeed, Vincenzio so admired his master that he set himself to copy not only Galileo's forward-thrusting, inquiring air, but his blunt, uncompromising speech as well.

"You should punish this professor," he said at length. "I tell you what, maestro, my good companion Pettirosso, who is like my own brother, and I—we will watch first this professor and then that one, and when we find the guilty one, we will tell you."

"No, no," Galileo said quickly. "It is better the writer remains anonymous, for if I knew his identity I might be rash enough to attack him."

"Then what will you do?" Pettirosso asked.

Galileo drained his wine cup before he answered.

"I think," he said, "I will make a public demonstration. That will teach them they cannot intimidate me with warning notes. Heretofore I have discreetly kept my proofs within the classroom—but now all Pisa shall see the great Aristotle proved wrong in broad daylight!"

"The experiment of the wooden balls!" Vincenzio exclaimed.

"*Esattamente!* But we shall use iron shot this time—a one-pound shot and a ten-pound shot, and we shall drop them from somewhere high— at least two hundred cubits."

"From the Baptistry?"

"No. From the Leaning Tower."

The word of the projected experiment travelled fast. The very next day the rector of the university called Galileo to his chambers, and fingering his white beard he spoke reprovingly.

"Galileo Galilei, I have heard of the public demonstration you plan for next week. Is this wise?"

"Why, sir, when I came here, did you not encourage me to disperse ignorance with the light of truth?"

"True, my boy. But have you never heard that it is dangerous to break idols in the marketplace?"

Galileo stared at the rector, scarcely believing his ears. Then he pulled the latest note from his pocket and laid it before his superior.

"Did you write this, sir?"

The rector read it with raised eyebrows, and then murmured, "My words were almost the same, weren't they? But I must have heard someone say them. No, I did not write it, but I would say it is a just warning, against which it would be foolhardy for you to proceed."

"And do you only warn me, too, sir?" Galileo asked. "Or do you forbid me the right to demonstrate my own discoveries?"

The rector sighed. "No, Galileo Galilei, I cannot do that. You may go ahead with your demonstration if you like, but take care you do not see your hopes buried in the holy ground of the cemetery of Campo Santo!"

The rector's words echoed in Galileo's ears on the day of the demonstration, as he stood upon the piazza adjacent to the Campo Santo, waiting for the bells of the Leaning Tower to strike the hour of noon. But he tried to be confident. Hadn't he and his assistants—just before dawn, while all Pisa was sleeping—conducted the experiment from the tower exactly as he planned to do it today? It was true that someone had probably watched them, since Vincenzio claimed he heard footsteps from the cloister of the Duomo, but nothing had come of it.

Now, with the sun almost at its zenith, professors stood lounging about the square talking and laughing, many of them casting derisive or hostile looks in Galileo's direction.

Townspeople who doubtless expected some kind of *spettacolo* were also present—mothers and their small children, idlers, and keen-faced priests whom Galileo hoped were Jesuits, since there were fine scientists among them. In the crowd he espied the gentle old rector and, sitting upon a stone bench close by, in the shade of the Duomo, Giovanni de Medici, his arrogant lips curved in a sneer.

The bells in the tower began to ring twelve o'clock, the laughter and stirring ceased, and all eyes were turned upon Galileo. He waited, however, until the last whisper of the bell tones had faded, and the bellringer himself had stepped out through the single, high door at the base of the tower and joined a young man whom Galileo recognized as Paolo Salviati. Then Galileo raised his hands and spoke in a loud clear voice.

"See here, each of my assistants holds an iron ball." He pointed to Vincenzio and Pettirosso behind him. "One iron ball weighs one pound, the other ten pounds. We shall carry them to the top of the tower and drop them down upon the area below the leaning side, which we have roped off. You who are disciples of Aristotle believe that falling bodies of unequal weight, if dropped from the same height at the same moment, will reach the ground at different times—"

"That's right," de Medici called from the crowd, "and the heavier body travels in proportion to its weight."

"I deny this is true," Galileo said, "and shall demonstrate the fallacy of Aristotle's reasoning. Watch!"

Amid a sullen murmur, Galileo strode into the tower, followed by Vincenzio and Pettirosso, and the trio climbed the six successive circular staircases which coiled dizzily around a core of empty space and ropes from the belfry.

Reaching the topmost gallery, above which loomed the bell tower itself, Galileo paused to catch his breath and noticed that Pettirosso alone had followed him.

"Where is Vincenzio?" he demanded.

"He'll be right along, maestro," Pettirosso assured him. "He stopped to look out the lower gallery door. Woman trouble! He thinks she did not come to see him perform today!"

"Vincenzio!" Galileo called. "We have no time to waste!"

The next moment his heavyset assistant panted up the steps, and indeed he did not look well. There were dark rings under his eyes and his handsome face looked pale.

"I told you, Vincenzio, you should not have exerted yourself last night," Pettirosso said with a laugh.

"Silence!" Vincenzio roared, then bowed subserviently to Galileo. "I'm very sorry, maestro. I am ready."

Galileo took from the pocket of his gown two square silk nets, and laying them flat upon the gallery floor, he carefully placed an iron ball in the center of each. Then grasping the corners of the nets, he suspended a ball from each hand, and stepped forward to the marble parapet. Vincenzio seized him firmly by the ankles, and Galileo leaned forward until he could see the crowd far below.

"Now watch!" he called down in the still noon air.

He held out the balls, and when his hands were on an even plane he released them at the same instant. Down they plummeted, the silk nets floating off almost invisibly while the balls grew smaller as Galileo watched them; then for an instant they too seemed to disappear, and he saw two simultaneous puffs of dust as the balls struck the earth.

"We have done it!" he said, smiling to his assistants, and pointed to another pair of one-pound and ten-pound balls upon the floor of the gallery. "Be ready with them."

Galileo hastened down the steps of the tower, half expecting that some of the spectators would come up to congratulate him; but he met not a soul, and when at last he came out through the tower door the old round-shouldered bell-ringer, who sat upon a bench a little distance away, looked at Galileo incuriously.

"It's impossible!" Galileo murmured. "Don't they understand?"

But already the greater part of the crowd had wandered away from the piazza, clearly disappointed by the exhibition, and as Galileo rounded the tower to the roped-off area, he saw that only a few of the professors and students remained. He looked up and saw Pettirosso and Vincenzio leaning over the balcony—doubtless they, too, were disappointed in the lack of reaction.

"Look, then," he cried to the little group, "did not the bodies strike the ground at the same moment?"

Two of the professors came over and shook Galileo's hand.

"Indeed, my boy," said one, "you have proven your point. You have won our admiration."

Galileo turned to the others.

"Are there any of you who have questions? My assistants are ready to repeat the experiment at once."

Nobody seemed to have any questions. Disappointed, Galileo looked up at his assistants on the tower and started to give the pre-arranged signal for quitting. Instead he uttered a startled shout.

For at that moment both students seemed to lose their balance—they slipped over the parapet and came diving down headfirst. There was plenty of time to observe the difference in their sizes—Vincenzio, full-fleshed and heavy, Pettirosso, small and birdlike.

And once again two bodies struck the earth at the same instant.

Galileo was sitting at his supper table that evening, unable to eat a morsel, when a messenger from the university brought word that the rector wished to see him.

The young professor found the rector behind his desk, looking grave in the dark robes and fur-trimmed hood of his office. Through the windows opening on the courtyard sounded a chorus of students' voices chanting:

"Grillo, mio Grillo,

Se tu vo' moglie dillo . . ."

"Many in the town believe the Devil hurled your assistants over the parapet," the old man said. "You yourself ran up to the tower directly after their fall, after stationing students at the tower door to see that no one escaped. Your inquiry was most thorough, I recall. The bell-ringer Aproino says that no one passed him all the time he was watching."

"He must have left his post when the accident happened," Galileo said, a desperate note in his voice.

"It could only have been for a moment or two—not long enough for anyone to descend the six flights from the top and escape. To make it worse, Aproino claims he heard the Devil stamp his foot."

"You don't believe that!"

"I am merely reminding you of the forces arrayed against you. There is bound to be an official investigation, and I fear you had better be able to explain what happened on that tower."

"I told you, my dear rector. They merely leaned too far forward and fell. When I was up there, I had Vincenzio hold my ankles because I, too, felt the downward pull."

"*Both* of them fell together—*accidentally?*"

"Why not? One could have tried to reach out to save the other—"

"Did you see one of them reach out? I stood by your side, and I failed to. The other witnesses say they did not merely fall over the parapet—they were *thrown!*"

"They imagine it—there was no one in the tower except my two assistants!"

"Do you really believe that, Galileo Galilei? *Then what became of the second set of iron shots?*"

Galileo gasped. "How did you know?"

"Do you forget that I followed you up to the gallery? I looked for the second set, because only a few moments before you said your assistants were ready to *repeat* the experiment. That meant they must have had duplicate shots in the tower. Is that not true?"

"It is true," Galileo admitted.

"Then you will have to explain to the authorities what happened to them. Many will say the Devil took them. You will have to prove he did not, and you know that I cannot lie in this matter."

Galileo passed his hand nervously through his red hair. "Perhaps if I knew where the sand came from . . ."

"Sand?"

"Scattered on the floor of the gallery. It wasn't there the first time I went up—I can swear to that!"

"You have only a day or two to think about it—the time it will take authorities to travel from Florence. I warned you that flaunting your discoveries in the faces of your colleagues might end disastrously. Now you must pay for that flagrancy."

"I will find the one who did it," Galileo said, his voice shaking.

"For your own sake, my boy, I hope you do."

Leaving the rector's chambers, Galileo walked the streets for a long time with despair in his heart, coming at last in front of the Duomo. There he watched an old woman come out of the church, stop, then go back and rub the dark-green bronze doors where a little lizard in bas relief shone like gold. Hundreds rubbed the spot every day, considering it lucky, and Galileo sighed, wishing that he were credulous enough to comfort himself so easily. But talk might help him to see a light. He turned his steps in the direction of Jofre Tarrega's.

A knock on the door brought Guilia, but this time the woman did not welcome him.

"Signor Tarrega has been ill all day," she said sternly, "but he said he would speak to you himself. Wait here."

His heart numb, scarcely believing his ears, Galileo stared at the closed door, until it opened again. Jofre Tarrega stood before him.

"I've been expecting you," Tarrega said, coldly ironical. "The rector has told me the news. What proud triumph you must have felt when you let go those nets and saw the two iron balls hit the ground at the same instant! But such *hubris* calls down its own destruction, and you have brought ruin upon yourself. I wash my hands of you, and so does Livia, who returned from Lucca in time to hear of this fiasco. You are no longer welcome in this house."

Galileo departed without a word and walked back the way he came. As he crossed the market place he came face to face with Giovanni de Medici. The young prince looked at him haughtily and laid his hand negligently upon his sword.

"Look at you now, Galileo Galilei—you are as mired as my machine at Leghorn! How much longer will you strut to your classes, *amico?*"

The prince's malice was like a dash of cold water. Galileo took a deep breath, and his mind took firm rein over his emotions.

He tried to pass on, but de Medici caught hold of his arm.

"Listen," he whispered, "I want you to know this, and it shall remain just between us. You can thank me for your predicament. *I wrote those notes!"*

"In Heaven's name, why?"

"I trusted to your hotheadedness. I knew that if you thought someone of the faculty wrote them, you would be sure to make yourself even more unpopular with some ill-considered defiance."

Instead of anger, Galileo felt only a curious relief. For now his course lay clearly ahead of him. He pulled himself away from de Medici's grasp.

"Then I have much work to do to mend the results of my own folly," he said softly.

Galileo went at once to the bell-ringer's small stone house, just outside the walls of the Campo Santo, and was admitted by the little man. Inside, at the fireplace, stood the law student, Paolo Salviati.

"Don't look surprised, signore," he said. "Guiseppe Aproino, the bell-ringer, is my uncle."

"I'm in great trouble, Salviati," Galileo said. "I wish to ask your uncle some questions, but I'm afraid he resents my presence."

"Uncle!" the young man said sharply. "You help the maestro, understand?"

The bell-ringer turned the palms of his hands upwards, and shrugged.

"Si, maestro?"

"I came to you before dawn this morning to ask for the keys to the tower, and returned them to you after the rehearsal. Has anyone else borrowed them since?"

"No, maestro."

"But the door of the tower is left open during the day?"

"Si. I open it at sunrise, when I ring the first bells, and close it at sunset when I ring the last."

"And are you there all the time?"

"No, no. Between sunrise and noon I work in the gardens."

Galileo nodded with satisfaction. "The rector says you heard the Devil stomp his foot."

"Si—twice I heard him."

"Twice?" Galileo paused, frowning. "Did you see me throw the balls from the tower, Signor Aproino?"

"No. A little girl ran into the tower and I went after her. I was inside when the Devil stomped."

"Now think carefully," Galileo said. "When did you hear the Devil stomp the *second* time?"

The bell-ringer scratched his chest thoughtfully. "Not much later."

"Before I came down from the tower?"

"No, just afterwards. I remember I was sitting on the bench outside."

"Before the students fell from the tower?"

"Si, before that."

"One more thing. The rector said that when the students fell from the tower you did not leave the door untended. But did you not run to see them?"

"The poor *ragazzos?* Si! But always I am in sight of the door. Nobody comes out, I swear! It was the Devil who pushed them—the Devil!"

Galileo bowed formally. "Thank you, Signor Aproino. I would like now to examine the tower again—with your permission."

The bell-keeper frowned.

"I will take him, Uncle," Salviati said.

The old man grumbled and produced a large key, and the student, after lighting a lanthorn, led Galileo out of the house.

Inside the tower, which was far more draughty and dank in the night than in the day, they paused and looked at the maze of ropes that led upwards through the dark floor, but two of them were tied to cleats upon a heavy, solid oaken frame.

"Why are those ropes cleated?" Galileo asked.

"To distinguish them. This one leads to a bell that is rung only on feast days, the other to a cracked bell my uncle does not ring at all."

Galileo seized the latter rope and gave it a tug. Nothing happened.

"It seems to be fastened," Galileo said.

"To a bar in the belfry—so that my uncle does not ring it by accident."

Galileo took the lanthorn from Salviati and led the way to the top of the tower where, his feet gritting on sand, he started a slow circuit of the gallery.

"May I ask, maestro, if you think Vincenzio and Pettirosso were murdered?"

"I know it."

The law student was silent a moment, then he said, "Two others came tonight to ask for admittance to the tower."

"Who?"

"The rector, and Giovanni de Medici. Uncle had to oblige them, and he climbed the tower with them. All they did was to walk round and round the balcony. De Medici seemed certain the Devil had been here."

"Ah," Galileo exclaimed suddenly, and holding his lanthorn close to a narrow gutter that drained the gallery, he plucked from the channel a small piece of thin leather.

"That tells you something, maestro?"

Galileo nodded, then rose quickly and ascended the iron ladder that led up into the belfry, where his lanthorn winked fitfully as he stepped among the dark shapes of the bells. A little later he descended.

"I'm ready to go now," he said.

The professor and the student walked back to the bell-ringer's house in silence, and as they were about to part, Galileo held up the lanthorn.

"I'd like to borrow this, Salviati. I have much yet to look for tonight."

"Of course. But where do you go?"

"To the Campo Santo."

"But what will you do in the cemetery?"

"Search."

"You may be in danger, I think. Let me come with you."

Galileo looked keenly at the gaunt face of his companion.

"Last week you pressed a sword to my chest, Salviati. Why now do you offer to befriend me?"

"You might have told the rector about my attacking you, and yet you held your tongue."

"Very well," Galileo said after a moment. "You may come along."

The moonlight was bright upon the urns and effigies in the cemetery, the grass soft and springy underfoot—grass growing from sanctified soil that had been brought in shiploads from the Holy Land. Galileo threaded his way among the graves and stopped finally in the shadow of the Leaning Tower.

"This would be the area, I think."

"What are you looking for?"

"The second set of iron shot."

Galileo searched until finally he discovered a hole in the turf, and embedded in it, the ten-pound shot. A few feet farther away he discovered the one-pound shot. He lifted the latter gingerly and examined it by the lamplight. Suddenly he pointed to some brownish stains on the surface of the iron ball.

"Blood."

"What does it mean?"

"It demonstrates the truth of my reasoning. Listen. Before dawn this morning, the murderer watched our rehearsal—we heard his footsteps in the Duomo—and he knew exactly what we were going to do. At sunrise, just after your uncle left to do his gardening, the murderer crept into the tower and hid himself in the belfry. At noon he watched me drop the two iron balls. Then after I left Vincenzio and Pettirosso at the top of the tower, he came out of his hiding place and struck the two students from behind with a sandbag he had brought with him. He must have succeeded in stunning little Pettirosso at once, but with Vincenzio, the larger one, he had trouble. His sandbag burst open in the struggle—I found a piece of the bag in the gutter a while ago. He managed to seize the smaller iron ball and struck Vincenzio's head—"

"But we found no blood on the balcony."

"He smuggled it out quickly with the spilled sand. Then, with Vincenzio and Pettirosso both unconscious, he propped up their forms against the parapet, keeping himself well concealed. When I reached the ground and looked up to see my two assistants leaning over, they were already unconscious."

"But why did he throw the second set of balls from the tower?"

"To make the crime look supernatural. Look what he does now! He runs to the opposite side of the tower, overlooking this cemetery, where there were no spectators, and tosses the balls down. The impact of their hitting the earth was the *second* sound of Devil's hooves that your uncle heard. The first thump, of course, was the landing of my own shot."

The law student held up his hands in objection.

"Then the murderer *pushed* Vincenzio and Pettirosso over the edge?"

"Yes."

"But how can someone throw away shot and push men from the

tower and then totally disappear? My uncle said no one came out, and you searched the tower from top to bottom immediately after."

"He escaped, of course, during the only few crucial seconds when it was possible—*when everybody's attention was drawn to the falling students!*"

"But he wouldn't have *time!*" Salviati cried. "After pushing over your assistants, he would have to run down six flights of stairs. By the time he reached the ground, the first shock would be over, and my uncle would be watching the door again."

"True, but right after the murderer pushed the two bodies over the edge, *he slid down the rope* that led to the cracked bell, the rope which your uncle had fastened to a stationary bar. Doubtless the murderer had come prepared to tie a rope thus himself, but your uncle had unwittingly provided just what he wanted. It would have taken him only seconds to descend. Everybody, including your uncle, was still absorbed in the spectacle of violent death, and the murderer was able to walk out of the tower unnoticed!"

"But maestro—who *is* he?"

Galileo stiffened as from somewhere in the city a dog howled in the night. Then he quickly replaced the one-pound shot in its recess in the earth and blew out the lanthorn.

"We now have a chance of catching him," Galileo said. "He will not dare leave these shots in the ground. Come, let us hide behind the hedge yonder!"

Galileo and his companion crouched low in the protecting shadow and waited. Time passed slowly; the moon swung lower in the hazy sky, and the shadow of the Leaning Tower crawled imperceptibly across the graveyard.

About midnight, as Galileo judged, they heard the swish of grass and a shuttered lanthorn, with one panel open, glimmered nearby.

The mathematician waited until the searcher had found the smaller iron ball and placed it within a bag. Then Galileo stepped forward.

"You won't get a chance to use it again," he said loudly.

For a moment the man was immobile; then as he tried to escape, Galileo lurched forward and pulled him to the ground. Salviati seized the lanthorn, opened all the shutters, and held it close to the man's face.

It was Jofre Tarrega.

"I knew you murdered my two students when I left your house earlier this evening," Galileo said, while Tarrega sat tight-lipped upon the coping of a grave. "You said then how proud I must have been when I released the nets and heard the iron balls strike the ground at the same time. *But nobody on the ground could have seen those nets at the height at which I used them, especially with the noon sun in his eyes.* That meant that either you, or the one who told you about it, was near me, in the belfry, watching the experiment from there. But the rector, who told you the news, was on the ground the whole time—so it could only have been you in the belfry!"

Tarrega growled. "I came here to investigate—to help you, Leo. I had nothing to do with the two deaths."

"Signor Tarrega," Galileo said quietly. "You can no longer keep your secret."

"What do you mean?"

"The professor who told Paolo Salviati that he saw me enter your daughter's room *thought he was telling the truth.* I'm sorry to say this, signore, but my whole life's work is at stake. Livia permitted Vincenzio Barbierini to enter her room at night. Vincenzio's stature is similar to mine, and his fair hair might look red in the moonlight. Also, he often affected many of my gestures and mannerisms, and could well have been mistaken for me by the professor who saw him.

"Last night Vincenzio visited Livia again. Doubtless you found out about it and went looking for Vincenzio. You saw us rehearsing in the tower and the plan of the murder of Vincenzio occurred to you. You knew how Vincenzio boasted of his conquests and you could not bear to let him defame your fine name or your daughter. So you killed him—and Pettirosso, too, because he was present and could have denounced you."

Tarrega's shoulders drooped and suddenly his face looked old—very old.

"Shall we go to the rector now, signore?" Galileo asked.

Without a word Tarrega rose to accompany them.

THE BEDLAM BAM

Lillian de la Torre

Lillian de la Torre died in 1993, fifty years after she described the first exploits of her detective, the famous lexicographer Sam Johnson. Her own 1975 introduction to the mystery "The Bedlam Bam" speaks eloquently of what she intended: "When James Boswell first met Dr. Sam: Johnson, in 1763, it was still a fashionable amusement to visit Bethlehem (pronounced Bedlam) Hospital and laugh at the lunatics; and the two friends once made such an excursion, though certainly not to laugh. Artists (notably Hogarth) and writers have transmitted to us their impressions of the lot of the madman in a society which still acted as if it thought a madman needed the devil beaten out of him. What would be the plight of a sane man mistakenly confined, and how could he regain his liberty? 'The Bedlam Bam' answers this question."

T o find my Tom o' Bedlam ten thousand miles I'll travel," chanted the ballad singer in a thin rusty screech, lustily seconded by the wail of the dirt-encrusted baby in her shawl.

"Mad Maudlin goes with dirty toes to save her shoes from gravel,
Yet will I sing bonny mad boys, Bedlam boys are bonny,
They still go bare and live by air . . ."

All along the fence that separated Bedlam Hospital from the tree-lined walks of Moorfields, ill-printed broadsides fluttered in the breeze, loudly urged upon the public by a cacophony of ballad sellers. As I flinched at the din, a hand plucked my sleeve, and a voice twittered:

"Poor Tom o' Bedlam! Tom's a-cold!"

I turned to view a tatterdemalion figure, out at elbow and knee, out at toe and heel, out of breech, with spiky hair on end and clawlike hand extended. As I fumbled for a copper, my wise companion restrained me.

"Let be, Mr. Boswell, the man's a fraud. No Bedlamite has leave to beg these days; they are all withinside. Come along."

Leaving the mock madman to mutter a dispirited curse, we passed through Bedlam gate and approached the noble edifice, so like a palace without, so grim within—as I, a visitor from North Britain, was soon to learn.

Behold us then mounting the step to the entrance pavilion. If "great wits are sure to madness near allied," as the poet has it, then what shall be said of that ill-assorted pair?—Dr. Sam: Johnson, the Great Cham of Literature, portly of mien and rugged of countenance, with myself, his young friend and chronicler, James Boswell, advocate, of Scotland, swarthy of complection and low of stature beside him. Believing London to be the full tide of human existence, he had carried me, that day in May 1768, to see one of the city's strangest sights, Bedlam Hospital, the abode of the frantick and the melancholy mad.

Entering the pavilion, we beheld before us the Penny Gates, attended by a burly porter in blue coat and cap, wearing with importance a silver badge almost as wide as a plate, and holding his silver-tipped staff of office. Beside the flesh and blood figure stood two painted wooden effigies holding jugs, representing gypsies, a he and a she. Though the woman was ugly, we put our pennies into her jug, and heard them rattle down; whereupon the porter passed us in, and we ascended to the upper gallery.

As we came out on the landing, our senses were assailed by a rank stench and a babel of noise, a hum of many voices talking, with an accompaniment of screech and howl that stood my hair on end.

A second blue-gowned attendant passed us through the iron bars of the barrier, and we stood in the long gallery of the men's ward. Around us milled madmen and their visitors in a dense throng, the while vendors shouldered their way through the crush dispensing nuts, fruits, and cheesecakes, and tap-boys rushed pots of beer, though contraband, to the thirsty, whether mad or sane.

Along the wide gallery, tall windows let in the north light. Opposite them were ranged the madmen's cells, each with its heavy door pierced with a little barred Judas window. Some doors were shut; but most were open to afford the inmates air. I peeped in the first one with a shudder. A small, unglazed window high up admitted a shaft of sunlight and a blast of cold spring air. For furnishings, there was only a wooden bedstead piled with straw, and a wooden bowl to eat from; unless you counted a heavy iron chain with a neck loop, stapled to the wall. No one was chained there, however; the fortunate occupant had "the liberty of the corridor," and perhaps stood at my elbow.

Others were not so fortunate. As we strolled forward, we saw through the open doors many a wretch in fetters, chained to the wall, and many a hopeless mope drearily staring.

"Here in Bedlam," remarked my philosophical friend, "tho' secluded from the world, yet we may see the world in microcosm. Here's Pride—"

I looked where he pointed. Through the open door of the next cell, I perceived one who in his disordered intellect imagined himself to be, perhaps, the Great Mogul. He sat on straw as on a throne, he wore his fetters like adornments, and his countenance bore the most ineffable look of self-satisfaction and consequence. For a crown he wore his chamber pot.

"A pride scarce justified," said I with a smile.

"For mortal man, pride is never justified. Here's Anger—"

The sound of blows rang through the corridor. In the neighbouring cell, a red-faced lunatick was furiously beating the straw on his pallet.

"What do you, friend?" enquired a stander-by.

"I beat him for his cruelty!"

"Whom do you beat, sir?"

"The Butcher Duke of Cumberland. Take that! And that!"

"Madmen have long memories," remarked my friend with pity. "The cruelties of the '45 are gone by these twenty years."

The noise had stirred up the menagerie. Pandemonium burst forth. Those who were fettered clanked their chains. Those who were locked in shook the bars. Some howled like wolves. Keepers banging on doors added to the hollobaloo. My friend shuddered.

"God keep us out of such a place!"

"Amen!" said I.

The tumult abated, and we walked on through the throng. A little way along, my friend greeted an acquaintance:

"What, Lawyer Trevelyan, your servant, sir. Miss Cicely, yours. Be acquainted with my young friend Mr. Boswell, the Scotch lawyer, who visits London to see the sights with me."

As I bowed I took their measure. The lawyer was tall and sturdy, with little shrewd eyes in a long closed-up face. The girl was small and slim, modestly attired in dove grey. At her slender waist, in the old-fashioned way, she wore a dainty seamstress's hussif with a business-like pair of scissors suspended on a riband. Her small quiet face was gently framed by a cap and lappets of lawn. Meeting her candid amber gaze, I was glad I had adorned my person in my gold-laced scarlet coat.

"How do you go on, Mr. Trevelyan? And how does the good man, your uncle Silas, the Turkey merchant?"

"On his account, Dr. Johnson, we are come hither."

"What, is he confined here?"

"Alas, yes. Yonder he stands."

I looked where he pointed. The elder Mr. Trevelyan was a wiry small personage, clad in respectable black. He had a thin countenance, his own white hair to his shoulders, bright black eyes, and a risible look. With a half smile, he listened to the tirade of a distrest fellow inmate, giving now and then a quick nod.

"He has no look of insanity," observed my friend.

"Perhaps not, sir. But the prank that brought him hither was not sane. You shall hear. Being touched with Mr. Wesley's *enthusiasm*—"

"Mr. Wesley is a good man."

"I do not deny it, sir. But my uncle has more zeal than prudence. He abandons his enterprises, and goes about to do good to the poor, in prisons and workhouses and I know not where."

"Call you this lunacy?"

"No, sir. Stay, you shall hear the story. Of a Sunday, sir, he gets up into the pulpit at St. Giles, just as the congregation is assembled. He wears a pair of large muslin wings to his shoulders, and 'Follow me, good people!' he cries, 'Follow me to Heaven!' Whereupon with jerks of his hands he flaps his wings, crows loudly, and prepares to launch himself from the lectern. But the beadle, a man of prompt address, pulls him back, and so he is hustled hither without more ado, and here he must stay lest he do himself a mischief. But never fret, Cicely, I have his affairs well in hand, by power of attorney and so on."

But Cicely had gone impulsively to the old gentleman.

"How do you, Uncle?"

"Why, my dear, very well. Reflect (smiling) 'tis only in Bedlam a man may speak his mind about kings and prelates without hindrance. And where else can a man find so many opportunities for comforting the afflicted?"

"Yet, dear Uncle, it distresses me to see you among them."

"Be comforted, Cicely. 'Tis only a little while, and I shall be enlarged, I promise you. Your cousin Ned will see to it."

A wise wink accompanied this assurance. Cousin Ned sighed.

"All in good time, Cicely."

Since Cicely seemed minded to canvass the subject further, we bowed and retired. The morning was drawing to a close. I was glad to leave the whole scene of madness, and return to the world of the sane.

Nor would I willingly have renewed my visit so soon, had not the dove-grey girl come to us in distress and urgently carried us thither to visit her uncle.

What a change was there! Two weeks before, we had seen him fully clothed and quite composed. Now as we peeped through the Judas window, we beheld him lying on straw in the chilly cell, his shirt in tatters, his white locks tangled, shackled and manacled to the floor.

"A violent case," said the burly mad-keeper. "I dare not unlock the door."

He dared after all, but only upon receipt of a considerable bribe, and upon condition that he stand by the door with staff in hand.

In a trice Miss Cicely was kneeling by her uncle's side, putting her own cloak about him.

"Alas, how do you, Uncle?"

The eyes he turned upon her were clear and sane.

"Why, very well, dear love," he said. "I have learned what I came here to learn, and more too," he added wryly.

"What have you learned, Uncle?"

"I have learned how the poor madmen here are abused, aye and beaten too, when their poor addled wits make them obstreperous. That staff (nodding towards the blue-coat by the door) is not only for show."

"Alack, Uncle, have you been beaten?"

"Beaten? Aye, and blistered, physicked, drenched with cold water, denied my books, deprived of pen, ink, and paper. And all for a transport of justifiable anger."

"Anger at what?" enquired Dr. Johnson.

"At my nephew."

"Why, Uncle, what has Ned done?"

"Ned has cozened me. You must know, Dr. Johnson, I am as well in my wits as you are—save for my ill judgement in trusting Ned. You see, sir, Mr. Wesley and his followers are barred from visiting Newgate Gaol—lest they corrupt the inmates, I suppose—and from Bedlam Hospital, lest they make them mad. Well, sir, being determined to know how matters went on behind these doors when they are closed, I resolved to make myself an inmate. I gave Ned—more fool me—my power of attorney and a letter that should enlarge me when I so desired, and by enacting a little comedy, with muslin wings, I got myself brought hither; in full confidence that Ned would see me released when I chose."

"Well, sir?"

"Well, sir, when I gave Ned the word to produce my letter and release me, this Judas Iscariot looks me in the eye, and says he, 'What letter? The poor man is raving.' All came clear in a flash. Ned has no intention of enlarging me. Why should he, when he has my power of attorney, and may make ducks and drakes of my fortune at his pleasure? Nay, he is my heir. What are my chances, think you, of coming out of here alive? Do you wonder I was ready to throttle the scoundrel? But they pulled me from him, and I have been chained down ever since. The keepers are bribed, I suppose. To my expostulations they turn a deaf ear. If not for Cicely, my plight need never have been known."

"Alack, Dr. Johnson," cried Cicely, "now what's to be done?"

"Have no fear, my dear. When next the Governors of the hospital meet, they shall hear the story, and he'll be released, I warrant you."

That very Saturday at nine of the clock we presented ourselves in the Court Room of the hospital. This handsome chamber is located above-stairs in the central pavilion, a gracious room with large windows overlooking Moorfields, a ceiling of carven plaster, and painted coats of arms about the walls.

Here sat the Governors, a stately set of men in full-bottom wigs and wide-skirted coats. My eye picked out Dr. John Monro, head surgeon, a formidable figure with bushy eyebrows, a belligerent snub nose, a short upper lip over prominent dog-teeth, a vinous complexion, and a bulldog cast of countenance; for upon his say-so, in the end, depended our friend's freedom or incarceration.

Four of us came to speak for him that morning: James Boswell, lawyer, Dr. Johnson, his friend, and Miss Cicely, his kinswoman. To strengthen our ranks, we brought a medical man, Dr. Robert Levett, Dr. Johnson's old friend, who for twenty years had dwelt in his house and attended him at need. He was a little fellow of grotesque and uncouth appearance, his knobby countenance half concealed by a bushy full-bottom wig. He wore a voluminous rusty black coat, and old-fashioned square-toed shoes to his feet. Thus ceremoniously attired, he came with us to speak as a physician in support of Mr. Silas Trevelyan's sanity.

Then they brought him in, and my heart misgave me. Gaunt, ragged, in chains, with his white hair on end—was this man sane? At his benevolent greeting to us, however, and his respectful bow to the committee assembled, I took heart again. As the blue-coated warders ranged themselves beside him, for fear of some disorderly outbreak, the gentlemen seated along the dais scanned him intently, and he looked serenely back.

Footsteps hurrying up the stair announced yet another participant, and nephew Edward Trevelyan appeared precipitately in the wide doorway—heir, attorney, and nearest of kin to the supposed madman, all in one.

The proceedings began. Dr. Johnson was eloquent, Dr. Levett earnest and scientifick, Miss Cicely modest and low-spoken. I was furnished forth with legal instances. Our one difficulty was in explaining how, if he was sane, our friend had gotten himself into Bedlam in the first place. We dared not say, in effect, "He came in voluntarily, as a spy." We skirted the subject, and concentrated upon his present state of restored sanity.

"We have now," said Dr. Monro, "only to hear from Mr. Edward Trevelyan, the inmate's attorney and kinsman. Mr. Trevelyan?"

Cousin Ned unfolded his length, rolled up his little eyes, and spoke softly in a deep resonant voice:

"Grieved I am to say it," he began, "my friends over there mistake my poor uncle's condition. He can be sly and plausible, sirs, but with me, whom he trusts"—Old Mr. Trevelyan stiffened, and Cicely put a dismayed hand to her mouth—"with me he speaks otherwise. His brain still swarms with lunatick fancies. He proposes to get upon the roof and with his wings elude them all, and a good job too, says he, for the Governor is a puppy that wants a cannister to his tail, and Dr. Monro is a cork-brained clunch—"

With a roar the uncle broke from his keepers and flung himself upon his nephew.

"Thou prevaricating pup! Thou lying leech! Thou Judas! Where is my letter that I gave thee for my safety?"

"The man is mad," growled Dr. Monro. "Take him away, and let him be close confined."

We four met again next morning for breakfast in Johnson's Court. We shared a loaf, and little Levett brewed pot after pot of tea, for which Dr. Johnson's capacity was vast.

"And now," pronounced Dr. Johnson, setting down his cup at last, "what's to be done next for our incarcerated friend, Mr. Silas Trevelyan? He cannot stay where he is. Chains and fetters would soon drive the sanest man mad."

"If we could perswade the keepers he is sane?" suggested Miss Cicely timidly.

"After Dr. Monro's verdict," said I, "how can we so? We can never get him away openly."

"Then we must bring him away covertly," said Dr. Johnson. "Can you not, Mr. Boswell, devise some bam that shall bamboozle the keepers and set Mr. Silas free?"

"Let me think. What do you say, sir, if we take a leaf from Shakespeare, and deliver our friend, like Falstaff, in a bucking-basket of foul linen?"

"Chain and all?"

"True, there's the chain."

"Take a leaf from *Romeo and Juliet,* and they'll undo the chain fast enough, I warrant you," mused little Levett.

Johnson frowned; then smiled: "We'll try it."

Accordingly we spent the best part of the day concerting our measures and assembling our properties. As the afternoon wore on, our physician was furnished forth with a bagful of flasks and vials, clean linen, and money to spend, and so departed for Bedlam to acquaint Mr. Silas with our plan, and put things in motion. We set our rendezvous there for midnight.

Punctually at midnight, we two, escorting Miss, drove up to Bedlam gate in a hackney coach. A cart followed us, with a large pine box for freight. Instructing our Jehus to stand, we rang the porter's bell. That functionary presently appeared, rubbing sleep from his eyes.

We soon saw that our precursor had opened the way for us by his authority as a medical man, plus, I doubt not, a judicious outlay of cash bribes. When we named our stricken friend, Mr. Silas Trevelyan, the fellow looked grave, passed us up the stair, and went yawning back to his hole.

At the barred gate on the landing, a second blue-coated warder was ready with the keys. They hung by a loop at his broad leather belt. As he selected and turned the right one, I scrutinized him narrowly, for upon his behavior depended, in part, the success of our scheam.

The fellow was tall and muscular, as befitted one who was often called upon to grapple with lunaticks. Little squinting eyes in a broad doughy face gave him a look more dogged than quick. True to his looks, he dogged us close as we entered the ward.

The long shadowy corridor was empty; the madmen had all been sequestered for the night. Eerie noises attested to their presence behind the locked doors: a snore and a snort here, a patter of prayer there, an occasional howl or screech of laughter that shocked the ear.

One door only was open, whence faint candlelight fell along the floor. Dr. Levett stood in the doorway.

"Be brave, my dear," said he to Cicely, taking her hand. "He is very far gone, and turning black. He has sent for you, only to give you his last blessing. Stand back, fellow (to the mad-keeper), these moments are sacred."

The warder, looking solemn, took up his stance by the door, and we passed within. Our friend Mr. Silas lay on his straw pallet, his eyes turned up in his head. Out of respect for his obviously moribund condition, his chains had been removed.

As Dr. Levett advanced the candle and pushed back the tangled locks, I saw the awful leaden blackness of the skin. Had I not been prepared for it, I should have been shocked. Even prepared, Miss Cicely clung to my hand as she whispered:

"How do you, Uncle?"

The dark eyes came into focus upon her.

"Ill, ill, my dear," he breathed. "The lawyer—is he here?"

"I am here, sir."

"Then write my last will—quickly. To my niece—everything to my niece."

His head dropped back. Dr. Levett held a draught to his lips. I drew forth my tablets and wrote down his bequest the briefest way. Faltering fingers signed it, and Dr. Johnson added his firm neat signature as witness.

"Take it, Cicely," murmured the testator. She slipped it into her bodice. "And," the failing voice continued, "may Heaven bless you. I forgive—"

The voice died, the white head dropped back, the jaw fell. Dr. Levett touched the slack wrist. Swiftly he closed the eyelids and drew the sheet over the darkened face.

"Our friend is no more," he pronounced gravely.

"What, dead?" ejaculated the mad-keeper, starting forward.

"Stand back!" cried Dr. Levett. "On your life, stand back! Such a death has not been these hundred years in England, for our friend is dead of the Black Plague! Look at his face—"

He flicked back the sheet and momentarily by the pale light of the candle revealed the blackened countenance; at which the mad-keeper started back with an oath.

"Now hark'ee, my friend," began Dr. Johnson portentously, "be guided by me: Were this known, there would be rioting within these walls; what keeper would be safe? Do you but keep silence, all shall be decently done by us, his friends. He shall be gone by morning, and the episode forgotten. Nor shall you be the loser," he added, fingering his pocket suggestively.

The fellow was stupid, which suited us; but so stupid that precious moments went past while we strove to make him see the supposed seriousness of the situation. Not so another keeper, a dark-visaged fellow with a squint who happened by. Hearing that Mr. Silas Trevelyan had but now died of the Black Death, he at once clapped a dirty handkerchief to his nose, and clattered off down the stair.

The first fellow was still mumbling when Dr. Levett settled the matter. He advanced the candle, clapped a hand to the fellow's face, and cried out:

"What, friend! 'Tis too late! You have taken the infection! You are all of a sweat, and turning black! (And so he was, glistening with ink from Levett's hand.) A clyster! Only a clyster will save you now! This way! To your own quarters!"

Speaking thus urgently, the physician steered the terrified fellow in the direction of his lair in the attick. We were left to do the last offices for the "dead," who lay motionless, looking more risible now than ever.

The supposed corpse was neatly laid out, cocooned in his winding sheet, when Dr. Levett appeared in the gallery alone, chuckling.

"A good strong enema—that will take care of the keeper," said he with a grin. "He'll be busy for a while. Come, let us go."

"Go!" cried Dr. Johnson. "Without the keeper, how are we to make our way through the barriers?"

"With his keys," said Levett, and produced them. "A clyster is a powerfully distracting operation. 'Twas child's play to get at the keys, though under his nose."

"Well done, Mr. Levett. Come, let us go."

Among us we made shift to carry the sheeted body through the barred gate, down the wide stair, and out at the portal, which the largest key unlocked, not without an alarming screech. A snore from the porter's lodge gave us Godspeed. Dawn light was greying the sky as we lifted our burden into the waiting cart. We eased the sheeted figure into the pine coffin. I lowered the lid, and Dr. Johnson screwed it lightly down.

"—in case we encounter the curious. 'Tis but until we get clear of the grounds," he reassured his friend in an undertone.

I noted with approval that underneath the bow of crape that mournfully adorned the lid, auger holes had been bored to provide the "corpse" air to breathe.

The carter, a scrawny pockmarked boy, was regarding our proceedings between alarm and superstitious awe.

"Is he dead? I'll have no part in it! Give me my money and get him out of my cart!"

By paying a double fee, we managed to retain the cart; but the carter took to his heels. I must perforce take the reins. Miss elected to share my lot. She could not be persuaded to leave her uncle in my hands, but sat herself determinedly upon his coffin. Dr. Johnson and Mr. Levett mounted the hackney coach without us.

We had wasted precious time. Before we could drive off, we were intercepted. Two fellows came up at the run. One wore the blue coat of a mad-keeper. I recognized the swarthy keeper who had sheered off so quickly. Now it became clear: The fellow was one of Ned's tools, and had run off, not to shun infection, but to inform; for his companion was Ned.

"Alas, my uncle!" said the false, mellifluous voice. "Why was I not notified? As his heir—"

"We have performed the last offices," said Dr. Johnson coldly from the coach, "and you shall hear further. We'll not bandy words at Bedlam gate. Drive on, Mr. Boswell."

I drove on.

How it fell out I know not, but I missed my rendezvous in the leafy walks of Moorfields. It was not the coach that overtook me, but a pair of footpads coming suddenly out of the shadows.

"Stand and deliver!"

A weapon glinted, and a rough hand pulled me from the high seat.

"Stay, you mistake," I cried; "here is no treasure chest—"

But the two fellows were up and slapping the reins, and off they went, cart and coffin and Miss and all; and as I stood dumbfounded, there floated back to me the girl's despairing cry:

"Cousin Ned!"

Here was calamity indeed. I could think of no better plan than to bellow "Stop thief!" which I did with a will. Wheels crunched on gravel, and the coach drew up beside me. Little Levett reached a hand and pulled me inside.

When he had heard my story, Dr. Johnson looked utterly grave.

"What have we done? We have delivered our friend, out of Bedlam indeed, straight into the hands of his enemy!"

"And his heir!" exclaimed Dr. Levett.

"No, sir," I corrected him. "Recall, sir, that as part of the comedy of the 'death bed,' I made his will. 'Every thing to my niece.' The girl is his heir."

"But does her venal cousin know that?"

"She knows it," said Levett wryly. "She need not lift a finger. She has only to let him be buried, and his fortune is hers."

"Great Heavens!" I cried. "That innocent face!"

"Innocent faces have masked murderous hearts before now," mused Dr. Johnson. "*Vide* Mary Blandy, *vide* your own Katharine Nairn."

"I'll never believe it," said I stoutly.

"Believe it or no, we must act to save him, and quickly."

"The more quickly," said Levett urgently, "that in too slavish imitation of *Romeo and Juliet,* I have made him helpless with a sleeping draught."

"Thus, then, the matter stands," Johnson summed up. "The lawyer thinks himself the heir. Perhaps he supposes he is in possession of his uncle's corpse. If so, he will bury him, thus rendering him a corpse indeed. Perhaps he has unscrewed the coffin lid and found a sleeping man. What is to hinder him from quietly doing away with him? Either way, he looks to inherit."

"And perhaps he is in concert with Miss, they'll bury him and split the swag," suggested Levett.

I shook my head vehemently.

"We must find him," said Dr. Johnson. "There is one hope yet. No one at all will inherit, if the old gentleman is not known to be dead. They cannot inter him secretly. Come, let us make enquiries. They all dwell together in a house in Jasper Street. To Jasper Street, coachman."

Jasper Street was nearby. There all was silent. No cart stood before the door, but as we stood knocking, a manservant trudged up. He stared.

"Hadn't you heard? I have just carried the news to our nearest friends. The master is dead of a mighty infection. They daren't keep him. His sermon will be preached as soon as may be, and so they'll put him hastily under ground."

"Where, friend?"

"At the parish church, where else, St. Giles Cripplegate."

Without further parley we drove off in haste. As we turned into the street called London Wall, we heard the great bell of St. Giles begin to toll. A few moments more, and we were there. The east transept door was nearest, and we entered in haste. A charnel-house smell seemed to taint the dusky air. It emanated from the opened vault before the Trevelyan monument, where soon the deceased must be inhumed.

Was he deceased? Within that plain pine coffin forward in the aisle, sleeping or waking, did he still live? Could we bring him off alive from this peril we had put him in?

My eye sought the chief mourner where he sat in his forward pew. Nephew Ned wore a black mourning cloak, and made play with a large cambrick handkerchief. Miss was not beside him.

Then I saw her, kneeling at the coffin foot in her dove-grey gown, clinging with both hands to the edge. As I looked, the sexton tried to detach her from this unseemly pose, but she shook her head and clung.

From the pulpit the sermon was already flowing over us in a glutinous tide. The deceased was a mirror of all the works of mercy, visiting the sick, the imprisoned, the distracted, and now gone to his reward in the blessed hope of the resurrection,

"For verily he shall rise again—"

Miss Cicely stood up suddenly. A long creaking rasp set my teeth on edge as the coffin lid was slowly pushed up, and a sheeted figure rose to a sitting position.

The parson gabbled a prayer, ladies shrieked, and Lawyer Trevelyan uttered a most unseemly curse.

Helped by Cicely, the supposed corpse put back his cerements and bowed to the startled company.

"I thank you, Reverend," said Mr. Silas coolly, "for your good opinion, and you, my friends, for paying me my honours, tho' prematurely. 'Tis too long a tale, how I came hither thus. Suffice it to say, I am neither dead nor mad, and I desire you will all join me at my house to break fast in celebration. You, nephew, need not come. You'll hear from me later. But you, dear niece, give me your hand. Come, friends, let us go."

So saying, in his madman's rags as he was, wearing his winding-sheet like a cloak, handing Miss Cicely, he led the way down the center aisle. We fell in behind him, and so the strange procession came to the house in Jasper Street. There the dumbfounded servants served the old gentleman his own funeral baked meats (hastily fetched from the nearby tavern).

Only when the general company had dispersed did we learn the full story of those hours between the time the coffin was stolen by nephew Ned, and the time we found it lying in the church to be preached over.

"The rattling of the cart awoke me," said old Trevelyan, "for your sleeping draught, sir (to Dr. Levett), was not so very strong. When I heard my nephew's voice, I knew my situation was precarious indeed. I kept silence, only thanking Dr. Johnson for his foresight in screwing down the lid."

"What is screwed may be unscrewed," remarked Dr. Johnson, "that was the most of my concern."

"That it was not," said Mr. Silas, "we may thank this brave girl here. She sat upon the lid, and would not stir, and between seeming stubborn grief and the menace of infection, she kept her cousin at a distance. She never budged from my side. Only after Ned had left my coffin in the aisle and was gone to instruct the parson and the sexton, did I hear the screws turn in the lid."

"How, with what, then, Miss Cicely, did you make shift to turn them?" asked Dr. Johnson.

"The scissors of a hussif, sir, have more use than snipping thread. But, sir," she went on, with a smile that irradiated her quiet face, "I dared not lift the lid while my cousin ruled. I still clung tight to the coffin, hoping, sir (to Dr. Johnson), for your arrival to protect us. When I saw you in the doorway, I whispered, 'Now, Uncle—' and the rest you know."

"A very pretty resurrection scene," remarked my friend with a smile.

" 'Tis not every man," added Mr. Trevelyan, "that lives to hear his own eulogy preached. I am your debtor, sir (to Dr. Levett), for that privilege. To you, gentlemen three, I owe my liberty; and to you, dear Cicely, having fallen into Ned's hands, I am well assured I owe my life. I have made you my heir in a mummery, my dear: you shall be so in earnest."

THE ESCAPE

Anne Perry

With the guillotine looming and death at every turn, the Paris of 1793 was a place of conspiracy and intrigue. Into a plot to rescue an aristocrat from the prison of La Force, Anne Perry weaves a traditional whodunit. Suspense, adventure, and the romance of a noble cause spice the brew as the author serves up the type of historical with which she's earned her reputation as a leader in the genre.

The rescue from the prison of La Force was very carefully planned. Sebastien had taken care of every detail himself, and no one had been told anything they did not have to know. By eight in the evening everyone was in his place.

Jacques was doing no more than driving the coach which had taken them all to the prison where the man they had come for was lodged, pending his trial before the Commander of Public Safety, and inevitably his execution by the guillotine.

He was a young aristocrat named Maximilien de Fleury who was there simply because his father's estates had been confiscated and it was necessary to indict him also in order that they could remain in the hands—and in the pockets—of the government. No other charge was known against him beyond those of idleness and wealth, in Paris in 1792, a crime unto death.

A bribe had been very carefully placed so that his family might visit him for one last time. A plea for clemency, plus several sous, had obtained the promise from a guard to find himself otherwise occupied, so that they might have time alone, during which some swift changes would take place. A very fine forgery executed by Philippe was to be substituted for their pass documents, and in the torchlight four of them would leave where three had come in.

Nicolette was very good indeed at distracting people's concentration by a variety of means, as seemed most suitable according to the nature and status of those whose attention was to be held. She was not a beautiful girl in the usual sense, but she could affect beauty in such a way that it beguiled the mind. One saw the grace and the confidence in her walk, the vitality in her, the imagination and intelligence, and a certain air of courage which intrigued.

She could discard it as quickly and be timid, gentle, demure. Or she could be weary and frightened and appeal for help. She had even aroused the respect of guards Sebastien had thought beyond the human decencies. It never ceased to surprise him, because over the last year he had learned to know something of the woman beneath the facade. She had joined the small group in the beginning, two years ago when they had just banded together, tentatively at first, to rescue a friend from one of the many prisons in Paris, before he faced trial and death. There were five of them, Sebastien, Nicolette, Etienne, Philippe the forger, and now Jacques.

Another rescue had followed swiftly, and then a third. By the end of 1792 they had snatched several more people from the Committee's prisons, and failed with three. This year they had attempted more, and succeeded.

Now Sebastien was walking beside Nicolette, her head bent demurely, as they passed the guards and gave them their papers, identifying them as Citizen de Fleury's sister and brother-in-law, come, with the jailor's generous permission, to visit him a last time. A few paces behind them Etienne followed, named in the same document as a brother. All of them, as always, wore a slight disguise so they would not easily be recognized again. Sometimes it was powdered hair, sometimes a false beard or moustache, a change of complexion with a little paint, a blemish, and of course different clothes.

They walked slowly; it was a natural thing to do in the cold, torchlit passages toward the entrance of the cells. Their feet echoed on the stone floor, and the darkness beyond the flame's glare seemed filled with sighs and whispers, as if all the pain of the thousands of inmates were left here after their shivering bodies had been taken out for the last time. Nicolette moved closer to Sebastien, and without thought he put his arm round her.

They presented their identification and their notes of permission to the turnkey and slowly, every movement as if in a dream, he took them, perused them, and passed them back. Then he lifted his great iron keys and placed one in the lock. The bolts fell with a clang, and he pushed open the door.

With a barely perceptible shudder Sebastien went in, his finger to his lips where the guard could not see it, in silent warning. De Fleury looked round, his face white with fear, to see who had intruded on him at this hour. It was only too apparent he expected the worst: a hasty trial and summary execution at first light. It was not uncommon.

"Maximilien!" Nicolette ran to him and threw her arms round him, her lips close to his ear. Sebastien knew she would be telling him not to show surprise or ignorance, that they had come to rescue him and he must follow their lead in everything they said.

Sebastien went after her across the icy, straw-covered floor and wrung de Fleury by the hand, his eyes steady, warning.

The turnkey banged the door shut. Sebastien's heart was in his mouth, his ears straining. The lock did not turn. The man's footsteps died away as he went back up the corridor. Etienne stood guard, shifting nervously from one foot to the other.

"Quickly!" Sebastien took off his cloak, a large mantle of a garment, and held it out to de Fleury. "Put it on," he ordered.

"They'll never let me out!" de Fleury protested, his eyes wild as hope and reason fought in his mind. "Three of you came in, they'll know to let only three of you out. And if you think finding the wrong one will make them let you go, you are dreaming. They'll execute you in my place, simply for aiding my escape. Don't you know that?" Some innate sense of honour forbade him accepting on these terms, but he could not withdraw his hand.

"We have passes for four to leave," Sebastien explained. "The turnkey has been bribed to be elsewhere, and it is the changing of the guard who let us in. Be quick."

De Fleury hesitated only a moment. Incredulity turned to wonder in his face, and then relief. He seized the cloak and swung it around his shoulders even as he was moving toward the door.

"Don't run!" Etienne hissed at him.

De Fleury stopped, twisting round to look back at Sebastien.

"You're supposed to be taking your last leave of your family," Sebastien reminded him. "You aren't going to gallop out!"

"Oh . . . oh yes." De Fleury controlled himself with an effort, straightened his shoulders, and walked with agonizingly measured pace out through the cell door and along the torchlit passage toward the entrance. Once he even looked back as if to someone he knew.

Etienne and Nicolette came close behind him, and Sebastien last, closing the cell door, the new pass papers in his hand, for four people.

Nicolette moved ahead to catch up with de Fleury, clasping his arm and clinging to it. Every attitude of her body expressed grief.

They were twenty feet short of the outer gates. The guards moved across the passage to block their way. Sebastien felt his heart beating so hard his body shook with the violence of it. It was difficult to get his breath.

De Fleury faltered. Was Nicolette leaning on him, or in fact supporting him?

One of the guards brandished a musket.

De Fleury stopped. Etienne and Sebastien drew level with him and stopped also.

"Here," Sebastien offered the pass to the guard. He took it and read it, looking carefully from one to the other of them. Their faces were full of shadows in the torchlight. Each one stood motionless, at once afraid to meet their eyes, and afraid not to.

This was the relief guard. They had not seen them come in. The paper was for the exact number of people, three men and one woman.

There was no sound but the guard's breath rasping in his throat and the hiss and flicker of the torches in their brackets.

"Right," the guard said at last. "Out." He gestured to the great archway and on shaking legs de Fleury went down, Nicolette still at his side. It had begun to rain.

Sebastien and Etienne increased their pace, passing into the wide street. Etienne took Nicolette by the arm almost exactly as the shot rang out in the air above them.

They froze.

One of the guards came running through the archway and across the cobbles, his musket held in both hands, ready to raise and fire.

Sebastien swiveled round. He was about to ask what was the matter, when he saw the turnkey behind them, and the ugly truth leaped to his mind only too clearly.

"Citizen de Fleury!" the guard accused breathlessly, looking from one to the other of them.

Before de Fleury could move, Etienne put his hand on his arm and stepped forward himself.

"What is it? Is something wrong?"

The guard stared at him, trying to discern his features in the erratic light.

Sebastien peered to see how far away the carriage was. Would Jacques have the coolheadedness to bring it forward even after he heard the musket shot? If not, they were lost.

The turnkey was coming out into the street as well, torch in his hand.

"Is it not bad enough we have to lose our brother, without bothering us at this time?" Etienne demanded, his voice shaking.

Sebastien heard the carriage wheels on the cobbles and saw the faint light on Jacques's pale hair. He turned back and caught Nicolette's eyes. He nodded imperceptibly.

Nicolette began to sink as if she would faint.

Sebastien started forward and picked her up, swinging past the guard and knocking the musket sideways and onto the stones. Etienne grasped de Fleury by the arm and as the carriage drew level, threw the door open and pushed him in with all his might. De Fleury fell onto the floor, with Nicolette on top of him.

There were shouts of fury from the archway and swaying light as the turnkey came up, yelling for them to stop.

Sebastien knocked the barrel of the gun into the air, and then hauled himself onto the footplate at the side of the carriage just as it turned and picked up speed, and a moment later a musket shot rang out, and another, and another. One thudded into the woodwork, but it was nearly a yard away. Please, God, Etienne was on the footplate.

They would call out the National Guard, of course they would, but by then de Fleury would be on the road to Calais, and they would be back in the familiar streets and alleys of the Cordeliers District, invisible again—if only they could elude them for the next hour.

The rain was heavier, driving in his face, making a mist of the dark streets, dampening torches, sliming the cobbles under the horses' feet. The wood under Sebastien's fingers was wet as he clung on while the coach swayed and lurched along the rue Saint Antoine toward the place de la Bastille. He could still hear the sound of gunfire behind.

Was Etienne on the footplate, clinging on as he was, or had he been flung off, and was lying somewhere on the road, perhaps injured, or even dead? Perhaps one of the shots had caught him?

Jacques could see better in the dark than he could! They were close to the river. He could smell the water and see the faint gleam of reflections on the surface. They must be on the quai de l'Hôtel de Ville. There were still shouts behind them, and another volley of shots. They were far too exposed in the open.

They swerved left into the Pont d'Arcole. The huge mass of Notre Dame loomed ahead on the Île de la Cité. They must find the narrow streets soon, the winding alleys of their own district.

They swept through an open square, more shots splattering around them, some sharp on the stones, others thudding heavily into the woodwork of the carriage. The driving rain was making it desperately hard to cling on. Sebastien was slithering wildly, his fingers bruised, his body aching. All his muscles seemed locked.

He was all but thrown off as they careered over the Petit Pont, across the quai Saint Michel, and finally into the narrow streets behind the Church of St. Severin.

When at last they stopped in the stable yard in the flaring torchlight, Sebastien was so numb he could barely let go. His fingers would not unbend. He saw Philippe's face white and streaked with rain as he ran out of the shelter of the doorway. The horses were shivering and streaked dark with sweat.

Sebastien dropped down onto the cobbles and almost fell, his body was so stiff, and hurt as if he had been battered.

"What happened?" Philippe demanded. "You look awful!" He looked at the coach, and his voice dropped. "It's riddled with splinters—a shot!" He lunged forward and yanked the door open, and Nicolette almost fell out. She was ashen.

Jacques scrambled off the box and came round the side; he too was soaked with rain, his hat was gone, and he looked exhausted and terrified. His eyes went straight to Sebastien.

"Etienne?" Sebastien asked the question which was in all their minds. "Where's Etienne? And de Fleury? Is he all right?"

Nicolette stared at him and shook her head minutely, barely a movement at all. "De Fleury's dead," she said in a small, tired voice. "One of the musket balls must have caught him. I don't even know when it happened. In the dark I didn't see, and he didn't cry out. In fact I never heard him speak at all. It could—it could have been the very first moment, when they were shooting at us before we even left the prison yard, or any time until we left them behind when we crossed the river."

There was a clatter of boots on the stones, and Etienne came round the back of the coach. He looked pale and very wet. There was blood on the sleeve of his coat, but he seemed otherwise unharmed.

Sebastien felt a surge of relief, and then instant guilt. He took the torch from Philippe and went to the coach, the door still swinging open as Nicolette had left it, and peered in.

De Fleury was half lying on the seat, the cape Sebastien had put round him in the prison crumpled, covering his body, his legs buckled as if he had been thrown violently when the coach had lurched from side to side as the horses careered through the darkness, shots screaming past them, thudding into the wood and ricocheting from the walls of the buildings on either side.

Sebastien held the torch higher so he could see de Fleury's face. With his other hand he moved the cloak aside. There was no mistaking death. The wide-open, sightless eyes were already glazed. He looked oddly surprised, as if in spite of all the terror of the prison, and then the sudden escape, the flight and the shooting of the guards behind him, he had not expected it.

Nicolette was close behind him. He handed her the torch and she held it, shaking a little, the light wavering, so he could use both hands to move de Fleury.

"What are we going to do with him?" she asked over his shoulder.

He had not yet thought as far as that. Other failures had stopped far earlier, before they had ever reached the prisoners, or else very soon after. Once before they had fled in rout, but the prisoner had remained behind, to face the guillotine. Decent disposal of the corpse had not been their responsibility. There were no churches open since the edict, and no priests in Paris openly. Religion was outlawed. You could go to the guillotine simply for harbouring a priest, let alone indulging in the rites of the faith.

Yet they could not simply leave him. They had offered him freedom, and now he was dead.

"I'll smuggle him outside Paris, as we were going to." It was Etienne's voice from the yard, behind Nicolette, his face wet in the torchlight, but he was beginning to regain his composure. "I'll bury him somewhere on the road to Calais." He grimaced. "At least that's better than a common grave with the other victims of the day's execution. Better a quiet coach ride toward Calais than a drive through the street mobs in a tumbrel."

"Yes, you'd better do that," Sebastien agreed. "Thank you." He leaned forward to straighten the cloak, to lift it and cover the face. In spite of the thousands who had died in the city since the storming of the Bastille nearly three years ago, the small gestures of decency still mattered—or perhaps because of them.

Etienne mistook his intention.

"Leave him there," he said quickly. "I'll take him out before dawn. Better in the dark. I'll make it look as if he's sleeping."

"Good," Sebastien acknowledged. "Thank you." He looked a moment longer at de Fleury's dead face. He felt guilty. Perhaps this death was better than the guillotine with all its deliberate horror, but that was little comfort now. They had still let him down. How had it happened? As always, no one else had known anything of their plans. They had been made only the night before. Why had the guard come back, and then followed them out to challenge them?

"I'm sorry," he whispered to de Fleury. He should leave him sitting up a little better. There was no point. It was a meaningless thing to do, but he still did it. It lent a kind of dignity.

Then he saw the hole in the back of the seat where the musket ball had come through. What an irony that the one ball that had penetrated through, instead of merely splintering the wood and lodging in the upholstery, should have gone straight to his heart. There was blood on the seat, dark and shiny. Sebastien put his finger to the neat round hole, then froze. He had touched the ball, embedded in the wadding. That was impossible!

His mind whirled, bombarded with realizations that ended in one terrible, irreversible fact. De Fleury had been shot from the front, from inside the coach! That could only be either Nicolette or Etienne—or just conceivably Jacques, if he had somehow tied the reins for a few moments and swung down from the box, and in the confusion and the dark Nicolette had not seen him.

But why? Why on earth would any of them, people he had trusted with his life over and over again, kill de Fleury?

Nicolette was standing at his elbow, still holding the torch. Etienne was still waiting.

"Yes," Sebastien said steadily, moving back and away from the carriage door. He slammed it shut, turning to face them. Nicolette lowered the torch. It must be getting heavy. "Yes, that's a good idea." He did not know what else to say. The question roared around in his head—which one of them—and why?

He did not want to know. The friendships were too deep and too precious. The betrayal was hideous. But he had to know. The suspicion would stain them all, and worse than that, they could no longer trust any life to whoever had done this. It explained the guard's return, the shots, everything else.

It was still raining. They were all standing there watching him. Nicolette, her hair wet across her brow, her clothes sticking to her, her dress sodden; Etienne with his arm still bleeding, holding it across his chest now, to ease the weight of it; Jacques frightened and puzzled; Philippe beginning, as usual, to get cross. He had been waiting for them since they left, not knowing what had happened.

Sebastien forced himself to smile. "Let's go inside and at least have something hot to drink. I don't know about the rest of you, but I'm frozen!"

There was a sigh of relief, a release of long-held tension. As one, they turned and followed him toward the light and the warmth.

Sebastien slept from sheer exhaustion, but when he woke in the morning, late and with his head pounding, the question returned almost instantly. One of them had killed de Fleury, coldly and deliberately. When the rescue had succeeded, in spite of the betrayal of the plan to the guards, they had shot him in the coach as they fled through the night.

How? None of them had taken a gun into the prison. It would have been suicidal. It must have been left in the coach, against the eventuality of the escape not being foiled by the guards. That still meant that any of the three of them could have done it, Jacques most easily—he had obtained the coach, that had been his task. But it would have been very hard for him to have left the box and come into the coach to perform the act. When they were in a straight road, Nicolette would have been likely to have seen him.

Nicolette would have found it the easiest. It was she who had ridden in the coach alone with de Fleury. When had she put the gun there? He sat at the table in his rooms eating a breakfast of hot chocolate and two slices of bread. It was stale, but bread was scarce these days, and expensive. He went over the events of the previous day, from the time Jacques had brought the coach until they had left from the prison of La Force.

There was no time when Nicolette had been alone. She had helped Philippe with the forged papers, getting them exactly right, and then she had been with Sebastien himself.

The question that remained was why? Why would Etienne have wished de Fleury dead? How did he even know him? If he had some bitter enmity with him, why had he not simply said so, and refused to be part of the rescue?

There was no alternative but to confront him with the evidence and demand the truth, at the same time hoping against reason that there was some explanation that did not damn him.

It was early evening when Sebastien knocked on the door of Etienne's rooms in the rue de Seine. He had put it off all day, but it could wait no longer.

The door swung open and Etienne stood in the entrance, smiling.

"Sebastien!" he said with surprise and apparent pleasure. "Not another rescue? It must be someone very important for you to try now, so soon after this fiasco."

"No, not another escape," Sebastien replied quietly. "An answer, if you have one."

Etienne's fair eyebrows shot up. "To what?"

"To why you betrayed us to the guard, and when that didn't work, why you shot de Fleury."

Etienne stood motionless, his eyes unblinking. Seconds ticked by before he spoke. He measured Sebastien's nerve, weighed their friendship and all that they had shared, the dangers, the exultation of success and the bitterness of failures, and knew denial was no use.

"How did you know?" he said finally.

"The ball was still in the hole behind him. He was shot from in front."

"Careless of me," Etienne said with a very slight shrug. "I didn't see it. Thought it would be so far embedded in the wadding you'd never find it."

"I wouldn't have, if I hadn't put my finger in."

Etienne still had not moved. "Why not Nicolette? She was in there with him."

"You left the gun in the carriage . . . in case. She had no chance to do that."

"I see."

"Why?" Sebastien asked. "What was de Fleury to you?"

Etienne moved backward into the room, an elegant room with mementos of a more precious age, when it was still acceptable to be * aristocrat, and have a coat of arms. One hung on the farther wall, two crossed swords beneath it.

"Nothing," Etienne replied. "Or to you either . . . compared with our friendship." He was not begging; there was something almost like amusement in his eyes, and regret, but no fear.

Then suddenly he darted backward with startling speed. His arm swung up and he grasped one of the swords from the wall and in an instant was facing Sebastien with it held low and pointing at him, ready to lunge. There was sadness in his eyes, but no wavering at all. He meant death, and he had both the will and the art to accomplish it.

They faced each other for a fraction of time so small it was barely measurable, and then Sebastien threw himself to one side and scrambled to his feet as Etienne lunged forward. The blade ripped the chair open where a second before he had been standing.

There was no weapon for Sebastien. The other sword was still on the wall, ten feet away and behind Etienne. There was a silver candlestick on the table near the wall to his left. He dived toward it and his hand closed over it as Etienne darted forward again. The blade flickered like a shaft of light, drawing a thin thread of blood from Sebastien's arm and sending a sheet of pain through his flesh.

He parried it with the candlestick, but it was a poor defense, and he knew from Etienne's face that it would last only moments. The sword was twelve inches longer, lighter, and faster.

His only chance was to throw the candlestick. Yet once it was out of his hands he had nothing left. He must work his way around until he could snatch the other sword. But if that was obvious to him, then it would be to Etienne also.

He picked up a light chair with his other hand, and threw it. It barely interrupted Etienne's balance, but it did bring Sebastien a yard nearer to the wall and the sword.

"You're wasting your time, Sebastien," Etienne said quietly, but for all the lightness of his voice, there was pain in it. He would not have had it come to this, but when he had to choose between himself and another, then it would always be himself. "I'm a better swordsman than you'll ever be. I'm an aristocrat, for whatever that's worth. I was born to the saddle and the sword. Don't fight me, and I'll make it quick . . . clean."

Sebastien picked up a Sevres vase and threw it at him.

"Damn! You shouldn't have broken that, you bloody barbarian!"

Etienne said with disgust. He slashed and caught Sebastien a glancing blow across the other arm, ripping his shirt and drawing another thin line of beaded blood.

Sebastien jumped over the footstool and dived for the other sword. Etienne saw what he was aiming for and leaped after him, but his foot caught the stool and he crashed down, saving himself by putting out his other hand. Had he not fallen, he would have speared Sebastien through the chest.

Sebastien tore the weapon off its mounting and faced him just as he rose to his feet again. The blades clashed, crossed, withdrew, and clashed again. They swayed back and forth, dodging the furniture, first one slipping, then the other. Sebastien was stronger and he had the longer reach, but Etienne had by far the greater skill. It could only be a matter of time until he saw the fatal advantage, and Sebastien knew it.

There had been far too much death already. Paris was reeking with death and the fear of death. There was so much that was good in Etienne, far more than in many that were still alive. He had courage, gaiety, imagination, the gift for inspiring others to give of their best, to rise above what they had thought they were and find new heights.

Then Sebastien again saw in his mind's eye the surge of hope in de Fleury's face when he knew why they had come to La Force, the gratitude, and then the surprise of death as he knew he was betrayed.

He stepped back and with all his strength tore one of the tapestries off the wall and threw it at Etienne. Etienne swore, as much for the damage to the fabric as anything else. He ducked so that it did not entangle him, and at the same moment Sebastien lunged forward and sideways and his blade sank deep into flesh. Etienne fell, taking the sword with him, blood staining his shirt in a dark tide.

Sebastien stood still, looking down at him. There was surprise in his victory, and no pleasure at all, not even any satisfaction. Etienne was dead with the single thrust.

Sebastien pulled out the blade and let it fall toward the body. He felt empty except for an overwhelming sadness, a heaviness inside him as if he could hardly carry his own weight.

As he had with de Fleury the night before, he bent to the body; only this was different, this was a man who had been his friend, a man he himself had killed. He wanted to say something, but all that filled his mind was, "Why?" Why could a man like Etienne have shot de Fleury?

Why could he not have told Sebastien, if de Fleury were some bitter enemy from the past?

Then he saw the paper in Etienne's pocket, just a small edge poking out. He pulled it, then opened it up. It was a large sheet of high-quality vellum, written in a copperplate hand. It appeared to be a legal document, but quite short, taking up only two-thirds of the page. After it were a dozen or more signatures.

He began to read:

Versailles, 5th June 1785

I, Maximilien Honore de Fleury, Vicomte de Lauzun, do herewith offer myself and all I have in solemn covenant with Satan, Lord of Darkness and of Lies, Master of Destruction, King of the Nether World, and Heir Apparent of this earth and all that is in it, that I may be of service to him in the seduction of innocence, the indulgence of appetite, the sacrifice of human flesh to his will, and the bending of minds to his dominion. For my loyalty to his cause he will reward me with pleasure and riches here, endless sensation and variety, and hereafter a place among the Lords of his Kingdom.

I pledge my soul to this cause, and write my name in my own blood . . . Maximilien Honore de Fleury.

In witness to this covenant we fellow servants of his Satanic Majesty do sign our names beneath:

Jean Sylvain Marie Dessalines
Jean Marie Victor Coritot
Stanislas Marie Delabarre
Donatien Royou
Joseph Augustin Barere
Etienne Jacques Marie du Bac
Ignace Georges Legendre

He stared at the page, unable to believe it. Etienne had been witness to this grotesque piece of . . . of what? Did these men really believe they had made a pact with the devil? Perhaps in 1785 it had seemed some kind of effete joke. Now no one joked about the devil, he was only too real. The stench of his breath was everywhere and the mark of his hand shriveled the heart.

People had turned on each other, killing and being killed. That Etienne, of all people, ironic, graceful, and brave, should have taken de Fleury's life to protect this grubby secret was tragic above all. If he had told Sebastien about it, Sebastien would have taken the paper from de Fleury, and made him promise on his life to keep silence. He could hardly tell his hosts in England of Etienne's complicity without exposing his own, and destroying his welcome also.

Sebastien shivered, cold through to his bones. Perhaps that was how pacts with the devil worked—you lost sight of the stupidity of evil, and the ultimate sanity of good. You destroyed yourself—unnecessarily.

He put the letter in his pocket. He would burn it when he got home. He turned round and went out of the door and closed it softly behind him.

THE BEST SORT OF HUSBAND

Susan B. Kelly

Susan B. Kelly's disarmingly witty entry to the Mystery Writers of America's Fiftieth Anniversary Short Story Contest (1994), like the real works of the heroine of the piece, Jane Austen, is as much a depiction of the manners of the time as it is a story about the lives of her characters. The piece took third place in the contest, which received hundreds of submissions from many parts of the world. To keep to the voice of her facetious narrator while working in all the details that make a mystery is a difficult undertaking that Kelly carried off with style.

A single woman with a very narrow income must be a ridiculous, disagreeable old maid.

EMMA

M y brothers, as you know, Jane, are quite desperate to be rid of me."

I nodded. I did know. I could even see their point. There is no condition worse than impoverished gentility. A lesser man might take himself into trade, forging his own vulgar riches and buying Nottingham lace by the yard for his wife. But a *gentleman*—one who has been to a good school and kept his terms at Oxford—is restricted in his choice of career: the army, the church, the law. None of these pays well since they are professions for gentlemen and assume a modest—or, preferably, immodest—private income.

It is, in short, a circular problem, since a gentleman without family money and property cannot earn a living as a gentleman—not if he wants to hunt.

It's a paradox which has vexed finer minds than mine and I do not intend to waste any more time on it.

It brings us, however, to the Crampton family and my visitor that day, Miss (Margaret) Crampton. She was the eldest of the four Crampton children and the only girl. Colonel Crampton had died ten years ago—an incident with a shotgun which had made the coroner harrumph a lot before returning an "Accidental" verdict. He had left some impressive debts of honour of which Mrs. Crampton had, until that moment, been happily oblivious.

Her family had reluctantly and meanly rallied round, obliging that lady, who was not a good manager at the best of times, to provide as well as she could for Mr. John, Mr. Richard, and Mr. George and—bottom of the pile, left to the sweepings, the gleanings, when all the rest had been seen to—poor dear Margaret.

Margaret, who had never had much hope of a husband, even before her father's disgrace.

It was not that she was exactly plain: Indeed, I found it hard to account for the fact that she was not at least as handsome as myself. Her features were regular enough—her nose not too long and sharp, as mine is, her eyes a soft and pretty grey, her mouth large and gentle and disinclined to sarcastic remarks, which is a good thing in a woman in need of a husband—but there was something undistinguished about the ensemble, something that made sure no eligible gentleman looked twice.

She had a good, fresh colour to her cheeks that morning and her soft, if overly fine, hair of that pale shade which is not unlike straw, and which was always inclined to escape from her bonnet at ill-timed moments of agitation and exertion, was threatening almost to tumble about her shoulders.

She had taken her bonnet off altogether, since we were old friends and very confidential. She looked sadly at it as it lay on her lap like a dead dog; it was old and shabby, although she dutifully trimmed it anew each spring.

We were sitting in the front parlour, the one with the creaking door which gives me warning of sudden eavesdroppers—maids coming in to shake dusters about ineffectually or Mama fretting over what to order from the butcher for dinner.

In fact, Mama and dear Cassandra had gone out to bully some of the local poor into being less feckless—indeed, less *poor*—and my guest and I were alone in the house—except for the servants, obviously.

She had agreed to take a dish of tea with me.

"It's not that I have anything against Mr. Bailey," she went on. "He is a gentleman of good fortune, it seems, and refined education. His manners are not objectionable. He has a good address."

"He lives in Curzon Street, I understand, and in Dorset."

"I meant," she said witheringly, "that he has a good upright bearing."

"Oh."

Well, it's an easy mistake to make. And Curzon Street *is* a good address, all the same. As is several hundred acres of Dorset.

"He's not even all that bad-looking," I ventured, "or so I've heard."

She shrugged. "In fact there is much to be said for him and his offer."

And single women have such a dreadful propensity for being poor, as I remarked to dear Cassandra just the other day, possibly not for the first time, since a well-turned phrase bears repeating.

"But we know so little of him," Margaret went on, "and now he turns up asking me to marry him, and John and Richard and George are determined to make sure I say 'Yes,' and will make my life a misery if I refuse him, unless I can come up with a really *sound* reason for doing so.

"You see, Jane," she concluded. "I *like* being single."

I sighed in sympathy, although I wasn't sure whom—principally— with. I can see that there is no greater burden for a young man than a plain and fading spinster sister, raised to do nothing useful but know a little French and point out India on a globe, draw a passable imitation of a landscape with three-legged cows, and bang out a few tunes on a twenty-guinea pianoforte.

It was hardly surprising, therefore, that John (etc.) had seized on Mr. Thomas Bailey like a good angel from heaven. Margaret was twenty-nine, after all, and getting to that time of life when ladies are assumed to be fast gathering dust on the shelf.

Gentlemen, I have noticed, seem to think that one husband is as good to their sister as another, so long as he's got money in the bank and the right sort of relations and doesn't spit in the street. They do not think a woman should have irrational prejudices in preferring Mr. James to Mr. Henry, or sandy hair to black, or a cavalry moustache to a clean lip.

Still, the temptation was always there: one's own home, a dress allowance, the superior title of "Mrs."; with the right sort of husband it was not to be lightly spurned. With the best sort of husband.

The question was, though: What was in it for Mr. Thos. Bailey?

"You are lucky, Jane," Margaret was saying, "in not being in such a precarious position."

Which I was, I readily admit. True, my sainted father had also died early (although not by his own hand!) and I had as fair a share of brothers as a girl might wish—rather more than Margaret, indeed—in addition to my elder sister Cassandra.

Like Margaret, I had no money of my own with which to buy a husband and, also like her, no real wish to possess such a commodity.

The crucial difference between us was that my brother Edward had been adopted in infancy by my rich and childless cousin, Mr. Knight, and had now come into his inheritance and was in a position, therefore, to offer Mama and us two spinster girls this small but comfortable cottage in the village of Chawton for as long as we should require it, and to guarantee us against starvation.

Which was just as well, since anybody less well equipped than I to go a-governessing is hard to imagine. I can see myself running amok and laying about me with a stick at all the Miss Julias and Miss Matildas that are inflicted on me; then being sent home on the first post chaise in disgrace, having broken Master Peter's pate when he answered me back.

"He is thirty-five," Margaret continued, musing almost to herself, "claims to have a clear four thousand a year. There are two children, of course. A boy and a girl."

"Yes," I said, since this was partly the point at issue. "What exactly did happen to his first two wives?"

It's not at all unusual, of course, to lose one wife in childbed, or to consumption, or any one of the thousand natural shocks that flesh is heir to, which is why middle-aged spinsters never lose hope, since there are always gentlemen coming back, as it were, on the market, only slightly shop-soiled. Occasionally they take the opportunity to marry some pretty young flibbertigibbet, but usually they want someone older and steadier, someone who will be a housekeeper and mother to their little orphans without producing more mouths to feed and backs to clothe and brains to cram with useless facts.

Two, though? Bad luck at the very least. And yet . . . if Margaret had been an heiress it would make sense, but she was not, far from it.

"He has gone on to Bath," my friend said, "and is coming back at the end of the month for my answer."

I began to see.

"I thought that since you, my dear Jane, are leaving for Bath at the end of the week . . ." She broke out suddenly, quite wringing her poor bonnet with her hands. "Oh, how I wish I could go to Bath! To spend the winter there in gaiety! What I would give!"

"But what am I to do? I'm not some sort of *spy*, Margaret."

"Just talk to his acquaintances. Watch him. Observe him at your leisure, and at his. Find out for me what measure of man this is that I am to tie myself to on such slight knowledge. Or, better still, give me a good reason—some vice, some sordid secret—" she lowered her eyes and her voice demurely, keeping up the seemly pretence that we single women know nothing of such matters "—some *woman* of the lower orders living under his protection—that will allow me to hang onto my respectable spinster state without fraternal reproach."

Well, I could hardly say no, could I?

But are they all horrid, are you sure they are all horrid?

NORTHANGER ABBEY

As chance would have it, I found myself that Friday being gallantly escorted to Bath by Mr. Richard Crampton, who had business at the Assize session the following week. Mr. Dick was the middle son, now twenty-four and a barrister, having qualified for this role in life by taking a degree at Oxford and eating the requisite amount of dinners at Gray's Inn.

I prayed earnestly that I would never have need of his services. It was to be hoped, for the sake of his future progress in his sphere, that he stood far enough away from the judge to spare him his bad breath.

Me, he did not spare.

Like all the brothers, Dick was a thickset, florid, somewhat *lumbering* young man of not above middle height. His sandy hair limped out from under his hat and hung over his meagre eyes with their invisible lashes. He had little conversation beyond horses, politics, and the recent wars against the French. Of the poems of Sir Walter Scott and the novels of Mrs. Fanny Burney or Mrs. Radcliffe, he had no opinion.

Of himself, he had a very good opinion.

He was a commonplace young man, like every young man I have ever met, except perhaps one, and he is dead. I am glad that, at almost forty, I may finally be considered safe from any matrimonial consideration whatsoever and may assume the chaperone's role by the fire with a glass of warm wine, although there was a time, when we first moved to Chawton, when I might have been induced to marry the Reverend Mr. Papillon, purely for the pleasure of being Mrs. Butterfly.

I was never put to the test, however, Mr. Papillon being very set on maintaining his bachelor state.

And all of which is quite beside the point.

Mr. Dick drove competently. The journey seemed to take forever.

He was inordinately proud of the fact that Captain John Crampton had been wounded in the leg at the battle of Vitoria three months earlier. I couldn't help thinking that Master Jack, had he been quicker on his feet, and a bit less *lumbering,* might have dodged the French sabre or musket or whatever it was, but I did not say so.

It was hardly *new* news, anyway. I know the latest excitement often takes a long time to reach our quiet corner of Hampshire, but John Crampton had been sitting at home with his leg up on a stool since mid-July and it was now early September. I had already heard several times how he had personally put Buonaparté's forces to rout and had had to throw a fake faint last time the story threatened.

Luckily, the Crampton brothers are the sort of men who are always expecting women to faint on them. Except for maidservants, obviously.

We finally lapsed into silence and I was able to peruse the volume of Cowper I had brought along with me for the journey in peace.

Young Mr. George, by the way, had opted for the church and had become positively unctuous since being ordained the previous summer. If all three brothers had gone into the same profession, of course, they might have helped each other on, but were they bright enough to think of that?

Were they—!

Although I suppose, between the three of them, they had everything pretty well covered.

Dear Margaret was worth more than all of them put together, and I was determined to help her out of her predicament if I could.

I loathe Bath, as everybody knows, but I had not been in the best of health all summer and Mama would simply not hear of my turning down the invitation to spend a few weeks in Queen Square with my brother Edward, and with Fanny, Lizzy, Marianne, and the rest of his girls, to bathe and drink daily in the spa.

At least this time I had something to keep me occupied. So no sooner had I settled in and supervised the unpacking of my trunk and the disposition of my gowns, than I donned a pair of pattens as insurance against mud, took my new pelisse in case it turned cold and a parasol against sudden sun, and, thus prepared for all eventualities, announced that I was just taking a brisk walk to the Pump Room to see if any of my acquaintance was in town.

I successfully fended off all offers to accompany me . . . except those of my brother Henry, who was still mourning the loss of his wife Eliza six months earlier and whom I had not the heart to gainsay.

Henry was no trouble as an escort, in fact, having little to say for himself these days and a great deal of sighing to do, which enabled us to proceed on our way in companionable silence. I was slightly surprised that he had chosen to bring his wounded heart to a bustling social place like Bath, but I knew that since Eliza's death he had been besieged by eager spinsters who could spot a well-to-do, gentlemanlike widower across thirty miles and without spectacles and who had no compunction about moving in for the kill. No doubt he had left Chelsea to escape from a particularly persistent specimen.

I had no difficulty in spotting Mr. Bailey at the Pump Room, since he was in the company of Richard Crampton, the two seeming very confidential. They were together too at the concert at the Assembly Rooms that evening and to be seen walking arm in arm in the Circus the following morning. They were like Mary and her wretched lamb, in that everywhere Mr. Bailey went, Mr. Dick was sure to go.

Presumably he was making sure that Bailey didn't change his mind about marrying Margaret or get entrapped by some widow of a certain age and uncertain income while no one was looking.

I contrived an introduction in the Lower Rooms the next afternoon, although Mr. Dick looked as if he would have avoided it if he could, mumbling my name and the apologetic, "A neighbour in Chawton." I then had a strained conversation with Mr. Bailey about the latest uses of electricity to treat gout, from which ailment, he hastened to assure me, he did not suffer. As I did not suffer from it either, the subject did not seem to be leading anywhere very fruitful.

An everyday sort of man, I concluded, as would make a respectable husband for a poor spinster and leave a bit over. His complexion was a little pockmarked when you got close up, but you would cease to notice that by the end of the wedding journey. He might be growing a little stout under his waistcoat, but what can you expect at five and thirty? At least the waistcoat itself was tastefully restrained—plain white marcella—which is by no means guaranteed these days, what with HRH the Prince Regent and his ornate friend Mr. Brummell setting the fashion.

He didn't have the ruddy complexion or well-veined nose of a two-bottles-of-claret-a-day man, and his hands, as he offered to lead me back to my seat after the interval, were the pale, soft, well-kept sort you don't associate with vice. I was beginning to think that I could be of no use to my friend in discovering Mr. Bailey's guilty secret.

Where so many hours have been spent in convincing myself that I am right, is there not some reason to fear I may be wrong?

SENSE AND SENSIBILITY

Henry seemed to take a fancy to him, though, and soon the two of them were swopping gloomy stories of dead wives over the foul-tasting water in the Pump Room every morning. I had not taken my brother into my confidence, but took the opportunity every evening to pump *him* in turn about what his new friend had said to him.

Henry's opinion was that Tom Bailey was a lonely, affectionate man, unlucky to have lost two wives in only ten years, who just wanted a nice woman to share his house and sit at the foot of his table, who needn't be handsome so long as she was good-natured and kind to his children and brought a few thousand pounds in the four percents to pay for her own keep.

Which was part of the problem: Margaret would be lucky to have two hundred pounds of her own and that not until Mrs. Crampton was dead. I did not mention this to Henry, who was not acquainted with the Crampton family or their situation.

So it was in his capacity as Henry's friend that Mr. Bailey was invited to a small private ball at Queen Square about ten days later. Mr. Richard Crampton, who was still in Bath despite the Assize being long over, was also invited as a Chawton man and my friend's brother. The Reverend George Crampton, who had recently arrived in town and who did not allow his clerical orders to prevent him from dancing *(lumberingly)* and drinking, had apparently invited himself.

Henry threw his head into his hands at the very mention of dancing and gaiety and determined not to attend, but Edward wasn't going to let that spoil anyone else's fun, and I personally was looking forward to tripping a measure and showing off my new spotted muslin . . . and exposing my bosom with the best of them.

I cannot imagine what it is like to lose a beloved spouse, of course, although I grieved long and hard for my father in the year five, but it seemed to me that Henry, who is of a naturally optimistic disposition, was beginning to show signs of recovering spirits and might have been badgered into attending the festivities had anyone tried hard enough, but as no one could be bothered, he was stuck with his original insistence that it would be too painful for him.

I was not particularly surprised, therefore, to find him hanging around in the anteroom to the best drawing room halfway through the evening, sipping punch and observing without being observed from behind a purple velvet curtain. I had danced every dance and was feeling tired, especially having had my left ankle repeatedly kicked by the Rev. George in the quadrille, so took the chance to sit with him for a while.

So it was in this manner, as in all the best novels of Mrs. Fanny Burney and Mrs. Radcliffe, that we came to overhear one of those odd and illuminating conversations that seem to occur only in books, this one being between Richard and George Crampton, carried out with the utmost safety—as they thought—under cover of the hubbub.

"Has Margaret been brought to consent?" asked Dick.

"Not yet, but she will, with promises of new bonnets and threats of our displeasure. It is for her own good, after all, and it's not as if she will have to tolerate him for very long."

"But she doesn't know that, and must not. My sister is a woman of such high moral principle, such refined and truly delicate and feminine sensibilities—"

"Yes, yes," George interrupted him. "How is the groom, more to the point?"

"Happily convinced that my father secreted a large fortune in gold and gems before his . . ."

"Accident."

"Quite. In a place where his creditors would never find them."

"Thus enabling us to provide Margaret with a suitable marriage portion. Have you drawn up the settlement?"

"I have."

"And is it watertight?"

"It is. The children will have to be provided for on his death, of course, but my sister will still be a very wealthy widow. He has no close family to kick up a fuss, as you know."

(I have noticed that these sorts of conversations in books always usefully have people telling other people things they already know.)

"Splendid!" George rubbed his hands together and I could hear the slap of sweat. Wet-palmed George, the Cramptons' maidservants called him when they thought no one was listening, and they should know. "Then I shall carry out the wedding service, quietly and discreetly as befits a double widower and an ageing spinster, then—"

"Then," Dick concluded for him, "the lawyer will have done his bit and the rector will have done his bit and it remains only for the 'wounded' soldier to do his bit."

"Which no one will suspect since our hero is laid up at home with a bad cut in the leg from the cowardly Frenchies and cannot leave the house."

They both laughed, and a few minutes later I heard them move off, back into the dance.

Well, I did say they had everything covered between the three of them. Pity there wasn't a fourth brother who was a doctor, to attest that there had been no foul play, and a fifth who was an undertaker—not that either of those was a suitable career for a *gentleman*.

I glanced at Henry to see how much he had heard or understood, but he was miles away.

"Eliza was always at her loveliest at social gatherings," he bleated. "I fell in love with her at such a private ball as this, all dressed in white, her glorious hair in those . . . curl things women used to wear in the nineties."

He began to cry.

"Henry?"

He hiccupped. "Yes, Jane?"
Too much punch.

I wrote to Margaret by the next post, laying all before her. I did feel rather pleased with myself at having succeeded in carrying out my commission and with such speed, although naturally I played down the role of good fortune in revealing the plot to me and emphasised my own skill and wit. Margaret could now confront her brothers with their iniquity or, perhaps, just rid herself of Mr. Bailey by letting drop the fact that there was no secret treasure, no dowry.

The confrontation need not be long delayed, since the Crampton brothers left Bath four days later, taking Mr. Bailey with them to get their sister's answer. I rather wished he might know to whom he owed his deliverance, but there was no real hope of that, and I got on with my holiday-cum-rest-cure, walking about with Henry and visiting the theatre and taking a little chaise out to Clifton one day.

I was surprised to receive a letter from Cassandra two weeks later, arriving the very day of my own departure from Bath. I thought any news she had to convey might have awaited my return. But this was too new, too exciting; she could not contain herself.

I learnt to my astonishment that Margaret Crampton and Mr. Bailey had been married by special license just five days earlier. So my dear friend had come to like him after all, chosen to accept his offer and link her destiny with his.

Of all the dreadful luck.

It was with sinking heart that I read on. I was sadly not at all astonished to learn that Mr. Bailey had met with a fatal accident while out riding the very next day. He had been quite alone, according to Cassandra, taking an early run on one of Mr. Jack's best hunters, which was in sore need of exercise with its master laid up.

"The poor creature must have bolted and stumbled into a rabbit hole," my sister wrote, "throwing its rider unconscious onto his head.

"If anyone had been with him, of course, something might have been done, but it was several hours before anyone feared for his safety and set out to look for him, and by then it was too late."

Cassandra, my dear kindhearted sister, was distraught on Margaret's behalf, imagining her sorrow and dismay, widowed not four and twenty hours after her wedding breakfast.

How, I wondered, could my letter have so tragically miscarried? The post was usually reliable. I blamed myself; I was in anguish. By what cruel fate had Margaret not been warned in time?

A large income is the best recipe for happiness I ever heard of. It certainly may secure all the myrtle and turkey part of it.

Mansfield Park

The hasty funeral was over and the new widow away in London by the time I reached home, so I was none the wiser and still full of self-doubt. I watched the post daily as it came to the Cramptons' mean house along the Winchester Road, expecting to see my letter, inexplicably delayed, arriving too horribly late. I wondered if there was any means of intercepting it, since for her to read it now . . .

It was not to be thought of.

She was dealing with the house in Curzon Street—although one would have expected Richard to volunteer for this sad task—consulting her husband's bankers and men of law and disposing sensibly of the poor children to boarding school.

She did not return for a month, and when she did I scarcely knew my friend, so stiff and formal had she become, actually *curtseying* to me instead of shaking my hand.

I remembered to call her Mrs. Bailey, although she hardly seemed entitled to the name after such a short tenure, and noticed that her gown, while obviously the deepest mourning, was also the latest style and the best silk. She had equipped herself with a little carriage, too, with the prettiest pair of ponies you ever saw and a footman in scarlet livery.

"Dear Jane." She unbent a little and took my hand as I murmured my shocked condolences. "How good it is to see you again. Always the dearest friend, always the best of *correspondents.*"

She moved to Bath herself soon after, and I occasionally see her there in the distance, out of mourning now and dressed in the height of fashion, surrounded by beaus and sycophants and flatterers, dining with the best people, reserving the most expensive box at the theatre for her exclusive use.

She has a new bonnet every week.

She has not remarried since she was, as she had told me, very satisfied with the unmarried state, and since widows, unlike spinsters, were not so very inclined to be poor. She seemed more than satisfied with her lot, having procured for herself the very best sort of husband.

She always waves if she sees me, although often she does not seem to see me, which is just as well, I think, since I am the only one outside the family who knows the truth and she is the only one who knows that I know and I value my skin as much as the next woman.

I have nothing more to say on this subject. I have novels to write. I think I shall set one in Bath one day, although there will not be any murders in it since murders are not my thing.

Fiction, whatever anyone says, is always much stranger than truth.

TRAVELLER FROM AN ANTIQUE LAND

Avram Davidson

Following hard on the heels of Jane Austen, a second literary eminence joins our cast, the romantic and mysterious poet Percy Bysshe Shelley. The author of the piece is an acclaimed science fiction writer whose contributions to the mystery field, though not numerous, were distinguished. (Avram Davidson died in 1993.) Shelley's poem "Ozymandias," from which Davidson's story takes its title, is printed on the last page of the story.

It was in April 1822, on the third day after his friend had sailed off into a lead-grey, oil-smooth sea only a few hours before the storm broke, that Tregareth, fearing the worst, made his way to Lord Gryphon's villa, to consult with him. Was not Gryphon the nominal head of the English *literati* hereabouts?

The time was past noon, Gryphon had already had his cup of strong green tea, and was lunching on the invariable biscuit and soda water as he lay abed. He looked up when the tall figure entered, long black hair in disarray, striking his fist into palm.

"Surely there is *some* news, Tregareth," Gryphon said. "Are they safe? Have they been . . . *found?*"

Tregareth shook his head. "I have no news, my lord," he said, trying to mask his agitation with formality. "Every vessel putting into Leghorn has been questioned, but there has been no sign of the *Sea Sprite,* of Shadwell or Wilson or the ship's boy. I thought that you might have had a letter, or at least a note, from their wives at the Villa Grandi, saying that they had arrived."

"I have had nothing!" Gryphon cried.

"Fulke Grant has heard no word, either. He blames himself, poor fellow—'It was to welcome me and get me settled that they sailed to Leghorn,' he says."

"Oh God, Tregareth!" Gryphon moaned, covering his fat, pale face with a trembling hand. "They have been drowned! They have surely been drowned!"

Tregareth, looking away from him, turning his gaze out of the window to the hot sandy plain, said sturdily, "It does not follow, my lord. Not at all. I conceive of at least two other possibilities—no, three. First, they may have been carried away off course—to Elba, perhaps, or even to Corsica or Sardinia. Second, assuming the vessel *did* come to harm, which Heaven forbid—though she *was* cranky and frisky—there were so many other craft at sea that evening—" Tregareth spoke more and more rapidly, his broad chest rising and falling as his agitation increased. "Surely it is not unreasonable that they have been taken aboard one of them and are even now disembarking in some port. And, third, I fear we must also consider the possibility that a piratical felucca may have ridden them down—pretending accident, don't you know, my lord—and that presently we shall receive some elegantly worded message which in our blunter English speech spells 'ransom'!"

Gryphon had begun slowly to nod; now his face had cleared somewhat. He reached for his silver flask, poured brandy into the tiny silver cup. "What must we do?" he asked. "You have been a sailor—in fact, if we are to believe your own account of it—wilder than any tale *I* dared to write!—you have been a pirate, too. Command me, Tregareth! Eh?" He drained the cup, looking at the Cornishman with raised brows.

Ignoring, in his concern, the implication, the other man said, "I thank you, my lord. I propose, then—in your name, with your consent—to obtain the governor's permission to have the coast guards scan the beaches. Perhaps some flotsam or wreckage will give hint of—" He did not finish the sentence. Gryphon shuddered. "And also, I will have couriers sent out on the road to Nice, enquiring of news, if any, of their having reached another port. In the event of their having been captured by brigands, we must await that intelligence."

Gryphon muttered something about—in that event—the British Minister—

Tregareth's grey eyes grew fierce and angry. "Let Shadwell's *wife,* my lord, let poor Amelia appeal to the minister and to diplomacy. Let *me* but hear of where they are constrained—give me a file of dragoons—or if not, just a brace of pistols and a stiletto—I have stormed the corsair's lair before!"

"Yes, yes!" Gryphon cried. He rose from bed, thrust feet into slippers, and, with his queer, lame, gliding walk, came across the room. "And I shall go with you! This is no coward's heart which beats here—" He laid his hand on his left breast.

"I know it, my lord," the other said, touched.

And, telling him that he must make haste, Gryphon thrust a silken purse into Tregareth's hands, bade him godspeed, and gloomily prepared to dress.

The two ladies met the Cornishman with flushed cheeks—cheeks from which the color soon fled as he confessed that he brought them no news. Jane Wilson essayed a brave smile on her trembling lips, but Amelia Shadwell shrieked, pressed her palms to her head, and repeated Gryphon's very words.

"Oh God, Tregareth! They have been drowned!"

But Mrs. Wilson would not have it so. She knelt by the side of her hostess's cot in the "hall" of the Villa Grandi—a whitewashed room on the upper story, not much larger than the four small whitewashed rooms which served for bedchambers—and taking the distressed woman by the hand, began to comfort her. Wilson was an excellent sailor, she said. No harm could come to Shadwell while Wilson was aboard. The storm had lasted less than half an hour—surely not enough to injure such a stoutly built vessel as the *Sea Sprite*. Tregareth added his assurances to Jane's, with an air of confidence he did not feel.

By and by the cries gave way to moans. Amelia pressed a handkerchief to her lovely eyes and turned away her head. Tregareth would have lingered, but Jane drew him gently away. They descended the stairs together. The sea foamed and lapped almost at their feet.

For a moment they were silent, looking out over the beautiful Gulf of Spezia to the terrace. To one side was the tiny fishing village of Sant' Ursula; to the other side, a degree nearer, the equally tiny town of Lorenzi.

At length Jane spoke. "Poor, poor, dearest Amelia!" she said. "She has been far from well. It is not only her body which is weak, you know, Tregareth. She has been sick in spirit, sick at heart. It is the loss of her dear children. To bid farewell to two such sweet babes in so brief a time—no, no, Tregareth, man knows nought of what woman feels. It is too much." And so she spoke, mantling her own concern for the missing. Even when she spoke her husband's name, it was only in connection with Amelia's illness.

"Did you know, Tregareth, that scarcely more than a week ago, when she was in truth barely able to turn on her couch, that we missed her one night? Wilson found her down below, her slippers sodden and her hem drenched, and she seemed like one who walks in a dream. I have not dared to part from her for even a moment since. We had better go back—but no word of this."

Amelia smiled at them as they returned, a sad and worn little smile. "I am ready to hear what you have to tell me, now, with more composure," she said.

And so Tregareth recounted to her what he thought she might safely hear. How Shadwell and Wilson came sailing the trim little *Sea Sprite* over the wine-dark sea to greet the poet Fulke Grant and his family. How Grant and Shadwell had fallen into one another's arms for joy. How they had settled the new arrivals in satisfactory quarters. And how, finally, it was decided that the *Sea Sprite* and the *Liberator*—Lord Gryphon's vessel—would return together, with Tregareth captaining the latter, while Gryphon stayed behind.

"Oh, why did you not do so, Tregareth?" cried Amelia Shadwell. "With a skilled sea captain such as you to convey them—"

It was the fault of the harbormaster, Tregareth explained. At the last minute he had refused clearance to the *Liberator* on some petty point or other. And so Shadwell and Wilson, by now impatient to see their wives once more, had sailed off alone, with only Antonio, the ship's boy, for crew. Not for worlds would he have told her of his fears. Of Wilson's being—for all his wife's pride—but a gentleman-sailor. Of how awkwardly Shadwell handled the craft. Of what others had said—

"Crank as an eggshell, and too much sail for those two sticks of masts," remarked the master of a Yankee ship, spitting tobacco. "She looks like a bundle of chips going to the fire."

And the *Liberator*'s first mate, a Genoa man: "They should have sailed at this hour of the morning, not the afternoon. They're standing in too close to shore—catch too much breeze. That gaff topsail is foolish in a boat with no deck and no real sailors aboard."

There had been only a slight wind. But in the southwest were dirty rags of clouds. "Smoke on the sea," said the mate, shaking his head. "A warning . . ." as the fog closed around the trim little *Sprite*. The air was sultry, hot and heavy and close. Tregareth had gone below to his cabin and fallen into a doze. He dreamed of Shadwell, his dark-fair hair only touched with grey, ruffled by the breeze, the light of genius in his eye, the look of exaltation on his face—a boy's face still, for all he was approaching thirty—a boy's fair skin and light freckles, and a boy's look of eagerness. The world had never gone stale for Archie Shadwell. . . .

Tregareth had thought, as he often did, of his own good fortune in being the friend of Shadwell and of Mrs. Shadwell; and somehow he found himself envying Wilson, who not only had a beautiful wife of his own—Tregareth's wife was dead—but the company of the beautiful Amelia Shadwell . . . and then he had fallen asleep.

And then had come the gust of wind—the *temporale,* the Italians called it—and the squall broke. It thundered and lightninged and he rushed on deck to help make all trim. In twenty minutes the storm's fury was spent, but Jane Wilson was wrong in thinking that was too brief a time for deadly damage. Twenty seconds could do for so light a boat as the *Sea Sprite*.

Thus three days had passed—three days of ceaseless enquiry. From Gryphon, Tregareth had gone directly to the governor, mentioned the name of *il milord Gryphon,* doucely slid the purse across the desk.

"A courier? As far as Nice? Of course! And the coast guards to patrol the beaches all about? Certainly!" The purse vanished. Orders were given, messengers scurried. Tregareth had left in a flurry of assurances, and come straight to the Villa Grandi.

He had intended to leave as quickly, to pursue his own search, to flag (and flog, too, if need be!) the coast guards into vigilance—for who knew if any of Gryphon's gold would trickle down to them? But Amelia would not hear of it.

"Tregareth, do not leave us!" she begged. And he, looking at her sweet face, could not refuse to tarry a little while. Jane summoned a servant to make fire for tea. Jane herself was busy pretending the matter was no more than that of, say, a diligence whose lead mule had delayed the schedule by casting a shoe; she bustled about with needles and thread. But Amelia would not play this game.

"Oh, Jane, in Heaven's name, be still," she pleaded.

"I am looking for the beeswax, to help thread my needles," Jane explained, hunting and peering. "I promised dear Shadwell to finish that embroidered shirt for him. Where can it be? Is that not strange? A great lump of unbleached beeswax—"

Amelia began to weep. "Shall he ever wear a shirt again? And this creature wants to kill me with her talk and her scurrying—"

But the next moment Tregareth himself was kneeling and holding her hand and vowing that Shadwell would live to wear out a thousand shirts, ten thousand. She smiled, allowed her tiny white hand to become engulfed in his great brown one. But she gave a little cry of pain.

"Why, what is this, Amelia?" he asked, astonished, opening her fingers, and looking at the scarce-healed marks there.

"I was sawing wood, kindling, for the fire," she said in a small voice; Jane and Tregareth exclaimed against such foolishness. There were servants. Amelia pouted. "They care nothing for me," she said. "Look at that slut, there—do you suppose she cares about me?"

The servant girl, perhaps sensing she was being mentioned, turned at that moment. She smiled. Not at all an ill-looking wench, Tregareth observed, almost abstractedly—though of course one could not even consider such coarse charms in the presence of lovely Amelia. The girl smiled. "The *signore* will soon return," she said.

Amelia spat at her, cursed, called her *puta,* struggled to rise.

"Madame!" cried Tregareth, shocked.

"She meant but to reassure you, dearest Amelia," said Jane, as the girl scuttled away, frightened.

"She did not mean to! She meant to scorn me! Does she think I am blind? Does everyone think I am blind? Do *you,* Jane?" But the hysteria passed almost as soon as it had come.

"Tregareth, forgive me," she said. "I am not well. Such sickly fancies cloud my mind. . . . Oh, I know that Shadwell must be living! So great a genius cannot die so young! No age ever had such a poet. Does not Gryphon himself agree? Was he not proud to have the little ship named after his own poem? Oh! I little thought, the day he carved his initials in her mainmast, that she would give us so much grief. . . . I have had such presentiments of evil—such a sense of oppression that I have not felt for years, not since poor Henrietta . . ."

Tregareth felt the little hairs rise on his neck. Never before had he heard the name of Shadwell's first wife mentioned in this house. It seemed—he scarcely knew why—it seemed dreadful to hear it now on Amelia's lips, on Amelia's smiling lips.

"Do you believe she drowned herself?" she asked. He could only stammer. "There are those who say—" Amelia paused.

"No one says—," began Jane.

But the sick woman smiled and shook her head. "Everyone knows of Shadwell and me, how we eloped while he was still a married man," she said dreamily. "Everyone knows that only Henrietta's death set us both free to marry. Everyone knows of Shadwell and Clara Claybourne," she continued. "First she bore Gryphon's illegitimate child, then she bore Shadwell's—everyone knows . . ." Her accusing eyes met those of Jane, who stood by, her face showing her pain. "But only you and I, Jane, know . . ." And she seemed to fall into a revery. Then she chuckled.

So pleased were they to have this sign of her mind passing to anything which had power to please her, whatever it might be, that they beamed. "Do you remember, Jane, your first night here? Were you listening? How Wilson said, 'To think that my wife and I are privileged to be guests under a roof which shelters two such rare geniuses! Archie, the author of that exquisite poem, *Deucalion,* and Amelia, the author of the great novel, *Koenigsmark*—' Do you remember, Jane, what Shadwell said?"

"I did not hear, dear Amelia. What did he say?"

"He said, '*Koenigsmark!* Ha-ha!' "

For days Tregareth rode the shores, scanning the waves, the scent of the salt sea never out of his nostrils. Some few bits of flotsam from the *Sea Sprite* had come ashore, but this was not proof positive. However, he no longer had doubts. He drove himself, unrelenting, in his quest. Not only grief for his friend spurred him on now, but guilt as well.

"You have travelled so far, Tregareth," Amelia had said to him; "you are, yourself, that '*traveller from an antique land*' who brought back word of Ozymandias. In the East, of which you are so much enamored, and of which you have made me so much enamored—do they have love there, as we know it? Or—only lust?"

Tregareth had considered, throwing back his head. After a moment he said, "In the East they have that which is stronger than either love or lust. In the East they have *passion.*"

She considered this. She nodded. "Yes," she had said. "For love may fade, and lust must ever repel. *Passion*. Do not think that our English blood is too thin and cold for passion, Tregareth."

Now he asked himself, again and again, spurring through the sand, was it covetousness to desire a man's wife for your own—if the man were dead? Would not Shadwell himself have laughed at such squeamishness? Would not Gryphon?

He almost did not see the coast guard until the man called out to him. When he did see, and reined his horse, he still did not imagine. Then the man gestured, and Tregareth looked.

And there on the margin of the sea he saw him.

"There is no doubt of it being Shadwell, I suppose?" Gryphon asked.

Tregareth shook his head. "None. Shadwell's clothes and Shadwell's hair, in one pocket Shadwell's copy of *Hesiod,* and in another, his copy of Blake."

Gryphon shuddered. He looked at a letter which he held in his hand. "From Mary," he said. He began to read.

" 'You have heard me tell that my grandmother, a Scotswoman, was reputed to have been fey, and to have visualized the Prince's defeat at Culloden before it happened. I, too, at times, have had presentiments of future misfortunes. I had them at the time of poor Henrietta's death. But never so strong as during this Springtime did I feel the burden. The landscape and seascape I saw seemed not of this earth. My mind wandered so, as if enchanted, and ofttimes I was not sure—and still am not sure—if the things I saw and did were real—or were the products of an ensorcelled mind, musing on ancient wrongs; and all the time, the waves murmuring, *Doom, Doom, Doom . . .' "*

They were silent. "What shall be done with the body?" Gryphon asked. "The nearest Protestant cemetery is in Rome."

Tregareth said, "Shadwell a Protestant? If ever there lived a man who was a pagan in whole heart, body, and soul— Besides, in this weather, it is out of the question to convey the corpse to Rome."

Distressed, almost petulant, Gryphon flung out his fat hands. "But what shall we *do?"* he cried.

"He was a pagan," said Tregareth, "and shall have a pagan funeral. The Greeks knew how. And I have seen it done in India."

Gryphon began to quiver. He reached for the silver flask.

The widow received the tragic news with an agony of tears. Presently she recovered somewhat, and said, "I knew it would be so. I have had no other thought. Now he is young forever. Now," her voice trembled and fell, *"mine* forever."

They parted with a gentle embrace, she accepting Tregareth's counsel not to attend the immediate funeral. Later, he said, when a second interment would be held at Rome, if she felt stronger . . .

Tregareth's emotions, as he rode back, were mixed. In great measure his activity on Shadwell's behalf had absorbed the grief he would otherwise now be experiencing at Shadwell's death. Moreover, thoughts he had earlier suppressed rose now and had their will. Had there not been, in Shadwell's friendship for him, some measure of condescension? Had Shadwell not indicated from time to time—though less openly than Gryphon—a lack of complete belief in the stories Tregareth told of his youth in Nelson's Navy and his adventurous career as the consort of buccaneers in India?

But—sharpest of all—Shadwell was dead! And he, Tregareth, was alive! It was dreadful about the former, but it was impossible not to feel gratitude and joy in the latter. As he rode between the forest and the sea, Tregareth felt the keenness of delight in the fact that he lived and could experience all the rich pleasures of the living world.

The body had come ashore near a place called Via Vecchio. A small crowd had gathered, but the dragoons scarcely needed to hold them back. The people looked on, half fascinated, half horrified at the strange scene, and kept crossing themselves.

Tregareth was in full, undisputed charge.

"I might have spared myself the trouble of bringing wood," he said. "See—not only is the forest there full of fallen timber, but here are all these broken spars and planks cast up on the shore."

He gave directions in loud and resonant tones. The workmen dared not resist, though they looked as if they would have mightily liked to. A pyre was soon built up, and the body lifted onto it. Tregareth heaped on more wood. One piece he glanced at, put it under his arm.

Gryphon was pale and ill at ease, but gentle little Fulke Grant did not even trust himself to stand, and remained sitting in the carriage.

"I think all is ready," Tregareth said. He cleared his throat. Hats came off in the crowd.

"Surely Shadwell's shade is watching us," he said, "as we prepare to bid farewell to his clay. Behold the verdant islands floating on the azure sea he loved so much, and which he took to his final embrace! Behold the ruined castles of the antiquity whose praises he sang in incomparable numbers, 'for the numbers came'! Behold the snowy bosoms of the ever-lofty mountain peaks! All these, Shadwell loved. Shadwell! *Vale!"*

He poured over the body a quantity of wine and oil, then took the waiting torch and thrust it under the pyre. The wood was tinder-dry and flared up directly. *"Vale,* Shadwell!" Tregareth cried again. He cast into the fire the copy of Blake which had been in the drowned poet's pocket. He tossed on a handful of salt, and the yellow flames glistened and quivered as they licked it up.

"Behold!" he exclaimed. "How peacefully the once-raging sea is now embracing the land as if in humility, as if to crave pardon! O Shadwell, thou—"

But here Gryphon interrupted him. "Tregareth, cease this mockery of our pride and vainglory," he said in a stifled, low voice.

Tregareth, his long black hair floating on the wind in magnificent disorder, looked at him with some surprise. Then he looked over to Fulke Grant. But little Grant, still in the carriage, now had the silver flask in his hand. The only sound he made was a hiccup.

Tregareth shrugged. He tossed in a handful of frankincense. The flame mounted higher. The heat grew more intense.

"I cannot endure to remain much longer in Italy," Gryphon said. "Every valley, every brook, will cry aloud his name to me. . . . We must go off together somewhere, Tregareth, you and I. For now I have no one left. America, Greece—somewhere far off." He sobbed aloud, then turned and walked away. The fire crackled and hissed.

Tregareth stood all alone by the pyre. Slowly he took from under his arm the piece of driftwood. It seemed a portion of a ship's mast. On it were carved the initials *G.G.* He clearly called to mind that happy day, only a short while back, when Gerald, Lord Gryphon, had carved the letters. The top of the piece was all rent raggedly. But on the lower part the breach was only partly so. The rest of it—

He could envision the scene. The sudden trumpets of the storm, the terribly sudden blast of wind, the foremast crashing down before the frightful pressure of the wind-caught sails, mast and sail falling as dead weight upon the gunwales, and the ship careening and filling and then going over, going down, as the sea rushed in and the lightning served only to make the blackness deeper. . . .

Tregareth ran his fingers over the smoother surface of the wood. Someone plainly had sawn half through the mast and then hidden the cut with unbleached beeswax of the same color.

He lifted his fingers, bent his head. Despite the wash of the sea and the scouring of the sand, Tregareth could still note the scent of the wax. He thought, for just a moment, that he could even detect the scent of the soft bosom in which the wax must have rested to soften it—but this was only fancy, he knew. It need not, however, remain only fancy.

Love, he reflected, can fade; and lust must ever repel—but passion is stronger than either.

He came as close to the pyre as he could, threw in the shattered section of the mast, and watched it burn fiercely.

Then he turned and went to join the others.

"I met a traveller from an antique land
Who said: Two vast and trunkless legs of stone
Stand in the desert. Near them, on the sand,
Half sunk, a shattered visage lies, whose frown,
And wrinkled lip, and sneer of cold command,
Tell that its sculptor well those passions read
Which yet survive, stamped on these lifeless things,
The hand that mocked them and the heart that fed;
And on the pedestal these words appear:
'My name is Ozymandias, king of kings:
Look on my works, ye Mighty, and despair!'
Nothing beside remains. Round the decay
Of that colossal wreck, boundless and bare
The lone and level sands stretch far away."

—SHELLEY, *Ozymandias*

BALMORALITY

Robert Barnard

The foibles and eccentricities of royalty play wonderfully into the caricaturist's hand. That we love to see the royals at the butt of a joke may have to do with how the mighty, if only in fun, are brought low. The real troubles of the current British royal family may have somewhat soured the fun, but in Robert Barnard's story we are safely in the Victorian past, where a very droll Bertie carries out a princely investigation.

I am going to write down a true account of the Merrivale business without help from my secertary because I know if it comes out I shall get blamed, especially by Mama, who blames me for everything that goes wrong in her circle, in Society in general—even, I sometimes think, in the country at large, as if I were somehow responsable for the national debt, the troublesome Afgans, and the viragoes who advocate votes for women. Nothing I say would influence Mama's opinion, in fact nothing anybody says does, but perhaps an account in my own hand, without the intervention of my secertary, will convince posteraty that I was entirely blameless. Here is the whole truth of the matter.

The story begins in a corridor at Balmoral Castle, built in a baronial but incomodious style by my revered father when I was no more than a boy (but learning!). In Scotland the summer nights are short, and the twilights almost seem to murge into the first lights of dawn (especially for those who have brought their own supplies to orgment the meager rations of wines and spirits). I was, I must admit, in a pretty undignified position for one of my standing. I was squeezed into an alcove, perched on a sort of bench, shielded by heavy velvet curtains. Not a comfortable position for one of my gerth. I would very much have prefered to stand, but I tried that and found that my shoes pertruded under the bottom of the curtains.

So far I had seen nothing I did not expect to see. I had seen Lord Lobway leave the comforts of his martial bed for the delights of Mrs. Aberdovy's. I had seen Lady Wanstone tiptoe along to comfort the loneliness of the Duke of Strathgovern. I have corridor-tiptoed in my time, or been tiptoed to, and I do not condem. I have nothing against adultary provided it is between consenting adults. Seducing a young girl is the action of a cad, unless she is very insistant.

What I had not seen was the figure of that frightful fellow John Brown. Now please do not misunderstand me here. I did not for one moment expect to see the awful gillie going to my Mama's bedroom. I do not suffer from the vulgar misapprehension about their relationship. In any case Mama's bedroom is at least a quater of a mile away, otherwise I would not have been hiding in the corridor! No, the door I was watching was that of Lady Westchester, and the reason was twofold: If I could catch John Brown out in a nocternal assingation with the lady, I could take the story straight to Mama (I already had my sorrowful mein well prepared) and that would perhaps see the end of his embarassing presence at her court; and secondly I have a definate interest in Lady Westchester myself, and I object to sharing her with a gillie. Her husband has been very willing to turn a blind eye (and even, since he sleeps in the next room, a deaf ear!) but I wonder whether he would be willing to do likewise for the repulsive Highlander? For when I heard Lady Westchester, in intimate converse with her best friend Mrs. Aberdovy, say "He's so deliciously ordinary!" that, I concluded, was who she was talking about. I had seen her fluttering her eyelids at him when he helped her to horse. And which of the other servants mix with Mama's guests on that level of familiarity (or impurtenance)? When she begged me not to trouble her that night (I had not noticed it was any trouble) then I concluded that her assingation was with one infinately lower than myself.

Dinner had been Oxtail soup, sole, foie gras, turbot, snipe, crown of beef, game pie, steamed pudding, and one or two other trifles I had just picked at, but dinner was hours and hours ago. I was just beginning to feel hungry when I heard the sound of a door opening. I peered through the heavy folds of velvet. It was not Lady Westchester's door. I was about to withdraw into my alcove when I saw a scene in the open doorway that gave me furiously to think. The door was Colonel Merrivale's, and coming out was a little bounder called Laurie Lamont, whose presence at Balmoral I found it difficult to account for. But what made my heart skip a beat was that I could see clearly that Merrivale was withdrawing his hand from the inside pocket of his jacket, while Laurie Lamont's hand was withdrawing from the pocket of his trousers.

Not an hour before Merrivale had been winning quite heavily off me and other gentlemen at poker.

Lamont scuttled off down the corridor and away to his room in some obscure corner of my Papa's Gothick pile, and I remained considering the scene I had just witnessed and hoping that the gastly gillie would make his appearance soon. I had waited no more than a few minutes when I heard footsteps. Looking out I saw that it was my own man! I shrank back, but the footsteps stopped beside my alcove.

"I would advise Your Royal Highness not to remain here any longer."

Well! He had barely paused, spoke in a low voice, and then continued on down the corridor. After thinking things over for a few minutes I emerged rather nonchalently and returned to my suite of rooms. Where my man awaited me.

"How did you know I was there?" I demanded.

"I am afraid, sir, there was a certain swelling which disturbed the hang of the curtain."

He has a clever way of putting things, my man. He meant there was a bulge. He is fair, tall, with an air that is almost gentlemanly and an expression that I have heard described as quizicle.

"Where had you come from anyway?" I asked.

"I was myself watching from another of the alcoves," he replied. I looked with distast at his discusting slimness. "I too had had my suspicions roused in the course of cards this evening."

I did not enlighten him as to which door I had in fact been keeping an eye on, or give any indication that the scene in the doorway had come as a complete bomshell to me. As he releived me of my clothes I let him continue.

"You remember, sir, that you summoned me to prepare some of the herbal mixture that you get such releif from, after too many cigars?"

"Shouldn't be getting short of breath these days," I complained. "I've cut down to just one before breakfast, and the odd cigarette."

"I rather fear that without noticing you have increased your consumption *after* breakfast, sir," he said. I allow my man great lattitude. He is invaluable in all sorts of little arrangements. "Anyway, the fact was I was in the card room for some time, during which Colonel Merrivale was winning quite heavily."

"Too damned heavily. I'm well out of pocket."

"Exactly, sir. And I noticed this Mr. Lamont. He was deep in converse with the Countess of Berkhampstead. She was telling him about her various ailments, and was so engrossed—predictably so, if I may venture to say it—that she was noticing nothing about him. They were by a mirror. By testing I realized he could see the cards of two of the other players. And I got the idea that he was making suttle signs to Colonel Merrivale."

"The damned rotters!" I exploded. "At Balmoral too! Windsor would be another matter, but Balmoral! I know Merrivale. He's brother to one of the Queen's Scottish equerries. Who is this Lamont fellow?"

"I have made enquiries about that, sir—talked to his man. He is active in civic affairs in Edinburgh, it seems. Has been pressing the case for a fitting monument in the city to the late Prince Consort. He has been agitating in the City Council and the newspapers for an Opera House, to be called the Albert Theatre."

"It will never happen. The good burgers of Edinburgh are far too mean."

"It may be, sir, that he doesn't expect it to happen, and that that is not the point. He has, after all, been invited to Balmoral. . . ."

"True. Mingling with those very much above his station."

"Quite, sir."

"Mama is too gulable. It's too much that people get invited here at the drop of the word 'Albert.' "

"I suspect it has been noted, sir, that the name is a sort of Open Sessamy."

"The bounders have to be exposed."

"Quite so, sir. But how?"

"I can charge him publicly with what I saw."

"Hardly conclusive, sir. And I see a difficulty: you were playing poker, for money, at Balmoral, sir."

He was his usual impurturbable self, but I huffed and puffed a bit, though nothing like as much as Mama would have huffed and puffed if she knew we had been playing poker for high stakes in what is vertually my late Papa's second morsauleum.

"Ah yes, well . . ." I said finally. "Might be a bit awkward. Though when I think how the Queen goes on about the company I keep . . ."

"Perhaps we should sleep on it, sir. By morning we may have thought of something."

"Nothing to do but think," I muttered, as he pulled my nightshirt over my head. I leapt between the sheets, burning my leg on the stone hot water bottle. "I'm not used to sleeping alone. Alix would have been better than nothing."

For my dear wife has no love of Balmoral, and generally siezes the time of our annual visit for a trip to see her relatives. I make no objection. If her relatives had been German Mama would probably find her visits to them admirably fillial, but as they are Danish she says she is being selfish.

Well, I spent a lonely night warmed only by hot water bottles, but I can't say that in the morning I had come up with any great plan. All I could think of was whether John Brown was in with Lady Westchester, and what they were likely to be doing. Mind you, I don't think my man expected me to come up with anything. When he said we he meant I. He's got rather a good opinion of himself.

"Well, sir," he said next morning, as he shaved the bits of my face that needed shaving, "it's a beuatiful day, and apparently the vote is for a croquy competition."

"Damned boring game," I commented. "Bonking balls through hoops."

"But you do play, sir."

"Oh, I can bonk with the best of them."

"Because I thought just possibly something might be made of it."

And he wisked off the towels just like the johnnie in the opera, and confided in me his thoughts.

The Arbroath smokies served at Balmoral are, I have to admit, unparalelled, and the kedgeree not to be despised. The sausages, bacon, and black pudding are inferior to what we have at Marlborough House, but the beefsteaks can be admirable. I breakfasted alone. If I take a small table and look royal everybody knows I am brooding on affairs of state and I am not disturbed. When I had eaten my fill I lit up my second cigar of the day and strolled out on to the sun-drenched lawns. It did not even destroy my good humour to see John Brown setting up the hoops and pegs and three seprate croquy lawns. Somehow I knew things were going to go according to plan.

Lord John Willoughby had been recruted to further the plot. Lord John is in fact alergic to croquy, but he was a fellow loser of the night before, and he was to be used as an apparently casual bystander. He had been approached by a deputation consisting of my man, and he had joyfully gone along with the idea. Those villians Merrivale and Lamont had been organised by Willoughby into opposing teams, and when I strolled up to Merrivale and said "Give me my revenge for last night, eh?" Lord Rishton willingly dropped out of the game and transferred to another team, which left me partnering the loathsome Lamont, with Merrivale's partner the delectible Lady Frances Bourne, whose only fault is her unshakable faithfulness to a damned dull husband. Still, if I couldn't partner her in any other sort of games, croquy it would have to be.

Willoughby, I'll say this for him, has a sense of humour. He arranged it so he stood on the sidelines of our game talking to Lady Berkhampstead. He was, too all intents and purposes, totally absorbed in her twinges of this and aggonising attacks of that. I let the game proceed until I was well-poised to shoot my red ball through the fourth hoop and Lamont was rather poorly placed for getting his yellow ball through the third. Then, as he was standing beside his ball shielding it from the gaze of spectators, I gave the sign and both Wiloughby and I stepped forward.

"That man moved his ball."

Laurie Lamont looked astonished, as well he might.

"I haven't touched my ball, sir. It's not my turn."

"I'll have no partner of mine cheating," I said.

"I saw him," said Willoughby, coming up. "He shifted his ball to a better position for his next shot."

"And where there's cheating, there's money on the game," I said menacingly. "I wouldn't mind bet—I strongly suspect that they've got a wager on this."

I looked meaningfully at Lamont, then equally meaningfully at Merrivale. I wanted both of them to understand *exactly* what piece of cheating was in question.

"And since no one would suspect Lady Frances of betting, I think we can take it that you, Merrivale, are the other culprit. Betting on a game of croquy in the grounds of the Queen's Scottish home! And cheating! You probably even have the wager on you, I'll be bound."

I knew they did. Lamont had his on him because he's one of these tradesmen chappies who won't leave loose money in their rooms even when they're guests of their Sovereign. Merrivale had his on him because his man had been pursuaded by mine to slip it into the inside pocket of his jacket that morning.

"I absolutely protest, sir," he now spluttered. "I have no money on me!"

He opened up his jacket, and pertruding from the pocket was an envelope. I extracted it and counted the money.

"One hundred and fifteen pounds. And no doubt you too have a hundred and fifteen?" Lamont squermed and kept his jacket tight-buttoned. I held out my hand and he took out the money. "Two hundred and thirty pounds. Well, well, well!"

It was the sum Merrivale had won the night before, shared equally with his accomplice. I pocketed it.

By now there were several bystanders, all curious to know what was going on. Lady Berkhampstead, interrupted mid-twinge, was loudly demanding to be told what was happening. I pointed to the Castle.

"Betting at Balmoral. I never thought to see this day. You sir—" I turned to Merrivale—"I would have expected to know better. You sir—" turning to Lamont—"I had no expectations of. I count on hearing that you have both left the Castle before nightfall."

There was a moment's pause. Merrivale spluttered, then the pair of them slunk in the direction of the Castle, their tails almost visibly between their legs. I walked over in high good humour to watch one of the other games.

"Just a little contratems," I said airily. "Regard our game as scratched."

That evening, when my man was poking and prodding me into my evening wear to make me presentable for the dreary horrors of a Balmoral dinner, he said:

"Colonel Merrivale's young daughter has been taken ill, and Mr. Lamont's mother. Quite a coincidence, sir."

I grunted my satisfaction, and in an interval of prodding said:

"That'll teach the Queen not to invite just any little squert who happens to suck up to her on the subject of Papa. I wonder if I should rub it in that she ought to be more careful who she invites?" I saw an expression pass over his face. I am very quick on the uptake. "Well, perhaps not. Perhaps I may just write an account of the whole busness for posteraty."

"That should make fasinating reading, sir."

My mind going back to the start of the busness and my concealment in the alcove, I said:

"Lady Westchester has intimated that I would be welcome tonight. Don't know that I shall take up the offer. Damned unpleasant not knowing who I'm sharing her with."

"I happen to know, sir, that the reason Lady Westchester was . . . unavailable last night was because her husband especially requested the favour of a night with her. The sort of ladies his lordship habitually consorts with are in particularly short supply in the Balmoral area."

"Really?" I said, rather pleased. But then I pondered. "That doesn't explain the other thing, though."

"Other thing, sir?"

"I heard her say of some man that he was 'delicously ordinary.' I'm damned sure she was talking about John Brown."

There came over my man's face that smile that people call quizicle.

"Oh that, sir. Is that what you suspected? Her ladyship has been heard to say that to several people. I think she intends the remark to be paradoxicle."

"To be what?"

"A paradox, sir, is something that is apparently abserd or impossible, but turns out to be true. Her ladyship was not referring to John Brown, sir."

"Oh?"

"She was referring to you."

For a moment he took my breath away. When the idea got through to me I felt immensely flattered.

"Well, I say, you know, that really is rather a complement, don't you think? I mean, here I am, with all my advantages, rather marked off by my birth, set apart all my life for a special task, and yet I manage to keep the common touch to such an extent that she can say that about me. I feel quite touched. She's right. I am ordinary. No one would call the Russian Emperor ordinary, would they? Or the Kaiser? She really has me summed up very well."

"I'm glad Your Royal Highness sees it that way."

"I do. I'm obliged to you for clearing up the misunderstanding. In fact I'm obliged to you for giving the other matter such a satisfactory outcome too."

I felt about my person for something with which to show my appreciation of his very special services. It is one of the drawbacks of being royal that one has very little use for ready money, so one very seldom has any on one. Fortunately I have always found that people feel just as well rewarded by a sincere expression of Royal gratitude. I clapped my man on the shoulder.

"Thank you, Lovesy," I said.

THE PASSION OF LIZZIE B.

Edward D. Hoch

In 1892 the most baffling crime in American history rocked Fall River, Massachusetts, and the rest of the nation. The Borden slayings were never solved, though volumes have been written in speculation as to the culprit. Less has been written about what became of Lizzie Borden after her acquittal for the murders. Could she have traveled to the Wild West of Edward D. Hoch's Ben Snow? Hoch builds his classical whodunit around the premise that she did, in a case that features his long-running cowboy detective.

It was in early July of '94 that Ben Snow left his horse Oats at a stable in Cheyenne and boarded a train for Omaha, nearly five hundred miles to the east. He'd been north to Canada and south to Texas, but had never visited the growing nation's midsection. Luckily, this stretch of track had not yet been shut down by the violence of the Pullman strike, and he was able to make the journey without incident. The man he was meeting had offered a nice financial reward for his time and trouble.

That man was named Cyrus Clant, and he was waiting at the station when Ben stepped off the train in Omaha. He looked Ben up and down after introducing himself and asked, "Where are your six-shooters?"

Ben smiled at the short, timid-looking man with the gray moustache. "Your letter stated you wanted someone to protect you. I've done that sort of work out West, but I imagined it would be different in Omaha. My guns are in here." He indicated the bulging carpetbag at his feet.

"That's good," the little man said. "Bring it along and we'll go to my place."

Clant resided in a house only a few blocks from the wide and winding Missouri River. It was in a section of modest Victorian-style homes. As he parked his carriage in front he pointed out across the river. "That's Iowa over there, Mr. Snow. We're right on the state line here."

"I've never seen this part of the country before," Ben admitted. He followed his employer into the parlor and found himself in a jungle of houseplants.

"My wife liked them," Cyrus Clant explained. "I'm in the process of thinning them out."

"Your wife?"

"She died last year of influenza."

"I'm sorry."

"Have a seat, Mr. Snow. That brings us to the reason I wrote you. I was told by a gentleman down Texas way that you—"

Suddenly a middle-aged woman entered the parlor from what Ben presumed to be the kitchen. "Good afternoon, Cyrus," she said.

He was visibly startled. "My dear, I didn't realize you were in the house. Ben Snow, this is Lizzie Benson."

"How do you do?" Ben said, rising to take her hand. She was a plain-looking woman with reddish hair and large attractive eyes, wearing a long black dress that reached to the floor.

"Shall I prepare some tea for you gentlemen?" she asked.

"That would be nice, Lizzie. Then if you could excuse us, we have some business to go over."

Cyrus Clant kept up a rambling conversation about the city and his successful hardware business until the tea was ready. After Lizzie announced she was off to do some shopping, he settled back with his cup. "Help yourself to the biscuits," he told Ben, "and we'll get down to business."

The front door closed and Ben saw Lizzie Benson's head pass by the front window. "Is she a neighbor?" he asked.

"No, no. She may become the next Mrs. Clant. The newspapers here often carry personal ads from eastern women wanting to move west and find a potential husband. When my dear wife passed away I was extremely lonely. I answered a few of these ads and the reply from Miss Benson was most cordial. After a few months' correspondence I invited her to journey out here and get better acquainted."

"She seems like a nice woman," Ben said, trying to be polite. In truth he had formed no opinion about Lizzie Benson.

"She's been in Omaha for a month now, living in a boardinghouse a few blocks from here. I find her a pleasant, agreeable woman, a bit on the quiet side. She seems to have a shrewd business sense, and has given me some good ideas for my hardware store."

"You wrote me two weeks ago, Mr. Clant. Might I assume your problem is connected with Miss Benson?"

The short man sighed. "There's a fellow working at my store, name of Seth Rankin. He's young, about your age."

"I'm thirty-five," Ben admitted. "Not all that young."

"Well, he's probably in his late twenties. Anyway, he's unmarried and his hobby is reading all those dime novels from back East. He reads stories about true murders too. He told me something about Lizzie Benson that I can't get out of my mind."

"What's that?"

Cyrus Clant rubbed his palms nervously over his trousers. "Seth thinks she's Lizzie Borden, the axe murderess."

Most eastern crimes made little impression upon people like Ben Snow who lived west of the Mississippi, but even he had heard of Lizzie Borden and the sensational murder trial the previous year at which she'd been acquitted of charges that she brutally murdered her father and stepmother. The eyes of the nation had been focused on the courthouse in New Bedford, Massachusetts, and even little children recited poems about the number of blows Lizzie struck with her axe. Still, the verdict of not guilty was cheered in the courtroom and almost universally hailed across the nation.

With the passage of time, that began to change. Lizzie went home to live with her sister at a different house in Fall River, and some people began to feel that she might indeed have been guilty, though the state had failed to prove it.

"I've heard of the case," Ben admitted, "but I don't believe I ever saw a picture of her."

"I have one here that I obtained from the local library." He produced an illustrated magazine and turned to an inside page where an account of the trial began. There were photographs of Lizzie Borden, her father, and stepmother. "You see the resemblance?"

"It's a poor picture. One can't be certain." Yet Ben had to admit that this could well be the likeness of Lizzie Benson, the woman he'd met just a quarter of an hour earlier. "But isn't Lizzie Borden still back East?"

"Who knows for certain? This article says she lives with her sister and is rarely seen. What could prevent her from placing that personal ad and coming out here under the transparent alias of Lizzie Benson?"

"Where was she living when you wrote her?"

"The letters went to a post office box in Taunton, Massachusetts. That's very close to Fall River."

"Why do you need me?" Ben wanted to know. "If you don't want to marry her, give her a ticket back East and be done with it."

"If she is Lizzie Borden, she might not appreciate being jilted."

"You're afraid of her?"

"When I was showing her around my hardware store she picked up an axe. It gave me a jolt, seeing her with it."

"All right," Ben decided. "I'll stay a week. By that time we should know if she's dangerous or not."

Clant drained the rest of the tea from his cup. "That will be just fine, Mr. Snow."

It developed that Clant had given Lizzie a part-time job, working at his hardware store three afternoons a week. The following day Ben found her there, dusting shelves and bins with a feather duster. She recognized him at once. "Hello again, Mr. Snow. You've decided to stay with us for a bit?"

He nodded. "I've taken a room at the Hotel Omaha till next week. Then I'll be heading back West."

"Are you a friend of Cyrus's?"

"An acquaintance. This is my first trip to Omaha and I decided to look him up."

She put down the feather duster and picked up a big metal scoop, using it to combine two bins of small nails into one. "I'm trying to get Cyrus to weigh these nails and package them in five-pound bags. That's the way some stores back East do it. Why spend the rest of your life selling things for a penny or two each?"

"You have a good business sense," Ben told her. "Did you work in a store back East?"

"No, not really. It comes natural to me, I suppose."

"Is your name Lizzie short for something?"

She paused in her work to stare at him. "My, you are full of questions, Mr. Snow. I use the name Lizbeth now, but Lizzie's what's on my birth certificate. I'm used to being called that."

"I guess we're about the same age, aren't we, Lizzie? I'm thirty-five."

"I don't mind telling my age. I'm a year younger."

"I've had a strange life, out West. I was born the same year as William Bonney—Billy the Kid. He was killed in '81, but a whole lot of people think he's still alive. Because I had a young face and was fast with a gun, folks got the idea I was Billy the Kid. It's caused me a great deal of misery in my life. Nothing worse than being mistaken for a killer."

"Why are you telling me this?" she asked. Her face had gone white.

"Just making conversation." He turned away and became interested in some brooms.

There were two full-time employees at Clant's hardware store. One was Seth Rankin, a stout man a bit younger than Ben. He was the one who'd first voiced his suspicions about Lizzie to Cyrus Clant. The other was a young woman, Theresa Sanchez, whose western-style skirt came to just below her knees, unlike the more proper full-length frock that Lizzie Benson wore. It was the Sanchez woman who approached him now, asking if she could help him.

"I'm just looking around," Ben told her. "Mr. Clant is an old friend of mine."

"Are you in town for the wedding?" she asked, pumping him for information he didn't have. She had a dark, musky scent about her, promising more tales than Scheherazade.

"I think the wedding's a long ways off," Ben told her.

Theresa Sanchez glanced back over her shoulder. "Not to hear her tell it! She's already acting like the second Mrs. Clant."

Ben spent the remainder of the afternoon drifting around the streets of the city. There was a big meat-packing plant, located conveniently close to the railroad that had brought him east, and a state school for the deaf. The downtown area was unlike anything farther west. Only once or twice did he see a slight bulge under a gentleman's coat that hinted at a hidden weapon.

He ate dinner at his hotel and read about the Pullman strike in the Omaha *Bee,* one of the city's daily newspapers. A few of the men around the lobby were reading the *World-Herald,* which seemed to be a younger paper edited by someone named William Jennings Bryan. One of the newspaper articles told about a new organization of businessmen named Ak-Sar-Ben, formed to promote interest in the history and progress of the city and the state. Ben studied the name for a minute or two before he realized it was Nebraska spelled backwards.

Finally he returned to the Clant home shortly before eight o'clock. Lizzie Benson had prepared dinner for Clant, and the two were seated in the parlor. The screen door was unhooked, and when he called to them he was invited inside.

"You should have joined us," Lizzie said, seeming more friendly than she had earlier.

"It was my fault for not inviting you," Clant insisted. "You must dine with us for the rest of your stay."

Ben accepted a glass of wine and was just settling in to join their conversation when they were interrupted by a knocking on the screen door. Clant went to answer it and Ben saw a police officer step inside. "Afraid I have some bad news, Mr. Clant. There's been a robbery at your store. One of your clerks has been hurt real bad."

"What? What's that?" His face dissolved into panic. "Is it Theresa?"

"It's Seth Rankin. He's been taken to the hospital, but it doesn't look good. He's unconscious and he's lost a lot of blood."

"Someone shot him?"

The officer shook his head. "He was hit in the head with an axe."

They took Clant's carriage to the hospital at once, with Lizzie remaining at the house. The store owner seemed extremely agitated and even Ben was unable to comfort him. When they reached the hospital, there was more bad news waiting. Seth Rankin had died of a massive head injury without ever regaining consciousness.

"Who could have done such a thing?" Cyrus Clant asked, appealing to anyone who'd listen. "There's never been trouble at my store before. I've never been robbed."

Ben drove Cyrus directly to the hardware store in the carriage. It was about a mile from the Clant house and the same distance from the hospital, on a dark street that seemed much more sinister to Ben than it had just that afternoon. A police officer was on duty at the front door and the interior was illuminated by gaslights. The place seemed somehow smaller at night than Ben remembered it, and as they entered he was startled by a plainclothes detective who'd been examining the floor behind one of the counters. He rose to the flickering light like some avenging angel and spoke to Cyrus.

"Good evening, Mr. Clant. It's Sergeant Hastley."

"Oh, Sergeant! You startled us. This is Ben Snow, a friend who's visiting from out West."

Hastley shook hands, demonstrating a grip of steel. "You one of them cowpokes?"

"Sometimes," Ben acknowledged.

Hastley was a broad, muscular man who wore a holstered Colt revolver conspicuously beneath the coat of his brown suit. "We've got a bad situation here," he told Cyrus Clant. "Looks like a robbery, but we can't be sure. What time was Seth supposed to close up tonight?"

"The store closes at six, but sometimes he stayed on later if there was work to be done. He was a good employee. I can't believe anyone would kill him."

"Were you here this afternoon?"

"We were all here. Lizzie was helping out, and even Mr. Snow stopped by. Wednesday is often busy, and my other clerk, Theresa Sanchez, was working too."

"Notice anyone acting suspicious?" He'd taken out a notebook and pencil.

"Nothing out of the ordinary."

"But it was a busy day with lots of money in the cash register?"

Cyrus Clant nodded. "A reasonable amount. I counted up before I left and there was around six hundred dollars. That's good for us. Is it gone?"

"The register was cleaned out," Hastley confirmed. "The officer on the beat was checking the shop doors and he noticed lights still burning in here. The door was unlocked and he came in. This was around seven-thirty, while it was still daylight. His first thought was that someone was after the guns you sell, but then he spotted Rankin's body behind the register here, right where I'm standing."

At the mention of the guns Clant walked over to the big padlocked case against the wall. It hadn't been tampered with. "You're certain it was an axe that did it, Sergeant?"

"It was right next to the body. One of yours, I'd judge. Looked new, with a little gilt decoration on it still."

Cyrus Clant nodded sadly. "We have a display of them over here."

Sergeant Hastley frowned as he walked over to look at the axes with their shiny blades. "See, that's the one thing makes me question the robbery motive. Wouldn't a stick-up man have brought along his own weapon?"

"He might have had a pistol that misfired," Ben suggested, leaning over to study the axes himself. "This display was handy so he grabbed an axe."

"If the pistol misfired, why go for an axe? The gun in his hand could have been used as a club."

"The man had no enemies," Clant observed. "Who else but a bandit would have a motive for killing him?"

"That's what I'm trying to figure out. Just you and Theresa Sanchez worked here with him, right?"

"That's correct—just the three of us. I mentioned that my friend Lizzie Benson was helping out today too. We were all in the store at one time or another this afternoon. Seth stayed on for a bit after six."

"You and Miss Benson left together?"

"We did. She went to her boardinghouse first to freshen up, then came on over to my place to help prepare dinner. She was there well before seven-thirty."

Sergeant Hastley nodded. "I didn't mean to imply the robbery and assault took place at that time. When the dying man was found some of the blood was already dry. I figure it must have happened shortly after you left at six. You were alone at your house then, Mr. Clant?"

"Well, yes—for a short period until Miss Benson arrived."

"I'll want to talk to her," the detective said. "What about you, Mr. Snow? Where were you just after six o'clock?"

"I had dinner at my hotel and then sat in the lobby reading a newspaper."

"Alone?"

"Alone unless someone remembers seeing me."

"Will you be staying in Omaha very long?"

"The rest of the week, at least."

"That's good. I may want to see you again." He turned to Cyrus Clant. "I'm finished here. Will you lock up?"

Clant nodded and dug out his keys. "Keep me informed, Sergeant. I want Seth's killer behind bars."

"So do we."

Clant drove the carriage back to his house. He seemed anxious to return to Lizzie but apprehensive at the same time. "It's the axe, isn't it?" Ben suggested quietly.

"Of course it's the axe! There are probably a dozen weapons in my store, not even counting the guns—hammers, screwdrivers, lengths of rope and chain, rat poison, black powder, knives of all sorts, saws, kerosene—but this killer has to choose an axe. Why?"

"The display was handy," Ben suggested.

"Or the killer was someone who knew how to handle one."

"That too."

He reined up the horse as they reached his house. "Do you think he caught Lizzie taking that money from the register?"

Ben considered the question. "If she needed money, I think she'd have simply asked you."

"I hope so!"

They entered the house and found Lizzie seated at the dining room table with a deck of cards, playing a game of solitaire. She leaped up as they came in. "I've been so worried! What happened? How is he?"

"Seth is dead," Cyrus Clant told her.

"Oh God!"

"You mustn't upset yourself about it. The police will find his killer."

"But an axe! What a horrible way to die! Was he conscious at all? Did he say who killed him?"

"No. He died before regaining consciousness."

Ben was watching her face, but it showed no reaction to this news. "I'm afraid it dampens our evening together," Clant told her. "I'm really very tired now. Mr. Snow, could you see Lizzie back to her boardinghouse?"

"Certainly."

She followed him to the stairs and they spoke a few quiet words together. Then she returned and picked up a lightweight black coat she'd worn over her dress. "I'm ready to go now, Mr. Snow."

The rooming house was close by, and they'd walked much of the way in silence before Lizzie finally spoke. "You don't like me, do you?"

"I barely know you, Miss Benson."

"Cyrus hired you to check up on me, didn't he?"

"Not exactly. It was something—" He let the rest of the sentence drift away. Suddenly he'd remembered that it was Seth Rankin who'd first raised the question of Lizzie's true identity.

As if she could sense the direction of his thoughts, she countered with a question of her own. "Are you really Billy the Kid?"

"Are you really Lizzie Borden?" he shot back, almost before he realized what he was saying.

She gave a short, sharp laugh. "Well, now the cat's really out of the bag!"

"It doesn't matter to me what or who you are."

She turned on him with a fierce passion. "That's right, and it shouldn't matter to Cyrus, either! I came all the way out here looking to start a new life. What difference does it make if I'm Lizzie Benson or Lizzie Borden or Lizzie Brown?"

"It shouldn't have made a difference until this evening. Now someone has been killed with an axe."

"I had nothing to do with that!"

He stared at her upturned face reflecting the glow from the overhead gaslights. She was not a pretty woman, but at that moment he would not have called her unattractive. "Rankin believed you to be Lizzie Borden. That might have been motive enough for you to kill him."

"Do you believe that?"

"I'm going to try to show Cyrus you're innocent," Ben said.

"That I'm not Lizzie Borden?"

"That you didn't kill Seth Rankin."

In the morning Cyrus Clant supplied Ben with Rankin's home address. The murdered man had lived alone in a small house out near the fairgrounds. "His wife went west with another man," Clant told Ben. "He mentioned it just once and then never spoke of it again."

Gaining entry to the locked house was no problem for Ben once he'd established that the police didn't have it under guard. The interior showed definite signs of a bachelor existence, with unwashed dishes and a pile of dirty clothes. It was impossible to tell if the police or anyone else had come there ahead of Ben.

He concentrated on searching a desk, but found little except ten-year-old correspondence received by Rankin's wife; there seemed to be nothing from her since she'd gone west. The only thing of interest was a letter from the U.S. Repeating Arms Company thanking Rankin for the store's recent large order. It was dated June 4, 1894, barely a month earlier. Ben wondered why Rankin rather than Clant would have placed a large order for anything. It was Clant's hardware store, after all.

Ben looked quietly through the closets but found nothing of interest. Some women's clothes were still there, as if Rankin had kept them for his wife's possible return. The most interesting discovery was the dead man's collection of dime novels and pamphlets carrying accounts of famous murder cases. One, *The Fall River Tragedy,* had been privately published just after the preceding year's Borden trial by a reporter named Edwin H. Porter. A quick glance through its pages showed the author had little doubt regarding Lizzie's guilt. He saw again the photograph that Cyrus had shown him. There was no denying the striking resemblance to Lizzie Benson.

He exited the house by the back door, careful not to be seen. He had borrowed a carriage used for store deliveries, and he drove it back through the busy streets of the city to Clant's Hardware. Inside he found only Theresa Sanchez on duty. "Mr. Clant and Lizzie have gone to the funeral parlor," she explained. "Poor Seth had no family here, and they're making the arrangements for burial."

"Wasn't there an ex-wife?"

"No one knows what happened to her," Theresa said with a shake of her head.

"Did you know her?"

"Not really. I may have seen her in the store once or twice, but she left not long after I started work here."

"I'm trying to track down some large orders Seth placed recently," Ben told her. "I wonder if you could show me your suppliers' invoices for the past two months."

Theresa moved past him to the counter, and once again he caught the musky scent of her perfume. She took out a spindle upon which were impaled numerous pieces of paper. "We keep them here for each quarter and then Mr. Clant files them away." Ben couldn't help noting that she stood exactly where Sergeant Hastley had said Seth's body was found. "He hasn't gotten to this batch yet."

Ben went through the invoices quickly, searching for one from the U.S. Repeating Arms Company, but as far back as the first of April there was nothing. He was about to give it up as a dead end when he noticed an oddity. The spindle had left its usual hole through each of the invoices, but those near the top had two holes, as if they'd been removed and then quickly impaled again without regard to the first hole. Almost all of the June invoices had two holes, suggesting that someone had wanted an invoice from the first few days of that month.

"How do you handle these invoices?" Ben asked. "You must return one copy with your payment."

"That's correct," Theresa Sanchez agreed, brushing the long black bangs from her forehead. "One copy is returned and the other copy filed on the spindle."

"Are there ever third copies?"

"Occasionally, but we rarely keep them unless there's a problem."

"You must have a ledger to record payments to suppliers."

"Certainly."

"Could I see it?"

Now she hesitated, apparently deciding she'd already gone too far. "You'd have to see Mr. Clant about that."

"Of course."

Cyrus Clant returned with Lizzie about thirty minutes later. His eyes were dark and he appeared tired. "It's a hard thing to do, bury a friend and employee."

"He handled himself very well," Lizzie assured Ben.

"I need to talk to you," Ben told him.

"Is it important?"

"It might be."

"Run along," Lizzie insisted. "I'll help Theresa."

"Well—just into my office for a few minutes, Snow."

Ben came right to the point as Cyrus closed his office door. "Have you ever done business with the U.S. Repeating Arms Company?"

"Of course. They manufacture Winchester rifles. We have some out in the case."

"Have you placed an especially large order recently?"

Clant thought about it. "Not that I know of."

"Theresa let me glance through the invoices on the spindle, but she wouldn't let me see the ledgers. Said I'd have to ask you."

"What does all this have to do with Seth's murder?"

"Perhaps nothing. But he received a letter from the company last month thanking him for the large order."

"What?"

"Can you look through your payments?"

Frowning, Cyrus Clant turned to the shelves behind him and took down a large ledger. "We don't have a regular bookkeeper, you understand. The books are audited each January." He went down the list for May and June, and suddenly frowned. "Here's a notation for U.S. Repeating Arms—a credit for a mistaken shipment that was returned. It says, '2000 Model 1892 lever-action Winchester rifles.' My God—I wouldn't sell two thousand Winchesters in twenty years!"

No, Ben agreed silently, but Seth Rankin might. "Obviously a mistake," he murmured. "Can I look through those records?"

"Go ahead. I have nothing to hide."

Customer invoices were kept in a separate file, and Ben turned quickly to that, trying to match up the incoming rifles with an outgoing order. It took him only a few moments to find it. "Here it is. The rifles were delivered by Rankin to a customer who signed himself Hank Yeltsa. Name mean anything to you?"

"Not a thing. You're telling me the rifles weren't returned?"

"It seems not. Seth Rankin entered a false refund from the company in your books, noting the return of a mistaken shipment. It balanced the original charge so you neither gained nor lost, but the company never got its rifles back."

"What did this man Yeltsa want with them? The Indian Wars are over."

"But there are others to take their place. I was reading in the *Bee* about this Pullman violence in Chicago—"

He was interrupted by Lizzie Benson, who tapped gently on the door and then entered. "Cyrus, do you have the key for the gun cabinet? Theresa thinks it should be dusted."

He got to his feet. "Here it is. I think we're done talking anyway, aren't we, Snow?"

"That's up to you," Ben said with a shrug.

Lizzie had hurried off with the key and Clant said to him, "What about her? That's what I hired you for, not this business about invoices."

"Do you think she killed Seth Rankin?"

"He knew her real identity."

"Or claimed to know it. Is that enough of a motive for murder?"

"To the real Lizzie Borden it might be."

Ben left him there, promising to return. He needed some fresh air, and a new perspective on things. Perhaps Clant was right. Perhaps the solution was the obvious one, and he just didn't want to admit it.

The afternoon newspaper carried reports of an armed clash between striking Pullman workers and two thousand deputies newly appointed by the United States marshal. The Chicago superintendent of police was incensed by the action, claiming the deputies were actually in the pay of the railroads and that they were nothing but "thugs, thieves, and ex-convicts."

Ben Snow read the item twice. On the third try he realized why it bothered him. Two thousand deputies. Two thousand Winchester rifles.

Was it possible?

If the railroads were buying weapons to arm the strikebreakers, they'd do it secretly, of course. Through a third party. Omaha might be just the right distance from Chicago. Far enough on the map, yet close enough by a special train.

Ben told Cyrus Clant he'd stop by the house after dinner, as he had on the previous night. He watched from across the street while Clant left the store with Lizzie and Theresa Sanchez followed behind them, pausing only to lock the door. But when they reached Clant's carriage Ben heard Lizzie ask for the key, claiming she'd forgotten her purse.

Ben crossed the street and moved quickly to the side of the building, careful not to be seen. Clant was pulling away with Theresa, calling out that he'd return for Lizzie shortly. She unlocked the door and reentered the hardware store. It was still bright daylight and she had no need to turn on the lamp.

He gave her ten carefully measured seconds and then stepped through the door after her. She'd just reached the display of axes beyond the counter where Rankin had been fatally attacked, and she was lifting one in her hand.

Before she could speak he heard another voice behind him and realized he hadn't been the only one to enter through the unlocked door. "Hold it right there, Miss Lizzie Borden!" Sergeant Hastley said, covering her with his revolver. "Move aside, Mr. Snow."

"What's going on here?" Ben asked innocently.

But Hastley ignored him for the moment. "Put down that axe, Miss Borden, very slowly. On the counter."

She obeyed him. "I only came back for my purse."

"Is it large enough to conceal an axe? What were you going to do with it later tonight, after Cyrus had gone to sleep?"

"That's not true!" she shouted. "You all try to say I killed them, that I'll kill again. It isn't so!"

Hastley smiled slightly. "Well, it doesn't matter now, does it?"

"Wait a minute," Ben interrupted. "How did you know she was Lizzie Borden? Through good detective work?"

"I know. I saw her picture."

"You were shown her picture by Seth Rankin. That was when you decided to kill him with an axe and frame her for the killing. Isn't that right, Mr. Hank Yeltsa?"

Sergeant Hastley was smiling as he turned the revolver and aimed it at Ben Snow's forehead. He was just an instant too slow. The little derringer hidden in Ben's hand fired once and it was over.

It was Cyrus Clant who forced his way through the ring of police officers to Ben's side sometime later. "They say you shattered his gun hand with a single bullet. That true, Mr. Snow?"

"It's one of the things I do for a living," Ben answered him.

"But why Sergeant Hastley? And how'd you know?"

"Rankin wouldn't have let just anyone into the store after closing last night. But he certainly wouldn't bar the door to a man who'd just bought two thousand Winchester rifles from him to arm the Chicago strikebreakers. The railroads paid Hastley for the weapons to conceal their own involvement, in case there was mass violence during the strike. He had Rankin order them through the store and pay the manufacturer directly, fixing the books so it would look like they were returned. Rankin knew too much, or maybe he wanted too much. Either way, Hastley decided to kill him. Knowing Lizzie Borden was in town gave him a perfect scapegoat."

"What made you suspect him in the first place?"

"Last night when we entered the store he was bent down behind the counter where Rankin had been hit with the axe. We may have thought he was examining the floor, but today I learned a spindle of invoices was kept on a shelf right at that point. The spindle's puncture holes hinted that one invoice may have been removed and the others hastily replaced. It seemed to me that a store employee needn't have been that hasty, but Sergeant Hastley might have been, if we almost caught him in the act."

"He was Seth's customer for the guns?"

Ben nodded. "The transaction no doubt took place on a railroad siding, where the weapons were off-loaded and put on a special train to Chicago. Hastley signed himself Hank Yeltsa. Yeltsa, H. That's Hastley spelled backwards. I read an item in the *Bee* about a new businessman's organization named for Nebraska spelled backwards and that gave me the idea. Maybe it gave Hastley the idea too."

"I don't know how to thank you, Mr. Snow," Cyrus said.

"I'll total up my bill and let you know."

Ben saw Lizzie only one more time, at the railroad station two mornings later. The Pullman strike had been broken by 14,000 government troops and the trains to Chicago and points west were running again. "I guess we're traveling in opposite directions," she said.

Ben Snow nodded. "I have a horse to pick up. How about you?"

"It would never have worked with Cyrus. I'm going back home to live with my sister. I should have known there'd be no new life for me."

"Maybe you didn't go far enough west."

She shook her head. "There'll always be someone who remembers the picture, and the trial. Someone who doesn't trust me around axes." Her face turned serious for a moment. "Thank you, Ben. He would have killed me the other night and framed me for Seth's murder."

"That was the plan."

She listened to a far-off voice. "I think they're calling my train."

"Lizzie—"

"No more of that! My name is Lizbeth Andrew Borden now, and shall be until I die."

Ben watched her hurry along the platform toward the rest of her life.

MIZ SAMMY'S HONOR

Florence V. Mayberry

What counts as an historical mystery is a subject of some dispute. Do stories whose action occurs within the author's lifetime fall into the category? If not, then Florence Mayberry's story is not historical, for though she has not stated the year, her protagonist is the elderly granddaughter of a Civil War veteran, and the story must therefore take place in the middle decades of the twentieth century. Whatever scruples others may have, however, we have no hesitation about including Florence Mayberry's story in Once Upon A Crime II. *It documents an era which in spirit, if not in time, is profoundly different from our own.*

Every night at six I went for the milk. On the stroke of six. Miz Sammy was exact about this. Miz Sammy was exact about everything and everyone, with one exception. The exception was Old Drunk Tom Canady, her good-for-nothing husband. What she saw in him, only the Lord and Miz Sammy knew.

Except, maybe, me, only nobody ever asked me since I was only around nine years old. One time Miz Sammy was showing me her heirlooms in her parlor and she picked up this tinted photograph of the prettiest grown-up boy I ever saw. That boy had big blue eyes, curly black hair, pink cheeks, and a daredevil smile. I asked, "Is this your boy?" And Miz Sammy said, soft as silk whispering against silk, "No, no, I've got no children. This is Mr. Canady. Taken a long time ago, soon after I first met him."

Long time or not, it was hard to believe that pretty boy could turn into the bloated, whiskery giant I'd seen staggering around town. Some folks said he drank because he came out of white trash, was only a riverboat cabin boy Miz Sammy had met up with that time she traveled by boat from St. Louis down the Mississippi to visit her folks in New Orleans. But along with that they did give a little sympathy for Old Drunk Tom, declared it could be a mite hard to live with high-handed quality like Miz Sammy, especially since her folks before they all died off never spoke a word to him after Miz Sammy married him. To Miz Sammy, they did, she was blood kin, but right in church one time her old daddy was heard praying out loud, "Thank You, Lord, for making my daughter barren."

Hard to blame the old man, my grandma said afterwards, because Drunk Tom was just plain no good. If it hadn't been Miz Sammy was quality, and a scorcher when she was mad, Tom Canady might have been rode out of town on a rail. He was mean in a fight, all right, carried a big knife, but there were plenty of stout men in our Missouri River town could've handled him.

Persnickety as Miz Sammy was, once I got to her house on time and once she gave me to understand she had seen to it the milk was also ready on the dot, waiting in the cool downstairs in the cellar, she often took her time about telling Poncey, her Negro hired boy, to fill my pail. Miz Sammy liked to talk to me, and I liked to listen. Lots of times she showed me her heirlooms. She was mighty proud of being a Blair. "Good blood brings honor, and nothing's more important than honor. Mind that, Louisa. Honor. Pay your just debts, don't be beholden to nobody. I may have to sell milk by the pint to pay mine, but they're paid, once I know where they're at." She probably meant by this any stray debt she hadn't heard about, run up by Old Tom whenever he could talk some fool into trusting him. "Just remember, Louisa, always hold your head high by keeping yourself square with the world. We Blairs ended up poor as Job's turkeys, but we had honor. Or else."

"Or else what, Miz Sammy?"

"We disowned 'em," she said flatly.

I was known as a saucebox at home, and it was on the tip of my tongue to ask how this fitted in with Old Drunk Tom, who didn't have anything, especially honor, what with charging up whiskey to Miz Sammy and getting her into debt she didn't know anything about. But maybe she figured if she finally found out and got them paid, why that kept Old Tom's head high.

I loved Miz Sammy's stories about the old days. About her granddaddy, Colonel Nelson Bedlington Blair, who had held a big chunk of the Missouri River country solid for the Confederacy. "He built this house, used to be a regular palace, parlor filled with fine furniture, handmade lace curtains on the windows, outside the lawn scythed smooth as velvet, parties with lanterns hanging from the trees, my mama decked out with real pearls, servants everywhere to take care of everything. And then that dratted war came. My granddaddy and daddy both fought in it."

She would sigh, and one night she said, "This house still has traces of that past time. In this very house, down cellar, there's a cell we never tore out, where granddaddy kept runaway slaves."

"Did your folks help 'em get free?" I asked.

"Land's sake, no! My granddaddy caught 'em, held 'em for their owners." Proudly, "We Blairs fought for the Confederacy, we were born and bred Southerners."

"I'm a Yankee," I said. "My grandpa freed the slaves. He did it in the Civil War when he was young. So if he'd been here then, he would have unlocked those slaves."

"Take your damned milk and scat home!" Miz Sammy shouted.

But that was just Miz Sammy's way. By the time Poncey got up the cellar stairs with the milk, she was feeding me sugar cookies and promising to show me the cell, iron bars and all, one of these days when she felt like climbing the stairs. Neither was I mad. All I cared about was getting a look at that cell. Imagine! Having your very own jail!

Miz Sammy was tall, close to six feet. She wasn't fat, but she was big. She had a proud lift to her head, and a figure that was all woman. Not that this meant anything to me back then. I was only nine and a girl besides.

Her blue eyes were wide-set. They could look deep into a person, but mostly they didn't. They just looked on Miz Sammy's own ideas. Her nose was straight and strong. And her mouth—I didn't like people hugging and kissing me, my mother said I was a "touch-me-not"—but I used to hope that sometime Miz Sammy would kiss me. Her mouth looked like if it kissed, the kiss would stay for keeps.

My mother said Miz Sammy would be handsome if she'd fix up. But lots of folks around town snickered about the men's clothes she wore when she worked in the cow barn or in the garden with Poncey. Behind her back, that is. Not to her face. When Miz Sammy got mad you could hear her cuss clear from her house surrounded by a two-acre lawn to the middle of town. Once when some white boys teased Poncey, she grabbed a couple and bounced their heads together. The fathers of the boys talked like they might join up and go have it out with Miz

Sammy, but that never got farther than talk at the front stoop of the drugstore. Miz Sammy was the daughter of Judge Courtney Blair, who was the son of Colonel Nelson Bedlington Blair. Our town was named Blairsville.

I always liked it when Miz Sammy's stories concentrated on those days when she was still rich. Everybody knew Old Drunk Tom had used up the money her daddy left her. But some folks swore she still had the family's diamond rings, fine gold jewelry, even her mama's pearl necklace hid out in her cellar. That whetted me up to get down cellar, maybe find where the treasure was. But even more than that I wanted to see that slave cell.

On this particular late afternoon, a hot summer evening when it hadn't rained for weeks, I ran to Miz Sammy's house, the milk bucket banging my bare legs. I stopped at the corner of the house and peeked around it to catch Poncey's signal. With Miz Sammy, it was as bad to be early as late. So Poncey always hung his red bandana on the outside knob of the back screen when it was exactly the time. Then, before I went inside, I would fold it up nice for him and hide it away.

The bandana was there, gently lifting in the breeze that was springing up. I tiptoed to the door, removed the bandana, and stuffed it down by the steps. Then I knocked on the porch screen and went inside.

The wooden striking clock on the shelf back of Miz Sammy's head said about a minute past six. Miz Sammy looked at the clock and then at me. "Well, Louisa?" she said, then squinted her big blue eyes and leaned forward. "What's that blood doing on your hand, miss? You fall and hurt yourself?"

Startled, I looked at my hand. Blood streaked the back of my fingers. "No," I said. "I didn't know it was there."

"No, *ma'am!*" Miz Sammy bawled. "What's the matter with your mother, not teaching you manners? Now that she's a widow, she ought to be learning how to be mother and father to you both and take you in hand."

"Don't you talk about my mother!" I said, banging the milk bucket on the table. I must have been a sight, skinny and freckled, my eyes glaring both mad and scared.

"I ought to blister you," Miz Sammy answered back, but very mild. "Go wash that blood off your hand. Poncey! Where did that dratted boy go? Poncey!"

I was standing by the window washing my hands and saw Poncey come out of his little cabin that was a few steps beyond the back porch of the big house. He had a white rag on his right hand with a big red splotch on it. Miz Sammy was hanging over my shoulder, looking too. When she spoke, no fight was in her voice. "I didn't know you were hurt, Poncey. You hurt bad?"

"No'm. Hit not deep, jist sprangled out."

"Come here and let me fix it. Right now, hear!" She turned to me with a curious, watchful expression. "How'd you get that blood on you, Louisa?"

I knew how. Off Poncey's red bandana. "I guess I got too hot running to be on time and my nose bled a little. I didn't carry a handkerchief."

She frowned. "Yes? Hum-m-m, well I'll pour out your milk and you better hike on home."

She took my bucket and opened the door which led to the cellar where the milk pans were kept in the cool. "Stay here, mind, don't follow me!" she ordered sharply, and shut the door hard behind her. She was back up in a few minutes and came out on the back stoop to watch me go. I felt her watching me like it was a shove. She made me stiffen and get so knock-kneed I almost tripped.

That's why I noticed the blood, from watching how I stepped. Big scattered drops of it led from the stoop to the outside cellar door which slanted against the house foundation. The cellar door was padlocked. Beside the padlock there was a splat of blood on the white paint.

On the way home I had to pass the old brick church which had been built by the Blair family before the Civil War. It was so run-down, bricks at its corners sloughing away, that it was no longer used. In the early twilight it had a brooding, scary look, as though all the dead people who had once attended it were hiding inside in the dimness to grab anyone who intruded on their church. It didn't help to see the ancient slave cemetery in back of it, its few moss-grown grave markers sticking up like snaggle teeth.

I ran past the church. By the time I reached home, I was out of breath, and milk had trickled between the pail and its lid from being swung.

"Landamercy," Grandma said. "The Booger Man after you?"

My mother came out of our room, brushing her hair. I knew she and Grandma were fixing to go to a social. "That goose chase you again?" She meant the old gander who had staked out a bug patch at the end of our lane. "If you'd face up to that goose with a switch, you could drive him off. You can't go around all your life being afraid."

What I said next, I didn't mean to say. "You'd run too. Because somebody's just been killed in Miz Sammy's cellar."

"Law, law!" Grandpa said, and shook his head in mock wonder.

"Shame on you, making up such tales," Grandma said.

"If anybody got in Miz Sammy's way, I wouldn't put it past her," Mama put in. "But who'd be silly enough to do that? Except, of course, that good-for-nothing husband of hers."

"Hum-m-m." This was Grandma, a deep back-of-the-head look in her eyes. "I've not seen Tom Canady lollygaggin' around town for a spell. Wonder if he's been up to something?"

"Saw him three days ago," Grandpa said. "Was at the barbershop getting his face steamed and hair cut. Been on a bender."

"When ain't he on one?" Grandma asked. "Louisa, what's this about somebody killed in the cellar?"

"Well," I said, "not really killed. Poncey's the one who got cut and he's alive and Miz Sammy's fixing up his hand. But he came out of the cellar dripping blood. There's blood all over the yard."

"Did Miz Sammy act like something terrible happened, or just like Poncey cut his hand working around?"

"Well—"

"This child is an exaggerator," Mama said. "With her two things equal ten. And if a drop of blood was shed, it'd be all over the yard."

"Maybe yes, maybe no," Grandma said. "Wouldn't hurt a mite for us to stop on our way to the social and say howdy to Miz Sammy. She might like to come along with us."

"Miz Sammy! Go to a social!" This was Mama. "She'll likely be pitchforking hay to the cows in the barn."

"Then we'll just pass the time," Grandma persisted. "If we hurry there'll still be enough light to tell if blood's spattered around."

Then and there I gave up my idea of walking as far as town with them. Maybe Poncey had washed away the blood. Maybe it wasn't his blood beside the cellar door, only browny-red spots of paint.

I hung around the front gate a few minutes after Grandma and Mama disappeared around a corner. Then I called to Grandpa that I was going up the street to play. He waved agreement.

I sauntered off, but once out of sight I ran. I cut back of the old church, had to slant across the edge of the slave graveyard, headed for Miz Sammy's cow lot near Poncey's cabin. The dark would help me hide if the grown-ups were standing around. And it was getting dark, faster than I liked. There was no moon and the stars only proved how dark the night was getting. At the corner of the church I ran blindly ahead. Next thing a murderous pain was in my foot and I was face down in soft spongy earth. I had tripped over a broken-off gravestone.

Fearful even to disturb the shadows, I didn't cry out. I lifted to one knee, hands crawling along the soft sod to gain support. My fingers fumbled over a soft cloth. I hung onto it for something to wipe off my feet and legs. Gone was my idea of eavesdropping back of Miz Sammy's house. I stood and stealthily retraced my steps. Still on the edge of the graveyard, back of the church, my bare feet stubbed on the hard, gritty ground.

As though it had waited for me to get near it, like a mean and clever dog at the end of a chain, a thought sprang at me. This earth I now walked over was hard and gritty, dry from lack of rain. But the sod around the gravestone I had tripped over was soft, loose. Why? WHY? Because that grave must have been dug up recently. Why? Nobody got buried there anymore. So why would anybody want to dig up a scary old grave with a broken headstone?

Under the hanging streetlight near our house I brushed my arms and legs with the cloth I had picked up, froze in mid-action. It was Poncey's red bandana. Its blood was dry, didn't rub off on me. But what had Poncey been doing out in the graveyard after dark?

I threw the bandana into a gulley and ran home.

That night, late, it rained. Hard, with thunder and lightning. It puckered up again while we ate breakfast and rained more. I had been planning to tell Grandpa about that fresh-dug-up old grave and get him to go look at it. But with the ground everywhere a loblolly of mud and Mama insisting I was an exaggerator, not even Grandpa would pay attention.

At breakfast Grandpa asked Grandma and Mama, "You women find Miz Sammy last night?" He winked at me.

"The house was dark," Grandma said. "And so was the yard. We couldn't've seen blood splotches if they'd been there. We went around back because Miz Sammy sets in the kitchen most of the time, but if she was there, she never answered."

When the rain stopped I put on my overshoes and walked down to the old church to examine the grave I fell on. It and another smaller grave were straggled out of line with the main graveyard. A bunch of chopped-off weeds were strewed around it. But with the rainwater running rivulets between the grave hummocks, everything muddy, the one I tripped over wasn't much softer than the others. I'd be called an exaggerator again. I should have kept that bloody bandana.

As I came down Miz Sammy's front walk early that evening, past the big scaly-white pillars of the veranda, around to the back door, my heart was beating fast. No red bandana was on the back doorknob. Poncey was even poorer than Miz Sammy. Likely had only one bandana, and I knew where that went.

"Come in, girl, don't let in the flies," Miz Sammy roared.

I went in. Poncey stuck his head from around the inside door to the cellar, said, "I gonna git it right now, Miz Sammy. Howdy, Miss Louizy."

I carried my bucket to the cellar doorway and stared past Poncey, trying to see below.

"All right, Louisa," Miz Sammy said sharply, "come sit right here at the table and wait. Hurry, Poncey."

Poncey vanished, shut the door solidly behind him.

The kitchen clock said ten to six. But for a wonder Miz Sammy paid no attention to the time. Just seemed in an almighty hurry to be done with me.

"Sit!" she repeated. "Now, don't bug those eyes out at me like a whipped pup. I baked some fresh buttermilk cookies, like to try a couple?" I nodded. Miz Sammy took two fat cookies out of a crock and handed them to me. I stared at her, and she stared at me. Then—I swear, it's the truth—she leaned over and lightly kissed my forehead.

"Well," she said, her cheeks real pink, which made her eyes look bluer than ever, "I'd like to know why I did that."

Before I had time to think up an answer, Poncey was back. He handed me my bucket, Miz Sammy took my money. With her other hand she pushed me out the back door. "I'll be right with you, Poncey," she said, and disappeared into the kitchen.

I stood on the steps, rubbing one foot on the other leg, thinking, dazedly, *Miz Sammy must like me, she must like me a lot.* Right after that I thought, *I sure would like to know what's in that cellar, I sure would.*

What pushed me into that second thought was, the outside cellar door wasn't locked. Its padlock lay on the ground beside it. Even a nine-year-old person might lift the door a crack, only a crack, and peek inside. And if that wasn't enough, the cellar was bound to be large enough to have hiding places. The door opening into the kitchen was at the middle of the house, the cellar entrance near one end. Even if Miz Sammy and Poncey came down to the cellar I could hunker down behind something.

I slipped around the corner of the house, hid my milk bucket in a shady flower bed. Whipped back, carefully lifted the slanted cellar door. Beneath it were shallow steps, a rough wall beside them blocking my view of the rest of the cellar. I raised the door higher, scooted under it, eased it down, tiptoed down the steps.

I was in a dim, hall-like corridor. Far down it, light from a high, narrow window revealed the corridor to be lined on each side with a series of alcoves. Odds and ends of furniture were stacked in one, boxes and trunks in another, a rake had fallen cattywise across the open side of another.

Where was the slave cell?

I tiptoed farther into the cellar, stopped as I saw a stair step angled into it, took a quick peek into the stair opening, and drew back. Miz Sammy stood at the top of the dim stairway. Poncey, a step down from her, his head blocking any view of me, was saying, "Hit's all right now, Miz Sammy, ever'thing quiet, hit's goan be fine for a spell."

I panicked, slipped across the corridor into an alcove, scrooged behind a ragged, busted-up sofa. Footsteps went up a step, the kitchen door shut.

A mouse skittered over a nearby board. I jumped into the middle of the corridor and was almost to the outside cellar door when I remembered I'd never have a better chance to see that old slave cell.

I tiptoed back. To left and right were the series of alcoves. Coal spilled from one. In another the faint light flickered on glass jars of canned fruit. The alcove with the rake held garden things, scythe, shovel, sacks of fertilizer.

And then I saw it. The alcove from which light filtered from the high, narrow window. This alcove was like the others, three heavy stone walls, no wall beside the corridor. But not open. Instead on that side were heavy iron bars, interrupted by an iron-barred door. The runaway slave cell.

I edged to it and stuck my nose between its first two iron bars. Inside was a cot, no other furnishing. A big man was lying on the cot. On his back, snoring, light from the high window touching his face. It was Old Drunk Tom Canady, Miz Sammy's no-good husband.

I said to myself, you better get out of here.

I ran back past the alcoves along the dim hallway and pushed against the slanted cellar door. It lifted slightly, then jerked against my thrust. It was now padlocked.

My breath whistled out. What would Miz Sammy, what would my folks do to me? What would I do if Old Tom woke up and saw me?

I took soft, sneaky steps halfway up the kitchen stairway and strained to hear movement. The kitchen was quiet. They had gone outside, found the cellar door unlocked, locked it. But maybe they would stay out awhile, give me time to slip through the kitchen, get outside, head for home.

A crack of light showed beside the door opening. Perhaps its catch was loose. I pushed it with my forefinger. The door swung open a few inches, and I almost jumped out of my skin.

There sat Miz Sammy at the table, her head on her arms, crying, her shoulders jerking. Horrifying, unreal. Like watching the Missouri River flood over its high bluffs to wash out the town. I caught the door's edge with my fingernails and closed it back to a crack.

Back down cellar I skittered to the alcove just short of the slave cell and across the corridor from it. This was beside the stairway, handy for escape. Also handy for Miz Sammy's milk pans, since a clean empty one sat on its broad shelf ready for morning's milk. I climbed up beside it so I could see better if Old Tom woke up. Too, I was hungry for the fading light from his window. I felt the cellar's dark creeping around me, ready to muffle me so not even a scream could be heard.

Whatever else could I do? I hated myself for being so little and stupid, with maybe no chance to grow up and get smart. Should I just stay hidden, wait for Grandpa and Mama to somehow find me? Or tiptoe right past Miz Sammy and take my chances on her skinning me alive?

Suddenly, from desperation, I saw what else I might do. I was small and skinny. The bars fronting the cell were about five inches apart. So were the three iron bars on the slave cell's window. I could slip through the cell's bars, shinny up the window wall, squeeze through the window bars.

But how climb about six feet to the window? The cellar walls were smoothed-off stone, no toeholds on them.

I recalled that board the mouse had scampered over, crept back to that first alcove I had explored, felt around until I found a stack of bed slats. I picked up one and went to the cell.

Old Drunk Tom still snored. I slipped the slat through the bars, sucked in my stomach, and turned sideways. My bottom snagged on one of the rusty bars and it rattled as I squeezed through. I didn't breathe for a minute, until a raucous snore released me.

The packed dirt floor of the cell was uneven, gouged out here and there. I found a handy rough spot beneath the window, braced the slat into it, put its other end against the window ledge. It formed a nice slanty climb.

On hands and feet, like a highbacked cat, I walked up the board until I touched the window ledge, steadied myself against its rough edge, reached with the other hand, and caught an iron bar. I let loose of the ledge and caught another bar. My full weight fell on them and I began to pull myself up.

Next thing I was sitting astraddle of the plank, two iron bars in my hands, splinters in my legs, and dried-out, rotten concrete sprinkled over me.

A heavy movement came from the cot. I looked over my shoulder. Old Drunk Tom was sitting up, his figure shadowy and menacing. "Hey!" he said. He gargled and hawked in his throat. "Fetch me one a my bottles, young'un. Old Tom's dry."

Better Miz Sammy than him.

I jumped off the board and headed for the cell bars. Next thing I was muffled against Old Drunk Tom's chest, his sour filthy breath floating around my head. "Say, maybe you come here to steal my whiskey, huh? What you doin' in my house? No young'uns round here, you been stealin' I'm gonna thrash your—"

I screamed. A miserable nightmare scream, barely peeping out of my mouth. Old Tom grabbed my ear and twisted. "Shut up! Scream agin 'n I'll stuff it down your throat, cram it through your belly!" He took one arm from around me, grabbed my shoulder, and shook me like I was a puppy, then slung me on his cot.

"Whose young'un are you?" His voice was thick, like his tongue took up too much room.

I couldn't speak. "Whose young'un!"

"Myra Newport's," I whispered.

"Old Josh Clark's widowed girl Myra?"

The mention of my grandfather brought courage. "He's my grandpa. You better leave me be. My grandpa keeps a shotgun under his bed. Loaded. He'll shoot you!"

One hand snatched me up. With the other hand he fumbled under the thin mattress. I saw the flash of a knife. "Sass me, I'll cut out your tongue. Lyin' too, why would Josh Clark's girl be in my cellar? You're some gypsy girl sneaked in here to steal."

"Is too my gran'pa, my gran'pa, my gran'pa!" I babbled.

He hesitated. Straightened, swayed like a high wind had struck him. Steadied and shook me again, then slung me back. My head struck the wall. "Your ole gran'pap come after me, I'll cut him worse'n I cut Ponce! I got a bellyful a being trounced around, locked up like some kinda animal. Looked down on like I ain't no man, jist some kinda animal. I'm gonna slice my way outa this damn jail!" He began to yell, "Samantha! Samantha! Git here afore I kill this sneakin' young'un!"

A door above us banged against a wall. Steps pounded down the cellar stairs. And there Miz Sammy stood on the other side of the bars, holding a lamp high beside her face. "Louisa!" Her voice sounded like it was squeezed out.

Old Drunk Tom yanked me off the cot, piniored my arms in front of him, put the tip of his knife against my throat. It pricked the skin. Stung.

"Tom, I'll let you out," Miz Sammy said quietly. "The key's in the kitchen, I'll get it. Set the child free."

Tom laughed. No fun in it. Deep, rough, like frogs inside him were trying to jump out. "No you ain't, you ain't gonna fool me no more. Onct this young'un's free, you'll take your time letting me out. You'll send Ponce for the constable, rouse up Josh Clark. Then I'll be nabbed onct I set foot outside. Neither you'll tell me where you had Ponce hide away my whiskey he stole, I won't git my whiskey. First you go bring me my whiskey, then mebbe I'll let go this young'un—"

"I'll get it," said Miz Sammy, turning toward the stairs. "There's a bottle in the pantry."

"Hold it!" he yelled. He laughed mean again, the frogs chunking up and down in his throat. The knife tip pressed at my skin. "Smart, ain't you? Allus been too smart, you and all them Blairs. But Tom's smarter. Thought you got all my whiskey outa that grave Ponce caught me scrabblin' in. Run off when I knifed him, but he come back later, dug up my bottles. Well, I got another hid back of you, over in them garden things. Got a bottle bedded down in a sack of fertilizer. Two more in that tub of shucked corn. You go git 'em, all three, or I'll slit this young'un's throat. Won't be my doin', it'll be yourn."

"Don't be a fool," Miz Sammy said coolly. "You do that, you'll end up not even drinking water. It's hard to swallow hanging from a rope."

"Woman, I got nowheres to go down, I already hit bottom. You reach me that whiskey or you'll have a murder in your hoity-toity damn house."

I felt squeezed into nothing as I saw Miz Sammy's broad shoulders droop like she just gave up. "Tom," she said. "Oh, Tom. What have we come to?"

This time his laugh lost its frog sound, sounded like a squawky trumpet. "Well, well. So I fin'ly got to show you who's boss."

"I reckon so," she said. "I'll go upstairs now and get the cell key. Then you bring out Louisa and get the whiskey yourself."

"No'm," said Old Tom, like licking on a stick of candy. "You'll not leave this cellar. You'll hand me them bottles. You'll poke 'em through these bars. This time I'm gonna drink in peace. I'm sick of drinkin' in jerks, scratching up a bottle at a time. Damn that Ponce anyway, spying, finding my grave hideout. Shoulda cut him for keeps."

"All right," Miz Sammy agreed. "But let Louisa go first. Louisa, how did you get in there?"

"I sc-scooted."

"Then scoot out. I'll fetch your bottles, Tom. When you have them, let the child go."

"Woman, I ain't crazy. This young'un's settin' right here till I drink my fill. Goin' no place, neither you. You kin set 'n watch."

"You're a fool! Josh Clark'll come looking for her. Any minute. She's expected home right after getting the milk."

"He comes messin' around 'n you call him in, me and this young'un'll both be outa here, her to Glory and me to hell," Tom said, mean. He flicked the knife's tip light and quick across my throat. It burned my skin in a fiery line.

Miz Sammy put the lamp nearer the bars, stared at me, her mouth tight in her white face. She turned, went swiftly toward the garden alcove just on the other side of the slave cell. There came the clatter of a spade or a hoe. She was out of our line of sight but now and again her shadow flickered on the corridor ceiling. I swiped at my neck, saw blood on my fingers. I was too scared to cry. I wondered if I could run fast enough, squeeze through the bars before Old Tom grabbed me. Knew I couldn't. Two of his big steps and he'd have me before I reached the bars.

In the alcove next door bottles clicked against each other. I thought I heard a splash, but wasn't sure: *Dear God, don't let Miz Sammy spill it all, he'll cut me sure if she does.*

"Git a move on!" Old Tom yelled.

And there came Miz Sammy against the bars, a bottle in her hand. She held it through the bars. "Where's t'other'n?" he demanded.

"Can't carry but one at a time with a lamp in my hand. And you can't drink but one at a time. Louisa's still with you, you've got what you asked for."

His laugh was almost a giggle. "Outsmarted by your ole man, huh? All that damn honor you brag your feisty folks left you with don't count for much tonight, does it? Set that bottle on the floor. Inside." She did. "Young'un, pick it up." I did.

Old Tom held the bottle in one hand, me with the other. "Uncork it," he ordered, then sniggered. "Maybe I oughta give her the first nip, Samantha, so she'll be more friendly." Miz Sammy drew a sharp breath, her face spooky in the lamplight. Nothing about her looked alive except her eyes.

I struggled with the cork, my fingers like rubber bands. Old Tom swore, shoved me toward the back of the cell. "Git in that corner and stay put. You run, I'll stick you."

He stood in the center of the cell. Uncorked the bottle, tipped it, took a long swallow. "Hell of a taste, musta turned on me. Been hid too long." He grinned, said, "But a second swaller always kills the first." He drank again.

He spat. Strangled, coughed. Dropped the knife, grabbed his throat. Staggered to the cot and fell on it.

"Louisa! Scat out of there!" Miz Sammy's voice was like a whipcrack.

Tom groaned. "What's in this, what'd you gimme?" He croaked, gagged. The cell smelled awful, with sweat and sour stomach. I slipped through the bars.

"Run for Doctor Masters up the street! Hurry!" Miz Sammy ordered. "Tell Poncey come help me! Tell him Tom's poisoned, we got to pour salt water down him." She looked savage, as though she hated me. "Scat, you little meddling fool! He's dying!"

He did die. That night. Miz Sammy had put a dose of bug poison in his whiskey, figuring to give him just enough to get me free. She and Poncey washed him out quick as they could, and the doctor ran down with his stomach pump. Doctor Masters testified to the police that the dose was mild, ought only to have made him sick enough to let me free, he had such fast treatment. But according to the autopsy, Old Tom's stomach, already half eaten up with whiskey, had been in no shape for bug poison.

There was never any question about Miz Sammy being exonerated. It was barely considered even any kind of manslaughter, what with everybody in town trying to shake her hand for saving a child. As for the child, well, you better believe that's the last milk I was ever sent for. Only ones happy about that were me and the old gander.

Miz Sammy on her part wouldn't shake hands with anybody. Kept swearing she was guilty of murder, tried to get her lawyer to set up a trial. Said it wasn't honorable for her to go free, asked if it had been Old Tom poisoning her instead of the way it was, would he have gone free?

Weeks later, Poncey found Miz Sammy down in the slave cell. Dead. Lying on Old Tom's cot, a broken glass on the floor beside it. Bug poison again. This time a strong dose and nobody to rinse her out.

A sealed envelope addressed to Poncey was beside her. It read, "This is for Poncey Jones from Samantha Blair." Poncey was afraid to open it. He got Doctor Masters to do it. Inside was a heavy gold ring with a big diamond in it. A carat or more. Her daddy's ring.

That was all the Blair jewels ever found.

THE 1944 BULLET

Jeffry Scott

Our final selection joins the present to the past, for it involves the journey of a contemporary Englishman to the war-destroyed village of his childhood. With its many reflections on the nature and personal significance of history, the story provides the perfect closure to this volume, which we hope you've experienced as a journey of a sort too.

I am not a dotard—lovely, antiquated word—but I can't carry phone numbers in my head, where until recently, forty or more awaited instant retrieval. And sometimes, not often, I go into a room or consult a file and for the life of me, cannot remember what the heck I was looking for. Momentary glitches, one hopes, insignificant. Really . . .

My long-term memory, by contrast, can be strikingly vivid, precise. Visions are fragmented, out of sequence, but I hear the voices, see facial expressions and details of clothing involved in events of half a century ago. It's worth adding that I am under sixty, if only just, and still play adequate squash and better golf. I pay for it next morning, hobbling to the shower, but that's natural.

Time may be the crucial factor here. Think of the years behind me as miles: I set out a child pilgrim among buildings looming too close and tall for their identity or purpose to be discerned—didn't the world seem much bigger when you were young? Looking back over the level plain of decades, one makes sense of the place left so long ago, seeing clearly. That's not a cliff but a cathedral, those giant sentries were trees in a park, and so on. . . . The same clarity applies to people of my young days, and their motives.

My memory reaches at least as far back as 1944, when I was eight years old. Back to Aybold Mains, and the Madwoman (but that was just village talk, she was homesick and neurotic, not crazy) who died by violence. And it lets, no, it forces me to hear again what my brave, beloved brother kept saying, when she was killed.

I wish to God that it didn't.

My heart turned over when I came downstairs that morning. Karen gave me an amused *What?* look but I didn't respond so she went back to her slice of toast and the *Daily Mail.* She had got used to being blond and gorgeous, with legs looking two yards long. I still couldn't get used to finding her in my home.

The snag being that Karen was hardly ten years older than my eldest daughter; they kept getting taken for sisters, which was less than comforting. But that wasn't what shook me. I had a nasty conviction that things were about to worsen, and the obvious reason for that was my eternal fear that she'd meet somebody nearer her age and tastes, so I ought to make the most of what I was seeing. . . . Then I turned to an inner page of the *Independent,* where a responsible broadsheet puts offbeat news, to find that the bad feeling wasn't about Karen at all.

Aybold Mains: The name jumped out and smacked me between the eyes . . . and in the belly.

Weird, because I'd loved Aybold Mains, it was my birthplace. Maybe the reflex of pain and dread was because I had been exiled from Eden. That village always touched a nerve, in much the way that one flinches at reminders of a friend who died too young, and badly, or a placid, benign kingdom destroyed out of spite.

"Look at this, Charlie!" Karen held up the *Daily Mail* with a frosted-pink, almond-shaped nail slanting towards a headline: TIME-CAPSULE TOWNSHIP JOINS THE NINETIES.

"Isn't that terrific? Tailor-made for a spot on the Prog." Beauty needs a flaw, and Karen's is to talk jargon when excited. She is a TV producer, in charge of what just about qualifies as a current-affairs show. I'd never been brutal enough to say so, but it was aimed at an audience with a shorter attention span than monkeys, if marginally greater intelligence.

"I shall get right on it," she said to herself. And to me, "Can't you see the possibilities? A town like Snow White's castle, wakened after a lifetime. It's thrilling."

"If you read a proper paper instead of a comic, you wouldn't talk rubbish." I rustled the *Independent* at her. "Same story's in here, but with facts. Aybold Mains isn't, wasn't, a town. Just a large village. And it hasn't been under a magic spell. The government sent the locals packing during World War II so generations of soldiers could learn street fighting there. Your enchanted village was a War Office battle school—a military slum getting hell knocked out of it since before you were born."

Part of me stood aside and groaned during the put-down. Good old Charlie, never hit a woman in his life. You don't have to strike people to hurt them. I sounded a pedantic, sneering old bastard, patronising a green girl. Karen is a graduate, she reached the upper levels of a stressful and demanding trade on brains and initiative, not looks. And she hated being reminded of our age difference. . . .

But all she did was retrieve her paper, taking rather a long time to put it away in the briefcase beside her chair. She looked all right when she straightened up again. "I forgot, you're from the west country. Did you ever visit that town—village—when you were little?"

I nearly told her that I couldn't have visited Aybold Mains because I lived there, damn it. Instead I said abruptly, "I shan't be around for a day or two. Got an out-of-towner."

"That's a bit sudden. I wish you had warned me." They worked Karen hard on that programme. Often the first production meeting was at six in the morning, with an edition recorded twelve hours later. Her free time was valuable; probably she had fixed a day off to be with me.

"I'd have told you last night," I lied, "but you weren't interested."

Karen had got back late, with a several-glasses-of-champagne buzz on. At a company party for network clients, she was taken aside and told of being pencilled in as executive producer; she was on her way. I would have rolled home roaring drunk and kept my partner up until the small hours gloating. She had just said, "It's a bit nice, you'll be proud of me yet," and gone to bed.

I hadn't told Karen I must go away, because until ten minutes ago, I was unaware of it. I had to see Aybold Mains, now that it was open once more. . . . No notion why, but certain it was needful.

Explaining to her was out of the question. "It's the Welsh branch office, our divisional finance controller has his knickers in a twist over redundancy payments." Karen looked so crestfallen that I felt a real swine.

Hardly surprising, since I was. Human nature being what it is, her disappointment irked me. "It's not Outer Mongolia, I'll be back in a couple of days."

"But you're a consultant, Charlie, and they're treating you like a junior."

"Stop sounding like a wife, doesn't suit you." I smiled to take the sting away, but it didn't, so I said she'd be late if she didn't get her skates on, that was no way to start her first day as executive producer–elect.

Karen's voice wavered between tears and anger when she went to the door. "Go for as long as you like! You always do this—if I'm up, you knock me down, and never say why."

It wasn't that, of course, though I preferred not to enquire what it was. Shelving the matter, I read the *Independent*'s report about Aybold Mains all over again.

The village had been the subject of a compulsory purchase order in 1944. In other words, the government made every landlord and householder an offer they couldn't refuse. The War Office—no mealy-mouthed stuff about Ministry of Defense in those desperate days—vowed we could all return home as soon as peace broke out. Not so; the army had stayed there ever since, in a No Go area for civilians.

Now Aybold Mains had been handed over to a consortium, comprising Peerless Parks, the Department of the Environment, and the Defense Ministry. Peerless Parks rang a bell; sure enough, it was part of the Ottermole Group. I phoned Ham Gradstone, their deputy chairman, asking if I might take a look at Aybold. Ham didn't know that my connection was personal, any more than Karen did. It was not something I had told . . . well, anyone, really.

As intended, he jumped to the conclusion that, as usual, I was scouting for unusual, vaguely worthy, risk-capital investment areas. "I'll get on the horn right away, Chaz. The place won't be ready until next year at the earliest, it's a bit of a mess at present," he warned. "Our tame archaeologist and minions are on site, though. I'll tell them to roll out what passes for a red carpet, lots of bowing and scraping."

Sorry about this, but the hackneyed quotation is inevitable: The past is another country where they do things differently.

So I have to explain a bit about me and my family. Dad was a marine engineer, away for months at a stretch. A naval reservist; he went back into uniform at the outbreak of war in 1939, swopping a sleek cargo liner for a destroyer which got torpedoed off Crete, keeping him away forever.

This sounds heartless, but there was little sense of loss for me. My big brother Steve was father figure and idol, thanks to Dad's extended absences. I was just a little kid, but I could tell that Steve was a hell of a fellow. Girls fancied him and boys admired him. A natural leader, as they say.

I must have been a millstone round a teenager's neck, but Steve found time for me. He taught me to play cricket and soccer, took me exploring in the woods, and showed me how to fish. He was very young to be man of the house, but he'd had plenty of practice while Dad was at sea.

I could talk about him for hours, but dwelling on my brother breaks my heart. Along with countless brothers, he died in the war.

Aybold Mains was a village like any other, no doubt. Not quaint, not even very pretty, sheltered in a Devon valley half a mile inland from the cliffs. Aybold prided itself, all those years ago, on being bang up-to-date, more suburban than rural. We had electricity, sewerage, and streetlights, just like a proper town. All thanks to a London tycoon who planned to set up light industry there, but went spectacularly broke once the infrastructure was in place. Dr. McPhee, parish council chairman, never mentioned Aybold Mains without tacking on, "a town in miniature," just as Homer's sea was always wine-dark. . . .

We had one of the five bungalows in Dane Street. They were widely spaced down one side, with fields on the other. The bungalows were super-modern, built in 1937, and there ought to have been many more, but the builder lost heart when all those grand London plans withered. Dane Street was a country lane with big ideas, a local joke being that it had more streetlamps than dwellings: which was true.

Next door lived the Artist and the Madwoman, as many villagers referred to them. The Artist was Hugh Feather, a World War I veteran and what used to be known as a remittance man. Remittance men were black sheep packed off to outposts of the empire, bribed with stay-away money. Feather's family was not affluent, so he was packed off not farther than the other end of the county.

He'd fought in the Spanish Civil War, and brought back the Madwoman. He called her Connie, short for Consuelo, I suppose. From patriotism or stupidity, she never bothered to learn much English. Forced to do shopping, she'd point and scowl, muttering what even a child of my age could perceive as curses when mime was insufficient.

She could have spoken like the lady of the manor and still daunted me. Her eyes rolled a lot. Her hair was like Medusa's, always in motion, blue-black ringlets and elf-locks stirring on her restless head. Bolder small children threw stones at her, if far enough off to run for their lives afterwards.

The Artist was more of a figure of fun, a toff who dressed like a tramp. He painted every day, without (sneered village art critics) managing a decent human likeness or a recognisable vase of flowers or bowl of fruit. People said he was a bit soft in the head, but smart enough to sponge off his family and never do a stroke of real work.

Living close, I knew Hugh Feather better than did most of my schoolmates. I liked drawing, and he taught me the rudiments of perspective and composition. It made me feel grown-up to be asked into his place, which happened rarely. The bungalow was shockingly untidy and grubby, but he had no end of curios and souvenirs, and he let me play with some; others were not to be touched, he decreed. Significantly, until recently I could recall only the fascination of his collection, not its details.

The Artist treated me as a valued guest, never talking down, while Connie lurked in the hall, grumbling incomprehensibly in the throaty manner of a cat preparing to fight. Despite which, such visits were much prized—and never mentioned to my friends.

Then came the war, and there was talk of leaving a white feather on the Artist's doorstep—"He's got the right name, that shirker!"—after the Home Guard was created and he refused to join. Dad, home at the time, told us that Hugh Feather had won medals in Flanders, and "risked another packet" fighting Franco in Spain. My father, I understand now, was a special man; I wish I had known him properly.

Pretty soon Feather got a job with the Ministry of Agriculture and Fisheries, roaring around South Devon on a motorbike. He didn't mind helping the war effort, he confided to Mum, but drew the line at killing any more people.

Typically, Aybold Mains sneered that it hadn't taken the Artist long to do well out of the war. For my part, I considered him far better value than our other close neighbour in the bungalow nearest the main street—PC Bell, the village copper.

Not long after Dad was killed, Steve got called up. He went into the army, and ended as a paratrooper. That left me, six or seven years old, as nominal man of the family.

PC Bell was a decent chap, but the police were short-handed and he was covering a larger area than before the war; even when available, he tended to be exhausted. So it was natural that when Mum needed help with the gardening, or a broken window mended, the Artist should lend a hand.

He'd drop in of an evening to hear the nine o'clock news on the wireless, when his wasn't working. And the motorbike took him far beyond Aybold Mains, which was a godsend to Mum, for he gave her lifts here and there (petrol rationing restricted us to two buses per day). With the Artist in our front room, it was like having a family again. I couldn't stay up for the news, but he'd give me a game of draughts before bedtime. So if I didn't pray for his wireless to misbehave, then I certainly hoped with fervour. . . .

It wasn't a bad time to be a boy. By 1944 southern England had turned into a vast armed camp. Even in our backwater we encountered sleekly towering trucks quite unlike boxy British ones, carrying the first GIs who tossed out the first sticks of gum.

One May morning, Mum was crying and shaking when I came downstairs. "We've got to go," she sobbed. "They're clearing us all out. They've given us three weeks . . . *and we own this bungalow.* How we'll manage, where we can go, it's beyond me, Charlie."

The government (which I took to mean Winston Churchill up there in London, living in Big Ben) wanted our home and every home, and the smithy-cum-bicycle-repair-shop where our glass-sheathed radio battery was charged every Wednesday, and the school, the church, the village hall, the Ploughman's Inn, and the Sun in Splendour. Streets and gardens and trees, birds, butterflies, and rabbits, everything.

It was as if I had been sentenced to death: unable to conceive of a viable life ahead of me. I had been out of Aybold Mains twice in my brief (though it did not seem so to me) life. To Exeter for a Christmas pantomime, and once to Torquay aboard a motor coach with the rest of the school for a boy scouts rally where Steve was getting a special award.

Somebody else took it even harder—the Artist's woman. I overheard him tell Mum that Connie was living up to the villagers' cruel nickname for her. "Connie thinks I'm trying to dump her," he said. "It's all a

conspiracy between me and the government and the army to winkle
her out of the blessed house. The crazy part—" Embarrassed, he started
again. "The silly part is that she hates England, hates this place. Probably hates me, God help us. But the bungalow represents security, I suppose."

Mum succumbed to similar if milder despair, at first. Then she pulled
herself together, and we packed stuff and threw stuff away, and the
pile of crates and cartons and bags and suitcases kept growing.

The entire community was in the same boat; eventually Aybold
Mains took on the air of a jumble sale with nobody buying. Items out-
worn, outmoded, or too awkward to take long distances were stored
in sheds and garages or simply left outside houses. We had to be gone
by the end of May. The majority of villagers, bloody-mindedly British,
reached an unspoken, shared decision to stick until the end, all leaving
on the final possible date.

And during our last week at Aybold Mains, an army corporal turned
up—my brother Steve.

Much has been said and written about the secrecy involved in that
D-Day invasion of Europe. But my impression is that virtually everyone in Britain knew or sensed what was coming. They didn't know the
date, June 6, but then General Eisenhower did not know that until the
last moment. What we were certain of was that a Big Show was im-
minent.

Steve told us that his commanding officer had let him slip away for
forty-eight hours. "Soon as I get back, all leave will be cancelled to stop
chaps shooting their mouths off in pubs." Steve was a man in more than
age now, attitude graver and harder, fitfully kind and attentive to me,
terse with Mum. Fanciful souls might say that my brother had a pre-
monition he would be killed. Then again, any soldier bound for the Nor-
mandy beaches would be unsure of his future.

At the start of this account, I spoke of long-term memory. For much
of my life I shrank from remembering Aybold Mains. Much of that was
due to feeling hurt because Steve was different the last time we were
together, disapproving in some mysterious fashion. Only relatively recently has the truth made itself clear—it was towards our mother that
he changed.

I know that they quarrelled when he came home. As when she and
Dad had fallen out, they'd shut up when I appeared. And Steve, hind-
sight insists, pumped me about Hugh Feather, the Artist. Mum hadn't

warned me to be discreet (for there was nothing about which to be discreet) so naturally I chattered. . . .

"Makes himself at home, then, gets his feet under the table," Steve suggested casually.

"Only when his wireless is bust. But he plays draughts with me every week."

"Bet he does," Steve agreed flatly. And from that moment I worried that he had turned against me, for unknown reasons.

It was a rotten reunion. When not drawing me about Feather behind Mum's back, he brooded constantly. And suddenly it was our last full day in Aybold Mains. . . .

The weather was sultry. After the midday meal, a hell of a row broke out in the Artist's bungalow. All our doors and windows were open for relief from the heat, so we could hear Connie in full cry next door. Though the language was closed to us, its abuse and reproach needed no translation.

It went on and on. At one stage frantic crashing and rustling took us to the kitchen doorstep. From the heaving of the privet hedge, Connie was trying to force her way into our garden, while Feather hauled her back. . . .

"See what you've started?" Steve snarled, and Mum, startled and then furious, exclaimed, "Shame on you, in front of the lad!" Their exchange baffled me.

"I'm off out of this," he grunted. "Want to come for a walk, kiddo?"

We rambled for miles, wandering around every part of the place where Steve and I had grown up. That made sense, since the government was expelling us until the war was over. It never occurred to me that he did not expect to return.

My feet hurt and my legs ached trudging down the main street in Steve's wake. The church clock struck five as we passed the Sun in Splendour, but an approaching storm created early twilight. Steve had his beret tucked under the shoulderstrap of his battledress tunic. His face was glazed with sweat. He hadn't said anything for a mile or more.

We turned the corner into Dane Street. PC Bell was tinkering with his bicycle by the front gate of his place. They chatted: Colin Bell and my brother were fellow cricketers before the war. Bell said he was staying on for a few days to liaise with the army. Already a cadre of infantry training officers and NCOs had begun exploring the village.

Dane Street fell away steeply from the main street. It wasn't very wide, and the fat, unkempt hedge on the side without houses narrowed it even more at that season. From the policeman's bungalow you could just make out the roof of our place, and no more than the rabbit's ears chimneys of the Artist's home.

We moved on, PC Bell lingered by his gate. It was a matter of sightlines. . . . Even when the shot alerted Bell, an apple tree obscured his view. Steve and I were, as the proverb goes, watchers who saw most of the game.

And what we saw, when we were nearly home, was Connie, the Madwoman, come hurtling into the road from their bungalow. Unaware of us, she made as if to go into our place, then halted. She cried out shrilly, evidently calling for Mum to come out.

I ran into a barrier—the back of Steve's hand against my chest. "Hold hard," he said.

I looked up, wanting to know why he was restraining me, why Connie was screeching at Mum.

The noise whipped my head round again. It was a sharp, vicious, cracking sound, like a whip. I was in time to see Connie collapsing in a heap.

Steve, reacting instantly, sprinted downhill to her. This was where memory processes always puzzled me. For when I thought of that afternoon I saw him not in khaki battledress but shorts, striped shirt, football boots, tearing towards the goal. Two periods mingled: my brother at about sixteen, on the soccer pitch, but in front of him lay an ungainly bundle in a floral-patterned frock.

Anyway, Steve went to her. Behind us, PC Bell shouted, "What's up?" or "What was that?" something of the sort.

Bell lumbered past, knocking me aside in his haste, just as Steve reached the body in the roadway and called, "Somebody's shot her, Colin!"

I hurried up. PC Bell, breath rasping in his nose, was going down on one knee beside Connie. I can't recall seeing the head wound. But there is a firm impression of blood on the roadway, one ringlet melting into a wetly shining worm. Suddenly Steve, having stepped back, grabbed me in a bear hug. His belt buckle smacked me in the teeth, and I was half stifled, choking on the smell of serge and metal polish while he whispered urgently, *"Don't look, don't look, kiddo."*

PC Bell gabbled, "She's dead, right enough, what in God's name happened here?"

"Search me," said Steve. "We were walking down and next thing, she just fell all of a heap. Didn't you hear the gun go off, Colin?"

"What do you think? 'Course I did!" Then: "Get the boy indoors, Steve, toot sweet."

My brother released me, spun me round, and swatted me hard on the backside. "Inside now! Don't let Mum come out. I'll be in presently." He wasn't to be argued with. I darted one more horrified glance at the corpse, my first really and truly dead body, and departed.

From the corner of my eye I saw PC Bell unbuttoning his blue tunic. I heard Steve offer, "Let me fetch that tarp, it'll be better." The Artist had borrowed a farm cart to move their furniture, and rolled up beside his bungalow's front gate was the tarpaulin to cover it. Steve, army hobnails ringing as he mounted the kerb, looked back, saw me peeping, and shouted angrily, "Get indoors, bloody little ghoul!"

So much for my direct, eyewitness experience of an unsolved crime.

Connie had been shot at near point-blank range (a few specks of propellant tattooing her forehead) with a .32 calibre automatic. That was all the authorities established, beyond murder by a person unknown.

Chance . . . If PC Bell hadn't seen us that afternoon, then Steve could have been among the suspects. As it was, the shot came within seconds of our saying farewell to the policeman, he was staring downhill along Dane Street an instant later—and observed that the two of us were still yards away from the dead woman.

The inevitable and prime suspect was Hugh Feather. But again, chance cleared him. Shortly before Connie died, a farmer from the next village called to sort out a query about tractor-fuel forms. Feather had dismantled his office in the spare bedroom, so they started delving in an already-packed tea chest. They were indoors together when the shot was fired. They heard no report, it was the shouting that alerted them.

The investigation must have been a nightmare. Policemen came from Exmouth, but the War Office was adamant—the village must be cleared next day. Residents and police alike were on a deadline. Steve gave the CID a statement and was on his way back to camp in Wiltshire that evening. Mum and I set off to her aunt's home, up-country, at first light the following morning. More than a week later a Bristol policeman questioned me all over again, but there was little I could tell him.

Long afterwards—on honeymoon in Ibiza, that long ago—I ran into PC Bell, there on a pensioners' package holiday. The murder was the single most dramatic event of his career, and it was natural for us to discuss it.

"A lot of odd fish were loose during the war," he said. "I reckon it was an army deserter, one of them foreigners, as it might be, Free French, or a Canuck or Yank, they was trigger-happy if you like."

The official theory had been that the killer waited behind the hedge opposite the Artist's bungalow. When Connie emerged, he poked the gun through the hedge, at the full extent of his arm, and shot her in the head. "You and your brother, rest his soul, had her in sight the whole time," Bell argued. "Your attention being on her, you never spotted the chap behind the hedge."

When I asked about motive, white-haired Bell was impatient. "Who knows? She was foreign, flighty. Not even a wedded wife, neither. Stands to reason she wouldn't think twice about romancing other fellows. Maybe some Spanish Gypsy like herself, they're hot-blooded. Crime of passion, stands to reason."

I didn't believe a word of it. Connie had been fixated on Feather. But former PC Bell, once nostalgic gossip dwindled, wanted to get back to the swimming pool and the cheap beer. So I didn't challenge his verdict.

As for the Artist, if he tried to stay in touch with Mum, I never knew of it; and I never saw him again. Steve's death on D-Day plus three broke her; she was in hospital by 1945 and bedridden for the rest of her short life.

When I arrived in Aybold Mains, it was at once exactly what I'd expected, and wholly surprising.

All those years I had imagined it violated and soured and ruined. There was a lot of that—the high street a wilderness of brambles and nettles and heaps of rubble unrecognisable as buildings; and a medley of smells, the reek of rotten plaster fighting the scent of honeysuckle smothering one ruin. Yet the church was intact and areas seemed no more than neglected. The Sun in Splendour pub looked much the same, apart from having a healthy, long-established bush growing out of its chimney. Most surviving houses were pocked by small-arms fire.

The army had enclosed the village in a tall security fence with rolls of razor wire along its base. Ellen Parkin was waiting where once soldiers had guarded the vanished main gates. Not only policemen look younger as one gets along in life—in her cutoffs and sun top I took Ms. Parkin for a student on a vacation job, but she was running the Aybold Mains project.

"Our masters in London told me to let you see everything," she said, "but it's not that simple. The army has been playing bang-you're-dead here since the forties, so the odd grenade or antipersonnel mine may have been mislaid. We've taped off patches that are still dodgy—stay out of them. Otherwise, feel free."

Ellen Parkin, Dr. Parkin actually, started pointing out village landmarks, orientating me. It rankled—I had not set foot here since boyhood, but I yearned to snap that having lived here, it was mine, and I didn't need lessons from an interloper.

Sensing constraint, she smiled apologetically and suggested, "You want to see for yourself, I expect."

"There's not much left of the place." Hearing myself, it sounded accusing, sullen.

Dr. Parkin nodded ruefully. "Oddly enough, the village stayed in better shape while the army was actively abusing it. They'd concentrate on a few buildings at a time, for the rough stuff with live ordnance, and kept the rest weatherproof, meanwhile. Some were used as offices and stores, and I suspect the instructors bagged others as unofficial officers' messes and so forth."

By then we were strolling along what had been the main street, a mixture of beaten clay and vestiges of fifty-year-old road surface scarred by tank tracks. "Until five years ago they trained soldiers here for Northern Ireland," she said. "You'll find places with Republican graffiti sprayed on the walls—'Smash H Block,' 'Brits Out'—for the proper Belfast ambience. This facility was abandoned after the last budget cuts . . . but the warriors held on to it long after it was needed. That's when the village finally died."

Her regret made me ashamed of earlier, childish resentment. "Where do you fit in?" I asked.

"Industrial archaeology is my specialty. I set up a new-style museum in Wales, at a derelict colliery village. Very popular with schools, and it puts new generations in touch with their roots." She coloured sheepishly. "Don't start me off! But John Buchan said it for me: If we don't know where we came from, how the heck can we see where we're going? Words to that effect, though he put it more elegantly."

I was liking her better. She said, "The idea here is to reconstruct a southwest rural community during World War II. Some of it will be fake—replica, to you. Reproduction propaganda posters, 'Dig for Victory' and all that, various artefacts we'll buy on the open market or borrow from other museums . . . wartime radio sets, kitchen gear, what-you-will, to fit up complete homes. We've already salvaged or excavated some interesting items. Excellent stuff is turning up in attics and cellars."

She broke off, with a concerned glance. "Are you okay? You look a bit seedy."

"I'm fine. All I need is fresh air. . . ."

"And peace and quiet," Ellen Parkin guessed aloud, not offended. "Look, nose around for a while, then have a picnic lunch with us. That place like a chapel is the village institute. The fabric's unsafe so we don't go inside, our trailers are parked in the yard behind—you can't miss us."

Dr. Parkin jogged away towards the building she had indicated; it was a sexist thought, but she looked just as good from behind as in front—not at all my image of an academic.

She'd been right, I did feel seedy, if that covered a kind of emotional vertigo. Aybold Mains was a defaced caricature of the place I had remembered for so long. And even in its ruinous state, it demonstrated that I had remembered half of it wrongly. But for the map, and Ellen Parkin's confirmation, I would have doubted its identity.

I went exploring, and soon enough I was at the top of Dane Street. Now it was no more than a tunnel plunging down through rampant brambles. The tall chimneys of the Artist's bungalow were barely visible among young trees. Somebody had hacked the briars aside, allowing passage for dwarfs or limber young people willing to scramble on hands and knees.

I stayed where I was. At the time (how we lie to ourselves, unknowingly) it seemed that locating our old home would be too painful. One hardly needed to look: It would be a tumble of bricks and roof tiles, another nonhuman corpse decomposing.

That was how I excused my utter inability to venture into Dane Street. Truly it never struck me that a queasy stomach and sweaty hands were symptoms of deeply buried fear. . . .

Lunch was a doorstep sandwich with an apple for dessert. Ellen Parkin's team had three trailers parked behind the village institute, as office, equipment store, and the last a workshop where finds could be examined. We ate outdoors at a trestle table.

The crew was young, enthusiastic, and bright, their names skidding off my forebrain as soon as they'd been introduced. Fortunately they were talkative, since I was struggling with . . . whatever it was. Anxiety attack, unless I was coming down with the flu. All I needed to do was turn my face towards the current speaker, and try to look intelligent.

Yet I took in information somehow. Because the village had been evacuated at relatively short notice, an unusually large number of artefacts were left behind—I could have told them that, of course. A boy remarkably unbowed by the treble handicap of a stammer, squint, and severe acne, positively glowed when telling me of discovering a shed at the heart of a briar patch with an Austin Seven car inside.

"I found a gorgeous model train layout, Hornby Double-00 gauge, in the attic of the pub," a girl struck in.

"Nearly losing a leg in the process," Dr. Parkin added drily. "Tina fell through the floor, the boards were rotten."

"But," Tina said proudly, "I fell *backwards,* so I didn't drag the train set down with me. Fantastic presence of mind."

"What mind?" somebody demanded, and they squabbled amiably.

Ellen Parkin spoke quietly. "Great kids . . . I'm letting them get treasure hunting out of their systems before we settle down to the slog and grind."

As if answering his cue, a lanky youth entered the yard, to mocking cheers from the rest. He was a living statue, naked except for shorts and the knee and elbow pads used by skateboarders. Shorts, protective gear, and skin alike were a dull, stony grey streaked with the black and brown of mud or worse. A miner's helmet swung from one hand.

"Unclean, unclean," Tina chanted squeakily, echoing the ancient warning against lepers.

Her joke seemed eerily appropriate. I don't hold with premonitions, ESP, any of that bag of tricks, but something insisted that the newcomer threatened me. It wasn't the boy, as such; he was a messenger or an omen.

I was scared. Not by him, he was only a horribly dirty teenager, but by his effect on me. First that vertigo on entering the village, perceptible enough for Ellen Parkin to remark on it, followed by vague depression and anxiety; now this outbreak of superstitious dread.

I wasn't right—and there surfaced a phrase from my childhood, an Aybold Mains euphemism for someone whose stability was suspect— I wasn't at all right. I'd never had a nervous breakdown. Was this how they commenced?

Dr. Parkin said something. By willpower, I smiled, asked her to repeat it.

"This is our tame Tunnel Rat. No, Leo, don't dare shake hands with the VIP." She chuckled helplessly. "Leo's forte is caving, so we use him for burrowing in confined spaces."

Teeth showed startlingly white in the filthy face. "Be right back. I've got to go and be hosed down."

When a scrubbed-looking Leo reappeared in clean shorts and T-shirt, he was carrying a small plastic box. Ellen Parkin groaned theatrically. "He's like a dog with a bone, every new face has to be shown Leo's great find."

He took it in good part, a schoolboy, no more than fifteen, chinless, beaky cast of features matching his good-school accent. As the other youngsters trooped back to work, Leo slid onto the vacated bench opposite me. "Tease away, Doc, this is the very best artefact uncovered so far." He blushed fiercely; well-bred kids aren't supposed to boast.

"Better look at this, Charlie, else we'll get no peace," Ellen Parkin sighed. "But I shall be showing you the really interesting material. We have pottery shards from the sixteenth century right up to bits of a Georgian tea service—smashed cup and saucer, nearly complete, a family heirloom that got dropped and swept up and thrown out in the back garden."

"Broken china," Leo scoffed. "Now if *this* little beauty could speak . . ." Perversely, he shielded the box with both hands. "All that Tunnel Rat guff means that I poke around in drains and sewers, sir. When people dropped things, they often rolled or got washed down through the kerbside gratings."

A thought elusive as an old tune flickered at the margin of my mind. I lost the thread when Ellen Parkin affirmed solemnly, "He has a terrific range of trouser buttons and kiddies' marbles."

"Charming," Leo muttered. He took his hands away. The box was made of hard, transparent plastic. The liquid filling it was clearish with a pink tinge. Drowned in that was an angular, orange-brown lump of metal.

"It's a pistol," Leo explained proudly. "Semiautomatic. I'm keeping it in a derusting compound Dad uses on his boat. The thing was sealed in the mud at the bottom of a drain, I'm scared it might crumble away if air gets to it for too long."

"Are you sure it's safe?" Ellen nagged. "It might go off."

Leo shook his head. "One, even if it was loaded, the ammo would be no good by now. Two, the whole thing's rusted solid, and three, it *isn't* loaded." He tapped the box's lid. "See, the slide's locked back, therefore the last shot was fired before it was lost . . . or hidden."

She shrugged, evidently reprising a familiar debate. "They were playing soldiers here for years, I'm surprised we've found just the one gun so far."

"Pistol," he corrected absently. And concentrating on me, "It's not service-issue." Leo spoke with certainty. Some youngsters collect stamps or go train spotting; he was a firearms buff.

"It's thirty-two calibre, I measured the bore. Colt made a thirty-two self-loader, but this just looks similar. The Spanish copied a lot of weapons, they made a Mauser look-alike—this could be from Spain, a Colt knock-off. Cheap thing, you can just make out a trace of silvering on the slide, but it was a thin wash, not proper nickel plating. See the butt, er, the handle? No sign of butt-plates, they'd have been papier-mâché or compressed fiber, completely rotted away."

I nearly blurted out, "They looked like mother-of-pearl, silver-white and shiny." My heartbeat stammered. Long-term memory had been vivid over the past decade, but patchy also. Now I remembered one of those fascinating objects I'd always looked forward to seeing in the Artist's bungalow. A silver automatic with a shiny white handle.

An unpleasant thought glided through the back of my mind: *Had* I just recollected the Artist's gun—or was it that I could no longer pretend to forget it?

Clearing my throat, guessing the answer beforehand, I asked, "Where did you find it?"

Leo jerked a thumb over his shoulder. "We call it Hidden Lane, it's first on the left coming from this direction, where I've zapped the brambles."

"Dane Street," I whispered.

Dr. Parkin, not noticing an avowed stranger's surprising knowledge, commented, "It was so overgrown down there that we might have missed it without the old county-council plans of the village. Dane Street is Leo's territory . . . below ground level."

He beamed at her. "I'd love to know how this pistol got into the drain. It had to be dumped there, Doc. Bet it was used in a holdup, maybe even a murder!"

It was, I told him, silently, *it was, and I know who did the killing.*

Ellen Parkin said sharply, "Enough, Leo, you'll make our flesh creep. Little boys and their obsession with guns, it's so uncool."

Leo picked up his precious casket. "It still deserves the star show-case when the museum's up and running. Sorry, Doc, got to be out of here—Mama's keeping lunch for me. Nice to meet you, sir. . . ."

When he was out of sight, Ellen Parkin said, "Sorry you got lumbered with that lecture, I could tell guns aren't your thing."

"Look, you'll think me very rude, but I don't feel terribly well. I'll come back again another day, but I really must get home."

That last word echoed in my mind during the journey. Never before had I thought of London as my home, though most of my life had been spent there. I had considered Aybold Mains my true home, but it was not. Home was wherever Karen was willing to live with me.

I got back to my place—our place—towards dusk, enormously relieved to see Karen's VW Cabriolet parked in the drive.

She opened the door before I could use my key. "What a surprise." She was nonplussed rather than pleased. Then her expression changed. "Charlie, what is it, have you had an accident?" She leaned past me, checking my car.

"Not that sort of crash, darling." My arms went round her.

Karen pulled away and drew me indoors. "Have you eaten, are you hungry, I can whip up an omelette. . . ."

Faking lightness, I said, "I'll settle for a great big Scotch, thanks."

"You look terrible. Sit down, I'll do the bar."

"You're not going out again, are you? I . . . I need to talk."

She swung round, making my drink slop, and laughed shortly. "God, you *have* had a shock."

"Sorry?"

She handed me the tumbler. "Nothing."

I took a stiff belt, and shuddered. "Better." It was a problem, knowing where to start and how to proceed. "I never told you much about where I grew up. . . ."

Karen was incredulous. "Charlie! You've never told me anything about yourself: what you think, how you feel, what you want. You're an island entirely surrounded by Keep Off and Mind Your Own Business."

Normally I would have shrugged that off. It had been a reflex action, not just with her, to keep personal matters personal. But now I said meekly—and sincerely—"That's right, I can't help it."

She folded her arms. She was barefoot, wearing an ugly, oversized grey sweatshirt emblazoned PROPERTY OF H.M. PRISON PARKHURT, which on her was a mini-dress. Karen looked *younger* than my daughter—and ageless. "If this is leading up to saying you need time on your own and we'd better live apart for a while, just cut to the chase."

I gaped at her, but she persisted, "Come on, it's always been a temporary arrangement, right? I have a key to this house, but that's just a roof. All your other doors stay locked and bolted. Can't give a lover the run of the place, she might get the wrong idea."

It was a revelation—I'd always been half ready for Karen to reject *me*. "You couldn't be more wrong. Maybe I am locked up, but there are reasons, nothing to do with you."

Her face hardened. "No, that came out wrong! I mean that today I found out my head has been scrambled ever since . . . hell, forever. Listen, Aybold Mains, your famous time-warp village—I was born there."

"But you come from Bristol . . . don't you?"

"Sort of. Bristol, then another aunt in Gloucester, and on to boarding school, that was Hampshire. I'm an orphan, sounds funny from a grown man. Got passed around like a parcel. Never mind where I've been, I started out in Aybold, it all goes back to there."

I told her everything. Dad and Mum and Steve, the Artist and the Madwoman, the expulsion from Eden. When I reached Connie's death, I needed another drink.

"Steve could always think quickly. Good athletes have that split-second faster brain, lets them catch the ball, save the goal, return the service, or whatever. I worshipped him, and I was just a stupid kid, but even so . . . I must have been on to Steve all along. Subconsciously I saw what he was up to, but I blanked it out. Same as forgetting that the Artist had a gun.

"All my life Aybold Mains has been . . . like a wound you know is so bad you daren't look at it. I thought it was because I'd been happy there until the government grabbed it and bashed it to pieces. But it wasn't that. Aybold was the place where I found out my brother was—"

I tried to name it. "Wicked," I chose, inadequately.

Chin on fists, Karen frowned. "You've lost me. You just said she, Connie, came out and got shot while you and your brother were miles away. Well, several yards, a dozen paces? And she was shot from close by. Steve couldn't have done it."

Her mouth pulled down at the corners. "Are you saying you lied for him, and managed to blot it out?"

My smile took her aback. I was grateful, for Karen had just shown me that it could be worse.

"No, I didn't lie for him. Lied to myself, maybe—but now I understand what went on, even though it's like a bit of old film that has been run so often you stop looking at it properly.

"We were walking down the hill. She came out of their bungalow. I looked up at Steve to see what he made of it, and there was the sound of the shot, and I looked back and Connie was falling down. Like her strings had been cut . . . So final, the way she collapsed, that I expected the earth to give way and let her keep going. Couldn't have imagined that, had to have witnessed it, it has to be genuine.

"Steve ran forward when she dropped. In my mind, he's playing football. So I didn't blank it all out. Football . . . because he kicked something. I didn't see what it was, then. It's taken me until today to work out—the football image came from him kicking the gun to the side of the road.

"I didn't notice a gun, but that must have been it. The boy Leo made me realise that. Brought back an extra fraction I had lost. When Connie collapsed, there was a flash of something silver. In her hand, or falling beside her.

"Don't you get it? *She shot herself.* It was the last day at Aybold for all of us, Connie and Hugh Feather had been arguing, she sounded distraught. She snapped, took the gun, and killed herself—in front of Mum. Connie had this idea that my mother was stealing her man, and she meant Mum to watch the consequence of that, have to live with it. Futile as well as twisted; if only she'd known—Mum was shortsighted as could be, but too vain to wear glasses. She never saw a thing."

I watched Karen absorb what she'd been told. "That's sick," she murmured. "Killed herself, partly to get at her enemy?" She hugged herself. "But I've known women capable of it."

"Steve caught on at once, probably spotted Connie raising the gun, which is more than I did. He knew PC Bell had only just lost sight of us when Connie pulled the trigger, and that Bell couldn't see her. So he ran forward and kicked the gun away from her body, meaning it to vanish down the storm-water grating by the kerb."

"Only it didn't go down."

"That's what always bugged me, subconsciously. I'd already seen the worst, her body lying there, and the blood, before Steve made such a fuss about hiding my eyes. But he kept telling me not to look. He wasn't protecting me, he was afraid I'd give the game away. He assumed I could see that silver gun lying on the drain grating. Any second, PC Bell would look around—*and see the gun.* The last thing Steve needed was me drawing Bell's attention to it.

"So he started the 'Don't look' thing. Then he hit on the pretext of fetching a covering for Connie, and nudged the gun into the drain with the side of his foot as he went by. I even heard it! That wasn't Steve's boot scraping the kerb, it was metal against metal, when the gun slipped between the bars of the grating."

Head on one side, Karen was tentative. "Don't explode, Charlie, but how can you be sure of a detail like that, a little sound, so long after?"

"I've told you, in patches that day is sharp as yesterday . . . sharper. Full color and stereo." I gestured helplessly. "When I try for recall it's no good, but now and then it just floods into my head. Today, seeing that gun, everything came back."

"Okay, I'll buy that. And the thing about thinking of football when your brother was running. I've often wondered whether memory doesn't use mental pictures as hints, like those crossword puzzles for kids: picture of an egg, and you're supposed to write E-G-G in the space. Similar to the symbolism in dreams . . ."

She leaned forward. "But you could be reading the whole thing wrong. Why would Steve cover up the suicide?"

"I'd like to think he wanted to keep scandal away from Mum. He had a split second to realise what had happened, and lost his head. There'd be an inquest, the coroner asking why Connie had killed herself. That could have uncovered her fear that the Artist was about to drop her and take off with Mum. Knowing Steve, he couldn't bear Mum getting linked to Hugh Feather. Not that she was, that's the tragedy: He was just being neighbourly."

I poured myself another Scotch. Karen sounded troubled. " 'I'd like to think,' you said. What do you really think?"

"I have this horrible hunch. . . . Steve could be damned ruthless. And he hated even the possibility of Mum and the Artist getting together. To him that was a betrayal of Dad.

"I'm afraid that when Connie shot herself, he summed up the situation and saw a chance to get the Artist out of Mum's life. When anyone is murdered, their partner's always the first suspect. All right, she was shot at close quarters—closer than anyone dreamed—but Feather could have followed her, out of sight behind their front garden hedge, and shoved the gun through. . . .

"Steve didn't know the Artist had somebody with him, to testify that he was nowhere near when the shot was fired. Most of the time those two were alone in the bungalow, they didn't go in for visitors." I set my drink aside, the stuff didn't taste good anymore. "Face it, if that farmer hadn't called, Hugh Feather would have been charged with murder. It's all academic, since he did have an alibi, but instinct tells me that Steve would have kept the truth hidden, even if that man hanged for it. *Because* he would."

Reading Karen's eyes, I nodded wearily. "A dreadful thing to say about my own brother. But part of me seems to have been saying it ever since Connie died. That's why anything to do with Aybold Mains upset me. For what it's worth—it only hit me today—if I'm distant and secretive and anything else that makes me a pain, it springs from that."

Karen took my hand. "Whether you're right or wrong about Steve, it must have been a hell of a burden."

"Telling you the whole thing has cut it down to size. I can handle a problem once I know it exists."

"If Leo keeps showing the gun to all and sundry, somebody's bound to make the connection."

"Doubtful. The community was scattered in forty-four, most of the people are dead and gone. PC Bell was in his sixties when I saw him last, and that was years back. Say the police do get on to it, I can't see them reopening the case. It's history."

"I still think, hope maybe, you've got this thing wrong," said Karen. "Surely the police knew the Artist had a gun and it was missing. Okay, he hadn't used it, his providential visitor proved that, but even country coppers aren't complete idiots. They'd work out that the likeliest person to have taken the gun was Connie. The next step would be suspecting that she committed suicide with it, but the weapon was overlooked or taken away afterwards. Didn't they search for it?"

"Not right next to her body. The drain was only a few feet away, and they envisaged a killer running off, discarding or hiding the gun as he went. There was no time for a proper search, the village was out of bounds from the next day onwards.

"And I doubt whether the police did know about that automatic. I knew, because Feather was looking for watercolour paints once, and they were in an old cigar box along with the pistol. After that, I begged him for a glimpse every time I went there. The Artist didn't have friends in the village, any callers went there on business, he had no reason to show them the thing.

"After Connie was shot, he wouldn't have said his gun was missing. Granted, he had a solid alibi, but why give the police a reason to question him all over again? He'd broken the law by keeping that thing; all firearms were supposed to be handed in after war broke out. The logical conclusion, since he'd been cleared and the police were looking farther afield, is that the Artist kept his mouth shut."

Karen looked me in the eye. "There's more, I can tell."

"My brother had to be aware that the Artist stood a strong chance of being accused of killing her. If it had gone that far, would Steve have spoken up to clear the guy? I shall never know."

She laid a cool palm against my cheek. "A burden," she said again. "This is a terrible cliché, Charlie, but it does help to share them."

When we reached the landing, Karen hurried ahead, yanking the spare bedroom's door shut. Not before I noticed the bed piled high with her clothes, and a brace of suitcases waiting to be filled. She kept most of her things in the wardrobe there, leaving the closet in our room for my gear.

We looked at each other. Karen said, "Don't ask."

There was no need. Had I kept to my original plan of spending several days at Aybold Mains, a farewell letter would have waited for me in an empty house. I'd have pleaded for her to come back, but the only decision of its kind greater than moving in with somebody is moving out again; and Karen isn't good at changing her mind.

It had been that close. I am trying to change, these days, and it seems to work. Karen, partly seriously, claims that I am too old to be a new man but that I qualify as a modified one. We might even get married.

Dr. Ellen Parkin sent an invitation to the opening of the Aybold

Mains project, with a tour of the museum in a repaired and refurbished Sun in Splendour. I pleaded a previous engagement. I'll never go back—except in my head.

Oh yes, that still occurs. Steve, poor Connie, PC Bell, and a small scruffy boy go through their eternal ritual. At last I understand its implications, but that makes the experience little easier.

And one level of my mind, aghast, wonders whether I remember the past—or if, imperious and uncaring, the past is remembering me.